BOOKS BY BENEDICT JACKA

An Inheritance of Magic

THE ALEX VERUS SERIES

Fated

Cursed

Taken

Chosen

Hidden

Veiled

Burned

Bound

Marked

Fallen

Forged

Risen

AN
INHERITANCE
OF MAGIC

===

BENEDICT JACKA

ACE

New York

ACE

Published by Berkley

An imprint of Penguin Random House LLC

penguinrandomhouse.com

Copyright © 2023 by Benedict Jacka

Penguin Random House supports copyright. Copyright fuels creativity, encourages diverse voices, promotes free speech, and creates a vibrant culture. Thank you for buying an authorized edition of this book and for complying with copyright laws by not reproducing, scanning, or distributing any part of it in any form without permission. You are supporting writers and allowing Penguin Random House to continue to publish books for every reader.

ACE is a registered trademark and the A colophon is a trademark of Penguin Random House LLC.

Library of Congress Cataloging-in-Publication Data

Names: Jacka, Benedict, author.
Title: An inheritance of magic / Benedict Jacka.
Description: First edition. | New York : Ace, 2023.
Identifiers: LCCN 2023006156 (print) | LCCN 2023006157 (ebook) |
ISBN 9780593549841 (trade paperback) | ISBN 9780593549858 (ebook)
Subjects: LCSH: Magic--Fiction. | LCGFT: Fantasy fiction. |
Paranormal fiction. | Novels.
Classification: LCC PR6110.A22 I54 2023 (print) |
LCC PR6110.A22 (ebook) | DDC 823/.92—dc23/eng/20230216
LC record available at https://lccn.loc.gov/2023006156
LC ebook record available at https://lccn.loc.gov/2023006157

First Edition: October 2023

Printed in the United States of America
1st Printing

BOOK DESIGN BY KATY RIEGEL

In memory of Cyril Keith Jacka

1927–2022

AUTHOR'S NOTE

Welcome to the beginning of my new series! I hope to keep working on it for the next ten years or so.

For those who have already read my Alex Verus novels, be aware that this world is a separate one, and the magic works in a very different way. This first book is designed to work as an introduction to the setting, but for those interested in knowing more, a glossary of terms is included at the back of the book.

I hope you enjoy the story!

—*Benedict Jacka, February 2023*

AN
INHERITANCE
OF MAGIC

CHAPTER 1

THERE WAS A strange car at the end of my road.

I'd only leant out of my window for a quick look around, but as I saw the car I paused. All around me were the sounds and smells of the London morning: fresh air that still carried the chill of the fading winter, the dampness of last night's rain, birdsong from the rooftops and the trees. Pale grey clouds covered the sky, promising more showers to come. Everything was normal . . . except for the car.

Spring had come early this year, and the cherry tree outside my window had been in bloom long enough for its flowers to turn from white to pink and begin to fall. The car was just visible through the petals, parked at the end of Foxden Road at an angle that gave it a clear line of sight to my front door. It was sleek and ominous, shiny black with tinted windows, and it looked like a minivan. Nobody on our street owns a minivan, especially not one with tinted windows.

A loud "Mraooow" came from my feet.

I looked down to see a grey-and-black tabby cat watching me

with yellow-green eyes. "Oh, fine, Hobbes," I told him, and shifted. Hobbes sprang up onto the sill, rubbed his head against my shoulder until I gave him a scratch, then jumped down onto the ledge that ran along the front of the building. I gave the car a last sidelong glance, then withdrew and shut the window.

I CLEANED MY teeth, dressed, and had breakfast, and all the time I kept thinking about that car.

Almost three years ago, the day after my dad disappeared, a white Ford started showing up on our road. I might not have noticed it, but a couple of the things my dad had said in that hastily scribbled letter had made me suspicious, and once I started paying attention I noticed that same Ford, with the same number plate, in other places. Near my boxing gym, near my work . . . everywhere.

It kept on for more than a year. I was worrying about my dad and struggling to manage work and rent, and while all that was going on, I'd kept seeing that car. Even after I got evicted and had to move in with my aunt, all the way up in Tottenham, I'd still seen it. I started to hate that car after a while—it became a symbol of everything that had gone wrong—and it was only my dad's warning that stopped me from marching out to confront whoever was inside. Sometimes it would vanish for a few days, but it'd always come back.

But eventually the gaps became longer and longer, and finally it didn't come back at all. When I moved out of my aunt's and here to Foxden Road, one of the first things I did was write down the description and number plate of every car on the street, then check back for the next couple of weeks to see who'd get into them. But every car on the road belonged to someone who lived there, and finally I came to accept that whoever it had been, they were gone. That had been six months ago, and ever since then, there'd been nothing to make me think they'd come back.

Until now.

I FILLED HOBBES'S water bowl, and then it was time to go to work. I zipped up my fleece and stepped outside, closing the door behind me. The black minivan was still there. I walked away up the road without looking back, then turned the corner.

As soon as I was out of the minivan's line of sight, I stopped. I could make out its blurry reflection in the ground-floor windows on our street, and I waited to see if it would start moving.

One minute passed, then two. The reflection didn't move.

If they were following me, they should have driven off by now.

Maybe I was being overly suspicious. After all, the men from two years ago had always used the same car, and it hadn't been this one. I turned and set off for the station. I kept glancing over my shoulder as I walked along Plaistow Road, watching for the minivan's black shape in the busy A-road traffic, but it didn't appear.

MY NAME IS Stephen Oakwood, and I'm twenty years old. I was raised by my dad, grew up and went to school here in Plaistow, and apart from one big secret that I'll get to later, I used to have a pretty normal life. That all changed a few months before my eighteenth birthday, when my dad disappeared.

The next few years were rough. Living alone in London is hard unless you have a lot going for you, which I didn't. To begin with, my plan was to wait for my father to come back, and maybe even go and look for him, but I quickly found out that just making enough money to live on was so all-consuming that it didn't leave me time for much else. For the first year or so, I was able to get a job with an old friend of my dad's who ran a bar, but when the bar closed, my money ran out. I got evicted and had to move in with my aunt.

Living with my aunt and uncle let me get back on my feet, but it was clear from the beginning that there was a definite limit as to how long they were willing to put me up. I couldn't afford a flat, but I could just about afford a room in Plaistow, so long as I worked full-time. And so after a stint at a call centre (bad) and a job at a different bar (worse), I found my way last winter to a temp agency that hired office workers for the Civil Service. Which was why, that morning, I took the District Line to Embankment and walked south along the Thames to the Ministry of Defence.

Saying I work at the Ministry of Defence makes my job sound more exciting than it really is. My actual title is Temporary Administrative Assistant, Records Office, Defence Business Services, and my job mostly consists of fetching records from the basement. One wall of the Records Office is taken up by a machine called the Lektriever, a sort of giant vertical conveyor belt carrying shelves of box files up from the level below. The basement is huge, a cold dark cavern with endless rows of metal shelves holding thousands and thousands of files. Every day, orders come down to change the files, at which point someone has to go down, put new files in, and take the old files out. That someone is me. In theory the position's supposed to be filled by a permanent staff member, but since being an admin in Records is pretty much the least desirable position in the entire MoD, no-one's willing to take the job, so they hire temps instead. For this, I get paid £10.70 an hour.

I've been spending a bit less time in the basement lately, due to Pamela. Pamela's title is Senior Executive Officer, a midlevel Civil

Service rank that puts her well above everyone in Records. She's in her forties, dresses in neat business suits, and as of the last week or two she seems to have taken an interest in me.

Today Pamela found me after lunch and put me to work sorting applications. It was a long job, and by the time I was done, it was nearly four o'clock. When I finally finished, instead of sending me back to Records, Pamela tapped the papers on her desk to straighten them, laid them down beside her keyboard, then turned her swivel chair to face me. "You started here in December?"

Pamela was giving me a considering sort of look that made me wary. I nodded.

"You said you were thinking about applying to university," Pamela said. "Did you?"

"No," I admitted.

"Why not?"

I didn't answer.

"It's no good just ignoring these things. You've missed the UCAS deadline, but you could still get into Clearing."

"Okay."

"Don't just say okay," Pamela told me. "That Records Office post won't stay vacant forever. If you do a three-year course and reapply, you could come in at the same role in a permanent position."

I tried to figure out how to answer that, but Pamela had already turned back to her computer. "That's all for today. I'll have another job for you on Friday."

I RODE THE District Line home.

As I stood on the swaying train, the conversation with Pamela kept going around in my head. It was the second time she'd suggested a permanent position, and the second time I'd avoided giving her an answer. Part of me wanted to be honest and tell Pamela that I didn't want a future in the Records Office. But if I said that, Pamela would either fire me or ask, So what are you going to do instead? and the only answer I had for that question was one I couldn't tell her.

The sad part was that by the standards of my other jobs, the Civil Service wasn't even all that bad. While I'd been living with my aunt, I'd been working at the call centre where I'd spent eight hours a day selling car insurance renewals. You know how when you ring up a company to cancel your service, you get put through to someone who tries to persuade you not to? Yeah, that was me. I say "persuade," but all you actually do is follow a script, and if you've never worked that kind of job, there's no way you can possibly understand just how mind-shatteringly boring it is. You pick up the phone and recite your lines, then you put the phone back down, and you do that over and over and over again, every single day. Compared to that, the Records Office was easy. At least box files don't yell at you for leaving them on hold.

But while the Civil Service wasn't that bad, it also wasn't good. The hours were steady and the pay was enough to live on, but it was meaningless and dull and I spent every day counting the hours until I could go home.

I stared at the ads on the train. In between posters for vitamin supplements ("Tired of Feeling Tired?") and for loan companies ("Discover Your Credit Score Today!") was one for a London university. "DO SOMETHING YOU LOVE" was written in big white letters, above a photo of three ethnically diverse students staring out at the horizon with blissful expressions. At the bottom right of the ad was a paragraph of small print titled "Funding."

I got off at Plaistow and went to the pub.

———

MY LOCAL'S CALLED the Admiral Nelson, and it's an "old man and his dog" type of place. It's a square building just off Plaistow Road, with windows on three walls casting patchy light into a wide room with a faded carpet and scattered tables and chairs. The people who come are a mixture of old East End, the new generation who've grown up here, a handful of Eastern Europeans, and yes, an old man with a big scruffy Airedale that lies at his feet and twitches his ears at the people who walk up to the bar.

My friends and I have been meeting at the Nelson ever since we got old enough that we could pretend to be old enough, and nowadays we go there every Wednesday and sometimes on Friday or Saturday too, sometimes to play games but usually just to talk. Our group's changed over the years, with new people joining and others drifting away, but the core's stayed pretty much the same. There's Colin, smart and practical and the one who always did best at school; Felix, tall with a scraggly beard and a cynical streak; Kiran, fat and generous and cheerful; and Gabriel, the youngest by a few months and who always seems to be going through some kind of personal crisis. We met in secondary school, and we've grown up together. Sometimes Kiran's or Colin's girlfriends will come along, but tonight it was just us.

"Ahhhhh," Gabriel said for at least the fifth time. "I don't know what to do."

"Dump her," Colin said.

"I can't just dump her."

"Dump her and tell her she's a slag," Felix suggested.

"I can't do that!"

"Well, if you're too chicken to dump her yourself," Colin said, "telling her she's a slag should do it."

"Oh, come on, guys," Gabriel said. "Seriously."

Gabriel always has some kind of issue; when we were younger it was either school, his parents, or girls, but nowadays it's always girls. All but one of his relationships have been horrendous train wrecks, and by this point I think all of us have decided that he just has some sort of talent for it. It always goes the same way—when the relationship starts he's excited, by a few weeks in he's looking stressed, then one day I'll walk into the Nelson and find him explaining to Kiran that the girl's tried to stab him or set his house on fire or something.

"Isn't this the same one who broke up with you two weeks ago?" I asked.

"She was waiting in front of my house Friday night," Gabriel explained.

"So?"

"Well, you know. If a girl's waiting outside your house, then . . ."

I waited for Gabriel to finish.

"You know," Gabriel said.

"I don't know."

"It means she wants to nob him," Felix said.

"No, it doesn't," I said.

"It kind of does," Kiran chipped in.

"Oh, come on," I said. "You're saying any random girl you meet outside your house—"

"After dark on a Friday night," Felix added.

"How does that matter?"

"It totally matters," Kiran said.

"Okay, okay," Felix said. "There's an easy way to settle this, all right?" He turned to Gabriel. "Did you or did you not end up nobbing her?"

Gabriel looked embarrassed. "Well . . ."

"See?" Felix told me smugly.

"Just because she's standing in the street—" I said in annoyance.

"I think the point Felix is making," Colin said, "is that there's some context here. She's not some random girl in the street."

"And you have to make a move," Gabriel added. "Or she'll think you're a melt."

"What?" Felix said, grinning at me. "You thought she was just there to talk?"

I rolled my eyes.

Felix tried to ruffle my hair, and I ducked away. "He's so cute," Felix said to the rest of the table.

"Oh, piss off."

"So I had to let her in, right?" Gabriel said.

"I know why *you* let her in," Colin said.

"So what should I do?"

The argument went back and forth, split about fifty-fifty between giving Gabriel serious advice and mocking him. We all like Gabriel, but even Kiran, nice to a fault, has long since figured out that the reason for Gabriel's problem is Gabriel. Still, he's our friend.

After a while the group divided, with Felix, Kiran, and Gabriel continuing the argument while Colin and I leant back on the bench. The pub was starting to get a few more people in with the evening crowd, though it was a long way from full. I was still on my second pint—I can afford to go to the pub, but only so long as I don't drink much.

"You all right?" Colin asked. "You're a bit quiet."

"Trouble at work," I said with a sigh.

"Your boss?"

"My boss's boss."

"I thought she liked you."

"She does," I admitted. "That's the problem. She wants me to go to uni and join the Civil Service full-time."

"I mean," Colin said. "You could."

"Yeah," I said, and fell silent.

Out of all our group, Colin is the one I'm closest to. His father's from Hong Kong—when the Chinese took over in 1997, he saw the way the wind was blowing and got out early, ending up here in London, where he married an English girl. The two of them had some issues, and Colin's mum moved out for a couple of years—they fixed things up eventually, but Colin had a hard time of it, and for a while he was a regular visitor around our house. We got pretty close, and we've stayed that way.

But nowadays, it's Colin who's got his life together, and I'm the one who's struggling. Colin's in his third year doing science at Imperial College, staying in college housing in Whitechapel. Felix did a gap year and is supposed to be at uni too, though as far as I can see he mostly spends his time trying to hook up with Chinese girls on dating apps. Kiran's midway through an electrician apprenticeship. And Gabriel . . . well, he's Gabriel. All of us are growing up and finding our paths.

Except me. For a while now I've felt as though I'm drifting, being left behind. Colin knows that, and that was the unspoken message behind his words. But he didn't push, and I didn't talk. We sat for another ten minutes before I finished my drink and headed home.

I OPENED MY front door to the sound of chatter and the roar of the TV. The noise was coming from the ground-floor bedroom that had once been the house's lounge—Ignas and Matis must be watching football. I went through into the tiny communal kitchen, grabbed some food and a plate, then went upstairs.

My house is an end-of-terrace two-thirds of the way up Fox-den Road, next to an old school that's been converted into flats, and it's rented out by the room by a Jamaican landlord with a view to squeezing the maximum number of people in and the maximum amount of money out. The other tenants are a group of Lithuanians who work long shifts at the local garage and grocery store. I had trouble breaking the ice with them at first but got some unexpected help when it turned out that the house had a rodent problem. Once Hobbes realised how good a hunting ground it was, he went on a killing spree, and there were dead mice and rats outside the door every morning and evening for a fortnight. The Lithuanians decided that Hobbes was wonderful, and we've been friends ever since.

Right now Hobbes was waiting at the top of the stairs; he meowed until I unlocked my bedroom door, then trotted in to head for his food bowl. I locked the door behind us, poured Hobbes some food, then sat on the bed to eat. My room doesn't have much space, but then I don't have much stuff. A bed, a wardrobe, a nightstand, one chair that's usually piled with clothes. Everything is old and badly maintained—cracked furniture, peeling paint, crooked skirting. Though one of the skirting boards is crooked for a reason.

Once I was done, I set the plate aside, then crouched down in the corner and pulled the skirting board free with a practised twist, revealing a dusty cubbyhole that held a faded envelope and a small wooden box. Hobbes watched with bright eyes as I opened the box to reveal two tiny spherical objects, each no bigger than a match head. They would have looked like ball bearings but for their colour—both were light blue, the colour of very pale turquoise. One rolled free in the box, but I'd glued the second onto a plastic ring. It looked a bit embarrassing, but it worked.

Those two little spheres were called sigls. Most people would think they looked like toys. The truth was, they were probably worth more than everything else in this room put together.

I slipped the ring onto my finger, sat cross-legged on the floor, and closed my eyes with a little sigh. This was the part of the day I looked forward to. Tomorrow I'd have to go back to moving box files around the MoD basement, but right now I had a few precious hours to spend on what I actually cared about.

Drucraft.

The first discipline of drucraft is sensing. Sensing is the foundation skill—you have to learn it before you can do anything else, which made my early training really frustrating since to begin with I was pretty bad at it. Back then, when I tried to practise, I'd do it by concentrating, like listening for a sound that's slightly too high pitched, or trying to see something that's a little too far away. But the harder I'd try, the more it would slip out of reach.

It took me a long time to figure out that the trick isn't to try harder; it is to get rid of distractions. You have to empty your mind of all the things that are crowding it. That tune that's been going around in your head, the plans you're making for tomorrow. Conversations that are bugging you, like the one with Pamela that I still hadn't quite forgotten. I closed them off one after another, shrinking them to nothingness, leaving an empty circle in my mind where everything was quiet and calm. It used to take me a few minutes; nowadays I can do it almost instantly.

Into that empty circle sprang an awareness. It wasn't quite a sound or a pressure—more of a *presence*, something you'd been half-aware of but hadn't been noticing. The strongest presence was the earth below, vast and diffuse and stretching away to the horizon, rising and falling with the curves of the land. That was very distant, though—much easier to sense were the currents within my room, following the lines of the walls and the furniture and swirling in the air. And easiest of all were the flows running through my own body.

This presence, what I was sensing, is called essentia. My dad taught me that it makes up everything, a kind of universal energy. You can't create it and you can't destroy it, but with the right art—and the right tools—you can use it.

When I first learned to sense essentia, it felt like a big indistinguishable mass. These days, the essentia in the air feels different from that in the walls or floor, and totally different from the essentia in Hobbes. The essentia flowing through me was the clearest of all—this was my personal essentia, and to me it felt comfortable, familiar, like a pair of old shoes.

But what makes personal essentia *really* special is that you can control it.

I focused my thoughts and sent a narrow flow down my right arm and into the sigl on my finger.

Light bloomed in the small room. The tiny sigl lit up like a star, casting a pale blue glow over the walls and ceiling. Hobbes watched lazily from the bed, light reflecting from his slitted eyes.

Channelling is the second of the drucraft disciplines. Your personal essentia is attuned to your body and mind, and with practice you can command it the same way you can your own muscles. Having it trickle into a sigl is a weird, slightly disturbing sensation, like feeling your own blood pumping out of your veins, and when I was starting out, I used to have this nagging fear that I'd somehow use too much and bleed myself to death. But as my personal essentia flowed out, ambient essentia from the air around me flowed in. As it seeped into my body, it attuned to me, taking on the resonance of my personal essentia until it was indistinguishable from that which I'd lost. An inward flow and an outward flow, perfectly balanced.

I scaled the essentia flow up and down, dimming the glow until it was almost too faint to see before bringing it to maximum brightness in a flash. Bringing it to full power was easy—the sigl had a maximum capacity that it could handle, and once I went past that point, then any more would just overflow, like pouring water into a sink that was already full. But bringing it to *exactly* full power without going over the limit was actually quite hard, and I spent a while practising, trying to see how quickly I could make the flow snap from full to nothing to full again without letting any of it go to waste.

I did some more exercises to wind down, channelling my personal essentia into various objects and pulling it back again before it could de-attune, and finally sending it flowing into Hobbes, setting up a kind of circuit where my essentia would flow into him while his would be drawn back into me. Hobbes put up with the indignity with a slight sneeze—he can definitely feel that trick, though he seems to tolerate it. Then it was time for shaping.

Shaping is the third, last, and hardest of the disciplines. I've been practising drucraft since I was ten, but I didn't manage to shape a sigl until I was almost nineteen. That had been a year and a half ago, and the sigl I'd created was the one resting in the box on my bed. After that had followed twelve months of waiting. Twelve slow, patient, *frustrating* months, until last September, when I'd created the sigl that was on my finger now.

I reached out to the ambient essentia around me, trying to gather it. It was much harder than activating the sigl had been—the flows in the air weren't attuned to me and wouldn't respond to my thoughts. I had to shape my personal essentia into a kind of vortex, creating currents that would draw in the free essentia until it was concentrated enough that I could use my personal essentia to "paint" it into strands, as though the free essentia were ink and my personal essentia a calligraphy brush. Even with all my practice, it was like trying to catch smoke, and it took me several minutes of patient work before I could shape it into a construct that hovered above my palm, like a woven knot of invisible lines.

An essentia construct is the first step towards creating a sigl, like a pencil sketch before a painting. I must have made thousands of constructs by now, but I still get a little glow of satisfaction from doing it well—I've come a long way since my father had to lead me through it step-by-step. If I wanted to turn this one into a sigl, the next step would be to shrink it, pulling in more and more essentia as the construct grew denser and denser to become the sigl's core. Of course, if I tried that right now, it wouldn't work. When you shape a sigl for real, you're creating matter out of pure energy, and that takes an *enormous* amount of essentia. The only place you find that is at a Well.

This particular construct was a project that I'd been working on since January. The idea was that instead of creating light, this sigl would redirect it, projecting a field that light would bend around. The result should be like a kind of invisibility sphere—as long as the sigl was active, no one outside the sphere's radius would be able to see in.

Or at least, that was the plan. The truth was, I had absolutely no idea if it was going to work. I had a pretty good understanding of how to make light sigls by now, but this was something totally different and much more complicated. Since I couldn't actually *see* the construct, I had to work by feel, which in practice meant dismissing the thing and re-creating it from scratch over and over again.

I had the feeling that I was going about this the wrong way. My father had made it sound as though professional shapers could make sigls pretty easily, so there had to be some trick I was missing. But without anyone to learn from, I had to figure it all out from first principles, which meant a whole lot of guesswork. For all I knew, if I went ahead and shaped this sigl, it'd do nothing at all.

That had been what had happened on my first try, three years ago. I'd practised and practised, but even so, when the time came to make the sigl, I failed and the essentia was wasted. I'd been close to tears, but my dad had laughed it off. He told me that everyone screws up their first time, that I'd done better and got closer than most. It had cheered me up, and I'd thrown myself into my practice, determined to get it right next time.

And then, when I'd finally managed it, he wasn't there . . .

I came out of my thoughts with a start. My room was dark; the sun had set while I'd been practising. Outside, the last traces of light were fading from the sky. Hobbes rose, stretched, and padded to the door, looking at me expectantly.

I let the construct unravel, then changed into my running clothes and went downstairs, slipping outside and closing the door as Hobbes trotted off across the street. I looked around for any sign of that car from this morning, but it was gone. Maybe it really had been nothing.

If you go around the corner of my road and turn left, you come into a little alley. To the left are gardens, honeysuckle and ivy spilling over fences made of wooden slats, while to the right are the back entrances of the shops that front onto Plaistow Road. Gravel crunched under my feet as I weaved around the rubbish bins; red and grey tiled roofs rose up all around, TV aerials and satellite dishes silhouetted against a dusky blue sky. Above and to the right was a block of flats, bikes stored out on the metal balconies. Lights shone from the windows, but it was a cold March evening and no one stepped out onto their balcony to see me go by.

The alley ended in a set of sheds. I climbed onto a recycling bin and pulled myself up, corrugated iron creaking under my feet as I crossed the flat roofs. The clouds and rain from earlier had passed away, and the sky was clear all the way to the horizon, fading from azure to a grey blue that mixed with the city's glow. I reached the end of the sheds and dropped down into a little open space closed off by garden fences and a brick wall on the far side. The ground had once been solid concrete, but dandelions and ryegrass had burrowed in and split it with their roots, turning it into a riot of growth. A wild cherry tree rose in one corner, still young but with new leaves pushing towards the sky.

Most people who saw my room on Foxden Road would think I was staying there because it was cheap. They'd be half-right, but only half. The main reason I was living here was this Well.

Wells are gathering points, places where essentia collects and pools, and the essentia here was so concentrated that I could sense it without even trying. It *did* feel like a well, a reservoir of energy and life and potential. It was tempting to use those reserves, to shape them into a new sigl, but I knew better. Three years ago, after I'd messed up my first try at a sigl, my dad had warned me that I should only use Wells that were full; this was a weak one, and it would take a full year to recharge. I'd got impatient and tried to use it early. The shaping had failed, the sigl hadn't formed, and I'd wasted five months of the Well's charge. It had been a painful lesson, but it had stuck.

Right now this Well was about a quarter full, and I knew from experience that it charged fastest in the spring and summer. By around September, I'd be able to use it to shape a sigl. And I had a *lot* of ideas for sigls. There was the invisibility sphere that I'd just practised creating. Or there was that idea I'd had for a darkness effect. From the basic starting point of something that generated light, I could see how you could branch off in a dozen different directions. I still didn't have a good feel for what was and wasn't possible, but there might be ways around that. With time and practice, I should have a good chance of getting one of my ideas to work by the autumn, and then . . .

. . . *and then what?*

I came back to earth with a bump. Yes, I could make another sigl. I might even be able to make one that worked. But what would I do with it? I had a lot of ideas for sigls, but none of them would put food on the table or pay my rent. Or find my dad.

I thought back to the conversations I'd had with Pamela and Colin. My friends were all going to university and getting jobs, while I was doing . . . what? I'd been practising drucraft for most of my life, and what did I have to show for it?

For a while now I'd felt as though I was being pulled between two worlds. In one world were my friends and my job; in the other were my drucraft and my sigls and this Well. I'd been trying to keep a foot in both, and it was getting harder and harder. Maybe I should do as my teachers at school had said, and what Pamela and Colin were nudging me to do now. Get a degree, start working on a career. It'd be hard and it'd mean going into debt, but I could do it.

But if I followed that path, there'd be a price. Between my job, my drucraft, all the problems that came with living alone, and spending enough time with my friends that I didn't go crazy, I was already stretched. If I added a uni degree on top of that, something would have to go, and I had a feeling I knew what that something would have to be.

It felt as though the "proper" choice, the one the world wanted me to take, was to give up my drucraft. Back when we'd been given careers advice at school, I'd heard a lot about following your passion, but the older I got, the more it felt to me as though there was another message under that, something harder and colder. As a kid, you're allowed to do things for fun, but the more you grow up, the more you get pressured to spend your time doing things that'll make you successful—the right A levels, the right course, the right activities on your CV. Everything to make money, to signal that you're a good employee.

Drucraft didn't make me money, and it *definitely* didn't make me look like a better employee. If my career was what I cared about, I might as well give it up.

But I didn't want to. Ever since I'd first pestered my dad into teaching me drucraft, it had been the one big secret I'd shared with him, the one thing we'd always done together. When he'd told me I showed talent, I'd thrown myself into it, practising every day after school without a break. I can still remember that smile of his when I got something right, the way his face would light up. He'd been so proud of me.

In his letter my dad had told me to do three things, and one of them had been to keep practising my drucraft. I'd done as he'd asked, but it had been almost three years. I'd been practising and waiting for a really long time, and it felt as though I was being left behind.

I sighed, then reached for the fence to climb back the way I'd come.

I WENT FOR a run, looping north through Forest Gate. Back when I was doing boxing, I'd go running every day. I'm not in proper training anymore—between my job and my drucraft I can't afford it—but I hate feeling unfit, so I try to squeeze in runs when I can.

As I ran, I thought once again about how unfair the whole thing was. As a little kid, I'd dreamed of having magic powers.

When I found out that drucraft was real and that I could use it, I'd been so excited. Except, surprise! You get to do magic, but the only thing you can use it for is to make a flashlight.

I knew that there was more to it than that. From what I'd heard, the more powerful sigls could do all kinds of amazing things—turn you invisible, give you superhuman strength, make your body as strong as steel. But to make those sigls, you needed powerful Wells and the knowledge of how to use them. Which meant that right now, my big magical talent amounted to something that came packaged with your smartphone as a standard feature.

I came out through the backstreets and rounded the north side of West Ham Park. Chestnut trees loomed up on the other side of the fence, the first pale green shoots beginning to sprout from bare branches. A city fox, caught in the middle of crossing the road, flicked his tail at me and vanished between two cars.

I've always liked London at night. The noise and bustle of the day fades away, and in the quiet you can feel the presence of the city. It has its own nature, kind of like its own essentia—old, layered, and complex, man-made construction on top of millennia-old earth. Generation after generation of people, with the plants and animals of old Britain living with them side by side. It's neat and chaotic and ancient and sprawling, and it's my home.

I passed Tanner Point and turned down Lettsom Walk, a little foot passage that runs alongside the railway lines connecting Plaistow to Upton Park. The walk runs straight as an arrow for a few hundred feet before twisting out of sight at the end. Up ahead, the white cranes and half-finished towers of the Plaistow construction site reached up into the night sky, red pinpoints gleaming in the dark. From the other side of the wall, I could hear the rumbling of an approaching train.

A soft footfall sounded behind me.

I twisted, suddenly alert. Plaistow isn't a dangerous area, but it's not exactly safe, either, and I've had to face down muggers before...

But there were no muggers. Or anyone else. The walk stretched away, clearly lit in the streetlights. Empty.

I looked around, frowning.

The Underground train came blaring along on the other side of the wall, its roar echoing around the houses. By the time it had passed by and was fading into the distance, rattle and bang, rattle and bang, any sound of footsteps was long gone. I started walking again, glancing around at the silent buildings.

There's a footbridge towards the bottom of Lettsom Walk, a cage of metal and brick that links the walks on either side of the railway lines. I climbed the stairs, wondering if I was just jumpy today. Half a mile to the east, the red taillights of the train shone in the darkness as it pulled into Upton Park. The wires above the tracks whickered and clanged, still vibrating from the train's passage. I reached the top of the steps and turned to cross.

There was a girl standing at the far end.

I paused, feeling that same echo of strangeness I'd felt this morning. The level part of the bridge is forty feet from end to end, and the girl was at the top of the far steps with one hand on the rail. She wasn't crossing; she was just standing there.

Most of the lights on the footbridge were burned out, leaving the girl's face in shadow. I couldn't make out her features, but she looked young. She didn't react to my stare, and something about her stillness sent a ripple of unease through me. What was going on?

I didn't move. Neither did she.

I shook myself and started forward, and as I moved, the girl did too. As we drew closer, I could see that she *was* young, maybe sixteen or so, small and light. She had fair skin and finely boned features, her head was covered with a furry hat, and she wore an elegant-looking long belted coat. But mostly what I noticed was that she was watching me, with a sort of curious, expectant look.

I walked past without slowing. As we passed each other, I heard her murmur in a wry voice, "Better get stronger."

I stopped dead. Turning, I saw that the girl was still walking away. She didn't look back, and as I stared after her she reached the other side of the bridge and disappeared down the steps I'd just climbed. Her footsteps rang out, their echoes fading.

I kept staring. What did she mean by . . . ?

Oh, screw this. I ran after her.

I reached the end of the bridge and stopped. The girl wasn't on the stairs. I jogged down a little further and leant out over the railing. From up here, halfway up the steps, I had a view up and down Lettsom Walk for more than a hundred feet in both directions.

Empty.

I stared down at the bare concrete. Where had she gone?

There were houses and cars along the other side of the walk, as well as some hedges, all more than big enough to hide a small girl. But she'd been out of my sight for less than ten seconds. She couldn't have moved that fast.

Could she?

I kept looking around, but nothing moved. At last I backed away, crossed the bridge a third time, and descended the steps on the far side. The walk beyond led to Plaistow Road and the way home. I kept checking over my shoulder for the rest of the journey back, but I didn't see anything more.

CHAPTER 2

THE CAR WASN'T there next morning.

I fed Hobbes, let him out, and had breakfast, glancing out of the window as I did. No black minivans. No mysterious sixteen-year-old girls, either.

Work went the same as usual, except that I passed Pamela in the corridor a couple of times, and each time it felt as though she had her eyes on me. She didn't say or do anything, but it still left me with an uncomfortable feeling, and this time it had nothing to do with jobs or universities. It was for quite a different reason: my looks.

Most people would say my looks are the most distinctive thing about me. I have wavy jet-black hair, large brown eyes, long eyelashes, and delicate, slightly feminine features; add it to my slim build, and when I was younger, I'd regularly get asked if I was a boy or a girl. As I grew I put on some muscle, but not much bulk, and even now, at twenty, I still was seen as a pretty boy rather than as a young man.

My looks got me a fair bit of attention while I was in school. Sometimes it was the nice kind, with girls trying to dress me up or ask if I was going to be a model. Sometimes it was less nice: I had to field the "Are you gay?" question a lot, which would usually lead into even less friendly questions, which would keep escalating until I did something about it. Apparently I get it from my dad: when I asked him about it, he said that when he was younger, he'd looked just like me. (He also told me that no, I couldn't be a model—male models needed to be five eleven, and I was probably going to top out at five eight, and I wasn't missing anything anyway, because modelling was a horrible job.)

It's got its pluses and minuses. People tend to be nice to me, even when they don't know me very well and I haven't done anything to deserve it. On the other hand, I've had a few unpleasant experiences where I've agreed to something, only to discover much later that what *I* thought I was agreeing to and what the *other* person thought I was agreeing to were very different things. Last September, after I moved out of my aunt's and back to Plaistow, I got a job at a bar in Hoxton. I hadn't looked very closely at what kind of bar it was, and, with hindsight, the fact that the guy didn't ask me for proof of age should have been a warning sign, but I had rent to pay and couldn't afford to be picky. It was only once I started that I realised what I'd actually been hired for—my shifts mostly consisted of getting hit on by men (and the occasional woman) more than twice my age. Most were willing to take no for an answer, but a couple of nasty incidents taught me that something about my looks seemed to attract the predatory type. I got out as soon as I could.

I didn't really think that Pamela was one of those. And nothing she'd done had been over the line. But I kept my distance all the same.

———

FETCHING AND CARRYING files is pretty mindless work, but there's one thing you can say for it: it gives you a lot of time to think.

All through that Thursday, as I moved box files around the basement, I kept thinking about that girl on the bridge. Her words had hit a nerve—I'd been feeling for a while now as though I wasn't doing enough. My dad had told me to keep practising my drucraft, but while I'd gotten better, I hadn't really gotten *stronger*.

When my father disappeared, I didn't just lose my remaining parent; I lost the only source of information about drucraft that I could trust. Without him I'd had to fall back on the Internet, and as it turns out, finding reliable information about drucraft online is really, really hard. Typing "drucraft" into a search engine takes you to pages with titles like "how to deal with friends or family members who spread conspiracy theories" and "our fact-checkers teach you how to spot misinformation." Any drucraft-related content posted on social networks like Twitter or YouTube or Reddit gets deleted, and when you try to look up the authors, you find they've been banned for "violations of our terms of service." Most sites won't talk about the subject at all, and when you ask about it, you'll get evasions or silence. It takes a lot of work to find people willing to talk, and even when you do, there's no guarantee that anything they say will be true. Here are some of the things I've "learned" about drucraft over the past couple of years:

- There are lots of Wells out there, scattered all over the country. *(Verdict: true.)*
- Different types of Wells draw upon different branches of essentia, and different countries are much better or worse for

finding Wells of particular branches. *(Verdict: not sure, but sounds plausible.)*

- New Wells are discovered with something called a "finder's stone." *(Verdict: false. I'd found my Well on my own.)*
- To make a sigl, you need something called a "limiter" that's powered by human blood. *(Verdict: definitely false. I'd made my two sigls on my own, no blood involved.)*

It's easy to say "get stronger," but that's pretty hard when you don't have any good idea of *how* people get stronger. The one thing that I was sure would help was getting more powerful sigls. But how?

The obvious way was to find more Wells. I'd spent a while last autumn trying to do exactly that, and I'd actually managed to find three, but none had resulted in a sigl. The first two Wells, out towards Upton Park, had both been weaker than my one on Foxden Road, and when I'd tried to use them, it hadn't worked. It hadn't been for nothing—those two failed shapings taught me some useful lessons—but it did seem that sigls needed a certain minimum amount of essentia, and if a Well wasn't over that limit, you weren't getting a sigl out of it.

The third Well *was* over that limit, but it was occupied. It was an old church in West Ham, and when I found it in October, someone had obviously just used it since most of its essentia had been drained already. It might have filled up since, but I was wary of getting too close. My dad had warned me that drucrafters were territorial, and you could get into a lot of trouble trespassing on a Well that wasn't yours.

But there obviously *were* other Wells out there—lots, if I'd been able to find four without even leaving my neighbourhood— so I should be able to find some if I kept at it. The problem was time. I spent eight hours a day at the MoD, the better part of two hours travelling there and back, another hour or two on drucraft. And then there were the little things. Calling the agency to sort out the latest error in my payslip. Going to the bank to get a document. Prowling around the supermarket looking for special offers. Having to stay home because the landlord had told us to let someone in. Chasing down the one person in the department who'd sign my time sheet. All the tiny annoying problems that people with better jobs and better lives probably don't have to deal with but which seemed to eat up whatever free time I had left. Hunting for Wells was a slow process, and I was stretched thin already.

There was another option. One thing that I'd learned from my research was that most people with sigls didn't make them; they bought them. And when the conversation turned to buying sigls, the same name kept coming up: the Exchange.

The Exchange is in Belgravia, a London district between Westminster and Kensington and Chelsea, and I finally managed to track the place down last year. I'd known right from the start that I wouldn't be able to afford a sigl—my bank balance for the last few months had hovered between £500 and £1,000, which in London is a month's living expenses at most. But even if I wasn't going to buy anything, I liked the idea of getting a look at what was on sale. One of the problems I'd been running into more and more over the past six months had been that I wasn't sure exactly what was and wasn't possible. If I could see what sorts of sigls other people had been able to make, it might give me a better idea of what I could do on my own.

But it turned out that none of that mattered because they wouldn't even let me in. I'd tried twice, and both times I'd been stopped at the door. Apparently the kinds of people who belong in these places have a specific look, and I don't have it. If I could make that invisibility sigl, I might be able to sneak inside . . . but

I'd only be able to sneak inside if it worked . . . and to know if it would work, I needed a better idea of what sigls could do . . . and to get a better idea of what sigls could do, I needed to get in.

So while finding more Wells didn't seem very realistic, the "buying sigls" plan seemed even worse. What did that leave?

Nothing.

I HAD TO stay late at work, and it was past seven when I came out of Plaistow station, walked down the hill, and turned off the side street leading to Foxden Road. The sun was setting in the western sky, its rays igniting the clouds in brilliant scarlet and gold. Cherry blossom petals were scattered on the pavement, and the temperature was dropping fast with the coming evening, the chill cutting through my fleece and making me shiver. A crow was perched on the telephone wires, watching as I passed below.

There was a girl waiting outside my front gate.

My mind flashed instantly to last night, but as the girl turned to face me I saw that she wasn't the same one who'd passed me on the bridge. This girl was about as old as I was, with fair skin and shoulder-length ash-blond hair. Her movements were quick and confident, and she looked me up and down in a self-assured sort of way.

"Well," she said at last. "You're better looking than I expected."

"Can I help you?" I asked.

"That's the question, isn't it?"

I opened my mouth to ask what she was doing outside my house, when another memory from yesterday jogged loose: Gabriel talking about why that girl had been waiting outside his house on a Friday night. Well, today was a Thursday, and it was technically evening, not night, but . . . .

"Do you know who I am?" the girl asked.

"Um," I said. "No?"

"Guess," the girl said with a smile.

"I'd rather not."

"Oh, come on. Here, I'll give you a hint. It's to do with your family. Your *well-connected* family."

That made me stop. *Wait.* Did she know something about my father?

"Who are you?" I asked.

"Lucella Ashford," the girl said, and waited expectantly.

I looked at her. The girl—Lucella—looked back at me.

"Okay," I said at last when it was clear that she was waiting for a reaction.

"As in, House Ashford."

". . . Okay?"

Lucella frowned at me.

"Not ringing any bells, sorry," I said. My brief flash of excitement was fading; it was looking as though she didn't know anything after all. Still, I had to check. "When you said 'your family,' did you mean someone called William Oakwood?"

Lucella looked at me as if I were an idiot. "Of course not."

"Right," I said, trying to hide my disappointment. I started to move around her.

"Where are you going?"

"I think you've got me mistaken for someone else."

"Don't walk away from me," Lucella said with a frown, and sidestepped to block my path.

I stopped with an internal sigh. In London, if a stranger comes up to you on the street, it generally means one of three things. First: they're looking for directions. Second: they want money. Third: they're drunk, on drugs, crazy, or all of the above. Lucella obviously wasn't lost, and she hadn't started to spin me a story about how she had to get home and needed three pounds for the bus fare or whatever, which just left "drunk/drugged/crazy." I didn't really want to know exactly which of those boxes she ticked, but unfortunately she was standing between me and my front door, so it was looking like I was about to find out.

Lucella and I stared at each other. The annoyance faded from Lucella's face, replaced by a thoughtful expression. "It's weird how you don't look like any of them," she told me.

Now that we were this close, I couldn't help but notice how pretty she was. Too bad about the on-drugs-or-crazy thing. "Excuse me," I told her.

"You do know what I'm talking about, right?"

"Not really, no."

Lucella stared at me for a second, then suddenly laughed. "Well, this isn't going how I expected."

"Look, I don't mean to be rude," I said, "but can you please let me through?"

"What? Oh." Lucella stepped aside.

I walked past. Lucella was eyeing me thoughtfully, but to my relief she didn't do anything. Now if I could just get indoors before she—

"You *are* a drucrafter, though, right?"

I stopped dead and turned. Lucella was standing with one hand on her hip, watching me.

"What?" I managed.

"You know, someone who can use drucraft?" Lucella asked. "A channeller, or a tyro at least? Because if not, then I *really* wasted my time coming here."

I didn't answer, and an interested look came into Lucella's eyes. "So you do know what I'm talking about."

"What are you doing here?" I asked.

Lucella studied me for a few more seconds, then seemed to come to a decision. "You know what, why not? Let's go inside."

I looked at her.

Lucella raised her eyebrows. "Aren't you going to invite me in?"

I hesitated. I didn't know what to make of Lucella, and part of me was still wondering if this was some sort of scam. But if it was, it was the most elaborate one I'd ever seen. Lucella was only the second person I'd ever come face to face with who knew what the word "drucraft" even meant, and I really, *really* wanted to find out what else she knew.

And even if she was just making it all up . . . well, she was a pretty girl about my age who seemed interested in me and wanted to come to my room.

"All right," I told her.

I pushed open the gate and walked up to the front door. Lucella made a waving gesture towards something or someone I couldn't see, and followed.

I CLOSED THE door behind us, breathing in the warm air. Chatter and the sounds of TV came from the front bedroom, and Ignas stuck his head out. He's a big guy with greying hair and stubble who works at the local garage and lives in the other upstairs bedroom with his wife. When he saw Lucella, his eyebrows rose.

"It's this way," I told Lucella, who took a long glance around then climbed the stairs. I followed her up and looked back to see Ignas grin at me and give me a thumbs-up.

Hobbes was waiting outside my room; he eyed Lucella suspiciously as we reached the landing. I unlocked the door and led Lucella in. "Well," I said, feeling suddenly embarrassed, "here it is."

Lucella stepped through the doorway, looked around, and stopped.

The silence stretched out. It was the first time I'd ever had a girl in this room, and all of a sudden I was uncomfortably aware of how small and dirty it was. "Well," Lucella said at last. "This is . . . different."

"Um . . ." I tried to think of how I could make a good impression. "Can I take your coat?"

Lucella handed me her coat—which I now noticed was lined with fur—without looking. Underneath it she was wearing a smart-looking blouse and skirt, and now that I looked more closely, there were rings glinting on her fingers. Standing there in my fleece and worn trousers, I suddenly felt very underdressed.

Lucella inspected the bed dubiously. "You don't have fleas, do you?"

"No," I said defensively. Well, okay, there had been that one time, but I'd learned my lesson about giving Hobbes his flea treatments.

Gingerly Lucella perched on the edge of the mattress. I scooped dirty clothes off the chair and sat down.

"So this is what a slum looks like," Lucella said, looking around curiously.

"This isn't a slum," I said in annoyance. "Why were you waiting outside my front door?"

Lucella leant back on her hands, her expression becoming thoughtful. "Because I've got a problem," she told me. "There are some people whose shoes I want to step into, and they aren't stepping out of them. You understand?"

"No."

"Okay. You know what House Ashford is?"

"No."

"What do you mean, 'no'?" Lucella said in irritation. "How can—ugh, fine. House Ashford is one of the Noble Houses of the United Kingdom. Not a Great House, but we're still a real House, not one of those old families who just call themselves one because their great-great-grandfather was someone important or whatever. We've got a seat on the Board. You understand?"

"Okay," I said slowly. I was starting to seriously wonder if this girl had a few screws loose. Maybe this was the kind of thing Felix and Gabriel meant when they'd say, "The cute ones are always insane."

"It's still kind of weird that you don't know anything about it," Lucella said, crossing one leg over the other. "I mean, you are related to us."

My thoughts came to a screeching halt. "What?"

"Well, not a real member, obviously, but still."

"Wait," I said. "You think I'm related to this House Ashford of yours?"

"Yes?" Lucella said, looking at me with an "Are you stupid?" expression.

I hesitated. A part of me still wasn't sure whether to believe Lucella or whether to decide that she was just crazy.

But if she was crazy, how did she know what a drucrafter even was? And how had she known that I was one?

"What I don't get," Lucella said when I didn't answer, "is how you don't seem to *know* anything. I mean, okay, you only had one parent to teach you this stuff, but still. You didn't even recognise your House."

"I think you've got me mixed up with someone else," I told Lucella. "My dad's definitely not from your House Ashford." That, I was sure about. My father's old-fashioned East London working class, and I didn't believe for a second that he'd raised me for nearly eighteen years while somehow hiding the fact that he was from some rich noble family.

"Not your father, your mother," Lucella said. "I mean, I'm assuming you get it from your mother's side?"

"Get what, my drucraft?" I said with a frown. "My dad taught me."

"Really?"

"Yes."

"Well, that's a bit less impressive, then."

"Okay, back up," I said. "You're saying my mother's from House Ashford? The same place you're from?"

"That I'm a *member* of," Lucella corrected. "And yes. Did she just not mention it or something?"

"She left when I was one."

"Yeah, but you still talk to her, right?"

"No."

Lucella laughed. "What, she just walked out on you and never called even once?"

I didn't answer.

Lucella paused. "Wait, seriously?"

I looked away.

"Wow," Lucella said when I still didn't speak. "And I thought my parents were bad."

I don't like thinking about my mother. When I was younger, I used to make up stories about her, imagining all kinds of reasons for why she might have left, and why she'd never got in touch. But as year after year went by and I heard nothing from her or from anyone else, the places those trains of thought led to became more and more depressing. When I'd ask my dad about her, he'd go quiet. He'd let slip a few things over the years, but not much. Though come to think of it, he had mentioned she'd come from a rich family.

As I got into my midteens, the whole thing started to bug me, and I started pestering my father about it, trying to get him to tell me what had happened. I probably would have worn him down eventually, except that right about then was the time *he* disappeared, and all of a sudden I had much more urgent problems. My mother became just another unsolved mystery, boxed up and pushed to the back of my mind and forgotten about.

Until now.

"You know, you're not what I expected," Lucella told me.

"What were you expecting?"

"Someone more like me, I guess," Lucella said with a shrug. "I grew up outside the family too, but at least my mother took me for visits. But it's like you've had no contact with them at all. I don't think half the Ashfords even know you exist."

"Was that why you came here today?" I asked. "You thought I'd know some of these people from House Ashford?"

"Something like that," Lucella said, swinging her legs.

"Yeah, sorry." I couldn't help but feel a little disappointed. Despite how weird it had been, I was realising that I didn't want this conversation to end. "Though . . ."

Lucella stared past me.

"Um . . . I know I'm not who you thought I was, but . . . it'd be really nice to have someone to talk to about drucraft and stuff."

Lucella blinked and looked at me. "What?"

"Um . . ."

"Oh, you thought I was about to leave?" Lucella said. "No. Actually, I think I'm going to help you."

That caught me off guard. "What?"

"I mean, you're not who I thought you'd be, but we still might be able to help each other." She glanced around the room meaningfully. "And I mean, you obviously need it."

"I'm doing all right," I said defensively.

Lucella raised her eyebrows.

"What kind of help?" I asked after a pause.

"A better place to live, some spending money, that kind of thing." Lucella eyed me critically. "Maybe clean you up a bit."

"Hey," I objected.

"Plus we could actually teach you some drucraft."

"What? How?"

"Same way everyone learns," Lucella said. "Tutors and drucraft schools."

I was suddenly very alert. "There are drucraft schools?"

Lucella laughed. "That got your attention. Yes, there are drucraft schools. I mean, they're just regular private schools mostly, but they have drucraft courses. I went to King's London—that's where everyone from House Ashford goes. Obviously you're a bit old for that now, but there's always uni. You're not going to Canterbury or Oxbridge, but we could probably get you into Maxwell or Queen Elizabeth or something."

My head was spinning: it was all too much to take in. I'd looked at university brochures from time to time, but never with any serious thought of getting in. But a university that taught *drucraft* . . . Being able to study that, as much as I wanted, without having to struggle to make a living day after day . . .

It was tempting. Too tempting. I looked at Lucella in sudden suspicion. "Why are you doing this?"

"I feel sorry for you, I suppose," Lucella said with a shrug. "But also, I might need you to do some things."

"What kind of things?"

"House Ashford has some . . . issues," Lucella said. "Questions of succession, let's say. Point is, we might be having some problems soon, and when we do, it'd be useful to have someone connected to the House who isn't in the House. Someone I can rely on. You understand?"

I looked at Lucella. Her voice was casual, but the way she was watching me wasn't. "Would this involve doing anything illegal?"

"Does that bother you?" Lucella asked.

"Depends on what it is," I said slowly. I was starting to wonder what I was getting myself into here.

"You want to be free, don't follow the rules," Lucella said lightly. "There are things out there more powerful than House Ashford."

Something about those last words made me look up sharply. Lucella wasn't looking at me, but just for a moment I had the sense of being watched.

The feeling was gone in an instant, but it left a sense of unease. I rose and turned to the window: outside, the sky was darkening. A crow was perched in the cherry tree, looking in at me through the glass with beady black eyes. I drew the curtain and turned back to Lucella.

The moment's pause had let me gather my thoughts. A little voice was telling me to say yes, that this was my big chance. Against that was caution. I didn't know what I was agreeing to, but something was telling me that it might be something I couldn't easily back out of.

But if I put all of that aside, the cold truth was that Lucella was right: I did need the help. At the moment I was just about keeping my head above water, but I had few savings and precious little safety margin, and it really wouldn't take much for things to go wrong. An accident, an unexpected bill, some mistake at work that cost me my job . . . any of those things could push me into debt, and once you get into that spiral, it's hard to get out.

"So?" Lucella said. "What do you say?"

"I guess we can give it a try," I said.

It sounded a bit half-hearted to me, but Lucella gave a satisfied sort of nod. "All right!" she said, clapping her hands. "Let's see what you can do."

"Do with what?"

"Drucraft, of course."

"Why does that matter?"

Lucella shook her head. "I keep forgetting how new you are to all this. Okay, pay attention." She held up a finger. "The biggest thing that children of Noble Houses are judged on is their drucraft. Looks count, brains count, but if a family head's sizing someone up, like for a marriage proposal or something, then the first two things they look at are their House and their drucraft skills. And that goes all the way down. If the armsmen and the servants are a bunch of plebs, well, people are going to think the House is weak. So if we're going to find some sort of place for you in House Ashford, you're going to have to measure up."

This world of hers sounds really weird. Still, the idea of a place where my drucraft was actually a selling point, and not something to hide, *did* sound nice . . .

"So let's see what you can do with a sigl," Lucella said.

I hesitated.

"You *do* have a sigl, right?"

"Yes . . ."

"Is it some crappy one that doesn't do anything but make light?"

I gave her a look.

"Wow," Lucella said. "You really are starting from the bottom."

"Can you go outside for a second?"

"Why?"

Because my sigls are behind the skirting board, and I don't want to show you where I hide them, I didn't say. To be honest, I was starting to get the feeling that Lucella wouldn't think my sigls were even worth stealing, but old habits die hard. "Please?"

"Oh, all right," Lucella said with a shrug. She got up and walked to the door. Hobbes was curled up in front of it, and

Lucella poked him with her foot to make him move, then went out into the hallway, closing the door behind her.

Hobbes gave me an unimpressed-sounding "mraaow," then looked at his food bowl.

"Later, okay?" I told him. I pulled out the skirting board, took out the box, reached inside for the two sigls . . . and hesitated.

My two sigls had been made twelve months apart, and you could really tell the difference. The older sigl was the first one I'd ever made, and it showed—you had to push nearly twice as much essentia through it as the newer one, but it wasted so much of it that it was only half as bright. I paused, my hand hovering between the two. Should I show her my best, or hold back?

I made my decision, took out the newer sigl in its plastic ring, put the box back in its cubbyhole, then replaced the skirting board and straightened up. "Come in," I called.

Lucella came back in, closing the door behind her, then looked at me and paused. "Oh."

"What's wrong?"

"When a boy asks you to step out of the room and come back, you kind of expect something a bit more exciting."

I felt my cheeks heat up. "Um . . ."

"Oh well." Lucella took a step forward and looked at the sigl in my hand. "Is that a plastic ring?"

"Yes."

"Where'd you get it, out of a Christmas cracker? Okay, okay, never mind. Light sigl, right? Let's see it."

I slipped the ring onto my finger and channelled a thread of essentia. A pale blue glow sprang up.

"Blue?" Lucella asked.

"Yes."

"Isn't white better?"

"It came out this way."

"Jesus." Lucella's eyebrows climbed. "What kind of made-in-China shit *is* this thing?"

"Can you stop it?"

"Fine, fine," Lucella said, waving her hand. "You have to admit it's kind of funny, though. I didn't know they even made sigls this bad."

"It's not that bad!" I said in annoyance. "It's a light sigl, it makes light. What else do you want?"

"Well, it'd help if it was actually bright enough to see with . . ."

I widened the flow of essentia through the sigl. The light doubled in brightness.

Lucella paused. "Did you do that?"

"Do you see anyone else around?"

Lucella gave me a suspicious look. "You aren't shining a penlight from behind your fingers or something?"

I was getting a bit tired of Lucella talking down to me. I thinned the flow of essentia down to almost nothing, causing the light to dim, then brought it up to half brightness again. Then I did it a couple more times, just to prove it wasn't a fluke.

"Huh," Lucella said. She actually looked mildly impressed. "Why didn't you tell me you were a channeller?"

"You didn't ask," I said. According to my dad, being able to channel was the point at which you were a "real" drucrafter, so I'd assumed that was what Lucella had meant. "What, did you think I could only sense or something?"

"Actually, I wasn't sure you could even do that," Lucella admitted. "Well, I guess you pass."

Huh. That was easy.

"That's so weird, though," Lucella said, bending close to stare curiously at the ring. "Why would anyone make a sigl like that?" She held out a hand. "Give it here."

I pulled my hand back and let the light from the sigl vanish. "Why is it weird?"

Lucella looked briefly surprised that I hadn't obeyed her. "Well, no one makes *blue* torch sigls."

"It came out that way."

"No one's that cheap," Lucella said with a laugh. "Or at least no House is. Did you get it out of some corp's bargain bin?"

"I made it."

"No, seriously, where did you buy it?"

"I *told* you, I made it."

For a moment Lucella looked as though she was about to make yet another joke, then she seemed to realise I was serious. "Wait," she said, her smile fading. "Really?"

I looked at her. Lucella stared back at me.

I waited. When Lucella didn't speak, I leant a little to the side. Her gaze didn't track my face, and I waved a hand. "Hello?"

Slowly Lucella turned to look at me. "What?"

"You said I passed?"

Lucella stared at me for ten seconds in total silence, then something in her expression changed. "Yeah, this isn't going to work."

"What do you—?" I began, but Lucella had already turned and pulled open the door. "Wait!"

Lucella shut the door behind her. I heard her footsteps trotting down the stairs, then the sound of the front door. Then silence.

"I thought you wanted to see what I could do," I said to the empty room.

Hobbes had been watching the entire conversation from the corner. "Mraaow," he said in a decisive tone.

"I kind of knew any girl I brought back to this room wasn't going to be impressed," I told him. "I didn't think she'd run away."

Hobbes looked pointedly at his food bowl.

I sighed. "Right, right, your dinner." The excitement that had started to build during my talk with Lucella was gone, replaced by a growing depression. Having your hopes raised and then dashed is much worse than having them never raised at all. For a few minutes there I'd started to believe that I'd found a way out. Now I was back to reality. Hobbes needed feeding, my bills had to be paid, and I had work tomorrow.

I shoved my sigl into my pocket, turned towards the wardrobe, then stopped. Lucella's fur coat was still lying on the bed. "Hey, she left her coat . . ."

Hobbes padded over to his bowl. His manner clearly conveyed that there were more important things to worry about.

I looked down at the coat, hesitating. Should I go after her? It was a cold evening; as soon as Lucella got out into the street, she'd notice her coat was missing. Maybe she'd come back.

Just as I thought that, Hobbes's head turned. A moment later, I heard the sound of the front door.

"That must be her," I told Hobbes.

Hobbes's ears flattened against his skull, and he backed away towards the window.

I frowned, started to say something, then stopped as I heard the sound of footsteps coming up the stairs.

Lots of footsteps.

Lots of *heavy* footsteps.

I stared, confused, as the footsteps grew louder and louder until they were right outside. My door swung open.

CHAPTER 3

THE MAN STANDING in my doorway looked like an ad for protein supplements. Muscles bulged from under a black shirt, and his shoulders were so wide he had to turn to fit through the door. Close-set eyes in a tanned face stared down at me in an evaluating sort of way. He looked like Vin Diesel from *The Fast and the Furious*, except uglier and with bigger muscles.

Staring up at the guy, I had one of those moments of clarity. At some point in this evening, I had made a really big mistake. Maybe it had been letting Lucella into my room; maybe it had been something I'd said; maybe it had been not locking the door when she'd left. But whichever it had been, things were about to go very, very badly.

Ugly Vin Diesel took a step into my room, and I got a brief glimpse of an equally huge guy behind him before Diesel reached for me with a meaty hand. I ducked and backed away, bumping up against the chair. Diesel took another step forward and grabbed for me again.

I blocked, and the impact lifted me almost off the floor. I

slammed into the wall, pain flaring in my back and side as shock washed through me. *Jesus, he's strong!*

"One piece," the second man grunted at Diesel. He was as big as his partner, with a shaven head and the look of a brawler, including a faded scar across his temple that looked as if someone had tried to scalp him with a pint glass. Between the two of them, I could barely see the door.

Diesel grabbed for me a third time and this time got a fistful of my clothing. He dragged me forward. "Easy—" he began, then his words cut off in a grunt as I hit him in the side. "Hey!" he growled, and shook me until I felt my bones rattle. "Quit it."

I hit Diesel's wrist, trying to break his grip. He scowled but kept his hold . . . right up until Hobbes's claws sank into his leg.

Diesel yelled in pain. Hobbes had latched on below the man's knee, tail bushed and eyes glaring, and he had his teeth and front claws sunk into the guy's calf while his back legs scrabbled and raked. Diesel dropped me and tried to shake Hobbes off, then when that didn't work he smacked him with a glancing blow that sent Hobbes flying.

Lucella's voice came from behind the two men, sounding annoyed. "Can you hurry this up?"

Diesel straightened up from inspecting his leg, swearing. "There's a cat!"

"I don't care if it's the Loch Ness Monster, get on with it!"

Lucella! A flash of fury went through me, there and gone in an instant as I tried frantically to think of something I could do. Something was nagging at me—a presence . . . ? *Is it . . . ?*

I concentrated, emptying my mind to feel the essentia currents of my room. Except that now, instead of swirling passively, they were flowing away from me, into those two men. There was essentia coming from them, but it was different, something vital and intense and alive . . .

I felt a thrill of fear as I realised what I was looking at. These guys were drucrafters. They didn't just weigh twice what I did; they were magically enhanced as well.

Diesel turned his glare on me and tried to grab me once again, but this time I was ready. I ducked under his arm and hit him in the body, quick punches that rocked him back. I was afraid, but the reflexes I'd earned from those hours in the boxing ring kept me moving. Diesel was big but slow: he swung with his right hand, and I stepped in, then got him under the chin with an uppercut. I heard his teeth go *click* and he staggered back.

The guy with the scar let Diesel bounce off him and shoved him back towards me. He couldn't get past Diesel to reach me; the room was too small and Diesel too big. I was one-on-one with Diesel, and for a moment this felt familiar. It was like a boxing match . . . okay, a boxing match against a guy twice my size, but I'd sparred with superheavyweights before.

I didn't let myself think about how those sparring matches with superheavyweights had usually *ended*.

Diesel closed in, and the small room became a whirl of motion. I caught a glimpse of Hobbes, looking dazed, crawling under the bed; Scar was scowling over the other man's shoulder. The wardrobe cracked, the wood splintering as Diesel thumped into it. My fists hammered his midriff—I wasn't seriously hurting him, but I could keep him at a distance. I was breathing hard, my blood up. One second at a time. Keep hitting him, keep pushing him back—

And then Diesel shoved me against the wall and punched me in the head.

Stars flashed, and the world turned into a blizzard of grey. I felt as though I was falling endlessly; blood roared in my ears. White and black lights flashed in my vision.

Gradually my senses came back. Pain was throbbing in my

head; it felt as though my skull was about to split open. There was a rushing in my ears, along with a buzzing sound; as the rushing faded away, the buzzing became words, fading in and out. "...taking too long," a deep voice was growling.

"...cat..." someone else complained from next to my ear.

"...don't give a..."

"...ran away..."

I struggled back to consciousness. I was upright: a big hand was sunk painfully into my shoulder, holding me up. I tried to move and caught my breath as a fresh spike of pain went through me.

I cracked an eye open a fraction. Light stabbed in, and as my vision adjusted, I saw that I was still in my room. Diesel's big hand was pinning me against the wall, and out of the corner of my eye I could see Lucella and Scar.

"...take him where?" Scar was saying.

"You let me worry about that," Lucella said.

Scar frowned.

"Is there something you're not understanding here?" Lucella asked.

"You said we were just keeping an eye on him," Scar told Lucella.

"Yeah, well, I changed my mind."

I felt Diesel shift to look at Scar. Scar shared a glance with the other man, then turned back to Lucella. "I think—" he began.

"You aren't paid to think."

"Aren't paid for snatching, either," Scar said.

"Fine, fine," Lucella said with a sigh, waving a hand. "I'll make sure there's a bit extra in it for you, all right?"

"How much?" Diesel asked.

"Not enough to be worth getting sent down for an all-day," Scar said.

I was still dazed and having trouble thinking clearly, but

everything I could hear was sounding worse and worse. I tried to move and pain flashed through my head.

". . . just asking," Diesel was saying.

"No," Scar told him. "You said—"

"I don't care," Lucella said deliberately, taking a step forward and staring up at Scar. "Now shut up and *do as you're told*."

Diesel and Scar were both twice Lucella's size, and from where she was standing, Scar towered over her. As she spoke those last words, though, I felt Diesel flinch. The effect on Scar was even stronger: he hunched down and shrank away.

Lucella stared at Scar for a few seconds longer, then turned away, apparently satisfied, and met my eyes. "Oh, you're awake."

I swallowed a couple of times before speaking. "This—" I began, then coughed. "This is your idea of helping me?"

Lucella started to answer, then paused.

"You said you felt sorry for me," I said. The anger clearing my head, burning away the cobwebs. "What was that, some kind of sick joke?"

"No," Lucella said with a slight sigh. She took a step closer, lowering her voice. "I *was* going to help you. It's just . . . look, remember what I said about having some shoes to step into? The last thing I need is more competition."

I stared at Lucella, not understanding.

I heard a voice call out from the direction of the stairs. "Think we should go," Scar said in a subdued voice.

"It's a shame," Lucella said. She picked up her coat, framed in the doorway against the light of the hall, then looked back at me. "I did kind of like you." Then she turned away and called over her shoulder to Diesel. "Let's move."

Diesel half lifted, half dragged me out of my room and down the stairs. This close, I could sense the essentia flowing through Diesel's body, radiating strength and power; he lifted me off the ground as though I were a football. Scar stomped down ahead of us, shouting something. There was movement, the scuffle of footsteps; I was dragged through the hall, and as we passed the door to the front bedroom, I saw Ignas, his eyes startled as they met mine.

Then we were out on the street. The cold spring air cut through me as Diesel dragged me along the pavement. A dark shape loomed up, and I twisted to see the side of a car. No, not a car—a black minivan.

Oh, I thought dizzily. *That was why it was there.* I was having trouble thinking; things had gone wrong too fast.

"Okay, put him in," Lucella was saying. The side door of the minivan rumbled open. "You go with—huh?"

The sound of raised voices came from the direction of my house. I twisted my head around to see Ignas and the two other Lithuanian men come spilling out of the door. Ignas looked down the road, saw us, and shouted something.

Lucella stared at them blankly. "What the hell?"

Ignas and the other men advanced down the pavement. Lucella shot Scar a glare. "I told you to take care of them."

"I was trying to tell you—" Scar began.

Lucella started to answer, then hesitated, looking back at the advancing Lithuanians; they'd already closed most of the distance. She swore and pointed at Scar and Diesel one after the other. "You, hold them off. You, get him in the car and drive. Now!"

I tried to break free from Diesel and got a cuff to my face that made me see stars. While I was still dazed, I was shoved into the front of the minivan; I heard the click of a seat belt and the slam of a door, then Diesel piled into the driver's seat next to me, the van creaking under his weight. The engine started with a growl. I caught a confused glimpse of Ignas struggling with Scar; Lucella was trying to get into the van, but Matis got in her way and she jumped back with a curse. Then the engine caught and the van pulled away from the kerb.

Suddenly everything was quiet except for the rumble of the engine. Faintly I could hear shouts from behind, but they quickly faded away. I tried to twist around to look.

"Sit down," Diesel said, not taking his eyes off the road.

"Where are you—"

"Shut it."

"Why—"

Diesel took his left hand off the wheel and balled it into a fist. I stopped talking.

The minivan rumbled to a stop at a junction. Diesel turned on the indicators, glanced left and right, then pulled out into Plaistow Road. The city lights rolled by: white and yellow windows, neon-orange streetlamps, the red and green of traffic lights. The van's engine growled, steady and powerful.

The pause was giving me the chance to collect my thoughts. I still didn't understand what was happening or what I'd got myself into, but I knew I had to get out of here.

But how?

People were passing by on the pavements, but I knew they couldn't see me through the tinted windows and shouting for help would just get me another punch. Could I dive out of the car? I'd have to undo the seat belt, pull the door open, then get out. No way I could do all that before Diesel could grab me.

I eyed Diesel covertly. With his bulk, he looked like a bouncer who spent his off hours at the gym. My head was still throbbing from that punch, and I had the nasty feeling that he hadn't even been using his full strength. If he'd hit me at full power with that sigl, he'd have broken my skull.

His sigl. Now that I knew what to look for, I could sense where it was—a node somewhere near the front of his chest, drawing in essentia in a steady flow. Could I get it away from him? I couldn't see how. Besides, he could probably beat the crap out of me without it.

A horrible feeling swept through me, fright mixed with hopelessness. How had I gotten into this? I was totally out of my league. A part of me wanted to just shrink down into the seat and do as I was told . . .

No. A flash of anger rose up inside of me. *Screw* these guys. What had my dad always said? The worse things got, the more you needed to keep calm. Figure out what you had going for you.

What did I have going for me?

He's driving and I'm not. As long as the car was moving, Diesel was distracted. He couldn't spare me too much attention without causing a crash.

What did I have in my pockets? Phone, wallet, keys, spare change. Use my phone to call the police? No, Diesel would just grab it. Scratch him with the keys . . . no, no, no. If only I had a sigl like his . . .

My sigl.

Hope sparked within me. It was still in my pocket, waiting to be used. But how? Lucella had laughed at it; all it could do was make light.

I looked left and right. The van smelt of upholstery and cheap coffee; outside, shadowy buildings were silhouetted against an overcast sky. Diesel's eyes flicked from the road to the car mirrors to me before going back to the road again. Red taillights showed from the car in front, dimmed through the tinted windows. The inside of the van was dark.

Light and dark . . .

The plan flashed into my mind in an instant. Slowly and carefully, an inch at a time, I began to slide my hand into my pocket. I could see the whites of Diesel's eyes, blurry in the darkness, and

I kept my movements smooth and steady so that he wouldn't catch them in his peripheral vision. My fingers brushed my sigl ring; I grasped the plastic between two fingers and drew it out. Once the ring was free, I waited for Diesel to check his mirrors, then slipped it on while he was turned away.

We'd been passing down a long dark street, but now from up ahead I could see the two-by-two neon lights of a motorway. Red traffic lights glowed; we were coming up to a slip road. The van purred to a stop behind three other cars. Past the glow of brake lights, a grey-brown concrete overpass arced across the night sky. The muffled rush of traffic filtered through into the van.

Diesel turned to stare at me.

Indicator lights flashed from the car ahead, illuminating the inside of the van in a faint strobe: blink-blink, blink-blink. Beyond, I could hear the whoosh of traffic on the overpass, cars accelerating down the slope and away into the night. Diesel was still staring and I held dead still. Had he seen my sigl? I wanted to hide it, but I knew that if I tried the movement would catch his eye.

The red traffic light glowed.

Come on, turn yellow, I prayed silently. *Yellow, yellow, yellow.*

The light stayed red. Diesel was still staring at me. Had he seen something?

Yellow!

The light turned yellow.

The cars ahead began to pull out one by one. Diesel turned his eyes forward and began to drive.

With a rumble, the minivan turned onto the slip road. The road followed a gentle curve, arcing to run parallel to the overpass and then to the merging point ahead. The cars that had been in front were pulling away as they sped up. Diesel pressed down on the accelerator; the growl of the engine rose in pitch, and the van shuddered as it gained speed.

I thrust my hand in front of Diesel's face and sent a burst of essentia through my sigl. Blue-white light erupted like a star.

Everything happened very fast.

Diesel screamed "FUCK!" and stomped on the brakes. The minivan's tyres shrieked, the vehicle fishtailing; the seat belt bit into my chest with a jolt of pain. Diesel fought blindly for control, overcorrecting then pulling back the other way; the minivan lurched and jerked, two of its wheels leaving the ground, nearly rolling over on its side before slamming back down and coming to a screeching, smoking halt. Diesel jerked with the impact, then scrubbed at his eyes, trying to get his sight back. Only then did he turn towards me, his face alight with rage.

But in the time he'd taken to do that, I'd unlocked my seat belt, opened the door, and dived out of the van.

I came down on the tarmac on hands and knees and was off like a sprinter from the starting blocks. I heard Diesel yell something, but I didn't stop to listen, and I was out of earshot in seconds. Cool air rushed past. There was a footpath running parallel to the slip road and curving away downhill, and I swerved onto it, settling into a fast run.

That fight with Diesel had given me some idea of what he could do. He was superhumanly strong, and maybe superhumanly tough, but he *wasn't* superhumanly fast. He was a bodybuilder, not a sprinter, and I was betting that I could run faster than he could.

I risked a quick glance over my shoulder and saw that the minivan had disappeared behind the roadside bushes. There was no sign of Diesel. Up ahead, the overpass was descending to merge with the access road; the red taillights of cars zoomed past, disappearing into the distance. Beyond, on the far side of the motorway, I could see a floodlit orange-and-white Sainsbury's sign, with a huge building peeking out from behind the trees.

And at that point I heard the growl of an engine.

My heart jumped and I looked back. On the other side of the bushes, the minivan was roaring along by the roadside. Through the tinted windows I could just make out a hulking shape hunched over the wheel.

Oh, shit. Too late, I realised that I'd been running right alongside the road.

Instinctively I sped up, but the minivan easily pulled ahead of me. Looking ahead, I saw that the bushes and the grass verge were thinning out: there was nothing separating the footpath from the motorway but a low kerb. The minivan's brake lights glowed and it turned left, bumping up onto the footpath in front of me and stopping with a screech of brakes.

I skidded to a halt, looking around. Before me was the van, to my right the motorway. The overpass and access road had merged and cars were zipping by across eight lanes of traffic. To my left was a high wooden fence. The minivan's door swung open, and Diesel clambered out.

I turned right and darted across the motorway.

A horn blared, but I was watching the traffic; one car zoomed by ahead, another behind, and then I was at the barrier that divided the two halves of the motorway. It was only a couple of feet high, a flimsy thing of grey metal. I vaulted it, then heard pounding feet and turned.

Diesel was right on the other side of the barrier. He reached for it and I feinted, making as if I'd hit him as soon as he tried to climb over. He checked, one hand on the metal.

Cars were slowing down behind Diesel, drivers craning their necks to look at the immobile minivan. I saw one guy mouth something angrily. "Stop running," Diesel shouted at me.

"Make me," I shouted back.

A truck roared past, the whack of wind blasting my hair. "You make me chase you and you'll regret it," Diesel shouted over the noise.

I stared defiantly.

Traffic rushed past all around us. Diesel looked around, seeming to realise just where we were. "Come on," he told me. "You don't want to get hit by a car."

"I've seen what you and your boss are like," I told him. "I'm taking my chances with the cars."

The false concern slid off Diesel's face. He set a foot onto the barrier.

I turned and fled across the other half of the motorway. More horns sounded; I came up short, let a car whizz ahead of me, then reached the far side and started running towards the Sainsbury's.

Snatching a glance back, I saw Diesel was still following. He was having more trouble crossing the road than I'd had.

Okay, let's see how badly this guy wants to catch me.

I ran back out into the motorway, crossing four lanes of traffic to get back to the dividing barrier. This time I made a big container lorry brake; its horn blared, and the driver shouted something that didn't sound friendly. I jogged along the strip of grass, checking back over my shoulder. Diesel was starting to look really pissed off, but he followed me again, lumbering through the rushing traffic.

As soon as he'd made it to the barrier, I ran back across to the side he'd just come from.

I heard Diesel yell something that sounded like "*Oh, come on!*" He tried to follow me again, but this time I'd timed my dash to be just before a clump of traffic.

There was the screech of brakes and a hollow thud. I glanced back to see Diesel bent over the bonnet of a car; he didn't look injured, but it had slowed him down. The Sainsbury's sign was right up ahead; beyond was a half-full car park and a huge supermarket, white lights and product aisles glowing from be-hind floor-to-ceiling windows.

I ran into the car park. The Sainsbury's was still open, and people were going in and out with trolleys and shopping bags. I entered through the sliding doors, slowing to a walk. Dozens of aisles stretched away to the left and right; I went up the nearest one, then crouched down at the first intersection, peering around the corner towards the entrance.

Diesel appeared in the doorway ten seconds later. He looked pissed off, but that car obviously hadn't hurt him much. He glared around at the checkout counters, then strode forward, heading for the aisle to my left.

As soon as he was out of sight, I rose and walked quickly back down the aisle. The shelves were high enough that you couldn't see over them. I walked past the checkout gates, through the slid-ing doors, and out into the night.

The car park was quiet. On the motorway, I could see a traffic jam and a few people staring in our direction. I turned right, jog-ging along the side of the car park and past a building site, then into a big retail park. Other shops loomed up in the night, and with each turning that I passed I felt a tiny bit of tension go out of me. Finally I saw a bus stop. A bus was just coming around the corner, and I recognised the route for one that would take me home.

I walked to the bus stop and stood behind two other people. The bus pulled up; I got on, touched my wallet to the reader, then found an empty seat. The doors hissed closed, the bus pulled away, and I hunched down, staring out of the window, ready to duck out of sight. I stayed like that, ready and alert, as the bus pulled out of the retail park and out onto a main road. Only when the lights of the last shops had disappeared behind me did I fi-nally relax.

CHAPTER 4

THE BUS HEADED south towards the river, beginning the long loop that would take it around Gallions Reach and then north-west towards Plaistow. The city lights rolled by, yellow embers in the darkness.

Now that I was safe, I was finally realising just how scared I'd been. That had been *terrifying*. What would have happened if I hadn't had my sigl in my pocket? Or if Ignas hadn't noticed what was going on? I'd probably still be in that van . . . or wherever they'd been planning to take me.

A cold and even more frightening thought occurred to me. Was this what had happened to my dad?

Looked at that way, the whole thing all made a horrible kind of sense. My dad had disappeared without a trace, and if I hadn't managed to get away from Diesel, I would have too. Lucella hadn't recognised my dad's name, but I couldn't believe that this was all just a coincidence.

The second thing I was realising was that I'd been far too passive and trusting. The more I thought about what I'd done this evening, the more I noticed just how many stupid mistakes I'd made. I shouldn't have let Lucella in, I shouldn't have shown her my sigl, and I *definitely* shouldn't have sat around like an idiot waiting for her to come back. And then once the goon squad had shown up, I should have yelled for help instead of trying to deal with it myself. I'd been lucky to get away at all.

Well, done was done. All I could do was make sure to be a lot less naive next time.

The final thing I was realising was that my head *really* hurt. I had bruises on my chest and shoulder, but my head was the worst, a throbbing pain pulsing outwards from the left side. It was bad enough that if I let myself focus on it, I actually wanted to throw up.

I wanted to check on Hobbes, but I couldn't go home: that was the first place Lucella and Scar would look. I needed somewhere to hide.

WHITECHAPEL WAS FILLED with noise and chatter, the air carrying the smell of discarded fruits and vegetables from the day's market. I found the building I was looking for and rang the bell.

Colin appeared at the door a minute later. He was wearing a T-shirt and tracksuit bottoms, and his hair was mussed. He seemed about to complain about how late it was, but as he got a look at me, his eyebrows went up. "Jesus, dude. What happened to you?"

"I need a place to crash," I told him. "Please?"

COLIN LIVES IN a big building used for student accommodation, with sets of three flats that each share a kitchen and bathroom. The room had a messy, lived-in feel, full of dirty clothes and empty bottles. I sat in the room's one chair, leaning against the desk to prop myself up.

"Here you go," Natalie said, handing me some tablets. "Ibuprofen." Natalie is Colin's current girlfriend, tall and heavily built with a plain, friendly face. I'd always thought of her as the tough-girl type, but since I'd come in she'd been showing an unexpected motherly streak.

"And some lemon tea," Colin said, putting a steaming mug down on the desk. "Drink that and I'll get you another one, all right?"

"Thanks," I said tiredly. "Sorry for ruining your evening."

Natalie laughed. "Don't worry, the movie was crap anyway."

"What are you talking about?" Colin said in outrage. "It's Jackie Chan! It's a classic!"

I closed my eyes, letting the sound of the argument wash over me. Now that I'd sat down, I wasn't sure I'd be able to get back up.

"Anyway," Natalie said eventually, and I opened my eyes to see that she had her coat slung over her arm. "I'll leave you to take care of him."

"Yeah, thanks," Colin said. "Sorry about kicking you out like this, I know it's pretty lame."

"It's all right." Natalie gave me a wave. "Take care, Stephen, okay?"

Colin escorted Natalie out. I heard the sound of the door closing, and Colin reappeared. "All right," Colin said. "Let's hear it."

Slowly and haltingly, I gave Colin an edited account of my evening. I didn't mention sigls or drucraft, which meant the story had some pretty big holes, but judging by the expression on Colin's face, just the bits I was telling him sounded unbelievable enough already.

". . . and then I changed buses at Stratford and came here," I finished.

"Wow," Colin said. "You realise what this means, right?"

"What?"

"You've officially beaten Felix for the worst date."

I gave Colin a look.

"Seriously, his thing with that girl from Singapore used to be first place, but you've definitely topped it. But okay, let me see if I've got this right. You invite some rich girl up to your room who tells you she knows your mum, then she calls in two heavies who beat you up and shove you in a minivan. You crash the minivan, play chicken with the driver on the A13, then give him the slip and catch a bus here. Right?"

"You believe me?"

"Well, if it was anyone else, I'd say it was a load of bollocks," Colin said. "But given that it's you, I can actually believe an evening with a girl would end up that badly."

"Thanks," I said tiredly. "I think."

Colin thought for a second. "You think this girl really knows your mum?"

"I don't know," I said. I took a swallow from the mug; the tea burned my mouth but made my head feel better. Hopefully the painkillers would kick in soon. "Maybe."

"Did you believe her?"

"Not at first."

"Then why'd you let her into your room?"

"Because . . ."

"Because?"

"What we were talking about last night in the pub," I said reluctantly.

Colin looked confused.

"You know . . . it's that kind of situation, and a girl's asking you to let her in . . ."

Colin stared for a second. "Wait, seriously?"

"I didn't know what to do, okay?"

"Okay, okay," Colin said. "I want you to stop and think for a second. You were taking relationship advice from Gabriel."

"I get it."

"You were taking *relationship advice* from—"

"Can you stop treating this like it's a joke?" I snapped.

Colin paused, the grin disappearing from his face as he took in how I was looking. "Ah, shit. You really are in bad shape, aren't you?"

I stared down at the mug, my thoughts going back to what had happened in my room. The weird thing was, Lucella hadn't come across as hostile at the start. Yeah, she'd been kind of insulting, but it had felt more like a recruitment pitch. It was only after I'd shown her my sigl that she'd changed.

We talked a little longer, but exhaustion was catching up with me and the conversation kept tailing off. At last Colin announced that I should get some rest, and laid out a spare blanket and an old sleeping bag. The floor underneath was hard, but I was too tired to care.

I SLEPT LATE. By the time I woke, sunlight was streaming through the blinds and Colin was gone.

I sat up with a wince; my neck had stiffened overnight, and the hard floor hadn't done my back any good, either. Colin had left a scribbled note on the desk telling me he'd gone to lectures and to take what I needed from the fridge. It's good to have friends.

I sent a text to work calling in sick. I hated to do it—not only did it mean I wasn't earning for the day, I was running the risk of getting fired. Job agencies are complete bastards and it takes hardly anything to make them kick you out. But I knew that if those guys could find where I lived, they could just as easily find where I worked.

I headed for the bathroom, pulling off my shirt, and took a look in the mirror. My left ear had turned a purplish red and I had a line of finger-shaped bruises on my shoulder, but my headache was mostly gone and I didn't think any of the bruises were serious. A hot shower eased my stiffness and left me feeling much better. Once I was done, I dressed in my dirty clothes and headed out, letting the door lock behind me.

TWO BUSES TOOK me from Whitechapel back to Plaistow.

I got off one stop before Foxden Road, approached cautiously on foot, then studied my road from a distance. No black minivan. Just to be on the safe side, I circled around to the other end and took a second look. Once I was sure the coast was clear, I walked up, glancing over my shoulder the whole time, and unlocked the door.

An eager "Mrrraow?" sounded from below.

"Hobbes!" I caught up the cat and hugged him, feeling my chest ease a little. I'd been really worried. Hobbes purred and licked my arm, then gave a questioning trill, as if to say, *Where were you and where's my breakfast?*

"Hey, hey!" a voice called. I looked up to see Ignas leaning out of the downstairs bedroom, a big grin on his face. "He's okay!"

The other two men poked their heads out into the corridor, all curious to see me, and I was deluged with questions in two different languages. I was ushered into the front room and handed a drink, and gradually, I started to piece together what had happened.

Apparently Ignas had been downstairs when Diesel and Scar had come in. Scar had told Ignas that they worked for the landlord, which Ignas had believed right up until the bumping and banging had brought him out into the corridor in time to see me being dragged out. At that point, Ignas had sounded the alarm, and Matis and Vlad had piled out, ready for a fight. After the minivan had carried me away, there'd been a brawl with Scar that had ended with him and Lucella backing off. The three men had filtered back into the house and, in the absence of any better ideas, had waited to see if I'd make it home.

All of them seemed very happy to see me, and I got a lot of handshakes and congratulatory slaps on my back. I found it all oddly touching. I hadn't felt as though I'd known the Lithuanians very well, but they obviously felt as if they knew me, enough that they'd been willing to fight to protect me.

Most importantly, there was no sign of Lucella. Apparently after the fight, she and Scar hadn't come back. Although somebody else had.

"Wait, wait," I said when I figured out what they were saying. "Someone else? Who?"

Matis said something in Lithuanian. He was Ignas's cousin . . . or brother . . . or maybe his cousin's brother, I wasn't sure. "Another," Ignas translated. "He ask for you."

"Was it a girl?" I asked.

The other man shook his head. "Boy."

I frowned. How many of these people were there?

At last Ignas and Vlad had to leave for work. Ignas was the last one to go, and as he did, I put a hand on his arm. "Ignas? Thank you. And tell the others thank you too."

"You're welcome," Ignas said with a grin. "Sorry we were slow, hey?"

"You weren't slow," I told him. If it hadn't been for Ignas, Lucella and Scar would have been in the van as well. I didn't think I could have escaped from all three of them. "If you ever need a favour, let me know."

Ignas just laughed and patted my head. I headed upstairs.

BACK IN MY bedroom, I fed Hobbes a double portion of cat food, then while he was happily munching I did what I could to tidy up. There hadn't been too much damage, largely because there wasn't much to break, although Diesel had splintered one of my wardrobe doors. I hoped the landlord wouldn't try to make me pay for it.

Oh, who was I kidding? Of course he would.

I'd just finished changing into some clean clothes when there was a knock on the door and Matis poked his head in. "Someone asking for you," he told me.

"The boy from before?" I asked.

Matis nodded.

I thought quickly, wondering whether to hide or stand my ground. *Stand*, I decided. And if this guy was going to try another kidnapping, I'd call for help this time. "Okay," I said. "Let's see who it is." I checked my pocket for my sigl and walked out onto the landing.

At the bottom of the stairs, illuminated in the morning sunlight spilling through the door, was a boy around my age with dark brown hair. I stopped with one hand on the banister, looking down.

"Hi there," the boy said. "Stephen, right?"

"Who are you?" I asked him.

"Tobias Ashford," the boy told me. "Mind if I come in?"

"Yeah, actually," I said. "I do." Last night's lesson was still fresh in my mind.

Tobias paused. "Okay."

"What are you doing here?" I asked.

"All right . . ." Tobias spread his hands. "Obviously getting off to a bad start here. I'm just here to talk, I promise. Hear me out?"

I looked down at the boy for a long moment. A bird called in the silence. "I'll hear you out," I said at last. "For now."

Matis clumped down the stairs, eyeing the boy as he passed. Tobias waited for him to get out of the way, then came up. I stood to one side as he walked into my room, then followed him in, stopping in the doorway.

Now that I got a closer look at Tobias, I could see that he was a little younger than me, maybe eighteen or so. He was an inch or so shorter as well, though he moved with a kind of springy energy that made him seem to take up more space than he really did. He had a quick, attractive smile, slightly spoilt by the sardonic twist that never quite left his mouth.

"Want to close the door?" he told me.

"No," I said, and leant against it, folding my arms. "I think I'm keeping it wide open so everyone in the house can hear any sound we make."

The boy blinked. "I'm, uh . . . not quite sure where to go with that."

"Now how about you tell me what you're really doing here?" I said. "And more importantly, how you know my address."

"Okay, okay," Tobias said. He sat down in my chair, heedless of the dirty clothes. "Give me a second and I'll explain. The first I knew that something had happened was when Lucella came home last night way too late with a couple of House armsmen whom she *definitely* shouldn't have been giving orders to. I tried talking to her and she blew me off. I had to lean on the armsmen to get the story, and even they didn't say much."

"So you know Lucella?"

"She's my cousin."

"Great," I said. "In that case, I've got a few questions for you. Lucella told me that she was from some noble family and that my mother's from that family too. Is that true?"

"Not a noble family, a Lesser House," Tobias corrected. "But... yes, that's true."

"How come this is the first time I've heard about any of this?"

"It's complicated."

"Complicated how?"

"I'm not really supposed to be talking about this ..."

"Try," I said flatly.

"Okay," Tobias said. He seemed to be choosing his words very carefully. "Most Noble Houses have at least one minor branch of the family that they use to marry in promising outsiders. It's how they make alliances and bring in new blood. Your mother is from ... one of House Ashford's branches."

I eyed Tobias. I had the feeling he was holding something back. "Does that mean I'm related to both of you?"

"Lucella's my first cousin once removed," Tobias said. "And you're Lucella's first cousin once removed." He gave a whimsical smile. "You're a little too distant to be part of the House, exactly, but ... welcome to the family?"

I looked at Tobias suspiciously. Cousins of cousins made us ... what? He didn't look much like me ... similar build, maybe, but that was about it. Though if we were that distantly related, that wasn't really surprising.

And wait, Lucella was my first cousin? Ew. Actually, come to think of it, did first cousins once removed count as incest? Well, after last night I wasn't touching Lucella with a barge pole, so it was a moot point.

"All right," Tobias said. "Could you at least tell me what happened last night? About all I could get out of the armsmen was that they drove you off in a car."

I had to laugh. "Your 'armsmen' punched me in the head hard enough to knock me out, then *dragged* me into a van. And they did it on your cousin's orders."

". . . Why?"

"I don't know," I said deliberately. "You tell me."

"But that doesn't make—" Tobias said, then paused. "Didn't she say anything? Give you some sort of explanation?"

"Yeah, actually," I said, watching Tobias closely. "Right at the end. She said the last thing she needed was more competition."

Tobias stared at me.

I tilted my head, waiting. "I'm guessing that means something to you," I told Tobias when he didn't speak.

"Just a second," Tobias said absently. He got up and started to pace before realising that the room wasn't big enough. Hobbes wandered up to me and head-butted my leg. I scratched him behind the ears, watching Tobias closely.

"Couldn't have been family," Tobias said to himself. He seemed to have forgotten I was there. "That's old news. Couldn't have been the engagement . . ." He stopped and looked at me, his eyes suddenly sharp. "Drucraft. It was something to do with that, wasn't it?"

I was silent.

"I'm right, aren't I?" Tobias said.

"She wanted to see what I could do," I said. I had the feeling I was on dangerous ground.

"I'll show you mine if you show me yours?" Tobias said with a grin.

I gave him a stony look.

"Tough crowd," Tobias said. "So what did you show her?"

I hesitated.

"The armsman said something about you blinding him with a sigl," Tobias said. "Was it that?"

"Yes."

"Anything else?"

I shrugged.

Tobias stared at me for a second, then shook his head. "Using a sigl doesn't make you competition. There's something you're not telling me."

I paused, wondering whether to tell the truth. It hadn't worked well the last time I'd done it, but I had to find out what was going on somehow . . .

"I told her I'd made it," I said.

Tobias raised his eyebrows, opened his mouth to answer, then stopped. "Oh," he said at last.

"Oh?"

"That . . . might actually do it."

"Okay, I want some answers," I said. "Why the *hell* would telling your cousin that I'd made a crappy light sigl be enough to make her call in a pair of goons to kidnap me?"

"All right, all right," Tobias said. He was making soothing motions, but there was a calculating look in his eyes that was making me suspicious. "This is going to take a while to explain."

"Then get started."

"Okay," Tobias said. "The head of our House is my grandfather, Charles Ashford. He's been running things for a long time now, but he's getting on and he needs someone to take over. Now, traditionally that would go straight down the family line. Unfortunately there have been some . . . issues."

"Issues?"

"Long story." Tobias gave me a brittle smile. "You wouldn't be interested."

I looked at him sceptically.

"So he's been looking for an heir," Tobias said. "And for a while now, it's been looking like it's going to be a guy called Calhoun Ashford. He's House Ashford's golden boy, and he's the kind of guy who *really* doesn't like anyone getting in his way."

"What's that got to do with Lucella?"

"Lucella is Calhoun's sister," Tobias said. "They're close." He gave me a meaningful look. "Very close."

I gave him a blank look.

"Anyway," Tobias said. "My guess is Calhoun heard about you and sent Lucella over to check out the competition."

"Why would—wait. They think I'm competition for *that*?"

Tobias nodded.

"*Why?*"

"Houses place a lot of value on drucraft," Tobias said with a twist of his mouth. "You want to be heir, you just *have* to be a strong drucrafter. Well, one of the ways they measure that is by what age you are when you manifest your first sigl."

"Manifest?"

"It means shaping a sigl without a limiter," Tobias explained. "Most nobles hit manifester level in their early twenties, or at least they say they do. Calhoun manifested his first sigl at sixteen, and he's supposed to be a prodigy. You made yours this year and you're what, twenty?"

I'd made it at nineteen, and it hadn't been my first one, either. But I'd learned my lesson about showing off. "Yeah."

Tobias nodded. "Twenty's not prodigy level, but it's enough to get you noticed, especially without proper training. And it's a *lot* better than Lucella. She's not even a shaper yet." Tobias laughed. "Kind of funny that you managed to trigger her that badly completely by accident."

"Yeah. Hilarious."

"Sorry. But you have to admit it's a good joke."

"No, I don't! I'd never even *heard* of your stupid House until yesterday! Now you're telling me that Lucella and this Calhoun guy both think I'm their rival? That doesn't make sense!"

"Calhoun's position isn't as secure as you think," Tobias said. "He might be first in line, but there are plenty of rumours floating around about him. It wouldn't take all that much to bump him down to number two, and he knows it."

I turned away, my thoughts whirling. This was insane. Only yesterday my biggest problem had been paying my rent. Now all of a sudden I had some crazy aristocrat after me?

I turned back to Tobias, who'd been watching me. "What if I told Lucella I wasn't a manifester?"

"She wouldn't believe you," Tobias said cheerfully.

"What if *you* told her?"

"She wouldn't believe me, either."

I scrubbed a hand through my hair. "I don't *want* to become head of some family full of insane nobles."

"I mean, you could tell them that," Tobias said. "Only trouble is, Calhoun would probably figure that instead of taking the risk of trusting you, he could just take you out of the running the old-fashioned way."

I tried to figure out what I should do. None of this was adding up. Last night I'd been sure that Lucella's attack had been linked to my father. Now Tobias was telling me that it was all about a House Ashford power struggle. I didn't know what to believe.

"You know," Tobias said when I didn't speak, "there *is* something you can do to get Lucella and Calhoun off your back."

I looked at Tobias with suspicion. "How?"

"The only reason Calhoun and Lucella were willing to try something like this is because you're off everyone's radar," Tobias said. "They probably figured that if you went missing, no one would notice. So all you have to do is change that. My family's holding a little gathering tonight for April first at our London house. There'll be plenty of other guests, and I can sneak you in."

"And then?"

"I'll introduce you to my grandfather."

"Your family just tried to kidnap me and now you want me to show up at their house?"

"Lucella doesn't run House Ashford," Tobias said. "Charles does, and this isn't the first time he's had to clean up one of her messes. The last time, he gave her a warning about what would happen if he had to do it again. You want to make her back off, this is how you do it."

"What, by telling on her to your grandfather?"

"You haven't met my grandfather."

I gave Tobias a look.

"Come on," Tobias said. "It's not like you're taking a big risk here. You go to a party, enjoy some free food, have a chat with Charles, then head out."

"Somehow I don't think it's going to be that easy."

Tobias shrugged. "So what's your plan? Wait for Lucella and Calhoun to come back and have another try?"

I was silent. I didn't trust Tobias. The longer I talked to him, the more I got the feeling that he was playing some game of his own. I didn't believe he was doing all this just to help me.

But he was right about one thing: I really didn't have a better plan. Approaching Tobias's grandfather sounded a lot better than just sitting around . . . and I *did* want to know more about my mother's family. Maybe I'd even get to see her.

"All right," I said. "I'll do it. On one condition."

"What condition?"

"There's a place I want you to get me into."

Tobias looked puzzled. "Where?"

I smiled.

CHAPTER 5

"THIS IS A complete waste of time," Tobias complained.

We were in Belgravia, standing in a square surrounded by white stucco-fronted houses. Down the road and across the square was an unobtrusive terraced building with a red door. It didn't look like much, but if what I'd heard was true, inside that building, you could buy any sigl ever made.

Tobias had not wanted to come here at *all*. I think he'd been expecting that the hard part would be persuading me to go along with his plan, and then, once he'd done that, I'd fall into line and do as I was told. He *definitely* hadn't expected me to demand a visit to the Exchange, and he'd spent a good fifteen minutes arguing that it wasn't worth the trip. I'd finally run out of patience and told him that either he got me into that building, or he could forget about me coming to his party. At which point Tobias had ordered a taxi with poor grace. I'd rather enjoyed the taxi ride—it had been ages since I'd taken one—but Tobias had sulked the whole way.

"I mean, if you don't think they'll let you in . . ." I said to

Tobias. There was a man standing in front of the Exchange's front door. He was wearing a nice suit, but his bulk and his stance marked him out as security.

"Of course they'll let me in."

I shrugged. "So what's the problem?"

"It's the Exchange! You probably can't even afford their catalogue!"

Yeah, he's Lucella's cousin, all right. "After you," I told him.

We walked down the pavement and up the steps. The security guard gave us a polite nod, his gaze resting a little longer on me. "Can I help you, sir?" he asked Tobias.

"Tobias of House Ashford," Tobias said shortly. "And guest."

"Right this way."

BACK WHEN I'D been trying and failing to get into the Exchange, I'd spent a while imagining what might be inside. In my mind, I'd built up a mental picture of something like a big expensive jewellery shop, with bright lights and shiny floors and glass cases full of sigls. So as I walked through the entry hall and into the Exchange, that was what I was expecting to see.

What I actually saw looked like a plush and very oversized living room. Thick red carpet covered the floor, while the walls were lined with velvet and held gold-framed paintings of landscapes. Private booths were set into the walls, each with padded seating and rounded wooden tables, and in the centre of the room were several floor-to-ceiling octagonal pillars with shelves that looked like standing desks. The air carried the pleasant smell of leather and old furniture.

I could see a scattering of other people: two groups of Chinese-looking men in the booths, leaning forward and talking earnestly, and a South Asian couple speaking with someone who looked like a member of staff. Their voices didn't carry: the fabric in the room had the effect of muffling sound. Even our footsteps were quiet.

Looking around the room, I had two immediate reactions. The first was that this looked really interesting and I wanted to spend more time here. The second was that I was really, *really* out of place. The instant anyone found out who I was, I'd be thrown out.

A man walked up to us. He had thinning white hair, wore a nice-looking suit, and greeted Tobias with a familiar smile. "Master Ashford, good to see you again. How long has it been, a year?"

"Something like that," Tobias said. "I'm just here to show this guy around."

"Ah." The man turned to me and extended his hand. "Marcus Taylor."

I took his hand and shook it. "Stephen," I said, trying to act confident. "I'm a family relation." *Apparently.*

"Welcome to the Exchange," Marcus said. "If it's your first time, would you like to see our catalogue?"

Marcus led us to one of the octagonal pillars. The shelf that ran around it held several copies of a glossy leather-bound book. Marcus handed me one, then faded into the background.

I looked at the book curiously—it had no title, only a gold stylised *E*—and flipped it open. At the front was a contents page.

- Introduction
- Light Sigls
- Matter Sigls
- Motion Sigls
- Life Sigls
- Dimension Sigls
- Primal Sigls

- Providers
- Conditions and Restrictions
- Index

Under each category were subheadings. The introduction had subsections titled "Well Guide," "Faraday Ratings and Carat Weight," and "Universal to Faraday Conversion." Under "Light Sigls" were subcategories titled "Light Sources," "Darkness Effects," "Power Sigls," "Diffraction," "Active Camouflage," "Duplication," "Illusion" . . . it just kept going. And that was just Light. The "Matter Sigls" category had as many entries as the Light one, and there were four more after that.

I felt like a little boy in a toyshop. I wanted to look at everything at once.

"You realise you can't actually afford any of these," Tobias said.

"You are just determined to ruin my fun, aren't you?"

"Fine. I'll stand here, waiting to see the look on your face."

The pages were glossy and smelt new. As I flipped through them to the "Light Sigls" category, I saw that each page was devoted to a different type of sigl, with prices and what looked like a maker's logo. It *did* look like a catalogue. The word "invisible" caught my eye; I stopped and paged back.

I'd reached the "Diffraction" category. At the top corner was a red rose with the name "De Haughton," and lower down was a zoomed-in, high-resolution photo of what looked like a blue sapphire. I started reading the text.

Phantom

For over 500 years, House De Haughton has been a worldwide name in Light siglcraft. Our first Phantom sigl was shaped at our family Wells in Lancashire in 1961, and ever since then we have worked to refine and improve upon the core design, striving to produce a personal concealment solution that is both affordable and reliable.

When essentia is channelled through it, the Phantom sigl creates a field that alters the wavelength of visible light around its wielder, temporarily shifting any rays into the radio range of the electromagnetic spectrum. The rays are then bent around the wielder, rendering them entirely invisible to outside viewing and enabling traversal of even the most dangerous areas in safety and security. As is standard for *diffraction* sigls, some visual distortion is inevitable, and incoming and outgoing light is of course affected equally: purchasers intending to make use of this sigl are encouraged to look at our range of vision-enhancing effects (page 76).

The Phantom J is our entry-level model and is recommended for those who intend the sigl for stationary use and to achieve concealment at ranges of 15 feet or more. The Phantom K incorporates features that reduce this minimum range to approximately 10 feet, as well as slightly reduce distortion. Finally, the more advanced Phantom L improves field adaption speed to the point that it can maintain effective concealment even at walking pace. The Phantom L also allows for variable essentia use, enabling the diffraction field to be expanded or contracted to cover nearby people or objects (recommended for experienced drucrafters only).

Phantom J	2.14 carat	£84,990
Phantom K	2.42 carat	£119,990
Phantom L	3.27 carat	£299,990

Purchase Information: Page 469

I started to turn to the next page and stopped with a jolt. They cost *how much*?

Tobias was watching me with a sort of malicious satisfaction. I counted the number of digits just to make sure I'd got it right, and had to struggle to stop my eyes from widening. These were the *affordable* ones?

Maybe some of the others were cheaper? I flicked through the pages, scanning prices. They weren't cheaper. Most were five or six figures, and the high-end ones were seven. After a few minutes of searching, the absolute cheapest I could find was a "torchlight" sigl that sounded pretty similar to my own. The manufacturer's logo said "Asmart," and it was priced at £499.

"Believe me now?" Tobias said.

I tried to figure out what to do next. I wasn't going to be buying any sigls, that was for sure.

"So can we go?" Tobias said. "Because we aren't—"

"Could you get me one of these catalogues to take home?"

"You don't need a catalogue to take home!"

I shrugged and looked off into the distance. "If you want me to come along tonight . . ."

Tobias gave me a black look and headed off. He returned a couple of minutes later with a copy of the catalogue in a fancy-looking bag. "Have you got any idea how much these cost?" he said, handing it to me.

"No," I admitted. "That was why I got you to buy it for me."

"All right," Tobias said. "You've had your fun. Now are you coming tonight?"

It was tempting to see how much more I could get away with, but I had the feeling I'd pushed my luck already. Besides, I *had* made him a promise. "I'm coming."

"Finally," Tobias said. He started to move towards the exit, then paused when I didn't follow.

"I didn't say I was coming right *now*," I told him.

"Oh, for . . ." Tobias bit back whatever he'd been about to say. "When?"

"When's the party?"

"Six. We'll want to be there between seven and eight."

"I'll stay here until six, then."

Tobias threw up his hands and left. I took my new catalogue over to one of the booths, sank into the leather seating, and settled down to read.

I STAYED IN the Exchange all afternoon.

Looking through the catalogue was fascinating. I'd had vague ideas about the sorts of things you might be able to do with drucraft, but seeing it all laid out like this made everything *so* much easier. Every page gave me a new idea.

As five o'clock approached, I looked up to see someone crossing the floor towards me. It was Marcus, the white-haired man who'd greeted us when we'd first arrived. "Stephen . . . Ashford, wasn't it?" he asked. "I hope you're enjoying your visit."

"Definitely," I said. "Any chance I could ask you about some of this stuff?"

"I'm afraid we're going to be closing soon."

"Can I come back tomorrow?"

"Members of House Ashford in good standing are always welcome here."

Something in Marcus's tone made me pause. Marcus was standing just a little way from the table, hands clasped in front of him, regarding me pleasantly. No one else seemed to be looking at us, and there was nothing I could put my finger on, but all of a sudden, I had the feeling of being watched.

Slowly I rose to my feet. "Maybe I should go."

"I think that would be wise," Marcus agreed.

I took my bag and left, the murmurs of conversation cutting off as the door of the Exchange shut softly behind me. The doorman's eyes followed me as I walked away.

I LEFT MY bag and catalogue at home and took a bus northwest.

The address Tobias had given me was on a street called The Bishops Avenue, in East Finchley. I'd never been there before, and once I reached the avenue, I started walking up it from the direction of Hampstead. The houses on the street seemed bigger than usual for London, set relatively far back from the pavement; most were half-hidden behind fences and trees. The sky had covered over with thick clouds, and the only sign of the sun was a sullen red glow in the west. A chill breeze swept down the street, cutting through my fleece and making me shiver. The night would be wet and cold.

I'd been walking for a few minutes when I sensed something up ahead. No, not ahead—across and to the left, in that house there. It was a Well, and it was strong. Very strong. I crossed the street, drawn as if by a magnet.

As I came closer, I realised that "very strong" had been an underestimate. This Well was *unbelievably* powerful. I was still hundreds of feet away, yet I could sense it as though it were right next to me, the essentia pouring out of it and suffusing the land and air. It made my Well feel like a puddle next to a duck pond. I drifted forward, a moth drawn to an open flame, my feet carrying me closer and closer . . .

A hand waved in front of my face. "Hey."

I came out of my trance with a jolt. Tobias was standing right next to me, giving me a quizzical look. "Why did you space out like that?"

I was too awestruck to be cautious. "The Well."

"You can feel it?"

"You *can't*?"

"If I concentrate, I suppose," Tobias said with a shrug. "We're not that close."

It seemed more than close enough to me. "Is it . . . yours?"

"Our family's," Tobias said. "The Bishop's Well. Sixth strongest in London."

Through the trees, I could see the walls and roof of an oversized house. It must be built around the Well, and I looked at Tobias with new eyes. I'd known that Tobias's family was rich, but feeling the strength of the Well somehow made it real to me in a way that it hadn't been before. "You grew up there?"

"Mm-hmm."

"How do you even sense anything?" I said curiously.

"Sense what?"

"Regular essentia, like in the air or the ground. That Well's so strong it drowns everything else out."

"You know most people don't bother learning how to do that, right?" Tobias said. "You don't actually need it to channel."

"But if you can't sense free essentia, you can't find Wells."

"I suppose?" Tobias said. "There are other people who do that stuff."

"How do you get new sigls, then?"

"You buy them from the Exchange."

I shut up.

"All right," Tobias said, glancing around. We were standing a little way down from the house's front gates. "We don't want to go in too early, so get comfortable while we wait."

The sun dipped in the sky, eventually sinking so low that its rays reached up to illuminate the clouds from beneath in a vivid bloodred. From time to time a car would pull up in front of the house, and there'd be movement as people went in. I watched the arrivals filter into the house. If things had turned out differently, would I have grown up there?

At some point I saw that Tobias was studying me. "What?" I asked.

"You don't look much like her," Tobias said.

"Who, my mother?"

Tobias nodded.

"Is she going to be here tonight?"

"No."

I hesitated. "Do you . . . know her very well?"

Tobias looked away.

"So do you?" I asked when Tobias didn't answer.

"Not really," Tobias said without turning around. "She travels a lot."

"Then—"

Tobias spoke over me. "You ask too many questions, you know that?"

I frowned at Tobias's back. *Okay, then.* "This whole thing is about who in your family gets to inherit, right?"

"That's what most things in our House are about."

"So, something I've been wondering," I said. "If Charles Ashford is the head of your House and you're his grandson . . . well, I don't know much about how inheritance works, but shouldn't you be in line already?"

Tobias still didn't turn around. "You're right," he said after a moment. "You don't know much about how inheritance works."

I gave Tobias a look. From the way he'd talked, I had the definite impression that Tobias was more closely related to Charles Ashford than this Calhoun guy was. So why was Calhoun the favourite to be heir?

I was getting the feeling there were some things about his family situation that Tobias wasn't telling me.

Actually, I had the feeling there was a *lot* Tobias wasn't telling me.

The sun sank until it was touching the buildings to the west; it slid behind their rooftops and in the space of a few minutes was gone. The shadows lengthened, and in the windows of the mansions all around, lights began to come on one after another. "All right," Tobias said. "It should be busy enough by now."

I could feel the pull of the Well, like a bonfire in the darkness. We headed for the front gate.

THE ASHFORD HOUSE was fenced in by high spiked railings that looked like wrought iron. A couple of LEDs glowed from a box on one of the gateposts; Tobias did something, and the gate swung open with a whir of motors.

Now that I got a closer look at the house beyond, I realised it was less of a house and more of a mansion. By London standards it was huge, built of stone and brick, with peaked roofs rising to three or four storeys, and wings and outbuildings that looked to have been added piece by piece over the years. Around the mansion were well-tended gardens. Lights glowed from the front door, but instead of heading towards it, Tobias turned aside onto a narrow flagstone path. The path wound between rhododendron bushes before leading to a small door set into the mansion's north wall.

I paused a few steps from the door. The path didn't stop: it kept going to another tall black fence and a barred gate that seemed to lead into the mansion's back gardens. The Well was in that direction, and it was close. Very close. There was *so* much essentia there . . .

"Don't even think about it," Tobias said.

I realised I'd been staring at the gate. I looked away quickly. "What?"

"Taking from the Well," Tobias said. He was giving me a knowing look. "You think you're the first one to have the idea?"

"You think they'd miss it?"

"Yes," Tobias said. "Yes, they would. Not that it'd matter, because you wouldn't even make it that far."

I measured the fence with my eyes. "Fence isn't that high."

"I'm not talking about the fence."

I looked at him.

"Not all sigls get advertised in the Exchange," Tobias said. "The Life sigls you would have seen in that catalogue are for humans. But there are ones designed to affect animals. Dogs, usually. You start with a regular guard dog, then enhance it. Stronger muscles, quicker healing, extra aggression. Sometimes they add other abilities too. They're called hellhounds."

I gave Tobias a suspicious look. *Is he making this up?*

Tobias just looked back at me with raised eyebrows. I turned to the gate and I cleared my mind, trying to sense.

The mass of essentia made it hard to pick anything out; it was like trying to hear while standing on a club floor. As I concentrated, though, I began to filter out the background noise, searching through the currents. Searching deeper, I realised I could feel something. It reminded me a little of those sigls I'd sensed yesterday, but it was different, wilder. And all of a sudden, I had the clear and definite impression of something beyond those bars, hidden in the shadows, cold and watchful and still.

I flinched, pulling back my senses and breaking the connection. I looked at Tobias.

"Our family had a bad experience with raiders a while back," Tobias said. "Ever since then, my grandfather's taken security seriously. *Very* seriously. Piece of advice? When you talk to him, don't make any jokes about stealing from that Well."

Tobias turned back to the door and unlocked it with a key. I took a last look at the gate, then followed Tobias into the Ashford mansion.

CHAPTER 6

THE DOOR LED into a narrow hallway. Off to one side, I could hear the hiss of a gas cooker and the sound of a knife on a chopping board. Tobias led me past, through the door at the end of the hall, and out into a wash of light and sound.

My first confused impression was that I'd walked into a room about the size of my entire house. As my eyes adjusted, I realised I'd been wrong: it was *bigger* than my house. It was some sort of living room or ballroom, floored in pale wood, with chandeliers hanging from above that made the whole room blaze with light. A staircase at one corner climbed to a raised gallery that ran from wall to wall.

The room was filled with people, divided into small groups. The buzz of conversation filled the air, and women were moving through the crowd with trays of drinks. No one turned to look as the door swung closed behind us; there was so much noise and bustle that none of them had noticed us enter.

"Let's see . . ." Tobias said, scanning the crowd. "Okay. See that guy up on the gallery?"

I followed Tobias's gaze. Above us and at the far end of the room, standing in front of the gallery bookshelves, was a young man. He was tall, slender, and handsome, with long straight features and—most oddly—white hair.

"The one who looks like an anime villain?" I asked.

Tobias snorted. "Yeah, I guess he does. That's Calhoun. Stay away from him."

I looked at Calhoun with new eyes. Was this the guy who'd sent Lucella to my house to get rid of me?

"All right," Tobias said. "I'm going to find my grandfather. Stay here and don't talk to anyone."

"Why?"

"Because I said so."

I gave Tobias a look.

"I mean it," Tobias said. "Just wait here for fifteen minutes without causing any trouble. Don't talk to anyone, don't go anywhere, and whatever you do, *don't draw attention*. You think you can manage that?"

"Yes," I told him.

Tobias walked away.

As I watched Tobias disappear into the crowd, I considered whether I wanted to follow his orders. It took me about two seconds to decide that my answer was no, at which point I started looking around for someone to talk to.

The men and women around me were a mixture of ages, though tilted towards the older end of the scale. The men wore suits of grey and blue and brown; the women wore outfits that I couldn't name but that looked expensive. Actually, all the clothes looked expensive—the more I looked around, the more I was realising that my jeans and fleece were making me stand out, and not in a good way. Maybe people would think I was one of the servants? But now that I checked, the men and women serving drinks were wearing smart black uniforms with blue-and-silver crests. I was dressed *worse* than the servants.

I scanned the room, looking for someone who seemed approachable. Most of the people were standing in groups, busy with their own conversations. There were a few older people who were alone, but none looked very friendly. Then the crowd parted and I saw a girl.

She was probably the most beautiful girl I'd ever seen. Maybe she fell a little short of the artificial perfection of the models you see on the Internet, but her movements had a grace and naturalness that no photograph could match. She was about my age, with blue eyes, hair that was so pale a blond that it was almost white, and very fair skin. She wore a square-cut white dress that left her lower arms bare, complemented by a few pieces of simple jewellery, and she stood with her back very straight. She saw me at the same time that I saw her, gave me a quick glance up and down, then stood waiting, as if to see what I'd do.

I hesitated very briefly, then walked across the floor. "Hi," I told the girl. "I'm Stephen."

The girl gave a small curtsey. "Johanna Meusel," she told me. She spoke with a faint accent, pronouncing each word precisely and clearly.

"Could I ask you a favour?" I said. "I've ended up at this party, but I don't really know who these people are or what's going on."

"Ended up?"

"Long story," I said with a smile.

Johanna laughed. "And you'll tell me if I help you? Well, all right. But just so you know—this isn't a party."

I looked around, then back at Johanna.

"Yes, I know what it looks like," Johanna said.

"It looks like a big crowd of rich people standing around drinking."

"But why do you think they're here?"

"Free booze?"

Johanna gave me an odd look.

Oops. That had obviously been the wrong thing to say. "Okay, why *are* they here?"

"Officially, it's an informal get-together ahead of the weekend summit," Johanna said. "Unofficially, it's about the embargo."

"The what?"

"You see the man at the centre of the crowd, against the far wall?"

I had to crane my neck to catch a glimpse of the guy. He was slightly overweight, with a navy-blue suit and receding iron-grey hair, and seemed to be lecturing the people around him.

"That's Arnold Hayes," Johanna said. "He's Executive Vice President at Tyr."

I gave her a blank look.

"Tyr Aerospace," Johanna explained. "It's one of the major US defence contractors. They and some factions in the US government have been pushing for Western European governments to limit their essentia sales. Now they're putting forward a proposal that any sales of sigls or aurum from Europe and North America should only go to NATO members. They claim it's to stop Russia from getting military-grade sigls, but that's not the real reason."

". . . It's not?"

"Well, it doesn't make any sense, does it? Russia's the ninth-strongest country in the world for Light essentia and the second strongest for Motion. They're a net exporter, not an importer. But China imports both of those, especially Light, and the US is getting worried about their military position, so they're trying to cut off the supply, using Russia as a pretext. But the European corporations and Houses don't want to do that, because China pays a premium for . . ." Johanna paused. "Ah, you look a little lost."

"Um," I said. "A little" was a massive understatement; I had *no* idea what Johanna was talking about. And she was talking casually, like all this was common knowledge. "How do you know all this?"

"I'm more curious about how you *don't*," Johanna said frankly. "This is pretty basic stuff."

"I'm not really into politics."

"You may not be interested in politics, but politics is interested in you," Johanna said with a smile. "Besides, House Ashford's involved in all of this. And you're one of them . . . aren't you?"

"I'm a distant relation," I said. *I think.*

"I haven't heard of any Stephens in the Ashford family tree."

"Do you know everyone in their family?"

"Most of them. Anyway, I think it's your turn. Why are *you* here?"

I hesitated, wondering what to say. A part of me felt that I should lie or make up some kind of crazy story. The way Johanna was acting was making me understand just how badly out of my depth I was here.

But I was pretty sure that if I tried that, I'd get found out. Besides, while Johanna might be strange, I was discovering that I liked talking to her. Unlike Tobias and Lucella, I had the feeling that she was actually being honest.

You know what, let's just see what happens.

"A girl called Lucella Ashford tried to kidnap me last night," I told her. "She showed up at my front door, we talked for a while, then I said the wrong thing and she got two of her armsmen to knock me out and carry me off in a van. I escaped, got told this morning that I could get Lucella off my back by going to Charles Ashford, and that's why I'm here."

"What did you say that made her try to kidnap you?" Johanna asked.

I blinked. "You believe me?"

"I mean, it's a little extreme, but these sorts of thing do happen," Johanna said. "Though I'm quite impressed you managed to escape on your own. It must have been very exciting."

I stared at her.

"So?" Johanna asked. "What did you say?"

"I, uh . . . Apparently Lucella was there because Calhoun had sent her to check me out, and I made her think I could be competition."

"That's strange."

"'Strange' is putting it mildly."

"I don't mean the competition part," Johanna said. "What's strange is that Calhoun would send Lucella to do anything. As I understand it, right now she's his biggest rival."

"His biggest—okay, seriously, *how* do you know all this? Are you related to them too?"

"Actually, yes," Johanna said. "My House is from Jena, in Thuringia. Thuringia came under Soviet occupation after the war, and my family fled to West Germany. While they were there, the sister of my great-grandmother met a man called Walter Ashford, who'd come to take advantage of the reconstruction. My great-great-grandfather didn't approve—he thought men like Walter were profiteers—but eventually Walter Ashford and my great-grandaunt were married and travelled back here to England. Their eldest son is Charles Ashford, and he's head of the family now."

"Oh," I said. That made sense, kind of. At least there was *one* part of this story that I could relate to and that didn't sound completely—

"Oh, and I might be marrying Calhoun," Johanna added.

"Wait, *what*?"

"That's the biggest reason I'm here, really. My grandmother and I are here to talk to Charles about the possibility of an engagement with Calhoun. Oh, and to meet him."

"You . . . haven't met him," I said carefully.

"Not before today," Johanna said, glancing up at the gallery, where Calhoun was still standing. "He's very handsome, isn't he?"

I looked at Johanna, lost for words.

Johanna gave me a smile. "You really are a bit out of place here, aren't you?"

"No kidding," I said. I'd known going in that I didn't belong; I hadn't realised how badly. "Didn't you say you and the Ashfords were related?"

"Only very distantly," Johanna said. "Calhoun's my second cousin once removed. If we tried to use each other's sigls, we wouldn't get even a flicker. But that's not really what you were shocked about, was it?"

"Not really," I admitted.

"This is how things work among Houses and the bigger corporations," Johanna explained seriously. "A marriage isn't just a relationship, it's a family alliance."

I shot a covert glance up at Calhoun on the gallery. He didn't seem to have noticed me. "Don't you get a say?"

"Of course I get a say," Johanna said. "If I absolutely refused to go along with it, well, Mama and Papa would have to accept it. But I'm a daughter of the Meusel family. I have to marry for the family's interests as well as my own."

"I think most girls here just marry whoever they want."

"Most girls don't have the privileges I have," Johanna pointed out. "The wealth I have, the education I received, the sigls I wear . . . there's a lot given to me, but there are things expected in return." She glanced up towards Calhoun and tilted her head. "Besides, I've got my own ambitions."

"So . . ." I said. "Right now, Calhoun's the favourite to become the next head of House Ashford, but it's not settled. Right?"

"That's right."

"If he wasn't heir, would you still marry him?"

"No."

I looked at Johanna.

"I've shocked you again," Johanna said with a slight smile. "But I'm just being honest. Calhoun's handsome, and he's supposed to be quite capable, but if he was just some talented outsider, then, no, my grandmother and I wouldn't be considering an engagement. And if Charles decides not to make him heir after all, then it'll be cancelled."

I started to answer, then paused as it suddenly occurred to me that by her own admission, Johanna was about one step away from becoming Calhoun Ashford's fiancée. Which meant she was an interested party too . . .

Oh, crap. Was that why she'd been so interested in what I'd said to set off Lucella? If she found out that I was a manifester, would she want to get rid of me as well?

Tobias had been right. I *should* have kept my mouth shut.

"Is something wrong?" Johanna asked.

"Um, no," I said, thinking quickly. At least Johanna didn't seem to be acting as though she thought I was a threat . . . yet. "Could I ask you one more thing? Apart from Calhoun, who are the other candidates to be Ashford heir?"

"Whoever Charles chooses, really," Johanna said. "At the moment it seems to be between Calhoun, Lucella, and Charles's two grandchildren. Though it's a little strange that Magnus isn't under consideration."

"Who?"

"Magnus Ashford-Grasser. Tobias's father. He married into the Ashford family from House Grasser of Munich. You'd think that if Charles was looking for an heir, he'd be the obvious choice.

But instead Charles is favouring Calhoun. If you ever find out why, I'd be very interested to know." Johanna glanced aside. "Ah, I have to go. It was nice to meet you."

"You too."

Johanna gave me a last smile and walked away. I watched her go with an odd mixture of feelings. Talking to her had felt like stepping through the looking glass and coming out again.

Except now that I thought about it, I *hadn't* come out. This was her world, not mine.

A growl from my stomach reminded me I'd had hardly anything to eat all day. If I was going to be waiting around for Tobias, I might as well see what the food was like. I started towards the tables at the end of the room.

I rounded a knot of people and came face to face with Lucella.

It's hard to say which of us was more surprised. Lucella looked as if she'd got ready for this party late and hadn't made much effort: she wore a fancy-looking dress that seemed to have been thrown on in a hurry, and there were a bunch of strands loose from her hair. She'd just taken a glass of bubbly wine from a tray, and she was staring at me.

So much for not attracting attention.

"What are *you* doing here?" I told her.

Lucella's eyebrows rose in outrage. "I *live* here!"

"Guess your family just has low standards, then."

"What are you—how did you get in?"

"You know, last night, I could have asked you the same thing."

People were turning to look at us. Lucella noticed, and a wary expression flashed across her face. "Keep your voice down."

"Why? Afraid of me making a scene?"

"You don't know what you're doing," Lucella snapped. "Who even got you in? Was it—"

And at exactly that point Tobias came walking up. "There you

are," he told me as he slipped between two people. "Where did—"
He saw Lucella and stopped.

The three of us looked back and forth at each other.

Lucella stared at Tobias. "You."

Tobias turned to me with a long-suffering look. "You just had
to stand still and not talk to anyone," he told me. "Was that really
so hard?"

"*You*," Lucella said again, her expression darkening. "You
little—"

"And that's our cue to leave," Tobias said. He grabbed my arm
and started towing me towards the stairs. "Hi, Luce, bye, Luce,
great catching up, let's do it again sometime—"

"*Stop right there!*"

Lucella's words sent a jolt down my spine, bringing me and
Tobias up short. I turned to see Lucella stalking towards us, her
eyes glittering. All of a sudden she seemed a lot taller and more
menacing, and she stabbed one manicured finger towards Tobias.
"You were planning this from the start, weren't you?"

"I don't know what you—"

Lucella's voice cracked like a whip. "*Answer me!*"

"Not at the start," Tobias said automatically. "You were dig-
ging for something, and I thought . . ." He trailed off with a frown,
as if he hadn't meant to say that much.

Lucella stared at him for a second, then gave a short, barking
laugh and turned to me. "You have no idea what's going on, do
you?"

"Don't listen to her," Tobias told me.

"'Don't listen to her,'" Lucella repeated mockingly, then looked
at me. "You never wondered why he came looking for you? Who
do you think gave me your address?"

I looked at Tobias.

"You need to go," Tobias told me. "Now." He pointed up.

"Through the gallery, into the hall, third door on the left. Knock and he'll let you in."

"No, he won't," Lucella said, stepping forward, her eyes hard as she stared at Tobias. "Both of you are staying right here."

I hesitated, feeling an urge to do as I was told. I shouldn't listen to Tobias; I should stay here and—

Wait. I shook my head, remembering what Lucella had done last night. Why the hell was I listening to her?

I ducked back into the crowd. Lucella whirled, startled, but she'd been focused on Tobias, and by the time she registered that I wasn't sticking around, I'd already put two or three people between us. I heard Lucella shout something and caught a glimpse of her looking angrily from side to side, then I was gone, walking quickly towards the corner of the room.

I was so preoccupied with Lucella that I didn't notice until too late that Calhoun Ashford was coming down the stairs. As I saw his white hair I stopped, but it was too late; he'd already seen me. His eyes passed over me—

—and moved on. Calhoun reached the bottom of the stairs and strode away in the direction of his sister, brushing past me as though I wasn't there.

I stared after him for a second, until the raised voices behind me reminded me that Lucella was still coming after me. I climbed the stairs that Calhoun had descended and walked swiftly along the gallery. People were turning to watch the commotion below, but I averted my eyes and nobody stopped me as I walked past them and through the door at the end.

The hallway beyond was decorated with paintings and wall hangings and felt quiet after the noise of the party. My feet creaked on the floorboards as I walked down the hall, counting the doors. When I reached the third on the left, I stopped and knocked.

A deep voice called out from within. "Come!"

I opened the door.

THE STUDY WITHIN felt small compared to the room I'd come from, though it was still much bigger than my bedroom. Bookshelves ran from floor to ceiling; the solitary patch of open wall was taken up by a huge map of the United Kingdom with spots marked out by pinned notes and glass beads. Two windows at the back were covered by drawn curtains. The room was dominated by a wooden desk the size of a dining table, covered in books and papers, with one chair behind it and one in front.

Sitting behind the desk was a man. He looked old—maybe midsixties—but his back was ruler straight and his movements measured and steady. He had receding hair and a neatly trimmed beard and was writing with a fountain pen. The scratch of the nib on paper was the only sound in the room.

I looked at the man curiously. Seconds dragged by. "Are you Charles Ashford?" I asked when he didn't speak.

The man kept writing.

"Um," I said. "Have I got the right room . . . ?"

"Sit," the man said without raising his eyes. He had an upper-class accent and spoke with a ring of command.

I hesitated, then walked forward and sat.

The man wrote for another thirty seconds while I watched. Then he set down his pen, stamped the paper with something that left a red imprint, and slipped the document into a leather folder. Only then did he look up at me with a pair of piercing blue eyes. "Well," Charles Ashford told me. "It seems the apple doesn't fall far from the tree."

I frowned. "Sorry?"

"Do you know why you're here?"

"My name's—"

"I know who you are, boy."

I paused.

"When you walked through that drawing room, you passed representatives of four major drucraft corporations and seven different Houses," Charles said. "I have meetings with them scheduled all the way through to midnight. However, right now, none of those meetings are taking place. Do you know why?"

I shook my head.

"Because I have to deal with you instead," Charles told me. "To clean up this mess that you, Lucella, and Tobias have collectively created."

"I didn't create anything," I said, nettled.

Charles raised his eyebrows. "And yet here you are."

I frowned.

Charles regarded me for a few moments, then nodded to himself. "What did Tobias tell you to say?"

"Lucella came to my house last night with—"

Charles cut me off with an irritated motion. "I didn't ask you what happened. I asked you what Tobias told you to say."

"The truth."

Charles snorted. "You're a fool if you think Tobias cares about *that*."

I was starting to get a bit pissed off about how Charles was acting as though the whole thing was my fault. I wanted to snap at him that Lucella had been the one to attack me . . . except I already knew what he'd say. *And yet here you are.* I was the one coming to him, not the other way around.

Well, if I wasn't going to get sympathy, maybe I could at least get some answers. "Tobias said that the reason Lucella came after me is because I'm a candidate to become the next head of House Ashford," I told Charles. "Am I?"

Charles looked back at me without expression. "What do you think?"

I thought about what I'd seen since stepping into this mansion. The wealth, the status, the conversation with Johanna. I looked across the desk at Charles. Would someone like him want to hand all that over to someone like me?

"No," I told Charles. I knew it was true as soon as I'd said it.

"Of course not," Charles told me. "You fail just about every possible criterion, especially the ones concerning education and social standing. I'm surprised you even made it into this room."

It was what I'd been expecting, but the way Charles said it still rubbed me the wrong way. "Okay, fine, since you brought it up," I said. "Before she tried to kidnap me, Lucella told me that there are schools that teach drucraft. Is that true?"

"Yes."

"Is there any way I could go to one?"

"No."

"Why not?"

"Because drucraft schools charge somewhere in the region of forty thousand pounds per year."

I stared.

"I assume that's a little outside of your price range," Charles said.

Looking at Charles's expression, I had a sudden flash of intuition. *He doesn't like me.* This wasn't about Lucella or his meetings. Charles had disliked me before I'd even knocked on his door. But why?

"Schools are free," I told Charles, trying to hide what I was thinking.

"Schools run by the British government are free," Charles told me. "Do you know why? No? Well, I presume you attended a state primary and secondary school. What were you taught there?"

"Maths, English—"

"Not the subjects. How were you taught to behave? What were the rules you were trained to follow?"

I thought for a second. I was coming to dislike Charles almost as much as he seemed to dislike me, but I had to admit, he was good at making you think. "I suppose . . . do as you're told. Show up on time, do the work, don't cause trouble."

"And why do you suppose you were taught those things?"

"I don't know," I admitted.

"Over the course of the eighteenth and nineteenth centuries, this country moved from an agricultural economy based upon farming, to an industrial economy based upon factories," Charles told me. "Factory workers must possess very specific skills. They must be educated to a basic minimum standard of literacy and numeracy, and they must be reliable, nondisruptive, and good at following instructions. Most importantly, they must do exactly what they are told, when they are told to do it. Industrialising countries lacked such workers, therefore institutions were set up to produce them. Replaceable parts for a machine."

I looked at Charles.

"Of course, you're too old to be going to school," Charles said. "So I imagine Lucella would have talked about universities instead. Where did she mention? Canterbury?"

"Yes," I said. I was getting a bad feeling about this.

"Canterbury University is the premier drucraft university in Western Europe," Charles said. "Oxford, Cambridge, and Imperial all have departments for drucraft theory, but not for practical courses. The students who go to Canterbury are the future ruling class of the United Kingdom. Children of Greater and Lesser Houses, corporate and political heirs. Canterbury is also very specifically *not* subject to the fee cap for domestic students, which means that its fees are set by market forces." Charles looked at me with raised eyebrows. "How much do you think it costs to study at a place like that?"

I was silent. I could see where this was going.

"Go on, guess."

"More than I can afford," I said flatly.

"Educational institutions exist to serve the needs of those who operate and fund them," Charles said. "In the case of this country's elite universities, the way they serve those needs is by functioning as a finishing school for the ruling class. A lower-tier university might see some profit in taking on a student such as you. A drucraft university would not."

The last traces of the hope that Lucella had planted last night flickered and died. I suppose, deep down, I'd always known it was a mirage. Some people get golden tickets and some don't. People like me are the kind that don't.

"What about my mother?" I asked Charles.

"What about her?"

"She works for you, doesn't she?"

"Yes."

"Is she here?"

"No."

"Then where—"

"In Leipzig." Charles glanced at his watch. "Assuming her flight was on schedule, she should have arrived about half an hour ago. She'll be spending the night before moving on tomorrow afternoon."

I stared at Charles.

"As you said, your mother works for House Ashford," Charles said. "As a result, she has an extremely busy schedule that leaves no time for distractions."

"What distractions?"

"Distractions," Charles said, "such as a boy who, apparently, does not know how to take a hint. Your mother has been free to contact you for a very long time. She has chosen not to. I suggest you respect that decision."

The words hit me like a slap to the face. The thoughts went out of my head, and all I could do was stare at Charles, who looked back at me with level eyes. I felt a pain flare up, like an old wound.

"Now," Charles said when I didn't speak. "There is the matter of Lucella's actions. My niece, much as I may regret it, is nevertheless a member of House Ashford, and until and unless she gives me reason to disown her entirely, I bear partial responsibility for her actions. What is your salary?"

"What?"

"How much do you earn in a year?"

"I get paid week to week."

"Then multiply your average weekly salary by the number of weeks in a year. I assume you're capable of multiplication."

I *really* didn't like this guy. "Twenty thousand, eight hundred and sixty-five pounds."

"Which, after tax, should come to a little under eighteen thousand," Charles said. He opened a desk drawer, took out a cheque-book, picked up his pen, and began to write. "In the unlikely event that you are financially prudent and do not spend the entirety of your spare income on drink, drugs, and flashy clothes, as most people your age do, you might save twenty percent of that." The pen finished scratching; Charles tore off the cheque and held it out. "This is a cheque for how much you could expect to earn and retain in a year. I offer it to you in recompense for my niece's actions, with the understanding that the matter will be closed."

I stared at the cheque. It was an instruction to pay Stephen Oakwood the sum of three thousand, six hundred pounds. "Or I could just go to the police," I told him.

"You are free to do so," Charles said. "In which case, you

would eventually end up in a court of law. With the quality of lawyers that you could hire versus the kind that my niece could hire."

I looked at the cheque, then back at Charles. "What's stopping me from taking this, *then* going to the police?"

Cold blue eyes looked into mine. "I would not recommend it."

I didn't move for ten seconds. Then I took the cheque and put it into my pocket.

Charles placed the cap back onto his pen and set it down. "Good."

The tone in Charles's voice sent a flash of resentment through me. It was the dismissiveness, as if everything was settled. "So now what?" I asked him.

"Now you can go," Charles told me.

"Can you . . ." I hesitated. "Can you give my mother a message?"

"I could, but I won't," Charles said. "You are, at present, a political inconvenience, for reasons you have neither the education nor the experience to understand, and which I have neither the time nor the inclination to explain. Extending your contact with my family would complicate matters needlessly. This may change in the future, but until it does, you will not return to this house without explicit invitation. Is that clear?"

"Yes," I said. I'd had enough of this guy. "Very clear." I got to my feet.

Charles picked up his pen and took out a new sheet of paper. "I expect you'll find my grandson loitering out in the hall," he told me without looking up. He'd already turned his attention to the document he was reading. "Tell him he's got fifteen minutes to find Lucella and bring her here. And let him know that once I'm done with her, he's next."

I walked out.

———

THE FIRST-FLOOR CORRIDOR in the Ashford mansion was empty and quiet. As I stood listening, though, I could just make out the sound of a familiar voice from down the hall. Tobias.

I paused, deciding what to do. I didn't especially want to talk to Tobias, and I wasn't feeling very inclined to run Charles's errands for him. On the other hand, I wasn't actually sure that I could find my way out of this place on my own without running into Lucella or something worse.

With a grimace, I started down the corridor. Tobias's voice was coming from a room towards the end with a half-open door. As I drew closer, though, I heard another voice answering him. It didn't sound like a casual conversation.

I hesitated for a moment. Then I crept forward, my feet making little sound on the carpet, and listened.

". . . see what the problem is," Tobias was saying.

"If you want to keep pretending to be some kind of master manipulator," a man said in a measured voice, "you're going to have to become much better at covering your tracks." His accent was a little like Johanna's, each word clear and precise.

"I don't know what you mean."

"You walked into Charles's study to demand an audience," the man said. "Did you really think he wasn't going to investigate? If he doesn't already know about your involvement, he will soon."

"It doesn't matter," Tobias argued. "Lucella used our armsmen last night—she can't cover that up. And Calhoun'll say he doesn't know anything, but everyone knows he and Lucella . . ."

"You stupid little boy," the man said dispassionately. "Calhoun is being groomed to be the next head of House, and he's excelled at every assignment he's been given. *That* is what matters, not a few rumours. As for Lucella, she may be a black sheep, but as long as she doesn't do anything to seriously damage House Ashford, the most she'll get is a slap on the wrist. The same is *not* true for you. The only protection you have is your status as Charles's grandson, and your . . . shortcomings . . . place limits upon that."

"My 'shortcomings,'" Tobias said bitterly. "And whose fault are they?"

"You need to be patient. Do as I taught you. Watch, and wait."

"Wait for how long? Once Calhoun gets engaged to the Meusel girl, it'll be too late."

"Engagements can be broken."

Tobias was silent for a second. "Who are Lucella's friends?"

The man's voice sharpened. "Do not ask that question."

"It was three years ago, right?" Tobias asked. "That was when everyone started treating her differently. I'm just saying, whoever these people are, if they could do all that for *her*, then—"

"Enough!"

Tobias fell silent.

"You do not understand what you are talking about." The man's voice was harsh. "If you have any ambitions to rise in this family, you will stay far, far away from Lucella and her 'friends.' And you will most *especially* not mention it to Charles. Understood?"

". . . Yes."

"Go."

Footsteps sounded from the room.

I moved fast, ducking down a side passage and hiding behind a cabinet. I heard Tobias's footsteps move out into the corridor, pause, start again, pause again. I waited thirty seconds, then stepped out.

Tobias turned to face me. "What are you doing there?" he asked sharply.

"Looking for a way out," I told him. "What are *you* doing there?"

Tobias gave me a narrow look. I glanced casually around. There was no sign of the man Tobias had been talking to.

"Oh," I added, as if I'd just remembered. "Charles wants you to fetch Lucella."

I saw Tobias perk up slightly. He looked at me as if waiting for more, but I didn't speak. The two of us stood in the corridor, watching one another, the sounds of the party echoing in the distance.

"So something I've been wondering," I said. "How *did* Lucella get my address?"

"How should I know?"

"She said someone gave it to her."

"Maybe it was Calhoun."

"That's funny," I said. "Because I passed right by Calhoun as he was coming down those stairs, and he didn't recognise me. Looked right at me too."

Tobias shrugged.

"So he cares enough to send Lucella to get rid of me," I said, "but not enough to find out what I look like?"

"I'm kind of busy," Tobias told me. "You want to get out of here, head that way down the main staircase."

I looked at Tobias. Tobias didn't meet my eyes.

"*You* were the one who told Lucella about me," I said. "That was why you were so quick to show up this morning."

Tobias looked away. "You got some way of proving that?" he said to the wall.

I kept staring at Tobias. "Fine," I said at last when it was clear he wasn't going to say anything else. "Oh, by the way? Charles told me that once he's done with Lucella, you're next."

Tobias looked around sharply, but I'd already turned and left. Tobias didn't follow.

───────

I TOOK A looping path around back to the living room to find that the party was still going. I got one or two glances as I wound my way through the crowd, but no one stopped me.

Lucella was up on the gallery, right next to the door that I'd used to leave the room the first time, in a position to ambush anyone who came out. As I watched, the door swung open, and Lucella pounced, only to come face to face with Tobias. Tobias said something and Lucella replied angrily, their voices lost in the chatter of the crowd.

Those two deserve each other, I thought. Lucella might have been the one to go after me, but it had been Tobias who'd sent her. Just as I reached the door, Lucella turned around, and our gazes met from across the crowded room. I saw her eyes flash and for a moment I felt a cold thread of unease, but then Tobias said something that made her look away, and before she could turn back, I was gone.

I left the house via the side entrance and walked out through the front garden. Night had fallen, and as I reached the gate the first drops of rain began to fall. I paused to look back at the mansion; lights glowed from its windows, and the sounds of the party drifted out, barely audible through the walls. It was the nicest house I'd ever been in, but I had no desire ever to go back there. The Ashfords might be my family, but in their different ways they'd all made it very clear that I wasn't welcome.

Well, screw them. I'd managed on my own before. I could do it again.

The rain was growing heavier, the droplets sharp and cold, driven by a biting wind. I turned away from the Ashford mansion to begin the long journey home.

CHAPTER 7

I WOKE UP the next morning in a melancholy sort of mood. Usually I sleep in on Saturdays, but this time I woke around six and couldn't get back to sleep. I ended up staring at my bedroom wall while the grey sky outside my window gradually brightened into white and blue.

My thoughts kept going back to last night. Despite everything that had happened yesterday—Tobias, the Exchange, the mansion—it was those two sentences from Charles that had stuck in my head. *"Your mother has been free to contact you for a very long time. She has chosen not to."* It didn't seem fair that after so much else had happened, that was what my mind kept coming back to, but it did.

My mother's disappearance had always been painful in a way that my father's hadn't. You'd think it would be the other way around—after all, my dad had raised me for eighteen years—but then, that was the point. My dad had been *there* for those eighteen years, while my mother had left before I was even old enough to remember her face. And when my dad had disappeared, he'd made it clear in that letter that he was leaving because he had to, not because he wanted to. He'd told me to stay safe and to keep practising my drucraft, and that he'd be back as soon as he could.

He hadn't come back, but somehow, it had never felt as though I'd been abandoned. It had felt more like . . . I don't know, like being sent on a mission. He'd left me with a direction and a sense of purpose, and during the bad times—and there had been some really bad times—that had counted for a lot. My mother hadn't left me a direction, or a letter, or anything at all. She'd just . . . gone.

Back when I was younger, I'd spent a lot of time telling myself stories about why my mother might have vanished like that, and the common thread in all of them had been that my mother had been forced into it somehow. Illness, danger, a family secret . . . it wasn't that she'd *wanted* to go, something had pushed her into it. But try as I might, I'd never been able to come up with a very good answer for why she'd never got in touch. And of course, there *was* a good answer, the same one Charles had slapped me across the face with. She hadn't done it because she hadn't wanted to.

I wanted to believe that Charles was lying. But the wealth of the Ashford family, the size of that house, the power of that Well . . . that hadn't been a lie. If you had a life like that, then surely you could find *some* way to send a message?

Unless it was to someone you didn't particularly care about.

I lay in bed, getting more and more depressed.

There was the soft thud of something landing on a mattress, along with the creak of springs. Something nudged my leg, and I twisted my head around to see Hobbes's yellow-green eyes. "Mrrraow?" he asked.

"Hey, you," I said tiredly, reaching over to scratch his head. Hobbes rubbed against my fingers, purring, then licked at my forearm with his sandpaper-like tongue.

"Ow!" I said with a laugh. "All right, all right! I'm up!"

I fed Hobbes, let him out, cleaned my teeth, and had a shower. And by the time I went down for breakfast, I was starting to feel that things weren't so bad after all. Okay, so I wasn't going to drucraft school, and, okay, I wasn't going to be getting any help from my family anytime soon, if ever. But now that I thought about it, none of that was actually anything new. What *was* new was that I had a lot more money and a drucraft catalogue, and all it had cost me was a few bruises. I was *way* better off than I had been a couple of days ago.

I made myself a big stack of toast, got a glass of water to go with it, then went back upstairs and lay down on my bed. Hobbes, who'd apparently finished answering the call of nature, squeezed through the window and curled up in the crook of my knees. I opened up my battered old laptop, put on a playlist, then pulled the Exchange catalogue out of its bag and laid it down on my bed. Then I glanced around my room and gave a contented sigh. It was a Saturday, and for once I had no work to do and no errands to run. It was just me, Hobbes, and my new catalogue.

I opened it and began to read.

Now that I wasn't in the Exchange and didn't have to keep looking over my shoulder, I could take my time and start from the beginning. The introduction had a table for converting between the "Faraday Scale" and the "Universal (Smithsonian) Scale," another table showing the relation between Faraday ratings and a Well's class, and a third showing the relation between the Faraday scale and carat weight. From context, the Faraday scale seemed to be for measuring Wells, while sigls were measured by carats.

Next was a confusing page about "sigl attunement." It claimed that all Exchange-traded sigls were the product of limiters confirmed to have an "attunement ratio" of at least two to one, and also that they were all "solid" rather than "threaded" unless specified otherwise. I puzzled over that for a while before giving up and moving on to the section titled "Fitting."

> All prices in this catalogue are inclusive of the sigl fitting process, including Board taxes, Exchange surcharge, shaping fee, and use of the provider's limiter. Fitting samples for all Exchange-traded sigl packages are extracted by qualified medical professionals at no extra cost. Certain providers may supply additional services as part of the sigl package, such as essentia reading, affinity consultation, transport to the Well area, accommodations, refreshments, and local cuisine. Which services are included in a sigl package vary by provider, and prospective customers are encouraged to examine the "Providers" section on page 451 before making a purchase.
>
> Sigl packages do not permit access to the Well itself.

I flipped to page 451.

The "Providers" section was a list of half-page and full-page spreads. Some of the names had "House" in them; others didn't. Weirdly, most sounded as though they were advertising some sort of package holiday, complete with glossy landscape photos: House De Haughton had aerial photographs of Lancashire, House Chetwynd had shots of forested hills in Shropshire, and something calling itself "Camlink" talked about its luxurious accommodations in Cambridgeshire and Lincolnshire for customers on "affinity programmes." They made it sound like a hotel.

Actually, what it really sounded like was someone trying to sell you a holiday experience. You were supposed to travel to the Well, stay in their hotel, eat a local meal . . . then get your "fitting sample" extracted, which sounded more than a little creepy but which was talked about in very casual terms, so maybe it was a standard thing in this world.

Putting it all together, it sounded as though sigls were made to order, and to make a sigl the buyer had to actually show up. My dad had told me a long time ago that if a sigl was made for someone else, it probably wouldn't work for you. I'd been able to use his—I'd learned to channel on an old crappy light sigl that he'd let me use—but I'd had the impression that had only worked because I was his son. That would explain why the Exchange didn't sell sigls premade. If it had been made for a stranger, you couldn't use it.

It also drove home to me just how rich the typical Exchange customer had to be. The high-end providers in the catalogue kept going on about their accommodation and food and entertainment. Maybe for these people, buying a sigl *was* like going on holiday.

Next I started going through sigl descriptions, looking for ones that I might be able to make myself. The first thing I wanted to know was whether my invisibility sigl design would work, but when I looked up "invisibility" in the index, it turned out there wasn't just one type of sigl that did that; there were four. Gloom sigls made the bearer harder to see by creating a field that converted incoming light into free essentia. Diffraction sigls, like the "Phantom" one I'd read about yesterday, bent light rays around the bearer. Transparency sigls, which I almost missed because they were under the Matter category instead of the Light one, worked by altering the transparency of the bearer, causing light to pass right through them. And finally, active camouflage sigls intercepted all outgoing light and altered its frequency to match the light coming in from the opposite direction.

All four had advantages and disadvantages. Gloom sigls were

the cheapest by far, but they weren't real invisibility; they just created a sphere of darkness that blinded everyone in its radius, bearer included. Diffraction and transparency sigls were "true" invisibility, but with drawbacks: the concealment wasn't perfect, and if you wanted to see while using one, you'd have to use a special vision-enhancing sigl as well. (Funnily enough, the manufacturers just so happened to provide sigls that did exactly that, for an outrageous price.) Active camouflage, since it affected outgoing but not incoming light, was the only one that didn't interfere with your own vision. Unfortunately, it was also insanely expensive—even the cheapest active camouflage sigl cost over a million pounds. It also had a note about requiring a "Board licence," whatever that was.

The design I'd worked out sounded a lot like the Exchange's diffraction sigls. Could I make one myself? I thought a bit, then got up to get a notebook and some materials. Hobbes made a drowsy noise of complaint and went back to sleep.

Some work with a notebook and pencil told me that diffraction sigls had a weight of between 1.2 and 4.9 carats. My own two sigls were so light that the kitchen scales couldn't measure them, but after some improvisation I decided that they were around 0.25 carats at most. Given that my sigls had used the full capacity of my Well, and assuming that the makers of the diffraction sigls were producing them with as little essentia as they reasonably could, this meant that my Well couldn't make a diffraction sigl. It didn't meet the minimum Faraday strength.

I sat back and looked at the figures with a surge of excitement. So long as I could match my sigl designs to ones in the catalogue, I now had a way to know in advance whether they'd be possible or not. It still wouldn't tell me *how* to make the sigl but was a huge step forward from where I'd been yesterday.

Hobbes had been waiting to see if I'd lie down again so that he could go back to sleep against my leg. When it became clear that I wouldn't, he yawned, rose, and disappeared through the window. Drucraft doesn't impress cats.

I spent the rest of the morning researching sigls that I'd be able to create with the Well I had. There weren't many, but there were some. The low end of gloom sigls should be possible, as would the weaker illusion effects. There was also a line of "dazzle" sigls, marketed as self-defence tools, designed to blind attackers with a flash of light and give the bearer time to get away. A few days ago I would have thought that sounded pretty weak, but my encounter with Diesel had taught me that blinding someone for a few seconds could make a big difference.

No laser beams. There were references to a "Military and Security" catalogue. Maybe the more powerful sigls were there.

By eleven o'clock I'd been at it for over four hours, and I'd only finished the "Light Sigls" section. I needed a break.

I left the house and walked to Stratford to pay in Charles's cheque. The bank had the usual Saturday morning queue, and I spent a while looking at the number on the paper. It was the most money I'd ever held.

I *had* thought about telling Charles to keep his money. It would have felt nice to tell him that I didn't need his help—only trouble was, it would have been a lie. The cold truth was that I needed all the help I could get, and I wasn't in any position to turn away a windfall, no matter who it was from.

Still, realising that Charles could make this kind of difference to my life, this casually, was . . . uncomfortable. It was a reminder of just how big the gap between us was. He'd said that the matter was closed. But if he ever changed his mind . . .

Well. I'd just have to worry about that when it happened.

I GOT HOME to find that the house was quiet. Ignas and the others were working their Saturday shifts, and Hobbes, unusually, hadn't come home for his midday nap. I got some lunch and set out again.

The catalogue had left me full of ideas for sigls, and I wanted to try them out. Invisibility might be out of reach, but one of those blinding sigls should be very doable, especially since I knew how to make light sigls already. But my Well wouldn't have enough charge for months, and those two at Upton Park were too weak. Which left only one option: the church.

The church with the Well is in West Ham, less than half a mile from my house. I got there around one and took a walk around the small triangular park surrounding the church itself, studying it from the outside. It was *really* old, built from brick and ancient stone, with a moss-covered roof and a central tower that wouldn't have looked out of place on a castle. The grounds held massive gnarled sycamore and lime trees, bare branches stretching up into the sky. On the south side, broken railings surrounded an overgrown cemetery; forget-me-nots and a few early bluebells peeked from around the weathered tombstones. An orange-and-black butterfly, a Painted Lady, alighted on the path, waving its wings before flitting away into the shade.

I could sense the essentia of the Well inside, but it felt very different from mine. If my Well felt radiant, this felt colourless, like a pool of pure water hidden in the grass. It seemed to have more "weight" to it than my Well, but it was a lot harder to detect, and I must have walked past it hundreds of times over the years without ever noticing anything at all.

But hard to detect didn't mean weak, and right now, the Well was holding about as much essentia as my own Well could hold at full charge. Maybe a little more. In theory, I could walk in and shape a sigl right now.

Two things held me back.

First, I didn't know if the Well was defended. The church's thick walls made it hard to tell if anyone was inside, but the times I'd gone by after dark, I'd seen lights in the windows. Whoever was tending this Well probably wouldn't have security measures as extreme as the Ashfords', but I still didn't think they'd be happy if I just strolled in.

But if it had just been that, I probably would have tried to sneak in months ago. The bigger reason I hadn't tried to use this Well was that it felt like stealing. It was one thing to use a Well that was abandoned, but this one wasn't abandoned. And it felt *especially* wrong stealing from a church.

I really wanted a new sigl. But did I want one badly enough to go in there and steal for it?

No, I decided. Maybe it would be different if I were desperate, but right now I wasn't. I'd found other Wells before, and I could do it again.

I turned around and headed home.

EVER SINCE THURSDAY, I'd been a lot more careful about approaching my house. I slowed down at the corner of Foxden Road, then stopped as I saw that there was a big black car just a little way down from my house, blocking the road with its brake lights on. From this distance it was hard to be sure, but it looked a lot like Scar and Diesel's minivan.

I drew back into the shadow of the building. As I watched, the minivan's brake lights went off, and it drove away, disappearing around the corner at the far end. I stayed in cover, waiting to see if it would show up again.

Five minutes passed. The van didn't come back.

Cautiously I approached, staying on the far side of the pavement where I could duck down behind cars. As I got closer to my house, I saw that no one was there. But there was something on our doorstep that looked like a package.

Uneasiness stirred in me. Foxden Road was bright in the afternoon sunlight, and there was no sound but for the whisper of the wind. Someone walking down the road would have said it was peaceful . . . but to me, it didn't feel peaceful. It felt wrong, and the focus of that wrongness was the thing on our doorstep.

Warily, I crossed the road.

The package on our doorstep was a brown cardboard box. But for the absence of labels, it could have been an Amazon delivery. On the top of the box was writing, and I leant forward to read it, keeping my distance as I did. There were just three words, written with enough force to score into the cardboard.

LEARN
YOUR
PLACE

A chill went down my spine. All of a sudden I knew that box was bad news, really bad news, like the feeling you get when you're watching a horror movie and you see something small and out of place. Whatever was inside, it was going to be something horrible, and I stood frozen, afraid to open it and afraid to run away.

A breeze blew across the doorstep, carrying a coppery smell. My nose twitched.

Slowly, I crouched down. I reached for the box, hesitated, then drew back the flaps.

At the bottom of the box was a matted heap of grey-and-black fur.

The scent of blood wafted out, stronger this time. I wasn't sure what I was looking at. Hesitantly, I reached into the box . . .

And then the heap of fur twitched just slightly, and all of a sudden my eyes seemed to snap into focus and I realised what I was looking at. *Hobbes.*

A wave of dizziness hit me; I swayed, my vision going grey. Little details jumped out at me, sticking in my memory with awful clarity. One of Hobbes's legs, bent the wrong way. Eyes closed tight. Something sticking out from his hips, a bulge under the fur where there shouldn't be one.

Grief and terrible fury swelled up within me. Who'd done this?

No. Fear washed away anger. *No time.* I pulled out my phone and frantically began to search for the number for the vet.

THE NEXT HOUR was a blur. Phone calls. Recorded messages. Emergency appointments. Transfer to a veterinary hospital.

It was only much later that things seemed to slow down enough for me to think. I was standing in the lobby of a veterinary hospital in Wanstead, a few miles north of my home. Display racks held rubber dog toys and pet-themed greeting cards. There was a nurse standing in front of me, talking.

". . . specialist is looking at him now," the nurse was saying. "Now, we should know more after the X-rays, but for the moment all I can tell you is that he's stable. Once our specialist's finished the evaluation, then he'll come out, and we should be able to discuss further options. Is that okay?"

"Okay," I said numbly.

"I know this is very stressful. Just try to wait patiently, and we'll tell you more as soon as we possibly can."

"What did the vet say?"

The nurse hesitated for just an instant. "We'll have to wait until after the X-rays. The specialist will come out to discuss options right afterwards, okay?"

I wanted to keep asking questions, but there was no point. "Okay."

"Also, I know you're very worried and this isn't really what you want to be thinking about, but one of the reception staff will be coming to you with a consent form and to talk about payment plans."

I didn't answer. The nurse said a few more things and left. I went outside.

The hospital was on the side of a main road, just north of a big junction. Cars whizzed past and people strolled along the pavement. I stood in the car park as everyone passed me by.

Now that I'd done all that I could, and I had nothing to do but wait, I finally had time to think about how this had happened, and my thoughts jumped instantly to one name. *Lucella*.

Hate boiled up inside me. I wanted to hurt Lucella, to kill her. But the hate was swallowed almost instantly by fear. What if Hobbes died? Was he dying on the operating table right now? Would I even know? The image of him going still, the breath leaving his body, stuck in my mind, playing in my thoughts over and over.

I walked back and forth in the car park, pacing from the low stone wall at one end of the car park to the side of the hospital. Wall to wall, back and forth. My thoughts jumped between fear for Hobbes and hate for Lucella and back to fear again. The traffic drove on by, uncaring. Other people came and went, some holding cat carriers, others with dogs on leads. Most looked happy, and something inside me wanted to scream at them.

At last the door to the hospital swung open. I glanced around as I'd done every time that door had opened, but this time it was for me. A man in his thirties dressed in surgical gear waved me over. Slowly I walked over, afraid of what I was about to hear. The man's face was hidden by a blue surgical mask, and I scanned his eyes for any clue as to what he was thinking.

"Stephen Oakwood?" the vet said. "And your cat is called Hobbes, is that right?"

I nodded, feeling sick.

"Ah, sorry, let me talk to you properly," the vet said, and pulled down his mask. He led me over to a holly tree and turned to face me, and as I saw the expression on his face, I felt something shrivel up inside me.

"It's bad news, I'm afraid," the vet said. He was tall, with a faint Midlands accent, and the sympathy on his face made it worse. "Hobbes has suffered very serious trauma. I understand that you didn't see what happened?"

I shook my head.

"The damage is a mixture of blunt force and crush injuries. Normally the most common cause for this kind of trauma is a road accident, but from the way the injuries are spread around the body, I don't think that was the case here. I'm afraid it looks as though he was beaten and kicked."

I imagined someone walking up to Hobbes as he lay dozing near my house, drowsing in the sun. He liked to sleep on the wall-tops of Foxden Road. In my mind I saw Hobbes starting awake as hands closed on him, trying too late to escape, then I saw him being thrown to the pavement, beaten and stamped on, the crack of breaking bones—

With a wrench I forced my thoughts away. "How bad is it?"

"First are the fractures," the vet said. "Left foreleg, left hind leg, ribs, and pelvis, nine breaks in total. They're serious but not life threatening. We can set them and splint the legs . . . we can't splint the pelvis, but fortunately it hasn't been twisted, so it should heal with cage rest. Unfortunately, Hobbes also has internal injuries, and those are . . . much more serious, I'm afraid. There's significant internal bleeding. The liver's certainly ruptured, and other organs may be too."

"Can you fix it?"

"We could schedule Hobbes for exploratory surgery with a view to full-scale surgical intervention." The vet seemed to be choosing his words carefully. "He'd have to be kept in intensive care, and it would probably require multiple operations."

"Please just talk straight to me," I said. "If you do that, is he going to live?"

The vet sighed. "I don't want to prejudice you, but . . . realistically, probably not. I've been present for maybe four cases of surgery on cats as severely injured as this, and three of them died in the perioperative period. We'll obviously do the best we can, but . . . I think if I try, he's probably going to die on the operating table."

I was silent.

"I should warn you that it'd also be very expensive," the vet said. "Between the operations and the weeks of intensive care, even if things went exactly to plan, the total costs could be five thousand pounds or more. I'm only mentioning it because it says on the form that Hobbes doesn't have insurance."

"And you're saying he'd probably die anyway," I said dully.

"Yes. I'm sorry."

I felt as though a black pit was swallowing me up. The car park felt very cold and very lonely.

"I know this isn't what you were hoping to hear," the vet said, "but honestly, I've looked at the X-rays and the tests, and I don't think there's any course of treatment that has any good chance of success."

I knew where this was going. "You think he should be put down."

"Obviously I'm not going to push you to do it," the vet said. "He's your cat and it's your choice. But he was in terrible pain when he was brought here. He's only sleeping now because of the anaesthetic. Once he wakes up, he'll have to be on constant pain relief. I think . . . on balance, surgical intervention is just going to drag out his suffering."

I was silent.

"Mr. Oakwood?" the vet asked.

Two choices stood before me, both impossible. A treatment that I couldn't afford and that probably wouldn't work, or having Hobbes killed.

But . . . no, there was a third choice. It was desperate, but I *was* desperate. Tobias's words last night: *"Stronger muscles, quicker healing . . . other abilities too. They're called hellhounds."*

"You said you could splint some of the fractures," I said. "Could you do that, then do what you can for the other injuries without surgery, so that I can take him home?"

The vet hesitated. "Yes . . . but without anything invasive, I can't treat the internal injuries. He'll almost certainly die within a few days."

"Then he'll die in his own home, peacefully, without having been cut open."

I was expecting the vet to argue, but he just looked a little sad and started explaining what I'd have to do about Hobbes's diet and care. It was only much later, when I was signing the waiver and getting the medications from the nursing staff, that I realised that the vet had probably been on my side. He'd started by recommending surgery because he was supposed to, but if he'd really thought it was the right thing to do, he wouldn't have given in like that.

They gave Hobbes to me in a plastic cat carrier. He was still unconscious from the anaesthetic, and his left legs were hidden under blue-wrapped splints.

I took a taxi home.

ONCE I WAS home, I hurried upstairs to my room and grabbed the Exchange catalogue. I flicked quickly to the "Life Sigls" section, searching for one that I remembered seeing. There were no healing sigls—if you tried to look them up, you got referred to the "Medical and Industrial Catalogue"—but there was a whole set of subcategories under "Personal Enhancement." Musculature, circulatory system, immune system, reproductive system, anaesthetic . . . *there.*

VITALIS

Gladeshire McKeon is the premier international provider for drucraft-enhanced health. Sourced initially from India and North America, our wealth of expertise in . . .

"Shut up," I muttered, and skipped ahead.

. . . monitors the bearer's physiological state and, when it detects blood loss, stimulates production of platelets and coagulation factors, rapidly stemming bleeding until the bearer can receive professional medical attention. In addition to this primary function, the Vitalis Consolidator can also utilise local essentia reserves to increase production of endothelial cells, speeding and reinforcing natural regeneration.

WARNING: The Vitalis sigl is not intended for long-term use and is not a substitute for professional medical care. Consult your doctor before making use of any Life sigls. Gladeshire McKeon is not responsible or liable for any publicly declared side effects of Vitalis. Potential side effects may include—

My phone buzzed, and I looked away from the catalogue to see that an unknown number was calling. Maybe it was the hospital. I hit the green button. "Hello?"

"Oh, there you are," Lucella said.

CHAPTER 8

I FROZE.

"So did you get my message?" Lucella asked.

"You," I managed to say.

"I'll take that as a yes."

I stared at the phone.

"You know how this whole thing started?" Lucella asked conversationally. "It was on Tuesday. I was having a bad day and didn't have anyone else to talk to, so I went to Tobias. I wasn't really expecting him to help, I just wanted to blow off some steam. But instead he gets this speculative look and starts talking about how there might be another candidate for heir."

What the hell is she talking about?

"Anyway, it sounded good," Lucella continued. "Bring in some new blood, maybe get another perspective, you know? Tobias might be a weasel, but he's always been good at ferreting things out. And with Charles favouring Calhoun, I figured we were both in the same boat. Instead, as soon as my back's turned, the little bastard decides he's going to screw *me* over too."

"I don't care," I told Lucella.

"Anyway, I'm guessing you've figured out by now what you were really there for," Lucella said. "Tobias just wanted you to tell Charles that his niece and nephew were being mean to you. I guess he thought that'd be enough to push him to the front of the line. Not that it worked. Oh, Charles was pissed off with me, but from the look on Tobias's face when he came out, he wasn't any—"

"Can you stop talking about yourself for once?" I asked her. "I don't care about your family politics. Was that you?"

"Did you not hear what I said or something? I told you, it was a message."

"*What* message?"

"To stay out of my way," Lucella said. "Charles cut my allowance and threatened to pull me out of Canterbury. Not that I care that much, but it's the principle of the thing. People like you don't get to make trouble for people like me."

"You—" I had to stop and take a breath; my voice was shaking. "You had my cat nearly killed for that?"

"Charles told both me and Tobias to stay away from you," Lucella said. "He didn't say anything about pets. So next time Tobias decides to involve you in one of his little plots, maybe you'll remember this and think twice, hmm?"

Lucella didn't even seem particularly angry. She sounded *casual*, which actually made it worse. "You think that's how this works?" I said through clenched teeth. "You can just do this and walk away?"

". . . Yes? Why, what are you going to do about it?"

"Go to the police."

Lucella laughed. She sounded genuinely amused. "You really have no idea how this works, do you?"

"If I tell them—"

"You realise I could have you arrested tomorrow?" Lucella

asked. "I go to the police and tell them that you tried to sexually assault me Thursday night. Then you followed me home, illegally broke into our house during a party, and then when that didn't work, you killed your own cat and texted me a picture as a threat. I tell them that, who do you think they're going to believe? You or me?"

I stared at the phone again.

"But talking to the police is annoying," Lucella said. "No, if you *really* got on my nerves, I think I'd just make you disappear. You like going out for late-night runs, right? One night, there'll be a plain black van parked somewhere on your route. You go past, someone comes up behind you and knocks you out, and no one ever sees you again."

I couldn't think of anything to say.

"You're a poor low-class white kid from East London with no friends and no family," Lucella said. "If something happens to you, no one's going to care. You won't get another warning." She hung up.

Slowly I lowered the phone. The "Call Ended" message was showing on the screen, and I stared at it until the screen went dark.

I looked down at the Exchange catalogue. It was still open to the page for the Vitalis sigl. The cheapest model cost £64,990.

I picked up Hobbes's cat carrier and walked out.

THE CHURCH WAS shadowed in the fading dusk. I did a circuit, checking it from all around. There was no movement, but I could see a light on in the southern windows.

I'd left this Well alone before because I hadn't been desperate. Now I was desperate. I was going to make a healing sigl for Hobbes, and to hell with anyone who got in my way.

The south door was locked. The main entrance wasn't. I slipped inside.

The inside of the church was solemn and quiet. Images of saints and biblical figures looked down from stained glass windows, and stone pillars rose to a vaulted ceiling. The floor was rough flagstone, worn smooth by centuries of footsteps. The air smelled of candle wax.

I took a glance around but nothing moved. The Well was at the far end, just in front of the altar.

I started forward.

A voice spoke from the shadows. "Good evening."

I jumped, turning. The man stepping out from behind the pillars was very tall, with striking features, black shoulder-length hair, and very dark eyes. He wore the black clothes of a priest, and he kept his hands clasped behind his back as he walked with a measured gait along the side of the wooden pews. "How can I help you?" he asked.

"I'm . . . visiting."

"Visiting who?"

I hesitated, trying to think of some plausible story. I've always been a bad liar.

The two of us stood in silence. My eyes drifted to the Well. I just needed a little time—

"You want the Well?" the priest asked. When I started slightly, he nodded to himself. "I thought so."

"I need to use it," I told the priest.

"You *need* to use it?"

Oh, screw this. "My cat's dying," I told the priest. "I'm going to use this Well to heal him. Don't get in my way."

The priest's eyes drifted down to the cat carrier. "Your cat."

"Yes," I told him defiantly.

The priest just looked at me.

Well, at least he wasn't laughing. "I'll fight my way past you if I have to," I told him.

"I see," the priest said. "And what will you do afterwards?"

"I'll use the Well to make him a regeneration sigl."

"By yourself?"

"Are you going to let me past?"

"I will give you a choice," the priest told me. "You may attempt to force your way past me. Or you may swear to respect the sanctity of this Well and not to tap it without permission. If you do, I will offer you some limited assistance." The priest held a hand out to me, palm up. "Choose."

I hesitated. "Limited assistance" didn't sound very helpful. Maybe he was just trying to make me back off.

I looked the man up and down. He was bigger than me, and young by priest standards, maybe early forties. But he was . . . well, a priest. He probably wouldn't be much good in a fight.

Except . . .

Was I *really* going to do this? Beat up a priest and steal from a church? It wouldn't be the first time I'd broken the rules, but I've always had an instinctive feeling that there's a difference between breaking the rules and doing something wrong. And this felt *very* wrong.

I could feel Hobbes's weight in the cat carrier. I couldn't lose him. The priest stood in front of me, waiting for an answer. Seconds ticked by.

I thought about running forward. My muscles tensed as I tracked the path across the floor that I'd take. Making a sigl would take time. I'd have to actually knock the guy out, or . . .

No, I realised. There were some lines I wouldn't cross, and this was one of them.

I straightened, letting my muscles relax. "Fine," I said. I felt tired, and disappointed in some way, as if I'd failed.

The priest nodded. "Bring your cat here."

I walked forward warily. The priest watched as I set the carrier down on the floor just in front of him. He was taller than I'd realised; up close like this he towered over me, and now that I got a good look at him he didn't seem particularly weak. Actually, he looked—

I caught movement out of the corner of my eye and turned sharply. From the darkness at the corner of the church, a pair of golden eyes were watching me. From the height it looked like a dog—a big dog?—but the shadows seemed to wrap around it and—

The eyes vanished. Frowning, I stared at the corner. I could just make out the stone of the walls, but whatever I'd glimpsed, it was gone.

"You are both safe," the priest told me. I looked back to see that he'd knelt on the stone and was opening the cat carrier.

I gave the corner a last wary look and then watched anxiously as the priest adjusted the carrier to slide Hobbes's head forward. Then he reached inside his breast pocket, took out a string of prayer beads, and sent a flow of essentia into Hobbes.

I blinked in surprise. The prayer beads were dark brown, with a crucifix hanging from them, but as I looked more closely, I saw that some of the beads were housings for things that looked like tiny gems. One was small and white, like a pearl, and it was emitting a stream of essentia that was flowing into Hobbes's head and spreading out through the cat's body.

"An infusion sigl," the priest said, as if reading my thoughts. "It directs Primal essentia into the subject's body. A poor substitute for healing, but it can ease suffering and preserve a creature that is close to death."

"Do you have some way to heal him?"

"Healing has never been one of my talents," the priest said absently. He hadn't looked at me since he'd opened the carrier. "I'm more curious as to what you thought you were going to do with this Well."

"Make a—"

"Regeneration sigl, yes. Have you ever manifested a sigl before?"

"Yes."

"To be used by someone else?"

". . . No."

"And do you know how to create a regeneration sigl?"

"I thought I'd figure it out as I went along." Most of my attention was on Hobbes. Was he breathing a little more easily?

"You would have failed," the priest told me. "Manifesting a sigl for your own use is very different from creating one for the use of another. Particularly another species."

"They do it with hellhounds."

"The techniques involved in creating hellhounds and other guard beasts have been developed and refined over many decades. Perhaps you might have been able to improvise something, but certainly not on a first try. And the essentia drain would have killed your pet while you struggled to figure it out." The priest leant back. "There."

I looked at Hobbes and felt a rush of hope. He *was* breathing more easily. He looked to be sleeping now, instead of being on the verge of death.

"Do not feel false hope," the priest warned. "Infusing a creature with essentia strengthens them but does not cure their injuries. It is a temporary reprieve, no more."

It was still more than I'd hoped for. "Thank you," I said. "I'm . . . sorry for what I said before."

The priest nodded and rose to his feet, then walked to the altar. "Even if you had succeeded in forcing your way past me," he said over his shoulder, "and even if you had somehow managed to hit upon a viable pattern for making a regeneration sigl for a cat, you would still have failed. Do you know why?"

"No," I admitted.

"Regeneration sigls require a Life Well. This is a Primal Well."

I was silent.

The priest turned to face me. "You didn't know?"

". . . No."

"Try to feel this Well's essentia. Can you tell the difference?"

"Well . . . yes." My Well on Foxden Road and the two lesser ones I'd found last year all had had the same feel. The Ashford Well had dwarfed them in strength, but it had still been similar in kind. This one was totally different.

"And you didn't consider that a Well with such different essentia might belong to a different branch?"

"I didn't think about it," I admitted. I was having that realisation a lot lately. I'd only ever had access to one Well, and it had made light sigls, so I'd just assumed that all Wells could make light sigls. Now that I thought about it, it was obvious—it could make light sigls because it was a Light Well. But it hadn't occurred to me to put two and two together.

I needed to learn more. I was making stupid mistakes, all because there were so many things I didn't know. And when I talked to other people, they didn't *tell* me what I didn't know, sometimes because they didn't care, but sometimes because the things I didn't know were so incredibly basic that it just never occurred to them to mention it.

"Wells such as this are quite hard to perceive," the priest said. "I do what little I can to assist with that. Probably unnecessary— few raiders would be interested in a low-class Primal Well—but old habits die hard. Did you happen to enter the church one day?"

"I noticed it from the outside."

"Interesting," the priest said. He sounded as though he were talking to himself. "Advanced sensing and shaping skills, combined with knowledge of some quite specialised sigls. At the same time, you seem extraordinarily ignorant of some of the most basic facts about drucraft."

"Can you help me?" I asked.

"Yes, but not in the way that you are looking for. Your cat is almost certainly going to die."

I flinched. "What?"

"I assume from the stitches and splints that you've already been to a vet," the priest told me. "You turned to drucraft only when that failed. Correct?"

". . . Yes."

"Medical drucraft in this country is advanced, but it is designed for humans. The Life sigls that those doctors use are heavily specialised for use on the human body. Drucrafters who treat animals are rare and mostly cater to the pets of the very rich. Your chances of finding one who could provide better care than a veterinary hospital and whose fees you could afford are effectively zero."

Rare, but not impossible. "So there *are* sigls that could heal him," I said. "Right?"

"Medics who expect to have to deal with emergency situations without access to proper facilities sometimes carry what are called mending sigls. They are designed to stem bleeding, particularly internal bleeding. A general-purpose mending sigl, one which was not specialised for use on humans, might be able to—"

"Could I make one?"

"Almost certainly not," the priest said. "Firstly, you would require a Life Well. At any one time, there are a little under a thousand of them in the United Kingdom, of which the permanent ones are almost all claimed. Finding a temporary one is possible, but even if you could do so, I do not know how to shape a mending sigl, and neither do you."

"I've shaped a sigl on my own before," I told him.

I'd expected the priest to challenge that, but instead he just studied me. After a moment, he smiled slightly. "Determination," he said. "A useful quality."

"So I need to find a Life Well, then figure out how to make a mending sigl from one," I said. "Right?"

"If that is your choice," the priest said. "You saw the infusion that I performed. Could you duplicate that without a sigl?"

I thought for a second, then nodded.

"You and your cat share a bond," the priest told me. "A spiritual connection formed by sharing essentia over an extended period. Personal essentia that you gift to him will be more effective than that shared by a stranger." He nodded at Hobbes, still lying unconscious in the cat carrier. "With regular infusions of essentia, he might live five to ten days. You have that long."

I stood there, thinking. A thousand Wells spread throughout the entire country . . . Could I do it?

No choice. I'd have to.

I bent down and snapped shut the door on the cat carrier. "Thank you for the help," I told the priest.

The priest nodded.

I picked up the carrier and left. When I reached the door, I took a last look back. The priest was standing in front of the altar, framed by the stained glass windows, watching me go.

I WAS VERY tired by the time I got back. The day had left me feeling battered, and I still had my bruises from Thursday night. I wanted to rest, but instead I opened up my laptop and brought up the calculator.

The priest had told me there were just under a thousand Life Wells in the UK. Dividing the population of London by the population of the UK, that would mean there should be a hundred or so in the city. Odds of finding one with a blind search in five days were fairly good.

On the other hand, if they were distributed by geography instead of by population, then I was dividing the *area* of Greater London by the *area* of the UK. Which gave me odds that were . . . much, much worse.

Well. Only one way to find out.

I knelt down by Hobbes and rested my hand on the cat carrier. "Just hold on," I told him quietly. Hobbes stirred slightly; his tail twitched, then he fell back into unconsciousness.

I walked out.

I SEARCHED ALL through the night.

I didn't have any real idea how you were supposed to find Wells. I could sense their essentia once I got close enough, but I knew from past experience that it had to be pretty close. For a street, that meant walking all the way down both sides, and for an open area, that meant quartering it, like a dog trying to pick up a scent. With no better ideas, I started at the borders of my neighbourhood and worked my way out. I combed the streets of Plaistow South, then went over the Greenway to the playing fields, now silent in the darkness. From there I worked my way west, towards the river.

As I searched, I thought about how I'd found Hobbes. Back in our old house, there'd been a family two streets over who lived in a ground-floor flat in a council block and had a load of old furniture mouldering away in their front garden. One day as I walked past, I saw that stretched out on the soggy old sofa was a mother cat, with five little balls of fur clambering over the cushions, scrabbling to climb the sofa and falling off into the grass.

Every morning that I walked past, the five of them would be a little bigger. I got into the habit of stopping to play with them, until they'd rush over to the fence each time they saw me. Then one day I saw a piece of paper stuck up in the window: KITTENS FOR SALE.

My dad said no: he had to go away for work, sometimes for a week or more, and he couldn't take care of a pet. I said I'd do it; he said I was too young; I kept arguing, and finally he threw up his hands and gave in. I already knew which one I wanted: the tabby who was the biggest of the litter and who was always the first to run over when he saw me. I carried him home in my arms, the kitten spending the whole journey looking around and trying to climb my shoulders. That had been three and a half years ago, and Hobbes had been a part of my life ever since.

In the three years since my dad had disappeared—during all the time that I was waiting for him, and struggling with money, and trying to deal with all the problems and loneliness and isolation that come with living on your own in a big city—Hobbes had always been there. When things had been at their worst, when my whole life had felt like a sea of grey with nothing to look forward to, he'd been the one bright spot of warmth and happiness. With my dad gone, he was the closest family I had. I couldn't bear to lose him.

I searched all through that night and found two Wells. Or what was left of Wells. Both were remnants, so weak that I could barely detect them, and what was left of their essentia was diffusing slowly into the ground. The priest had talked about temporary Wells; maybe this was what they looked like once they'd been used up.

One of the Wells had what I was coming to recognise as Light essentia, shining and weightless, like my one on Foxden Road. The other was something I'd never felt before. The traces that were left gave me a weird feeling of . . . focus? Perfection? In any case, it didn't feel like those sigls that Scar and Diesel had worn, which meant it wasn't Life.

By the time the sky started to turn grey, I was tired, dispirited, and cold. A whole night's work for nothing. I headed home.

Hobbes was awake and in pain; as I opened the door, he gave a pitiful meow. I stroked him, gave him some of the painkiller the vet had prescribed, cleaned up his mess, tried to feed and water him, then poured essentia into his body as the priest had done. By the time I was done, Hobbes was asleep again.

I wanted to sleep as well. Instead I wolfed down some food and headed back out.

I searched from dawn to dusk, and this time I found three Wells, though not the ones I was looking for. Another Light Well, this one with a fragile, ephemeral feel, weak and not even a quarter full. Another with a kind of essentia I didn't recognise, tapped and empty. And one that was full, hidden away down one of the tributaries of the River Lea. It was pristine and untouched, the essentia swirling and mysterious and quick, and at any other time I would have been thrilled. But it wasn't a Life Well, and with a heavy heart I turned away.

By the time the sun started to dip behind the buildings, I was utterly exhausted. I'd been awake for thirty-six hours straight and I was actually falling asleep as I walked. I somehow made it home without getting into an accident, fed and treated Hobbes, and fell asleep the instant my head hit the pillow.

I WOKE EARLY on Monday morning to pouring rain. I grabbed my umbrella and went out again. The temp agency kept calling until I muted my phone.

I searched out west towards Upton Park, working without a break all the way to sunset. I strained my sensing ability to its limit and didn't find a single Well.

Hobbes was looking weaker and still wasn't eating. I tried to get some liquid food down his throat, only for him to vomit it up in bile and blood. Then I went out again, pacing the streets in the darkness.

ON TUESDAY I decided to stop eating. Having to prepare food was a distraction and digesting it was making me feel sluggish. I'd be able to concentrate better without it.

I found three Wells. None were Life.

Hobbes started to have trouble breathing.

WEDNESDAY, AND I finally found a Life Well. Unfortunately, someone else had found it first. Its essentia was drained and scattered, not enough left even to practise with.

Hobbes got worse.

THURSDAY. ONE WELL. Not Life.

FRIDAY CAME.

CHAPTER 9

ON FRIDAY I snapped.

I woke early—I was too worried about Hobbes to sleep well anymore—and rolled sideways to check on him. Hobbes was sprawled on his side, his breaths shallow and quick; his pulse was weak, and his lips and gums were pale. He barely registered my touch, his eyelids fluttering before closing again.

I laid my hand on his side and sent a surge of essentia into his body. Over the last couple of days I'd worked out a way to increase the amount of essentia I could channel; it felt like lighting a kind of invisible fire inside my body and channelling the heat it produced. I didn't really understand how it worked, but it seemed to increase my personal essentia flow a lot, and within a minute or so Hobbes's breathing eased.

I was sure by this point that these infusions were the only thing keeping Hobbes alive. Every time I did them, the effect on Hobbes's health was instant. The problem was, they were wearing off a little faster every time. I'd already had to increase the rate from two times a day to three times a day, and at this rate it wouldn't be long before I couldn't leave his side at all.

I got up, staggering slightly as a wave of dizziness hit me. The new technique was taking it out of me . . . or maybe it was the lack of food. The gnawing feeling in my stomach was painful, but it did help me focus. I drank some water and headed out.

Today I was searching north, towards Forest Gate and Leytonstone. I had it down to a routine by now. I'd scan a map of the area on my phone, ignoring the sea of missed calls and messages, then work out a route that would trace every street while doubling back as few times as possible, like one of those puzzles where you had to draw a line without taking your pen off the paper. Then it was just a matter of walking the route.

The problem was endurance. Sensing wasn't difficult, but it did take effort, and by this point I'd been doing it eighteen hours a day for nearly a week without a break. Maintaining my concentration was getting harder and harder, and my focus was starting to slip. Each time that I caught myself doing it, I'd imagine Hobbes dying and use the spike of adrenaline to force myself to focus again. When *that* didn't work, I imagined the casual way Lucella had ordered Hobbes's death, and let the memory fan my anger into white-hot hatred. Hate and fear were the twin whips that drove me onward, keeping me on my feet when nothing else would.

But while hate and fear spurred me, they also broke the state of inner calm that I needed to use my sensing. Each time that I used them to shock myself awake, it was a little harder to get back to the right frame of mind. I was going slower today than I had yesterday, and I knew that tomorrow I'd be slower still.

I found one Well in the afternoon. It was full, but with the same heavy, earthy essentia that I'd sensed in one of the Wells I'd found on Tuesday. It was also sealed off, inside a tall, blocky building with barbed wire on its walls. A sign above the door said "LVS Services," with a smaller notice saying that they were a subsidiary of "Maar Gruppe." I went home to treat Hobbes, then dragged myself out again as the sun set, forcing myself to keep searching as evening turned into night.

And then, just when I wasn't expecting it, I found one.

The Life Well was tucked away in a cluster of trees in Wanstead Park, next to a huge pond. The water was cold and dark, a chill breeze rolling off it and hissing through the branches overhead. The essentia inside was vital, powerful, alive . . . and untouched.

But there wasn't much of it. The Well was very weak.

Over the past few days, I'd spent what few precious spare hours I had working out ideas for the priest's mending sigl. I'd made and remade essentia constructs, trying to figure out how to make a healing sigl. The design that I'd come up with was my best guess, but it was still only a guess. I had no idea whether it would work.

I took a deep breath and began.

It felt wrong right from the start. I wasn't used to working with Life essentia, and the techniques I'd learned from shaping Light sigls didn't work in the way I expected. The essentia didn't flow straight; it kept on trying to grow and branch on its own. I had to use a heavier hand than I'd wanted to, and by the time I'd finished with the construct stage, the construct felt threadbare and the Well reserves very small. I took a deep breath, started to shrink the construct, and prayed.

The construct began to take shape, but I could see immediately that the Well's essentia was running out too fast. I kept working, reinforcing the lines of the construct one by one, but the essentia was draining too quickly and I'd underestimated how much this sigl would need. Still, I was getting close. Just a little more and I could start to manifest . . .

The essentia flow thinned, and the essentia construct flickered. It was only two-thirds of the way there. "Come on," I whispered, and strained harder, pulling in all the essentia I could.

The essentia flow continued to drop. The construct wavered. "Come on. Come on, come on." It wasn't over the critical point. If I tried to force it now, nothing would happen. "Just a little more. Just a little more—"

The essentia dried up. The last strands were pulled in, and the flow stopped. The construct shook wildly. I tried desperately to force it through . . . and failed. The construct collapsed, the essentia pouring outwards, spreading out and sinking into the land around, the earth soaking it up like water.

"No!" I shouted. I cast about, but there was nothing left. The Well was empty. It would take months to refill, if it refilled at all.

I threw back my head and screamed. The sound echoed off the water of the pond, bounced back from the silent trees. I'd been so close! If only there had been a little more . . .

And then the reality of it hit me. It had taken me six days to find this Well. To find a stronger one would probably take even longer. Hobbes wouldn't survive six more days. He wouldn't survive three.

It was over.

I broke down then. I'd been driving myself all week with the hope that if I pushed hard enough and desperately enough, I could keep Hobbes alive. It had all been a lie. He was going to die, and it was my fault.

I curled up under the tree and cried myself to sleep.

WHEN I WOKE, it was the middle of the night. The sky was clear, and the spring chill had leached into my bones. Cold is worse when you're hungry, and when I tried to get up my numbed feet made me fall over. I spent a while rubbing feeling back into my limbs before pulling myself upright.

Despite the cold, I felt calm. I knew what I had to do. I was finding Wells too slowly, and it was because my sensing was too weak. I'd been straining and driving myself to look for Wells, but that was wrong. You didn't get better at sensing by trying harder; you did it by removing distractions.

I just hadn't been taking it far enough.

The sky stretched out above me, black and clear, stars twinkling through the London lights. A crescent moon shone down, framed by a pale aura. I stared into the void, looking inward. Over the past few days, I'd tried to keep my mind empty, but the thoughts and worries were still there. Hobbes, Lucella, Charles, my mother and father. I had to get rid of them all.

I started with Lucella, the thoughts and memories a mass of images tinged with emotion, hate and anger and fear. Normally I'd try to banish that mass, move it to the edge of my mind, where it'd be less distracting. Instead, this time, I methodically gathered the thoughts and memories together, and crushed them. It was like taking a glass sculpture in your fist, and squeezing. The sculpture shattered into splinters, the splinters into razor-sharp shards. Pain stabbed through my mind, but I kept squeezing until there was nothing left but dust.

Then I moved on to the next one.

I went through everything that was distracting me: worries, memories, images, plans. As the shards of each one sliced across my thoughts, my mind became clearer, sharper. As the void within grew bigger, so did the void without, the night sky getting larger and larger. At some point it flipped, and I wasn't looking *up* into the sky, but *down*. The blackness hung beneath me, and all that was holding me up was the clutter in my mind. Each time I destroyed another piece, I slipped a little deeper.

The stars burned with a cold fire, infinitely far and within arm's reach. I could see colours in the endless dark. No, not dark, it had its own colour, all colours. I was almost falling. Only one thing was holding me back. I reached out to crush that too, then realised what it was. Hobbes.

I paused. The stars blazed. The strand linking me to Hobbes was the last thing holding me back. Just a little more, and I'd be able to walk among them.

No, I decided. Slowly, inch by inch, I drew myself back. The connection to Hobbes became a tether that I pulled myself along, hand over hand, until I blinked and found myself on the ground again, staring up at the sky.

I looked around with new eyes. Currents of essentia flowed through the earth, followed the lines of the streets, traced patterns through the sky. I picked out the ones that I needed and began walking south, watching the colours shift lazily in the dark.

The city was quiet, the only noise the occasional rush of a passing car. Charles Ashford loomed up out of the night, a giant twice my size. He told me to go west, to use the Wells there to shape a sigl that would bring death in the form of a golden mace. I told him that wasn't what I needed, and he grew angry and changed into my mother, who walked by my side for a while. She had no face, only a black plane, but she spoke without words, talking of webs and shadows. I tried to keep up but with so many more legs she could move faster than I could, and eventually she outdistanced me and disappeared beyond the lights.

The last person I met was my father and he didn't say anything at all, just walked the rest of the way along with me. At some point I realised that he'd drawn a sword; he held the blade in one hand and the scabbard in the other, offering them to me. I touched the sword and made it disappear; he nodded, then pointed with the scabbard to the south.

I blinked. I was alone on an empty street. Where my father had pointed were the black railings of West Ham Park. Green trails of essentia curved into the park, disappearing into the night. I climbed the fence—my body felt very light—and dropped down into the darkness on the other side.

The Life Well was in the northeast corner, hidden in the middle of the greenhouses. It was sheltered and enclosed, a concentration of emerald light, trails of essentia drifting lazily to converge at its heart. I must have walked past the place a hundred times without ever sensing it. I settled down and got to work.

It went much faster this time. The essentia construct took form before me, a pattern of glowing green threads. Now that I could see it, I realised that the design I'd been using wouldn't work. I reached out with my finger, tracing lines in the air, re-shaping the construct into something denser and more complex. More channels, so that the essentia could flow more smoothly. A focusing array, so that the flow leaving the sigl would be concentrated on a single part of the body. Once I was done, I leant back and studied the construct before giving a nod. *There.*

I started to pull in essentia from the Well. The construct flared and brightened, its lines glowing with emerald light. Essentia poured into the pattern above my palm, growing brighter and brighter, denser and denser. It felt as if it needed more help, and I drew upon my own personal essentia more heavily, feeling it burning inside me like a white flame.

I don't know exactly how long it took. It could have been minutes, or hours. But when it was done, I was left kneeling between the greenhouse tables, staring down at a tiny spark of green cupped in my palm.

I blinked and looked up to see that the sky was turning grey. Dawn was breaking. I squeezed under the greenhouse fence, crossed the park, and climbed the gates, my precious cargo wrapped carefully in my pocket. Then I went home.

I let myself in with my key. Hobbes's spirit was wandering around my room, and I shooed him back into his body before settling down. Now that I studied it more closely, the sigl looked like a tiny sphere of emerald, a little bigger than my other two, pale green with a wavy pattern at its centre. I channelled through it and saw Life essentia flow into Hobbes's body.

It was difficult. Hobbes's body was quite close to death, and I knew that if I pushed too hard, I'd kill him. The only feedback I had was the sense of his own essentia, and I used it as a guide, pushing harder when what I was doing seemed to be working, easing off when it felt as though the strain was too much. A couple of times his spirit tried to leave and I told him that I needed him to stay, until he finally seemed to accept it and it merged with his body again and stayed that way.

When I was done, Hobbes wasn't in pain anymore, but his breathing was still very shallow and weak. Once again I fanned the essentia inside me into a white flame, burning something that couldn't be seen or felt, and poured heat and life into Hobbes's body until he was breathing easily again.

At some point my father had come in and started talking to me. "... hey," he was saying. "*Hey.* Can you hear me?"

"I need to heal Hobbes," I told him.

"Jesus, dude, you look like you've been through a famine. When's the last time you ate?"

"Monday, I think," I told him. "I couldn't eat before, I needed to reach the stars. It's fine now."

"Reach the—you know what, just stay there." My father disappeared. I kept adding small flows of essentia to Hobbes while I waited for him to return. I was *really* tired.

My father showed up again with a steaming bowl. The smell made my mouth water, and I suddenly realised just how hungry I was. "Here," my dad said, handing it to me. "Eat slowly."

I took a bite. It tasted amazing. "Wow," I said. "What is this?"

"It's plain white rice. Don't eat too fast or you'll throw up."

"Okay." I looked at my father's features and blinked. "Why do you look Chinese?"

"Because I was born that way, you dickhead."

"Oh," I said. "You're Colin." Now that I focused on his face, I could see that it was him. "That actually makes much more sense."

"Yes," Colin said patiently. "Yes, it does. Now how about you get some sleep?"

"You're made of essentia too, you know. I just couldn't see it before."

"Uh-huh. Take your shoes off."

"Hobbes'll need food and water," I told Colin, swinging my legs onto the bed.

"I'll handle it. Now go to sleep."

"Okay," I agreed. I put my head down and was out like a light.

I WOKE UP a couple of times during the day. Both times there was a bowl of rice sitting by my bed, and I'd eat a little, check to see that Hobbes was okay, and fall asleep again.

When I woke up for the third and last time, it was late afternoon. Colin was sprawled in the chair, one leg crossed ankle to knee, reading on his phone. "Well, that took long enough," he said, looking up. "Have you been skipping sleep as well?"

"Yes," I admitted. The rice bowl beside my bed had been re-filled again, but I was feeling full. "So what are you doing here?"

"What the bloody hell do you think?" Colin said. "We've been trying to figure out if you're alive or dead! You didn't answer your messages, and you didn't show up on Wednesday. After Kiran called half a dozen times, we decided someone was going to have to come around. I came by yesterday and that Ignas guy told me you'd been in and out at crazy times all week, looking worse and worse. Left him my number, and he called at the crack of dawn."

"Oh," I said. I suppose that kind of thing *does* happen when you just stop answering your phone.

"So, I have to ask," Colin said. "Have you gone insane?"

"I did, but I came back. Is Hobbes okay?"

"See for yourself."

I peered over the bed to see Hobbes lying on the floor. He looked as though he'd tried to get onto the bed but hadn't been able to manage the jump with his broken legs. But his ears were pricked up and his eyes open, and as I looked down at him, I knew instantly that he was feeling better. Hobbes looked up at me and gave a companionable sort of "mrow," and the sound of his voice sent a warm rush of relief through my chest.

"Okay," Colin said. "I think it's time you told me what the hell's been going on."

"Um. What do you think it looks like?"

Colin gave me a deadpan look. "Stephen, I have *absolutely no fucking clue* what this looks like."

". . . Okay, that's fair."

"Kiran thinks you've joined a cult, Felix thinks you're on the run from debt collectors, Gabriel's just happy he's now only the *second*-most dysfunctional one, and I thought you'd finally found a girlfriend," Colin said. "At least until I saw you. You *definitely* haven't found a girlfriend."

"Not a girlfriend, a girl," I said seriously. "I met her ten days ago."

"Wasn't that the crazy one?"

"No, Lucella was nine days ago. This was the girl on the bridge. I think she's sixteen or something."

"Sixteen?"

"I *told* you, she's a girl, not my girlfriend. Now will you listen?"

Colin leant back with a long-suffering look. I sat up cross-legged on the bed and began to explain. "She told me I needed to get stronger." Ever since I'd woken up today, everything seemed much simpler. "I should have just listened to her from the start, but instead I got distracted by everything that was happening. A lot of those things were ones I did have to deal with, but I wasn't thinking about them the right way, and that was why everything kept going wrong. I didn't actually have a plan, I was just kind of reacting to everything that happened."

"How about you have some more to eat?"

"I'm too full, I'd just throw up. So when I went to talk to Charles? That's what I mean about not thinking about it the right way. I went to him because Tobias told me to and because I couldn't come up with any better ideas. But since I didn't have any real power of my own, Charles didn't actually have to give me anything he didn't want to, and I couldn't do anything when Lucella went for me afterwards."

"Stephen, I have literally no clue what you are talking about."

"Okay," I said. "You know how you've been not-so-subtly hinting for a while that I should get my life together?"

"I was *trying* to be subtle."

"The problem is I've been trying to do too many things," I said. "I've been doing all the things I feel I'm supposed to do, and I don't actually have time to do all of them, so I've been doing them all badly."

"No man can serve two masters?"

"Yeah, that. Anyway, I'm going to focus on my drucraft from now on."

"That weird hobby you used to do with your dad? Oh, nearly forgot." He dug something out of his pocket. "Here's your green shiny thing. What is it, costume jewellery?"

"It's a sigl," I told him, accepting it. "I used it to heal Hobbes."

Colin looked at me.

"You don't believe me," I said.

"Sorry, dude," Colin said. "And . . . maybe sleep on it before you quit your day job, all right? So you're not making life-changing decisions when you're sleep deprived and hallucinating?"

"All right."

"Right," Colin said, getting to his feet. "Now don't take this the wrong way, but I've had enough of spending my Saturday watching you sleep, and I am going to the pub. In the meantime, could you maybe try to get through a whole week without half killing yourself?"

"I'll try," I said. "And thanks."

Colin left. Looking around, I saw that he'd left me some water to drink and changed Hobbes's litter tray. Come to think of it, he must have kept on making and warming up fresh food all day long. He really was a good friend.

Hobbes gave a plaintive meow, and I lifted him onto the bed. His pelvis was hurting him, and I carefully arranged him until he wasn't in pain anymore. Then I lay back on my pillow with my hands behind my head and concentrated.

Ever since I'd woken up, I'd been seeing faint shimmers of colour at the corners of my vision. I'd thought they'd go away as I woke up and recovered a little more fully, but they hadn't. On a hunch, I quieted my thoughts and sensed.

Colour sprang into the world. Pale gossamer threads were

floating all around me, through the air and the walls and through the glass into the street outside. They ranged in colour from iridescent to silvery grey to a white that was so faint that it was hard to see.

Essentia. I was seeing essentia.

I stared down at my hand, channelling, and saw a shining white light well up at my palm. I'd never been able to *see* my personal essentia before.

Why was I seeing it now?

I puzzled over it for a while. Come to think of it, hadn't I been doing that last night? That had been how I'd been able to see the flaws in that mending sigl. They hadn't been hallucinations and I hadn't gone crazy. The fact that the mending sigl worked proved it.

But what did it mean?

I WENT BACK to the church the next day.

I'd meant to set out early, but by the time I'd woken up, infused essentia into Hobbes, and had some breakfast, it was later than I'd thought. I was moving more slowly than normal, and I kept having dizzy spells. Maybe I really *had* pushed myself too hard.

By the time I reached the church, the bells were chiming and the service had started. I dawdled outside in the April sun, watching the bees buzz around the dandelions. Once the congregation began to filter out, I walked in.

The priest was standing near the altar, speaking to a few of the worshippers who'd lingered after the service. "Ah," he said as I walked up. "The boy with the cat. You know, you never did tell me your name."

"It's Stephen. And you never told me yours."

"Father Hawke," the priest replied. "Did you have any success?"

"My cat's alive," I told him. Up close, I could see the church's

Well clearly. It shone with a clear, pale light, like pure water. I wondered if my own Well would be that beautiful.

Father Hawke started to say something, then paused.

"You told me last time that I didn't know very much," I said. "Do you know where I could find someone to help with that?"

Father Hawke was looking at me with an odd expression.

"Um," I said. The women who'd been talking to Father Hawke were giving us curious looks. "Hello?"

Father Hawke blinked. "I'm sorry?"

"What we were talking about last Saturday," I said carefully. I didn't want to say the word "drucraft" where we could be overheard. "I'm looking for a teacher."

"A teacher . . ." Father Hawke repeated absently, then shook his head slightly and seemed to come back down to earth. "Yes. Just a moment." He disappeared through a door for a minute, leaving me to wait, then returned and handed me a business card. "Here."

The card had a name and a nearby address. "Thanks," I told him.

I took a last glance back on my way out. Father Hawke was still watching me, and there was a strange look on his face. I slipped out the door, then went home.

IT WAS MIDAFTERNOON when I finally got back to my room. Hobbes was fed, watered, and treated, and was sleeping with his eyes tight shut; his fractures weren't hurting and shouldn't wake him. I'd talked to Ignas and reassured him that yes, I was okay, and yes, I'd stop starving myself, though I'd had to eat something in front of him to prove it. The dizzy spells kept coming, but I'd found they weren't as bad if I sat down. Outside, the sun shone down upon Foxden Road. For the first time in a week, I had time to think.

I lay down on my bed, opened my notebook to a blank page, and began to write.

Problems

1. *My drucraft isn't strong enough.*

2. *My father is missing and I've got no idea how to find him.*

3. *My mother is missing and I do know how to find her, but she doesn't seem to care about finding me.*

4. *Lucella's my enemy and might at any point decide to come back and screw me over.*

5. *Tobias is also my enemy and might also at any point decide to come back and screw me over.*

6. *Charles Ashford might also become my enemy and decide to screw me over.*

7. *If 4, 5, or 6 happen, I'm probably not strong enough to stop them.*

8. *I've been fired.*

9. *I'm going to run out of money.*

10. *I still want to get revenge on Lucella/Tobias/Diesel/Scar/ Lucella again/the Ashfords as a whole, and yes, I know expecting to get my own back against them is probably a pipe dream at this point, but seriously, fuck these people, especially Lucella.*

I set my pen down and studied the page. It was a pretty daunting list.

Okay, let's try to break this down.

Problems four, five, six, and seven were the same thing, really—they were all just different variations on "some arsehole from House Ashford decides to ruin my life." It was hard to say which Ashford I should be most worried about. Lucella was probably the most likely to come after me, but also the most straightforward. Charles seemed the least likely to try anything, but by far the scariest if he did.

Problems eight and nine were also basically the same thing. I'd gone through the messages on my phone to find a list of texts and missed calls from the temp agency. The last message, sent on Thursday, informed me in frosty tones that my placement at the Ministry of Defence had been cancelled, and not to call them back. I knew the agency wouldn't be in any hurry to find me anything new.

Problems three and ten I'd just have to ignore for the moment, not so much because I *wanted* to as because solving either one felt completely impossible. If my mother wasn't interested in talking to me, then there wasn't much I could do to change her mind, and launching some campaign of revenge on the Ashfords was so obviously stupid I wasn't even going to think about it. I wasn't happy about it, but for now both of those would just have to wait.

Letting problems one and two wait, on the other hand, felt like a bad idea. My drucraft not being strong enough was starting to bite me, really hard. And as for my father, he'd told me to wait for him, but it had been three years. If he was going to come back on his own, it should have happened by now.

All right, I decided. I picked up my pen, crossed off three and ten, drew circles around one and two, then drew bigger circles around four to seven and eight to nine. Then I sat back and looked at the four circles. Which was the most urgent?

The Ashfords, I decided. I still didn't know exactly how many enemies I had in that snake pit of a mansion, or what they were going to do next. Lucella, Tobias, and Charles had made it sound as though they were done with me for now, but even if I trusted them—which I didn't—the key words were "for now." To me, what the Ashford situation really felt like was a ticking clock. At any point in the future, someone from House Ashford could decide to come after me again, at which point I'd suddenly have another bunch of drucraft-enhanced goons like Diesel and Scar kicking down my door. How would that turn out?

Badly. I'd been lucky last time, but I wouldn't be lucky forever, and that meant I needed to find some way to defend myself. Sooner or later that invisible clock was going to run down, and when it did I had to be ready.

The next most urgent problem was money, and while that wasn't quite so immediately dangerous, it was inevitable in a way that the Ashfords weren't. After all, I didn't *know* that the Ashfords were going to come after me—they might just go back to ignoring me, the same way they'd ignored me for the previous twenty years. But if the number in my bank account dropped below zero, then the bank *wasn't* going to ignore me. Neither was my landlord.

The obvious answer was to go back to what I'd been doing. Find a new agency job, try to get my life back to the way it had been, and generally keep my head down and hope for the best. It might even work . . . for a while.

Except that was exactly what I'd been doing wrong for the past three years. I'd been thinking in terms of "for a while," and all the time my list of problems had just grown and grown. I needed some way to pay my bills, but whatever I did, it had to be something that helped *solve* my problems, instead of just putting them on hold.

And last of all was my father. I still missed him as badly as ever, but nothing that had happened in the past couple of weeks had brought me any closer to finding him. In fact, if I believed Tobias and Lucella, none of this whole business with the Ashfords had anything to do with my father at all.

But I *didn't* believe them. It just didn't make sense that my father could disappear without a trace, and then, by some totally random freak coincidence, someone tried to make *me* disappear almost three years later. There had to be some kind of link, and that meant that at least one of the Ashfords knew a lot more than they were telling me.

But it's one thing to know someone's lying to you, and another to do something about it. And even if I could track down whoever had made my father disappear, what could I do about it? If they could do that to my father, they could do the same to me.

I sighed, put my pen down, lay back on my bed, and stared up at the ceiling. What should I do?

Colours shimmered at the edge of my vision. I cleared my mind, and they sprang into focus, wisps of silvery essentia swirling lazily in the air. I frowned at them, thinking.

Maybe I was looking at this the wrong way. What did I have going for me?

Drucraft.

It was my one big advantage, the one thing I could do that everyone else couldn't. It might be weak right now, but it had potential to be much more. Combat and defence sigls could help protect me against the Ashfords, and they could give me a fighting chance if I ran into my father's enemies too. As for money . . . well, I'd seen the wealth in that mansion. If drucraft could make them that rich, there had to be some way I could earn a living from it.

And drucraft gave me the possibility of something more: independence. Lucella, Tobias, and Charles had all offered me things I wanted—money, knowledge, family—but now that I looked back on it, it felt as though every time I'd accepted one of their offers, I'd got the short end of the stick. And as long as I kept on dealing with them on their terms, that was never going to change. They had all the power, which meant they got to set the rules.

Maybe this was how rich people stayed on top. They didn't run around doing things themselves—they made sure their position was better than everyone else's, then got other people to do stuff for them.

But if I could get my drucraft to the point where I had some power of my own, I could get away from that. I wouldn't have to beg the Ashfords for table scraps, then sit around waiting while they decided whether to pay me what I was owed or just stab me in the back. I could accomplish things on my own. And if I ever found out what had happened to my father, I'd actually be able to do something about it.

So my list was wrong. I didn't actually have ten problems. I just had one.

I picked up my pen again and began crossing out the list line by line, starting from the bottom and going up. Once I got to *my drucraft isn't strong enough*, I stopped, circled it a couple more times, then set down my pen and nodded to myself. One problem, one solution. Much better.

It's funny how a single decision can change your whole life. But now that I thought about it, I'd been building towards this for a while. What had happened yesterday had made me realise just how much of my time I'd been spending on things that didn't matter. I didn't really care about my job or going to college.

What *did* I care about?

I wanted the power to protect myself and Hobbes and live my life as I chose. I wanted to find my father and have a family again.

And I wanted to develop my drucraft to be the best that it could be.

The path to the first two lay through the third. So I'd dedicate myself to my drucraft. Simple.

I sat back against the wall, stretched, and looked out through the window. I felt lighter, as if I'd cut myself loose from something that had been weighing me down for a very long time. The sunlight shone down onto Foxden Road, sycamore branches casting shadows that swayed in the breeze. Out there, a new path was waiting. I didn't know whether it was the next step in my journey or the first, but for the first time in a long while, I was excited to find out.

I walked out through the door and into a new chapter of my life.

CHAPTER 10

WELL, I THOUGHT, *this looks like the place.*

I was in Upton Park, a mile or so east of Plaistow. The house I was in front of was bigger than average for this street, with a side extension. The number on the door matched the one on the card Father Hawke had given me. Above the number was a name: Maria Noronha.

I walked up to the house. Another dizzy spell made me pause; I could hear chatter from inside, children's and women's voices speaking a language I didn't recognise. Once my head cleared, I rang the bell.

The voices from inside tailed off. I heard footsteps approaching the door, then silence. Looking at the door, I saw that it had a peephole. I tried to look unthreatening.

There was a pause, then the rattle of a chain. The door swung open.

The woman standing in the doorway was in her thirties, small and pretty, with Indian looks, brown skin, and long black hair. Even though it was a Sunday afternoon, her clothes were neat and fashionable looking. She looked like a junior bank manager, or maybe a lawyer. "Hello?" she asked.

"Hi. I'm looking for Maria Noronha?"

"You've found her," the woman told me. She spoke formally, with a slight accent. "Who are you?"

"My name's Stephen Oakwood. Father Hawke sent me."

"Who—oh." Maria sighed. "That man is *so* annoying. I hope he's not giving out my home address to everyone who walks in." Maria gave me an appraising glance. "Well, you don't look like trouble. What can I do for you?"

My looks come in handy sometimes. "I'm trying to find someone to teach me more about drucraft," I said. "Could you help?"

Maria looked puzzled. "I'm . . . not really a teacher. I'm an essentia analyst."

"A what?"

"For Linford's," Maria explained. "It's one of the big UK drucraft corporations. When customers are looking to buy a sigl package, they're matched up with an essentia analyst. We do essentia readings, give them advice on sigl choice, instruct them in its use, coordinate with the shaper and the medical team, that kind of thing."

"Oh," I said. "Okay." I thought for a second. "So if I wanted to learn the basics, who'd be a better person to go to?"

"Drucrafters usually learn the basics from private tutors or in-house teachers."

"Would *they* teach someone like me?"

"Probably not," Maria admitted. "Maybe he did know what he was doing sending you here after all. All right. I'll give you a reading and answer your questions. Payment in advance."

"Payment?"

"My freelance rate is a hundred pounds an hour."

I stared at her. "*A hundred pounds an hour?*"

"And a reading is two hours," Maria added. "It's not very high by professional standards."

"I'd have to work ten hours to be paid that much!"

"Well, that tells you something about how much your time is worth compared to how much my time is worth."

"I can't afford that much," I told her. Well, *technically* I could, but that was nearly as much money as I could save in a month!

"You get what you pay for."

I tried to bargain and got nowhere. I wanted to just walk away, but I was uncomfortably aware of how many blunders I'd already made through not knowing basic information. I had to learn this stuff from somewhere.

"Fine," I said at last with bad grace. "I'll get the money."

Maria looked quite unconcerned. She could obviously tell that I didn't have any better options. "Come around and knock on the side door when you do."

"Here," I said twenty minutes later, holding up a slim wad of notes.

The side door to Maria's house led into a one-room extension with windows looking out onto a well-tended garden. There were a couch, a desk, a faded armchair, and—for some reason—posters on the wall with anatomy diagrams of the human eye.

Maria held out her hand for the money, but I didn't give it to her. "Not yet," I said.

"I did say 'in advance.'"

"I'll tell you what I need," I said. "Then *if* you can help me, I'll pay you. You can start the two hours from there."

"And you want me to just sit and listen?"

"I'm paying *you* to tell *me* things. Why would I pay someone to listen to me talk?"

Maria looked amused. "I can see you don't go to therapy."

"What?"

"Never mind. All right, I'll be generous since this is your first time. My children have dinner at seven. You've got until then." Maria clasped her hands in front of her and gave me an inquiring look. "So tell me about your situation."

"I'm a . . . well, I guess you could say I'm a new drucrafter." I'd already thought about how I'd answer this. "My drucraft skills are pretty good, but I don't know much about this world or how I fit into it. I'm trying to figure out what I can do to make a living."

"When you say your skills are good, do you mean you're a channeller?"

"A manifester," I said. I'd mentally debated whether to admit this or not, but in the end, I'd decided to take the risk.

But Maria only looked mildly interested. "Oh? Are you from a Noble House?"

"Why?" I said guardedly.

"I thought they were the only ones who trained up manifesters that young." Maria shrugged. "Well, anyway. What types of channelling are you familiar with?"

I gave Maria a fairly thorough answer, going through the exercises my father had taught me as well as the tricks I'd learned from Father Hawke. As I did, I watched Maria very carefully to see how she'd react. I remembered how Lucella had flown off the handle when I'd told her what I could do.

As it turned out, though, what Maria was interested in was something quite different.

"A white flame?" Maria had been sitting, relaxed, behind her desk; now she leant forward, suddenly intent. "Those enhanced infusions you did, it felt like burning a white flame?"

"Yes . . ."

"Have you had any physical symptoms since then?" Maria's voice was sharp. "Fainting, dizziness, exhaustion, nausea?"

"Dizzy spells," I admitted. "And I've been pretty tired. But I haven't been getting much sleep, so I thought—"

"Are the dizzy spells getting worse?"

"I don't think so?"

"Dear God." Maria slumped back in her chair. "You nearly gave me a heart attack." She looked up at me. "*Never* do that trick again. Understand?"

"Why not?"

"That idiot of a priest. This is what happens when you have amateurs holding Wells . . . All right. Do you know the Five Limits of drucraft?"

I shook my head.

"The second limit is called the Primal Limit, and it says that humans can't use drucraft from any of the branches on their own. You can transform free essentia into personal, but you can't transform that personal essentia into anything else. Only a sigl can do that. A sigl does two things: it turns your own personal essentia into a spell effect, and it amplifies that effect by drawing on free essentia from your surroundings. Understand?"

". . . Yes."

"Now," Maria said. "Primal drucraft is the exception. To make light you need a Light sigl, and to change something's mass you need a Matter sigl, but you can perform Primal effects without a Primal sigl. It'll be weaker, because you won't have the sigl's amplification, but you can do it. It's why some people don't think Primal drucraft really counts as its own branch, but anyway. One of those Primal effects is called "heart's blood," and it's supposed to be a way to convert a part of your own *self* into essentia. People who've done it describe it exactly the way you did, burning their own life essence to make a white flame. It gives you a lot of personal essentia, very fast, and if you do it too much *it kills you*. If you go over a certain line, you drop dead, and nobody knows exactly where that line is."

"Oh," I said. "So these dizzy spells . . ."

"Soul sickness," Maria said. "There's no cure except bed rest and time. But if it hasn't got any worse, you should be fine. Just don't do it again!"

I thought about that for a second. "I guess that *was* worth paying for."

"Well, I'm glad you think so. So now that I know you're not going to drop dead on the floor of my consulting room, let's get started and I'll give you an essentia reading."

I handed over the money to Maria—I had to admit, she'd earned it. Maria opened up a desk drawer to reveal what looked like a collection of sigls in plastic housings, each of which had a cable attached. I'd been expecting her to ask me to channel or do some exercises, but all she did was ask me to take one of the sigls and hold it in my hand.

"What's it doing?" I asked curiously as I looked down at the sigl. It was pale blue and very small, and looked like one of my own Light sigls.

Maria plugged the cable into a small handheld device. "It's a measuring sigl."

I focused, seeing as I did that a tiny flow of essentia was being pulled through my hand into the sigl. "It's pulling in my personal essentia?"

"Oh, you can feel that?" Maria said. "They're minimum-strength continuous sigls. No attunement, so they can't actually do anything, but the reader lets me know how much of your essentia they *would* be using." The device in her hand beeped, and she took the sigl away, replacing it with a pale red one. "Next, please."

Maria went through a series of sigls. The early ones all pulled only a thread of essentia. Later ones pulled more.

"All right!" Maria said eventually, setting down the device. "All done."

"So what did that do?"

"I was measuring your essentia capacity and affinities."

"Affinities?"

"How good you are with the different branches," Maria explained. "You'll have a much easier time working with essentia that matches your affinities, and a much harder time with essentia that doesn't. The kinds of sigls you can buy from UK providers have enough attunement that they'll work even through a bad affinity, but it still helps. And if you really are a manifester, then you'll do much better working with your affinities instead of against them." Maria glanced down at her notepad. "Now, if this was a proper fitting, I'd give you a full report, but since it's not and we're on a clock, I'll just give you the short version. You have a strong affinity for Light, a weak affinity for Matter and Dimension, a weak disaffinity for Life, and a strong disaffinity for Motion."

"Is that normal?"

"The Dimension affinity is a little unusual, but apart from that, it's very standard, yes."

Maria's manner was quite casual. I wasn't ready to relax just yet, but it didn't look as though she was going to react like Lucella. "So I'll do better trying to manifest at Light, Matter, and Dimension Wells?"

"Yes, but don't get too caught up on it," Maria said. "Your affinities are just starting points, and they'll change over time. If you take another reading in a few years, they'll probably all have shifted. Your essentia capacity, though—that stays the same."

"Essentia capacity?"

"The rate at which your body converts ambient essentia into

personal essentia, measured by the number of sigls at the Lorenz Ceiling that you can keep active at the same time," Maria said. "Basically, it's how many sigls you can use at once. It's correlated with your skeletal mass. Average in this country is 2.4 for women and 2.8 for men."

"What's mine?"

"Just under 2.5."

"So . . . below average?"

"Yes."

"Is there some way to improve it?"

"Not really," Maria said. "You can raise it a tiny bit with practice, but given your channelling skill, you've probably done all that already. Think of it as like your height. After a certain age, you're not getting any taller."

That didn't sound good. "Does it matter very much?"

"It doesn't matter at all," Maria said. "I mean, how often are you going to *need* to use two or three sigls at once?"

I started to relax. I'd been worried that a low essentia capacity might make me weaker in a fight.

"Unless you're getting into a fight," Maria added.

"Oh, *come on*!"

"Let me guess," Maria said with a smile. "You're one of those boys who wanted to grow up to be a combat drucrafter."

"It's not about what I want! There are—" I stopped. I didn't want to tell her about the Ashfords. "There are reasons."

"Well, whatever they are, if you had ambitions about joining the Board security forces or something, you'll probably have to give them up. I think their minimum for a combat drucrafter is 3.0."

I looked away in frustration. With the way Lucella had acted, I'd started to think that I might be something special. But it seemed as though the more people I talked to, the less impressive my abilities were turning out to be.

"Why is this bothering you so much?" Maria asked.

"It just doesn't seem fair," I said, not meeting her eyes. I didn't want to say what I was thinking, because it sounded so childish. *It's not enough that I'm poor and on the small side, I have to be weaker at drucraft too?*

"Of course it's not fair," Maria said. "Essentia capacity is mostly inherited, and nothing about inheritance is *fair*. Some people are taller, some people are stronger. You just have to play the hand you're dealt."

I didn't answer.

"You really are upset," Maria said. "Look, if it makes you feel any better, my essentia capacity is 2.1. That's about as far below average for women as yours is for men. I promise you, it hasn't made my life worse in any way that's mattered."

You didn't have a couple of guys break into your bedroom ten days ago. I took a breath and got control of myself. "Is it going to make it harder for me to use drucraft?"

"No, not at all," Maria said. "Think of your essentia capacity as strength, and your drucraft skills as dexterity. Even if you were an essentia cripple—that's what they call anyone with a capacity below 2.0—it wouldn't affect your sensing, channelling, or shaping in any way."

Well, that was something. Okay, time to get down to what I'd really come here to ask. "Some people have been acting as though the fact that I can shape sigls is a really big deal," I said. "Is it?"

"That's . . . actually quite a hard question to answer," Maria said slowly. "It's certainly *unusual*. It's a very specialised skill, and most of the ones who can do it come from Noble Houses. Honestly, for most people, it just isn't all that useful."

"It's not?"

"Less than five percent of the sigls in this country are made by manifesters," Maria explained. "The rest are made by shapers, using limiters. I suppose you were thinking of making your own sigls? Because I'm afraid that isn't really how things work anymore."

I looked at Maria, puzzled.

"I'll give you an example," Maria said. "How many medical drucrafters do you think are manifesters?"

"Some?"

"None," Maria said. "Or so close as to make no difference. The average medical drucrafter in this country is a doctor who went to medical school, then got a contract from one of the big medicorps. Then he'll start to specialise." Maria gestured up at the posters on the wall. "Let's say he focuses on glaucoma. He won't know how to make a Life sigl that treats that, but he doesn't need to. His sponsor will pay for him to go to India, where he'll meet some nice essentia analyst like me who'll work with shapers to make him his own set. By the time he finally goes into practice, he'll have spent more than ten years learning everything there is to know about glaucomas and about using Life sigls to treat them. He'll have a lot of debt, but he'll be paid very well."

"Uh," I said. "Okay."

"Now imagine you try to do that on your own," Maria said. "You don't have a Life Well to make sigls from. Even if you did, you wouldn't know how to make the specialised sigls that medical drucrafters use. And even if you could get past *that*, you aren't a doctor. It would take you years and years of work and a huge amount of money, and even after all that, you still wouldn't be good enough."

I was silent.

"Drucraft isn't about lone practitioners these days," Maria explained. "It's a globalised economy."

"But if I just wanted to learn medical drucraft, I could start with simpler things," I argued. "Like . . . a mending sigl."

"Even a mending sigl, which is just about the most basic

medical sigl out there, is still a very complicated piece of shaping," Maria said. "People use limiters for a reason. There's no way you'd be able to make one on your own without training."

But I did, I thought but didn't say. "Could I get training as a shaper?"

Maria hesitated. "We do offer training contracts to potential shapers, but there aren't many places and there's a lot of competition. Unless you've got a really strong academic record, I think you'll have a difficult time."

"But I already know how to shape sigls."

"I'm afraid the bottleneck in sigl production isn't shapers," Maria said. "There are maybe twelve thousand Wells in this country of D-class and higher, and they only produce so much essentia per year. You can't get more essentia, but you can always get more people."

I sat and digested that. "So you're saying I have this really rare ability, but it's not actually particularly useful for anything."

"I mean, it's a nice thing to have on your CV," Maria said with a smile. "But I think you'd be better off focusing on something more practical."

"Like what?"

"Well, there *is* one career in the drucraft world that I think could work quite well for you," Maria said. "Locating."

"Locating what?"

"Wells. There are around five thousand permanent Wells in the United Kingdom. They can grow or shrink, and there's a fair bit of turnover among the weaker ones, but for the most part they're a fixed asset. But most Wells aren't permanent—they're temporary. A permanent Well is like a fruit tree; it produces year after year. Temporary Wells are like . . . hmm, like wild mushrooms. They pop up in different places, and after you harvest them, you have to go somewhere else to find a new one.

"Locators are the mushroom pickers. They travel around, looking for Wells, and when they find them, they call them in to whichever sigl provider they work for. Then the provider sends out a team to drain it or to secure it, depending on how strong the Well is. The locator gets paid a finder's fee depending on the Well's class, and the fees for the stronger Wells can get pretty high. And you don't need a degree."

I thought about that for a second. "What's the catch?"

"What do you mean?"

"If a job doesn't need any qualifications, that usually means it's really bad."

Maria laughed. "That's a bit of an exaggeration, but I can see where you're coming from. Locating isn't a bad job, but there are some hurdles. First, you'll need a finder's stone. It's a continuous Light sigl made in such a way that it only activates in the presence of ambient essentia. The closer you get to a powerful concentration of essentia, like a Well, the brighter it glows. Sort of like playing 'hot and cold.'"

"How do you get a finder's stone?"

"Linford's can provide you with one."

"For free?"

Maria gave me a pitying look.

"Right," I said sourly. "So before you can earn money, you have to *have* money."

"Welcome to how the world works," Maria said. "But it's not as bad as you're making it sound. Corporations will 'stake' you with a finder's stone. Linford's offers all of the sigls in its locating line with no money down, so long as you sign on with them and have a good enough credit score. Then once you're earning finder's fees, you pay back the cost of the finder's stone in monthly instalments."

"Mm," I said. I'd learned to be wary of the words "no money down." "What if you can sense Wells *without* a finder's stone?"

"We offer no-stake contracts too. But if you want to get anywhere as a locator, you need a finder's stone."

"Why?"

"They're a lot more reliable," Maria said. "Sensing isn't taught
very much these days, apart from the basic level that you need to
channel. Drucraft organisations used to do it for religious reasons, but nowadays you can just get a finder's stone and skip it."

I frowned.

"Look, if you really do want to make a living in the drucraft
world, becoming a locator is the best way to get on the ladder,"
Maria said. "It's long hours, and you'll have to get used to pushing
through dry spells, but you can earn a lot if you work hard. And
there's a lot of room for working your way up. I know for a fact that
some of the shapers at Linford's got their start as freelance locators. You just have to prove yourself first."

"Okay," I said. I couldn't help but feel that Maria was pushing
this job just a little bit harder than she should be. "Is there a short-
age of locators right now or something?"

"Definitely," Maria said with a nod. "With everything that's
been happening in the past couple of years, demand for essentia
has shot up and supply hasn't. There's more and more pressure to
find temporary Wells as soon as possible."

"And there aren't any . . . problems?"

Maria hesitated. "I don't want to put you off . . ."

I gave her a look.

"As I said, essentia's a limited resource. That means competition."

"What kind of competition?"

"Signing on with a recognised sigl provider gives you access to
the Well Registry," Maria said. "That lets you check to see if a
Well's been claimed, and claim it in the name of your sponsor if
it hasn't. Once a Well's claimed, then that should be that. In

practice . . . it's very common that we'll respond to a claim, and when our site officer arrives, there's nothing there. Either there's no sign of a Well at all, or it's been recently drained. Usually the locator tries to tell us that the Well was full when he got there, but someone else stole it." Maria shrugged. "They're always hoping we'll pay them anyway. We don't, of course."

"But?"

"But . . . it is true that there are certain groups out there who watch for new Wells to appear and move on them before they can be secured. How likely that is depends on the Well's rating. No one's going to go chasing across London for the sake of a D-class, but once you get up to a C-plus or so . . . well, those are worth real money. From what I hear, it can get a little rough."

That didn't sound very encouraging.

Maria checked the slim watch on her wrist. "We're almost out of time. Do you want me to begin registering you with Linford's? You'll need references and a background check, and the sooner you start on those, the better."

"Just one thing," I said. "From how you were describing it, a finder's stone is basically a visual aid for detecting essentia. Right?"

"That's right."

"Is there some way to do the same thing without one?"

"There are some specialised sigls . . ."

"Not with a sigl," I said. "Or any other kind of tool. Just seeing essentia on your own."

"You're really determined to avoid paying for a finder's stone, aren't you?" Maria said. "Sorry, no way around it. If you want to see essentia, you'll need a sigl."

I looked at Maria, seeing the faint swirls of essentia in the air behind her, and nodded.

"So do you want to register?" Maria asked.

"Could you give me a reference?"

"Maybe," Maria said with a smile. "Now, shoo. You've had more than your two hours and I've got children to feed."

BY THE TIME I got home it was early evening, and the sky outside my window was darkening to a beautiful shade of dusky blue. I fed and treated Hobbes, who meowed at the attention. He was doing much better, which was a relief—after what Maria had told me, I was going to be a lot more careful about that infusion trick. Once I was done, I lay down on my bed with my hands behind my head and stared up at the ceiling.

A locator, huh? The more I thought about the idea, the more I liked it. I already wanted to spend more time looking for Wells. It'd let me earn a living from something I needed to do anyway.

I'd come a long way in the last two weeks. Between Maria, Father Hawke, Johanna, and Charles, I felt as though I was beginning to understand the drucraft world. But there was one big piece missing.

I'd been vaguely wondering if seeing essentia the way I'd been doing over the last couple of days was a normal thing. Maybe it was something you just naturally developed once your sensing got good enough, and the stress and pain of that night had pushed me over the edge. But Maria seemed absolutely convinced that it was impossible. She might be wrong—well, she *was* wrong—but she obviously knew far more than I did. So what was going on?

One thing was for sure: I wasn't telling anyone about it. I still had a very vivid memory of what had happened the *last* time I'd revealed an ability that I wasn't supposed to have, and until I knew a lot more I was going to keep my mouth shut and my eyes open. For now, I decided to get an early night. Tomorrow was going to be a busy day.

CHAPTER 11

I woke early the next morning. Once I'd had breakfast, I lifted Hobbes onto my bed, into a spot where I could keep an eye on him, then knelt down next to the loose skirting board and pulled it out. Yesterday I'd made a decision. Today I had to figure out how to put it into practice.

I took out the envelope from the cubbyhole and sat down on my bed. Inside the envelope was a single sheet of paper that smelt of dust. I unfolded it and began to read.

Stephen,

Something's happened and I'm going to have to disappear. I can't tell you the details, but understand that I'm doing this for your protection, not because I want to.

Men will come looking for me. Stay away. It's me they want, not you.

I'll come back as soon as I can, but I don't know when that'll be. Until then, keep practising your drucraft.

Love,
Dad

I finished reading and looked down at the handful of faded lines. Even scribbled as they were, they didn't cover even half the page.

My father had written those words in May, the same year I'd turned eighteen. That had been almost exactly three years ago. He'd said he'd come back as soon as he could. Should I keep waiting?

No. It sounded like a big decision, but the truth was, it was something that had been at the back of my mind for a long time. I couldn't keep sitting around hoping that things would get better on their own. If I wanted to solve my problems, I'd have to do it myself.

But how?

One of the things I'd tried in those first few months had been going to a detective agency. They'd looked for my father and found nothing. Lack of money had stopped me going further, but even then, I'd gotten the definite impression that it wasn't going to help. Whoever these men coming after my father were, they were *serious*, and if they hadn't been able to find him, a high street private detective probably wasn't going to do better.

But while I didn't have any way of finding my dad, I might have a way to find the people looking for him. I still had the licence plate number of that white Ford, and a detective agency should be able to do something with that. But they wouldn't do it for free . . . which brought me back to the next problem. Money.

I took out my old laptop, brought up the calculator, and started budgeting. With the cheque from Charles Ashford, I had a little over £4,400 in the bank. The vet bill came to almost £1,600, not counting any return visits. £200 had gone to Maria. My rent was £540 per month—our landlord had put it up again. Add in travel, the electricity bill, the gas bill, council tax, phone payments, groceries . . .

I had enough money for two months. *Maybe* three, if I ate cheaply, stopped going to the pub, and generally lived as frugally as I could . . . though that was assuming no disasters, emergencies, or anything else that would lead to extra expenses, which, given my last couple of weeks, was probably optimistic. After that I got into debt-and-overdraft territory, which scared me. There's a reason credit card companies try to get you on the hook—once you fall into that pit, it's hard to climb out.

So for now, I could forget about hiring a private detective, or for that matter spending any money that I didn't absolutely have to. I had about two months to get out of the red. Maria had told me that being a locator could earn me enough to do that. Was it true?

I opened up my browser and went to the Linford's website.

The Linford's site was big and confusing. The details of locating and Wells weren't on the public part, but Maria had given me a guest log-in that allowed me low-level access. I navigated to the "Fees" section and found what I was looking for.

FINDER'S FEES

Well Strength (Faraday Scale)	Well Class	Light, Primal	Matter, Motion, Dimension	Life
1	D	£190	£220	£250
2	D+	£600	£700	£780
3	D+	£1,200	£1,300	£1,500
4	C	£1,900	£2,200	£2,500
5	C	£2,800	£3,200	£3,600
6	C	£3,800	£4,300	£4,900
7	C	£4,900	£5,600	£6,300
8	C+	£6,150	£7,000	£7,900
9	C+	£7,500	£8,500	£9,600
10	C+	£8,900	£10,200	£11,500

The table kept going, with the fees scaling up to eye-popping amounts. A strength-20 Light Well would earn you £28,000.

Strength-32 Wells, which was the point at which the class ticked up from B to B+, had finder's fees of between £60,000 and £80,000. Even if I never found anything above the first few ranks, I'd only need to find one C-class Well per month to earn more than I had from my last job.

It sounded amazing. Actually, it sounded a bit *too* amazing. Those numbers felt really high for a job that was just supposed to be a way to get your foot in the door. I clicked through to the section on finder's stones.

Just as Maria had said, finder's stones were Light sigls that glowed in the presence of high concentrations of ambient essentia. And they weren't cheap—even the most basic model cost £1,999. The website claimed you could pay nothing down if you passed the background and credit check, but that required signing up for monthly payments that added up to even more than buying the sigl outright. The whole thing gave me a bad feeling and I decided I'd rather trust my own sensing than pay thousands of pounds to Linford's. Maria had made it sound as though relying on sensing was worse than using a finder's stone, but I'd just have to manage.

The good news was that I had a plan. To find my father, I needed money; to strengthen my drucraft, I needed sigls; to make a living as a locator, I needed finder's fees. Finding Wells would let me solve all three problems at once.

And I didn't have to start from scratch, either. I'd found several Wells last week. At the time I'd ignored all of them except the Life ones, but I remembered where they were. It was time to get something back for all that hard work.

"Motion," I muttered. "Why did it have to be Motion?"

Channelsea is one of the places in London where nobody goes. It's a little enclave of riverside and mudflats, bounded by the

Greenway on one side and railway lines on the other, and centred upon an old chemical plant that's been rusting away for years. There are a lot of places in London like Channelsea, areas with no shops or houses or tourist attractions that most people never go into because there's nothing there.

At least, as far as they know.

Right now I was standing in a jungle of plants and leaves and branches. I was less than fifty feet from the Channelsea River, but the undergrowth was so thick that you wouldn't know it. Plants pressed in from all around, sycamore and lime trees blocking out the sun, while nettles, chickweed, and cow parsley clogged the ground. The place was secluded but noisy. The wind rushed in the trees, the sounds of the river echoed through the undergrowth, and every few minutes the air would shake to the sounds of a low-flying aeroplane or an Underground train from across the water. And at my feet, at the centre of the small clearing, was the Well.

I'd found this place by pure luck. I'd been passing Channelsea House last Sunday when an old memory had come back to me of exploring with Colin, and I'd turned off the Greenway to follow the riverside path, pushing through the overgrowth until the rusting shapes of the gasholders had appeared on the other side of the river. Then I'd squeezed through a break in the wire-mesh gate set into the concrete barrier that ran alongside the path, and found the Well in the little patch of unused ground between the barrier and the old chemical plant.

The essentia in this Well was very different from mine. It gleamed pale yellow in my sight, swirling like a whirlpool, currents and eddies forming and changing and branching off. It definitely wasn't a Light or a Life Well, and it didn't look like the Primal one I'd seen at Father Hawke's church, either. That left Dimension, Matter, and Motion. My instincts told me that it was Motion. Which, according to Maria, was the branch I was worst at.

It was a bit annoying, because having taken another look through the catalogue, I was getting the feeling that Motion might be the best out of all the branches for self-defence. Motion sigls could generate attacks of blunt kinetic force, as well as heat-based effects that could burn or freeze. There were even knife- or sword-type effects that created a razor-thin blade that could slice straight through things, though those sounded horrendously lethal and had warnings plastered all over them. Best of all, there were movement sigls that let you jump long distances, levitate, or fly.

But I was getting ahead of myself. Most of the really exciting Motion sigls had carat weights of 1.5 and up, which according to the catalogue needed a Well class of at least C+. I wasn't sure exactly how strong this Well was, but I had the feeling that it was probably a D, or a D+ at the very most.

I *had* thought of just waiting until my registration at Linford's was done and trying to sell it to them. But Linford's only paid £220 for D-class Motion Wells, and while that wasn't nothing, I had the feeling that a new sigl would be more helpful than an extra couple of hundred pounds. And there was always the chance that this Well might be a permanent one, in which case I could keep coming back year after year.

I settled down with my back against a tree, pulled the catalogue out of my backpack, and opened it up to the "Motion" section.

AN HOUR LATER, I closed the catalogue with a sigh. Based on the options in the catalogue, I'd narrowed my choices down to three: slam, jump, and mighty blow.

Motion sigls all seemed to revolve around kinetic energy, either generating it, redirecting it, or neutralising it. I'd picked these three sigls because they seemed to be the simplest—all of them converted essentia into kinetic energy to do something very straightforward. Slam was a short-range blast of compressed air, mighty blow was designed to enhance a punch or kick, and jump created a kinetic thrust that could either fling you through the air or accelerate you into a sprint. And with carat weights of 0.3 to 0.5 for the low-end models, all three were effects that even a D-class Well could stretch to.

There was still the slight problem that I didn't actually know *how* to make any of those sigls. I was pretty confident in my ability to make light sigls by now, and I'd somehow managed to make a mending sigl on my first try, but for all I knew, that could have been a one-off. Realistically, there was a pretty good chance I was going to screw this up.

So with that in mind, I decided to stay away from jump and mighty blow. Both sigls were designed to enhance the wielder's own body by boosting a punch, a kick, or a leap, and it felt to me as though messing that up could lead to really bad consequences—if I applied the force to the wrong spot, I'd end up dislocating my own limbs. Slam, on the other hand, sounded relatively safe. From the description it didn't seem to have the power to hit very hard, so even if the worst happened, I shouldn't be able to seriously injure myself. There was still the "strong disaffinity for Motion" problem . . . but what did that really mean, anyway?

I put away my catalogue and got up to find out.

FORTY-FIVE MINUTES LATER, I'd found out. "Strong disaffinity for Motion" meant that the essentia in the Well hated me.

Sweat dripped from my forehead, and I shook my head quickly to fling it away. The essentia construct above my palm shimmered and started to unravel again, and I quickly twined my personal essentia through it to hold it together.

When I'd made my light sigls, I'd done it slowly and carefully, not moving on to the next step until each part of the construct was exactly right. I'd tried to do the same with this one, and it wasn't working, because the essentia *wouldn't stay still*. It wasn't like sketching in pencil, it was like wrestling a dozen angry snakes, and whenever I got one part of the construct right, another part would start to unravel and change.

The good news was that my new ability to see essentia was making a huge difference. Back when we were fourteen or so, Colin had gone through an electronics phase and talked the rest of us into scrounging up the materials to make circuits. Felix and Gabriel had given up quickly, Kiran had taken to it really well, but for my part I'd struggled—I could understand the theory, but I had trouble putting it together. It was only once I tried soldering the things myself that it clicked. You could *see* the way the current would flow through the circuit, and figure out how the whole thing would work from there.

Trying to make an essentia construct with my new sight felt the same way. Instead of having to second-guess everything, I could just look at the construct and see how the finished sigl would work. I'd redesigned the construct half a dozen times by this point, and if I'd been doing this blind, it would have had so many flaws by now that it would have been useless. As it was, I was pretty sure it'd work.

But it'd work only if I could finish the shaping, which I wasn't at all sure was going to happen. The main reason I'd redesigned the construct so many times was because I'd had to *remake* the construct so many times, because it kept falling apart. Worse, I obviously hadn't recovered as much as I'd thought, because my dizzy spells were coming back, and they were getting stronger. If I dragged this out any longer, I was going to faint.

I swept my personal essentia into a whirlpool, gathering in the Well's reserves for what would have to be the last time. This time, instead of waiting for the construct to stabilise, I started shrinking it immediately, the design spinning as it condensed. The strands of essentia fought me, trying to slip out of shape, and I worked frantically to push them back as the construct grew tighter and tighter. The construct shrank past the critical point where there was no going back, more and more essentia flowing in.

I kept drawing on the Well's essentia as the construct grew denser, closer and closer to becoming real. The Well was half-empty. A tiny spark of yellow appeared on my palm, and I pushed more and more, frantically trying to hold the pattern in my mind, fighting the dizziness as I went further and further . . .

The construct gave one final rebellious shudder, and it was done. The balance shifted, and all the remaining essentia in the Well poured into it like a flood, the construct condensing and crystallising, becoming set. The flow cut off.

I swayed, half falling and catching myself with my free hand. My head was swimming and I felt sick. I took quick, deep breaths, focusing on my lungs and trying not to throw up. Only once I'd got control of myself did I look down at my open palm.

A tiny, faceted, pale yellow gemstone winked up at me. It was maybe a fraction bigger than my light sigl. "You," I told the sigl, "had better be worth it." I did *not* want to do that again.

I NEARLY FELL over twice on the way home, waves of dizziness greying out my vision and forcing me to grab on to the nearest tree or wall. Maybe I really had been pushing myself too hard.

But once I got indoors, a shower and a lie-down made me feel much better, and after an hour's rest I felt well again.

It was time to see what my new sigl could do.

"All right," I told Hobbes. "Motion sigl, mark one, test one." I'd cleared my floor, then pushed my chair into the corner and balanced an empty Coke can, rescued from the rubbish bin, on the seat. "Ready?"

Hobbes, perched on the bed with his splinted legs sticking out to one side, gave me an affirmative "Mraaa."

According to the catalogue, the slam effect used kinetic energy to compress air, which was then released explosively outwards, creating a blast of concussive force. The blast would start to spread and diffuse almost immediately, meaning that the range would be very short, but it still sounded useful.

"Let's do it," I said. I'd rigged up a crude ring out of wire and Blu Tack, out of which the Motion sigl gleamed like the world's most mismatched piece of jewellery. I slid the ring onto my finger, clenched my fist, and aimed it at the Coke can. "Here we go." I channelled a flow of essentia into the sigl.

Nothing happened.

Hobbes gave me a quizzical look. I tried again. No result.

"Mraow?"

"I don't get it," I told Hobbes. I held the ring up in front of me and channelled a third time. I could see my personal essentia flowing down my arm and into the sigl, and free essentia from the air around was being pulled in. It was doing *something*, I just couldn't tell what.

Maybe Motion sigls activated differently from Light or Life ones. How *would* you activate a force attack, anyway?

Well, it wasn't like there was anyone to see me embarrassing myself . . .

I held out my hand with the palm facing the Coke can, channelled essentia into the sigl, and shouted "Hadouken!"

Nothing.

"Expelliarmus!"

Nothing.

"Forzare!"

Nothing.

"Magic missile!"

Nothing.

"Kamehame . . . ha!"

The air stirred slightly.

I blinked. *Wait, that actually worked?*

"Mrrraaaaow," Hobbes said with amusement.

"Stop acting like this is funny," I told him. I channelled into the sigl again, trying to put more energy into it. "Kamehame . . . *ha*!"

Definitely a stir of air.

Okay, this was ridiculous. I'd barely even seen that show. Why would shouting *that* word do anything when . . . ?

Wait. With all the others, I'd attempted to use the sigl instantly. For this one, I'd instinctively tried to charge it up. I tried again, but this time, I channelled essentia in a steady build, trying to gather power.

I felt the difference instantly. Energy and pressure seemed to build at my palm, growing stronger and stronger. Eventually it seemed to reach a maximum, like an elastic band drawn back to its limit, and I aimed my palm at the Coke can and let go.

There was a *whuff* of displaced air and the curtains flapped. The Coke can went flying off the chair, smacked into the wall, and fell to the floor.

"All right," I said with satisfaction. I replaced the Coke can and went back to try it again.

—————

I SPENT MOST of the day playing with my new toy, then got a full night's rest and went out again early the next morning. Most of the Wells I'd found last week had been empty, nearly empty, or inaccessible, but there'd been one other usable one: a fragile, ephemeral-feeling Light Well in Canning Town.

The shaping went much more smoothly this time. This was partly because I was making a design I already understood, but I was also coming to realise that Light Wells were just *easier*. The essentia seemed to respond naturally to my thoughts, arranging itself as I wanted.

The sigl I made this time was a flash effect, designed to blind attackers with a burst of light. I'd learned some lessons from practising with the Motion sigl, and I didn't try to make it a continuous flow: instead I shaped the sigl so that it functioned as a tiny capacitor, storing up energy over a half second before releasing it all in an instant. The result consumed a lot more essentia than my old light sigl but was *much* more powerful. It was the first time I'd tried to shape a sigl with that kind of capacitor element, but I was able to get the design to work quite easily.

I was starting to fully appreciate just how big an advantage my new essentia sight was. Being able to see my own constructs let me spot mistakes as I made them, instead of only finding out once a sigl was misshaped and worthless. Without that, making that slam sigl would probably have taken me a good three or four attempts, which would have meant either finding more Motion Wells, or waiting for years to get that much essentia out of the one at Channelsea. As it was, I'd done it in a single try.

Maybe this was how corporations and Houses were able to make sigls so easily? But Maria had insisted that essentia sight had nothing to do with it. It was confusing.

In any case, once I started practising with my new sigls, I quickly realised that my drucraft skills had some major gaps. I was good at sensing and shaping, but the way I'd got good at them had been by being slow, controlled, and patient. My new flash and slam sigls were designed for fights, which meant that they needed to be used in a hurry. And once I started trying to do things in a hurry, it became very obvious that being slow and patient did not work *at all*. To use a slam sigl to hit a moving target—like, say, a Coke can tossed into the air—you had to channel a burst of essentia into the sigl very fast, while maintaining concentration on your aim. After missing the can twenty-five times in a row, I decided to try a mock battle, and that evening I went back to that secluded spot in Channelsea to stage a pretend drucraft fight. I imagined that I was being attacked by a couple of guys and that I had to use my slam and flash sigls to fend them off.

I'll spare you the details of my performance. Short version: it was pathetic. My combat channelling skills were so bad that if I'd been fighting for real, I actually would have done *worse* than if I hadn't had any sigls at all.

In the end I decided that I was just going to have to take this seriously. My bank balance was dropping fast, and I was itching to get out there and start hunting for Wells, but I remembered what Maria had said about competition. Between my soul sickness and my lack of experience with my sigls, I wasn't in fighting shape. If I found a Well and someone else showed up aiming to take it from me, things would go badly.

So the next day, I started on a training programme. I'd get up early, go for a morning run, then spend most of the day practising with my two combat sigls. I'd push myself until I felt the dizziness starting to come back, then rest until I was feeling better again.

It was very, very boring. Much as I love drucraft, doing the same channelling exercise hour after hour is pretty mind-numbing, and after a couple of days I wanted nothing more than to quit and do something else. What stopped me was the memory of being trapped in that van. The only reason I'd made it out of there had been because I'd been able to activate my sigl *instantly*; if I'd been even a second slower, Diesel would have had time to knock my hand away or shut his eyes. In a boxing match, being able to throw one kind of punch well is better than being able to do a dozen kinds of punches badly. There'd been a guy at my old gym who'd pretty much only thrown jabs, but since he spent *so much* time throwing jabs, he could do them hard enough and accurately enough that he was actually one of the tougher guys to beat. And so I kept practising with my new sigls until channelling essentia into them was totally reflexive and I could do it in an instant.

Two weeks passed.

My soul sickness wore off, the dizzy spells becoming rarer and rarer until they stopped completely. I got in touch with Maria and confirmed that she'd put my application through to Linford's. Hobbes recovered steadily, his bones starting to knit. I got plenty of sleep, and this time made sure to check in with Colin and the others so they wouldn't worry. I didn't hear anything from Lucella or the Ashfords, which suggested that they weren't coming after me. At least, not yet.

I also made use of the time to come up with a better solution for mounting my sigls. The plastic ring was too fragile, and the wire one too insecure. I couldn't afford the prices that the local jewellers charged, but it turned out that the local hardware store had a wide stock of cheap steel rings of various shapes and sizes. With Ignas's help I was able to bore holes in the rings and mount my sigls into them, recessed so that even if the ring was bashed into something, the metal would take the impact.

By the end of the fortnight, I had four mounted sigls and was confident with all of them. My slam sigl could throw out a blast of force to a distance of two or three feet. It hit as hard as a solid jab and should be enough to stun and disorient someone, particularly if I caught them off guard. My flash sigl could project a burst of blinding light in a cone which I could either widen for easier aiming or narrow to extend its effective range. And then I had my light and mending sigls, which weren't much use in a fight but might be helpful outside one.

It wouldn't be enough to beat someone like Diesel or Scar. Not with those strength sigls, and especially not if I had to deal with both of them at once. But the next time someone tried to just walk up and grab me, they'd get a nasty surprise. I'd gone from "mostly harmless" to "mildly threatening" in less than a month, which was really quite fast.

Still, I knew I had a long way to go. I'd been reading the Exchange catalogue from cover to cover, and there were some sigls in there that I thought *would* give me the ability to beat Diesel or Scar, but they were all much more powerful than anything I had or that my Light and Motion Wells could provide. I needed more.

As the last week of April came around, I decided I was ready. I was as comfortable with my combat sigls as I was going to get, there was no sign of activity from the Ashfords, and I hadn't had any dizzy spells in four or five days. If I was going to make it as a locator, now was the time.

The question of finding Wells had been hovering at the back of my mind for a while. I still wasn't sure how reliably I could find the things, and the more I looked into it, the more it seemed as though there *was* no reliable way to find the things. But I did have one big advantage: my essentia sight.

I'd been experimenting with my new sight in between my training sessions, and the more I learned about it, the stranger it felt. More and more, I was starting to think that my first guess— that this was some normal outgrowth of sensing that you just naturally developed once you were good enough—had been wrong. By this point I'd tested my sensing in every way I could think of, from feeling the flows of essentia in my room, to spotting Hobbes through the walls, to seeing how many paces I could get from my Well before I couldn't pick it up. And no matter what I did, my sensing felt about as strong as it had been before. Maybe my range had improved a tiny bit, but if it had, it had grown the same way that the rest of my drucraft skills had grown, in a very small, incremental way.

My new ability felt totally different. It wasn't like a learned skill, it was like . . . well, like having been blind and suddenly being able to see. My sensitivity was the same, my range was the same, but instead of having to feel essentia, I could see it. It didn't feel like a natural outgrowth. It felt like something completely new.

I searched online and found nothing. It wasn't like other aspects of drucraft, where you could usually find *some* people talking about it, even if most of what they said was wrong. Searching for phrases like "essentia sight" got you no results at all, even on the few drucraft sites I'd found that seemed more or less reliable. At last I decided I didn't have the time to keep chasing dead ends. My essentia sight worked, so I should stop looking a gift horse in the mouth.

And it was quite a gift. My new sight wasn't as useful for sensing as it was for shaping—it didn't do anything to increase my range, so I couldn't actually pick up a Well from any further away—but it still helped. The extra clarity made it much easier to tell the difference between an area with a Well, and one that just happened to have a lot of essentia floating around. Instead of having to carefully sift through an area's "background noise" to make sure I wasn't missing anything, I could take it all in at a glance.

And so that Sunday the twenty-fourth, I began actively hunting for Wells.

CHAPTER 12

FROM THAT DAY on, I quickly fell into a routine. Each morning, I'd wake up, take care of Hobbes, then have breakfast while looking at a map and deciding where to go—I didn't have a good idea of the best places to search yet, so I tried to cover as wide a range as possible. I'd leave around nine to miss rush hour, search until one, then come home for lunch and spend the afternoon practising with my sigls, studying the catalogue, or doing research. Once the sun had set, I'd have dinner and go out for my second search of the day, coming home around midnight to go to bed and start all over again the following morning.

It was hard work, but I enjoyed it. April is the time in England when everything starts to sprout and grow, and the trees that had been bare at the beginning of the month were now covered in green. The cherry blossoms were in full bloom, leaving drifts of petals on pavements and in gutters, and the bluebells and daffodils were bright spots of colour in the parks. The weather stayed fine, and I ranged back and forth around East London, in the beauty of the London spring.

The only thing stopping it from being really fun was my lack of money. My bank balance felt like an invisible number hovering over my head, ticking steadily down and pushing me to keep searching, hoping for a break. But luck wasn't with me, and while I found a few Wells, all were either locked away and inaccessible or empty. Every night I came home empty-handed, while every day the number in my bank account shrank a little more.

On Wednesday afternoon, I came home to some good news: an email telling me that my application to become a "registered locator" for Linford's had been approved. As part of that, I now had log-in details to the Well Registry.

The Well Registry was something I'd read about on the Linford's website: it was some sort of official record that decided who had the rights to use a Well. Right now I had read-only access, which I immediately put to use. The interface was simple enough— you just scrolled around a map of the United Kingdom, tapped a spot, and sent off an information request. The app would pause as it consulted the database, then spit out a result of either "registered" or "no data."

I checked a couple of random patches of street and got "no data" results, then scrolled over to Father Hawke's church. The "thinking" icon on the app spun briefly before the church flashed up purple as "registered." The Ashford mansion turned purple as well. I tried several more random locations before putting in the coordinates of my own Well. The result was a grey "no data," suggesting no one else knew about it. The same applied to the Well at Channelsea.

Okay, so that part seemed to be working. The next part was figuring out how to register Wells myself.

There was a "Claim" button on the app, but it was greyed out. I tried to activate it and got a message saying I needed a verification code. How was I supposed to get one of those?

I went back to the email from Linford's and read the small print.

"HEY, HEY, THE runner's back!" Felix called as I walked into the pub. "Did you give the phone hounds the slip?"

"I told you, I'm not on the run from debt collectors," I told Felix as I sat down on the bench.

"Could have fooled me," Colin said.

It was just me, Felix, and Colin today. Gabriel's relationship with his not-girlfriend had (to no one's surprise) crashed and burned, and Kiran was helping him pick up the pieces. I got a glass of water and sat down at our usual table.

"So what is it this time?" Colin asked. "You stop eating again?"

"It's not that," I told him. "It's the job with Linford's."

"You're still doing that?"

"He said so last week," Felix said with a yawn.

I've never had a good handle on exactly how big a secret dru-craft is supposed to be. My dad told me to be discreet, but he also told me that it was okay to tell people occasionally, so long as I trusted them and was careful. In the past I'd admitted to Colin and the others that drucraft was a thing I did, but only in a way that suggested it was some weird hobby that I got up to in my spare time. As of last week, though, I'd started to change that. I'd told Colin and Felix about Linford's and about how they would pay for Well locations, though I'd been careful not to give any details.

But details or no details, I knew that by telling Colin and Felix that I was trying to get an actual *job* in drucraft, I was crossing a line. The problem was that I didn't know exactly where that line was, or what would happen if I got caught on the wrong side of it. Right now, though, I was feeling pressured enough that I was willing to push things. I needed someone to talk to, and these guys were the closest friends I had.

"My application got approved," I told Colin. "They say I can start, but . . ."

"But what?"

"They're charging me fees before I can work," I said reluctantly.

"Course they are," Felix said with amusement.

"How much?" Colin asked.

"A hundred and thirty pounds for a licence application fee, a hundred and eighty pounds for a grant of licence fee, then forty pounds for a processing fee," I told him. "Plus another sixty for a background and credit check."

"Sounds about right," Felix said. "Don't you remember when Kiran signed up with Uber? He had to pay all that stuff too, *and* he had to shell out an extra hundred for a private medical."

"How's anyone supposed to be able to afford all this if they're not earning already?"

"Go into debt," Felix said with a shrug. "It's like with student loans, isn't it? They want you on the hook so you'll work harder."

"Okay," Colin said. "I don't want to come across as *more* cynical than Felix—"

"Cheers," Felix told him, taking a drink.

"—but shouldn't you be used to this stuff?" Colin went on. "I mean, you've been working how many years?"

I was silent. Because of course Colin was right; most of my jobs had screwed me over one way or another. The bar in Hoxton had underpaid me week after week, and when I'd complained, the manager had snidely suggested that I should be making up the difference in tips. At the call centre everyone had monthly targets, and if you didn't make yours, you had to do unpaid overtime until you did. The Civil Service had been the best of a bad bunch, and even then the agency had made it clear that if I took too many sick days, I'd be fired.

"I thought a drucraft company might be different," I said at last.

"What?" Colin said. "You thought a company selling fake shit would be *better*?"

Colin's always been the type to think that if you can't measure something, it doesn't exist, and I know he sees drucraft as a joke. It's meant I've never had to worry too much about him finding out that it's real, but it does get a bit annoying from time to time. "It's not fake."

"If you say so, dude," Colin said. "So now the bloom's off the rose, you thinking about going back to a proper job?"

"No," I told him. The extra fees were painful—I had £1,672 in the bank as of this morning, and this would wipe out nearly a quarter of that—but there wasn't any way around it. I couldn't register Wells on my own.

"Look," Colin said. "I know this drucraft stuff was a bonding thing with you and your dad, kind of like with mine and martial arts. But just because it was good for you doesn't mean you can do it for a living."

"You can, though," Felix said unexpectedly.

"Really?" Colin said, giving Felix an exasperated look. "Are you doing this just to troll him? Like when Gabriel got sucked into that MLM thing and you told him to go for it because you thought it'd be funny?"

"Oh, yeah, I forgot about that," Felix said with a grin. "That was hilarious."

"You know about drucraft corps?" I asked Felix.

"Well, yeah?" Felix said. He nodded at Colin. "They recruit from his uni."

"No, they don't," Colin said.

"There was one with a stall at your milk round, remember? You had one of their brochures."

"That was some engineering firm."

"Whatever," Felix said with a shrug, and got up to go to the bar. "Same again, right?"

"Look, don't listen to him," Colin said once Felix was gone. "This company of yours smells like a total scam."

"They pay a lot for high-value Wells," I argued.

"And how are you supposed to find them?"

"With the finder's stones they sell you."

Colin gave me a look.

"I'm not buying one," I added.

"So how are you supposed to know if these places with good feng shui or whatever are 'high value'?" Colin asked. "I mean, if they tell you it's worth ninety-nine pence, can you pull out a ruler or something and prove them wrong?"

"No," I said with a sigh.

"And can you sell it to anyone else?"

"No," I admitted. I'd already discovered from reading the small print that any Wells I registered would be in the corporation's name, not mine.

Colin looked at me with raised eyebrows.

"I get what you're saying," I told him. "But I've looked online and it does seem like you can make decent money from this."

"Yeah, that was what Gabriel said about the MLM thing too," Colin said. "Said there were guys taking home a thousand pounds a week, but when you talked to him, it turned out it wasn't anyone he actually *knew*."

"All right, here we go," Felix said, returning to our table and putting the glasses down. "Pint for me, pint for Colin, and a glass of water with a pink straw for Conan the Barbarian over here. I tried to get you a paper umbrella but they used them all up at the hen party last night."

I held up a middle finger to Felix and took my drink. "Anyway, it's a real job," Felix told Colin. "It's just kind of shit."

"Come on," Colin said. "They're just going to take his money and never pay him."

"Nah, they pay," Felix said. "Just less than minimum wage. That's why they have to bus in guys from Eastern Europe to do it."

The argument went on for a little while longer. Colin made a couple more attempts at nudging me back towards the Civil Service, but I didn't respond and he eventually took the hint.

At last Colin announced he had to get home, and Felix and I decided to follow him. "Hey, listen," Felix said as Colin headed out. He'd had more to drink than Colin and looked a little flushed. "If you do keep working for these people, don't spread it around, okay?"

I looked at Felix in surprise. "I thought you said it was a real job."

"Just because something's real doesn't mean you're allowed to talk about it."

I SPENT THE rest of that evening thinking about what Felix and Colin had said. I was pretty sure Colin was wrong about Linford's being a scam—they couldn't *totally* cheat their locators, or no one would work for them. But from long experience I knew that it was really, really common for companies to make "mistakes" with payslips, particularly for employees that they didn't very much care about keeping around.

It was Felix's last comment, though, that stuck. What *would* happen if I talked to the wrong person about drucraft? I didn't know, and that bothered me. But I decided that from now on, I'd be more careful about bringing it up, even with my friends.

BY THE NEXT day, though, my long-term concerns were quickly eclipsed by my worries about not finding any Wells. I'd wanted to make a third combat sigl, but as the days kept passing and the number in my bank account kept shrinking, I started to think I'd have to sell the next Well I found instead. Then when I still didn't find anything, I began to wonder if I'd even be able to do *that*.

But then, on Friday, my luck finally turned.

ON FRIDAY MORNING, I found the second-most powerful Well I'd ever seen. It was in Chancery Lane—I'd decided to go into Central London on a whim—in the centre of a densely built block of buildings. There was no way in, but it didn't matter: I could feel the Well from halfway down the street. It was incredibly strong, almost as powerful as the Well at the Ashford mansion, a glowing beacon of Light essentia that shone like a bonfire in the night.

Unsurprisingly, it was not open to the public. Old buildings rose up all around it, white and black and red, peaked roofs pointing to the sky. Craning my neck, I could just see the branches of a tree, which made me think that the block must have a little park or courtyard at its centre, but there was no way to get close enough to tell. I tried my app, and the area pinged as "registered." Yeah, no shit.

I looked the buildings up and down. It *might* be possible to climb up. Or, failing that, there was probably a door or window somewhere that'd give me a way in. My imagination spun me a fantasy of what I could do if I had that much essentia and the time to use it.

But that was only if I made it to the Well. The strongest sigls in the Exchange's catalogue were priced in the millions, and I was pretty sure this Well was strong enough to make them. How much security would you put on something that was worth millions of pounds a year?

A lot.

Yeah, I should not even be thinking about this. Still, as I turned away, I couldn't help but take a last glance back at the topmost branches of that tree. Maybe someday.

"ALL RIGHT," I said softly to myself. "Jackpot."

It was past midnight on the same day. I'd started doing my evening searches later and later—the quiet and stillness made it easier to focus on my sensing, and the darkness also came in handy for getting into places where you weren't strictly supposed to be. Right now I was in Victoria Park, a big stretch of trees and grassy fields about three miles west of my home. I'd been following the canal path to the south when a half-glimpsed trail of essentia had drawn my eye. I hadn't been quite sure if it had really been there or if I'd imagined it, but I'd trusted my instincts and climbed the fence into the darkness of the park. I was glad I had.

Victoria Park has a small lake towards its western end, where bridges run out across the water to an island with dirt paths and picnic tables. The Well was at the island's shore, under a beech tree. It was a Motion Well—I recognised that swirling, pale-gold essentia instantly—and it was strong. Nothing like the monster I'd seen in Chancery Lane, but stronger than any of the Wells I'd used. Best of all, it was full, and unclaimed.

I rose from where I'd been crouched next to the Well and bounced up and down on my toes. I still wasn't great at estimating Well strengths, but I guessed that this Well was somewhere around four or five times the strength of mine. That put it somewhere around the middle of the C range, which meant a finder's fee of £3,000 to £5,000. Even at the low end, I could live on that for months.

There were two problems. Firstly, this place was about as public as you could get. It was deserted right now because it was nighttime and the park was closed. But the island was crisscrossed with paths, and off to the east I could see the shadowy shape of a big Chinese pagoda that I knew was one of the park's main tourist attractions. Come Saturday morning—which was about six hours away—this place would be swarming with people.

And that was bad, because while the Well might be worth thousands, I couldn't sell it. I'd paid my money to Linford's, but they hadn't yet activated my account.

I hesitated, thinking. I could call the Linford's contact number and try to register the Well off the books, but I had the nasty feeling that if I did that, they'd either pay me less or pay me nothing at all. I could give up on selling this Well and try to make a sigl from it, but I'd had a hell of a time making my last Motion sigl, and the essentia in this Well looked even more hyperactive and chaotic. Besides, my bank balance had sunk low enough that I was more worried about paying my rent.

In the end I decided to sit on it. The Well had gone unnoticed so far—with a bit of luck it'd stay that way just long enough for Linford's to process my account. Until then, I made a mental note to keep checking this spot on the registry, just in case.

SATURDAY SEEMED TO crawl by. I had trouble concentrating on my sensing and kept bringing up the app on my phone to check that spot. I found one more claimed D-class Well, but my thoughts kept drifting to that island in Victoria Park.

Then, about an hour after sunset, I tapped the button for the five hundredth time, and instead of the "no data" result, the icon kept spinning.

I frowned and pressed the button again. Had I put in too many requests? I knew there was a limit on how often I could send queries. The icon kept spinning; I quit the app, reloaded, and hit "Check Location" again.

It spun for a second, then flashed purple.

Shit!

I abandoned what I was doing and rushed to Victoria Park.

I SPENT THE whole bus ride wanting to kick myself. Why had I been so greedy? I should have just called Linford's last night. Sure, they would have paid me less, but I would have probably at least got *something*. Now I was going to get nothing at all. Once I was close enough, I jumped off the bus and ran the rest of the way.

By the time I reached the park, it was pitch dark. It had been a sunny day, and stars twinkled down out of a clear sky. There was no moon, and Victoria Park was a sea of darkness.

I climbed the fence, dropped down onto the grass, and ran towards the island.

There was no way I could sell the Well's location now—the best I could do was use the essentia for myself. I'd been glancing through the catalogue, and a C-class Well should be strong enough to create some sort of levitation sigl. I didn't know *how* to make a levitation sigl, but it seemed like it was one of the more straightforward designs, so maybe—

I stepped onto the bridge and a figure appeared out of the darkness ahead to block my path. I stopped dead.

"Park's closed," the figure said. A woman's voice.

"What are *you* doing here, then?" I shot back.

"I work for a maintenance company. I'm watching the area."

Yeah, right. "You mean the Well?"

I saw the woman stiffen. It was hard to see the movement in the darkness, but I'd been watching for it. And as the seconds ticked by, she stayed silent, instead of asking *What well?* like a normal person.

"So you're the one trying to steal it," I said.

"Steal it?" The woman's voice climbed in indignation. "It's mine!"

"I found it first."

"No, you didn't! It wasn't registered."

"I still *found* it first."

"Well, did you register it?"

I was silent.

"So then it's not yours, is it?"

The woman's face was still only a shadow. I wondered how old she was. "Fine," I said, and started across the bridge.

"What are you doing?"

"If you're going to take this Well, I'm going to use it first."

"What?" She moved to block me. "No, you're not!"

I stopped. "Or you'll do what?"

"I'll . . ." The woman hesitated.

We were only fifteen feet apart now. I still couldn't make out the woman's features, but she was smaller than I was. It would be pretty easy to blind or stun her from here. Or just punch her out, for that matter.

"I'll call the police," the woman announced.

I snorted. "And tell them what? Now get out of my way."

The woman drew back slightly. "No." She sounded afraid but didn't budge.

I hesitated. I could definitely drop her if I attacked from here. But . . .

But now that I was actually in a position to do it, I realised I didn't like the idea of hitting a woman smaller than I was. Okay, well, not *any* woman—if it were Lucella, I'd have done it already. *Was* she like Lucella?

Seconds ticked by. We stared at each other in the darkness.

"Ugh," I said at last. "Fine. Let's talk."

GETTING THE WOMAN to agree to walk a hundred feet or so to the light was an argument in itself. I had to flat-out tell her that it was a choice between that or a fight, and even then it took me ten minutes to get her to the gate on the west side of the park, where streetlights cast a glow over the canal bridge.

I'd been revising the woman's age down and down the longer we talked, but when she finally stepped into the light, I realised I'd still overestimated. She was around the same age as me, pretty and athletic looking, with African features, straight black hair, and dark clothes that seemed like they'd been chosen as a compromise between looks and practicality. She watched me warily from across the splash of light.

"Were you trying to sound older than you were?" I asked.

"None of your business," the woman—girl—said, folding her arms. She had an upper-middle-class accent. "How old are you, anyway?"

"None of *your* business."

We stared at each other across the circle cast by the streetlight.

"Okay," I said. "I'll answer your questions if you answer mine. Deal?"

"Fine," the girl said. "Who are you working for?"

"Myself."

"I don't believe you."

"Well, it's true." I might be registered with Linford's, but they weren't paying me. "Who are *you* working for?"

The girl hesitated. "Mitsukuri."

Who?

"My turn," the girl said. "Are you a raider?"

"I don't even know what that is," I said. "So no. What's your name?"

She frowned. "Why do you want to know?"

"Because if I'm going to keep talking to you, I want something to call you other than 'suspicious-looking African girl.'"

"*You're* suspicious!"

"Still waiting. Also, that was two questions."

She made an annoyed noise. "Ivy. And I'm not telling you my surname, so don't ask."

"Are you using any sigls right now?"

Ivy hesitated, and I watched her very closely. This one was a test. I'd been focusing on Ivy since we started talking, and I could see the glow of an active sigl coming from her head. It looked to be set into some kind of hair ornament, and it was sending a steady flow of essentia down into her eyes, creating some complex effect that I couldn't identify.

"Yes," Ivy said at last. "All right. If you're not working for anyone and you're not a raider, why were you looking for Wells? And answer properly this time."

"I did answer properly," I told her. "It's not my fault you didn't believe me. I signed on with Linford's, but they're not letting me register Wells yet, so I'm waiting to sell this one. Or I *was*, until I saw someone else was trying to take it."

"I still don't believe you found it first."

"It's a Motion Well," I told her.

". . . You could have just guessed that."

"And it's under the beech tree on the west side of that island."

Ivy was silent.

"Believe me now?"

"You still didn't actually register it," Ivy said. "It's not my problem if Linford's are slow."

"So you're saying the only way I'm getting anything out of that Well is if I fight you for it?"

We stood staring at each other for a few seconds more, then I saw Ivy let out a breath. "Twenty percent."

"Of what?"

"That's a class-six Motion Well," Ivy said. "The finder's fee is four thousand, eight hundred pounds. I'll pay you twenty percent."

Apparently Mitsukuri paid better than Linford's. "Fifty percent."

"Twenty percent is *generous*. You're getting paid a thousand pounds to do nothing."

"Nine hundred and sixty. And I could still just take it myself."

"You just admitted you can't sell it. And there must be some reason you don't want to shape a sigl there, or you'd have done it already."

I hesitated, weighing my options. Nine hundred sixty pounds was a lot less than what I'd been hoping for, but it was a lot better than nothing. Besides, I was developing a reluctant liking for Ivy. She'd probably been pretty scared coming into this—she was a small girl on her own in the middle of a dark, empty park, facing a guy bigger than she was—but she'd still stood her ground. The more I thought about what fighting my way past her would actually mean, with Ivy hurt badly enough that she couldn't stop me using that Well, the more unpleasant it felt. I had the feeling that if I started doing things like that, I wouldn't like the kind of person it'd turn me into.

"Fine," I said. "Twenty." I felt a little bit of relief as I said it.

Ivy hesitated, then nodded. "Okay. I'm going to wait at the Well for the Mitsukuri team to show up."

———

We walked back along the park avenue towards the bridge. Ivy still kept a watchful eye on me, but she wasn't staying quite so far away anymore.

We were just about to turn onto the bridge when Ivy stopped dead and threw out a hand towards me. "What are—" I began.

"Shh!"

With a frown, I obeyed. Ivy crept forward. The bridge had Chinese-themed posts along its length, painted in gaudy colours, and she peered out from behind one of them, looking out onto the island. I craned my neck, squinting, but the island was pitch dark.

Ivy pulled away, motioning to me to back up along the avenue. "Trouble," she whispered once we were a little way back. She hurried off along the avenue back the way we came.

I caught up with her. "What trouble?"

"On the island. I think they're raiders."

A path opened up to our right, and Ivy disappeared down it. I jogged after her until I caught up. The path ran around the west side of the lake, and Ivy was crouching in the gloom, peering out across the water at the island. I stopped and did the same.

The island was a black shadow in the darkness. I could make out the bridges, visible by their contrast against the lake, and in my essentia sight I could see the Well itself, a swirling golden glow that cast no light. I couldn't see any raiders, though. Seconds ticked by, and I started to get suspicious. Was Ivy just pretending?

Then I heard voices from across the water. A young man's voice, followed by another. A light flickered: a smartphone screen. It swung around and winked out almost immediately, but in that brief glimmer of light I made out at least three shapes. Then it was gone and the island was dark again.

Carefully Ivy backed away into the shelter of the trees. "They *are* raiders," she said. She seemed to be talking to herself. She pulled out her phone and started typing.

"Hey," I asked in a low voice. "Ivy."

Ivy didn't take her eyes off her phone. In the screen's glow, I could see she was chewing her lip.

"Ivy!"

"What?"

"What's a raider?"

"They drain other people's Wells and sell the essentia . . . Oh, come on!" Ivy made a frustrated expression. "Why aren't they answering?"

"What, the people you work for?" I asked. "Why not just call the police?" *Like you threatened to do with me?*

"They'll be too late. You can drain a Well in an hour. Besides . . ."

"Besides what?"

It was hard to tell, but Ivy looked uncomfortable. "Mitsukuri won't pay for a Well if the police are there."

I gave her an unimpressed look.

"We haven't got long." Ivy took a deep breath and turned to me. "Can you help me chase them off?"

"Help you?"

"I'm not losing this Well too," Ivy said fiercely. "You were acting tough before. Or do you just do that to threaten girls?"

I thought for a second, eyeing Ivy.

"Well?" Ivy said. She sounded tense.

"Fifty-fifty," I told her.

"What are—" Ivy stopped and made an angry noise. "Fine. Fifty-fifty. *If* you actually help."

"Deal."

———

WE WALKED TOGETHER back towards the bridge, moving a lot less stealthily this time. "How nasty are raiders?" I asked Ivy quietly.

"What do you mean?"

"As in, if we lose to these guys, are they going to give us a kicking and walk off? Or are they going to cut us up with machetes?"

"Machetes?"

"It's what the gangs in my neighbourhood use."

We'd reached the bridge, and I felt Ivy stiffen. "They've seen us."

I didn't ask how she knew. "If I say 'eyes,' close your eyes tight," I told her quietly.

"Why?"

"Just do it."

We started across the bridge.

Under the surface, I was a lot less confident than I was acting; a part of me knew that walking up like this on a gang had the potential to end very, very badly. But a bigger part of me didn't care. It felt as though ever since I'd stepped into the drucraft world, I'd spent my time being threatened and pushed around and dictated to by everyone and their mother, and I was sick of it. Diesel had beaten me up, and I'd run away. Hobbes had nearly been killed, and I'd just had to take it. These guys had nothing to do with any of that, but they were yet another bunch of people using what power they had to make my life just that little bit worse than it would otherwise have been, and I'd had enough.

Before we were halfway across the bridge, dark shapes appeared at the other end. We slowed to a stop. "Can you see them?" I said quietly to Ivy.

"Four," Ivy whispered. "They're pretty young."

That's good.

"And, um, the one on the right just pulled out a machete."

That's bad.

"Ey, ey!" one of the raiders called at us. "You in the *wrong* neighbourhood, boys."

The raiders began to advance across the bridge. It was only wide enough for them to come two at a time. Just like Ivy had said, the one on the right was holding something that looked a lot like a blade, while the one on the left had something else. "What's the left one holding?" I whispered to Ivy.

"Stick," she whispered.

All right. I took a deep breath and made my decision. I felt adrenaline start to surge through me.

I heard a klunk as the guy with the machete struck the railing with the flat of his blade. He kept rapping it as he advanced, in time with his steps: klunk, klunk, klunk.

I held my ground. The raiders stopped just a little way apart from us.

I looked at the raiders, measuring distances. One more step forward, and they'd all be in optimal range for my flash sigl.

One of the raiders shouted suddenly in a deep voice. "Ogun!"

"OGUN!" the three behind him chorused.

"Ogun!"

"OGUN!"

I felt the hairs on the back of my neck rise—a sense of being watched. The wind died, leaving the park in silence.

"Ogun!" the leader called.

"OGUN!" came back.

Beside me, I heard Ivy catch her breath. The leader took a step forward, his stick lifted to the sky.

"Eyes," I told Ivy.

The leader opened his mouth again. I closed my eyes and triggered my flash sigl.

The flare was bright enough that I could see it even through my eyelids. The bridge erupted in screams and yells.

I opened my eyes again to see that the raiders were in chaos. The machete guy was clutching at his face and shouting, and I charged my slam sigl and fired. There was a *whuff* and he went down. The machete fell with a clatter, and I grabbed it and tossed it into the lake.

A shout made me look up; another raider was charging. He was going for a tackle, but he was still half-blind from the flash and I was able to sidestep the rush. One of his hands caught my arm; he tried to pull me in, but there was no way I was getting into a wrestling match. I put a right cross into his face and then an uppercut to his chin, and he dropped.

Something glanced off my ribs, hard, and I felt a jolt of pain. I spun to see the fourth raider drawing back for another punch. Behind him Ivy was struggling with the stick guy, but then the raider drove in and I got my arms up into a guard.

I just had time to notice that his right hand was glowing dark red with essentia before the punch landed on my forearm. Pain exploded from the blow; it felt like getting hit by an iron bar. I stumbled back, the guy driving in at me. His fist hammered into my guard like a lump of metal; I came up against the side of the bridge with a thump, and the raider drew back for a knockout blow.

I was hurt and off balance, but the pause gave me just long enough to recover. As the raider came in, I triggered my flash sigl right in his face.

The raider screamed and staggered back. I hadn't got my eyes completely closed and spots danced in my vision, but I could see well enough to tell that the raider had his back to the other side of the bridge. I took a run and shoved him in the chest, sending him over the railing and into the lake with a thunderous splash.

A shriek made me spin around. The guy Ivy had been fighting was down, but she was backing quickly away from—

—a monster?

A spike of terror shot through me. The thing was seven feet tall, vaguely human shaped but made out of pure shadow. The air around it seemed to get darker and darker until the core was pitch black; looking into it felt like staring into a void.

Ivy backed past me and I began to back away too. The monster gave a low, chuckling laugh and advanced slowly. I looked around wildly, my heart hammering in my chest. I could see the whites of Ivy's eyes; two of the raiders were still down on the bridge; the one I'd knocked into the lake was floundering in the water.

"*Run*," the monster said in a throaty voice and stepped closer. Except we'd got turned around in the fight; we were backing onto the island. Ivy and I stepped back off the bridge at the same time as the monster drew closer and—

Wait. I'd seen three raiders. Where was the fourth?

A sudden suspicion flashed through my mind, and I focused on the monster, clearing my thoughts enough that I could use my essentia sight. And as soon as I did, I realised what I was looking at. It wasn't a monster; it was a spell.

"*Run*," the monster said more loudly.

I could hear Ivy's quick breathing and knew that if I broke and ran, she'd do the same. No matter how much I told myself that this had to be one of the raiders, the primitive part of my brain was screaming *darkness, scary thing, run away*.

The monster took a step off the bridge, coming down on the island. Its movements were confident and sure.

A thought flashed into my head: *it can see.* That darkness had to be one-way, or light couldn't be reaching its eyes. And if light could reach its eyes . . .

I triggered my flash sigl, sending a blaze of radiance into the darkness.

I heard a curse, and the monster staggered back onto the

bridge. All of a sudden, the illusion was broken and my fear vanished. It wasn't a monster, just a guy covered in shadows. He straightened up and swore at me.

I aimed with my left hand, channelling into my sigl. Air slammed into the raider with a *whuff*, and he staggered back.

I walked forward, left hand raised, and fired another slam into the mass of darkness, aiming for where the head should be. Now that the fear was receding, I could see the effect more closely, understand how it worked. There was a sigl somewhere around the guy's chest, converting outgoing light into free essentia. It grew weaker quickly, which was where the creepy shadow effect came from, but now that I could see that he was at the centre of it, it was easy to aim. *Whuff, whuff, whuff.* I kept firing slams into him, knocking him back with blows of compressed air, hammering him until he broke away and scrambled back to the far side of the bridge. The raider who'd been lying on the bridge made it to his feet just in time to see the other guy run past; he gave me one look and ran away too.

I was left in the middle of the bridge. The shadow-man raider was the only one still there, a mass of darkness at the far side.

I heard Ivy call "Hey!" and looked around: she was handing me the stick from the guy she'd knocked down earlier. I took it and turned back.

"You ain't shit!" shadow guy yelled at us.

I turned side-on to the raider. With my free hand, I beckoned. Ivy stepped up next to me.

The raider hesitated, then backed away. The island was ours.

THE RAIDERS HUNG around for a while, circling the island like wolves. From time to time they'd try to creep up to one of the two bridges, but every time Ivy would spot them and give warning.

Apparently there were only three left—the fourth one must have run away and not come back.

With odds of only three to two, and having lost their weapons, the raiders didn't seem keen for a rematch. At last the beams of electric torches cut through the night, along with the sound of men's voices, and the raiders turned and vanished into the darkness.

The men drew closer, their torch beams splashing over the bridge. "Your guys?" I asked Ivy.

"Yes," Ivy said. She called out something to the man at the front in what sounded like Japanese; he said something back in the same language. Ivy advanced and met them on the bridge.

I kept my distance, watching warily. The adrenaline rush from the battle was wearing off, but I didn't want to relax just yet. At one point I saw the man look over at me and ask Ivy something; she replied and he nodded, then pulled out a tablet and started typing into it. I backed away to the other side of the island as more men crossed the bridge and started setting up fences around the Well, then I watched them from the darkness, thinking.

For some reason, my mind kept going back to that moment at the start of the battle. It had felt almost like fighting in front of an audience, as though someone or something had been watching.

I shook it off. Maybe I was imagining things.

At last Ivy came walking over. "Done the handover," she told me. "I think we were in time. They don't think the Well was touched."

I nodded.

"Give me your number," Ivy told me. "I'll text you when the money comes through."

I held up my phone so that she could see the screen. "Fifty-fifty," I reminded her.

"Yeah, yeah," Ivy said in an annoyed tone, typing into her own phone. "Not that you deserve it, after you tried to steal it."

"If I hadn't tried to 'steal' it, you'd have been alone on that island when those raiders showed up," I told her. "How do you think that would've ended?"

Ivy made a scoffing noise but didn't answer. Glancing over, I could see that the Mitsukuri people had finished fencing off the Well.

All of a sudden, I just wanted to go home. I started to walk away.

"Hey!" Ivy called after me.

I paused and looked back.

"What's your name?" Ivy asked.

I gave her a grin that I knew she'd be able to see. "Not your turn to ask a question."

For a moment I thought Ivy was going to stick out her tongue. I walked off into the darkness with a smile.

CHAPTER 13

I WOKE UP next morning stiff and aching. My arms and side hurt, and inspecting myself in the bathroom mirror revealed big purple bruises in the places where I'd been hit by that iron-fist guy.

I tried using my mending sigl, but it didn't help. Apparently a sigl designed to stop you from dying from internal bleeding didn't do much to heal bruises, which I suppose shouldn't have been a surprise. I was in for a painful few days.

But I still went downstairs in high spirits. I'd fought my first real drucraft battle. And my opponents hadn't been pushovers, either—they'd been a small gang with weapons and sigls of their own. I'd won, and it felt good.

As I ate breakfast, I replayed the fight in my mind. On the whole, I thought I'd done pretty well. With hindsight, I should have realised earlier that shadow-man had been a human being and not a monster, but it's a lot easier to be calm and rational about that sort of thing when you're *not* getting attacked in the darkness of a moonless night. And at least I'd only frozen rather than screaming. Mental note: *next time you see Ivy, remember to make fun of her for screaming.*

The big thing I was lacking was defence. That battle had gone well, but a big part of that had been because those raiders had let me blind all four of them with my opening move. I could really use some sort of sigl that'd let me keep enemies at a distance. Or maybe something closer ranged, that I could use if I got tackled or grabbed . . .

I went upstairs and spent a while leafing through the catalogue. As usual, most of the sigls that seemed like really *good* answers to my problem were incredibly expensive. Even more annoyingly, all the best defensive sigls seemed to be from my two weakest branches, Life or Motion.

Still, I wouldn't know if it was possible until I tried. As I headed out for the day's search, I decided that the next time I found a Life or Motion Well, I'd keep it for myself.

I'D BEEN EXPECTING to sit on that decision for a while, but life is unpredictable. As it turned out, I found a temporary Life Well that very same day.

One nice thing about my new routine was that it was leaving me with a lot more energy. With my old jobs, the combination of work, errands, my commute, my drucraft, and all the other little things had meant that I was constantly short of time. Lack of time led to lack of sleep, which left me constantly stressed and tired. I was still working long hours, but the flexible schedule made it much more forgiving. Yes, my side and arms hurt, but I could just go easy on the searching for a few days and give myself time to recover. And instead of having to spend ten hours a day in the train and office, I could rest in my room with Hobbes, give my muscles a break, and do shaping practice instead.

At the moment, my shaping practice was focused towards making a new type of Life sigl. While my victory on Saturday night had raised my spirits, it had also made me think back to the fight that I'd lost against Diesel and Scar and the strength sigls they'd been using. I'd gone through the catalogue, trying to figure out what they'd been using, and the closest match I could find was a model called Ajax, one of a broader category of Life sigls described as "enhancement." I had access to a Life Well now, so in theory I should be able to make my own. The question was how.

I started with my mending sigl, since it was the one example of a working Life sigl that I had access to. As far as I could tell, it worked by strengthening a particular bodily system, which in this case must be the one that handled blood clotting. Or maybe the one that managed the body's internal organs . . . or healing in general . . .

. . . actually, I had no idea. In fact, the more I looked at the sigl, the more I realised that I didn't understand how it worked at all, which was pretty bizarre given that I'd been the one who'd, you know, *made* it. I had a vague general idea of the shape of the essentia flow and how it was transformed, but the longer I studied the design, the more little details I noticed whose purpose I didn't really understand. It made me wonder yet again exactly what had happened the night I'd shaped it. How could it have seemed so straightforward back then, and so impossibly complicated now?

But while I didn't really understand how the sigl worked, I did think I understood it well enough to make a copy that would strengthen a different bodily system instead. I wasn't sure *which* system it would end up affecting, but I was hoping I could figure that out by trial and error. But before I could give that a go, I heard back from Ivy.

———

IVY'S TEXT POPPED up on my phone on Wednesday morning, just as I was finishing breakfast. The money's come through, it read. How do you want to be paid?

I swallowed my food, picked up my phone, and typed a response. Shall we meet up somewhere?

Ivy's response came back almost immediately. What for?

Me: To sort out the details.

Ivy: Or you could just send me your bank details and I could pay you directly. You know that online banking exists, right?

Me: Well, yes. But it's nice to talk face to face.

Ivy: I don't see why. It's not like I know you.

Me: We just met each other on Saturday night.

Ivy: I've met you. That doesn't mean I KNOW you.

I rolled my eyes, put my plate in the sink, then resumed texting.

Me: Okay, fine, send the money online. What do you need, the account number?

Ivy: And the sort code.

Me: Done.

I sent the data, then brought up the banking app on my phone and waited. Somewhat to my surprise, I got an activity pop-up almost immediately. On the screen was a notification saying C/R: BACS: £2,400.00.

Me: Got it. Thank you.

Ivy: You're welcome.

Me: Do you want to meet up again?
Ivy: Why?

I thought for a bit.

Me: Honestly? Hunting for Wells is kind of a lonely job and it'd be nice to have someone to talk to. You're the first other locator I've met and you seem to have some idea of what you're doing. I'd like the company and we might be able to help each other.

There was a minute's pause before the "..." indicator appeared, indicating that Ivy was typing another message.

Ivy: How do I know you're not just trying to take advantage of me?
Me: Well, I haven't so far.
Ivy: The first time we met, you threatened to attack me and tried to steal my Well.
Me: It wasn't "your" Well. I found it before you did.
Ivy: I've only got your word for that.

I started to type a long message about how I'd known exactly where that Well was and what kind of essentia was in it, which should *prove* that I was telling the truth, and anyway if I'd actually wanted to screw Ivy over, I could have just . . .

. . . no. I held down the Delete key until the whole message had disappeared.

Me: Why is it so hard for you to believe that I mean what I say?

There was another pause, then the "..." indicator appeared again. It disappeared and reappeared several times, as though Ivy was deleting her words and starting again. When her message appeared, it was a short one for how long it had taken to write.

> Ivy: I have to be careful.
> Me: Well, so do I.
> Ivy: You're a boy.
> Me: Honestly doesn't help as much as you'd think.
> Ivy: You're still a lot safer than I am.

I thought about pointing out that being a boy made me *more* likely to get beaten up or stabbed, not less, but something told me that Ivy probably wasn't interested in hearing that. Instead I tried to put myself in her shoes. Why was she being so cautious?

Well, we *had* kind of got off on the wrong foot.

> Me: Look, I'm sorry about how I came across when we first met. I wasn't trying to threaten you.
> Ivy: Could have fooled me.
> Me: I said I was sorry. Anyway, for all I knew, I was the one in danger from you.
> Ivy: How would you be in any danger from me?
> Me: You could have had a couple of guys hanging around just out of sight waiting to attack me as soon as you gave the word.
> Ivy: That doesn't sound very likely.
> Me: You'd be surprised.
> Ivy: Fine. Apology accepted, I guess. But you'd better not do that again.

I leant against the wall with a smile and kept on typing.

> Me: Besides, you were the one trying to sound like you were about ten years older.

Ivy: I was not.

Me: Then how come your voice went up as soon as you stepped into the light?

Ivy: You're imagining it.

Me: If you say so.

Ivy: Honestly. If I'd known you were the kind to get scared that easily, I wouldn't have been so worried in the first place.

My smile faded.

Me: What do you mean?

Ivy: You see a girl on her own in the middle of the night, and the first thing you think of is that she's got a couple of men waiting to attack you?

Me: Turns out it does actually happen.

Ivy: If you say so.

I stared at the screen. Maybe I was imagining it, but that last line seemed to carry a sort of amused contempt. All of a sudden I didn't want to talk to Ivy anymore. I stuffed the phone into my pocket and headed upstairs.

I spent a couple of hours working on sigl designs, but it didn't make me feel any better. Ivy's last few messages kept going around in my head, and the more I thought about them, the more they bothered me. Lucella's attack had taught me a harsh lesson: at any moment she or one of the other Ashfords could decide to come back and do something horrible, and if they did, I'd be hard-pressed to stop them. I felt very alone and very vulnerable, and a part of me had been hoping that Ivy might be someone that I could talk to about all of this.

Instead, Ivy had proved Lucella right. Lucella might be my enemy, but despite that—in fact, maybe *because* of that—she'd given me the hard truth instead of the comforting lie. People like Lucella really *could* do things like this to people like me and then casually walk away. And if I tried to tell anyone, they'd either think I was making it up, or they wouldn't care.

I really was on my own.

Hobbes stirred against my leg. I looked over at him, smiled, and scratched his head. Hobbes purred, snuggled down against me, and went back to sleep.

Okay, not completely on my own. I stroked Hobbes a little longer, then turned back to my notebook. There was work to be done.

WITH THE MONEY from Ivy, I had enough of a buffer that I could finally take the first step towards searching for my dad. I spent a little while researching private detectives, then went to the firm that sounded the most trustworthy and told them what I wanted. The quote they gave me wasn't cheap, but at least it was in the hundreds, instead of the thousands. I put some money down and was told that they should have a report in a week or two. In the meantime, I had a sigl to make.

IT WAS TWO days later.

"Okay," I said to Hobbes. "Enhancement sigl, mark one, test one."

I was standing in my room. As was traditional at this point, Hobbes had been moved up to the bed to watch. His fractures were healing, but he wasn't yet up to jumping: fortunately he seemed to understand that, and now when he wanted to get up onto the bed, he just sat there and meowed insistently until I picked him up. My new sigl was around my neck, held by a piece of string and some Blu Tack.

My new Life sigl was a little emerald teardrop. In the end I'd largely copied my mending sigl, reproducing the details of its design without fully understanding why they were there. I'd managed to identify the part of the sigl that caused the essentia that flowed out of it to affect blood coagulation; after some testing, I'd figured out a way to alter that so that it would strengthen and enhance a body's muscles instead. The idea was that the essentia would flow *only* through my muscles, bypassing nerve and vein and bone. It should deliver its energy to my muscle fibres, and nowhere else.

I hoped.

"Okay," I said again to Hobbes. "We ready?"

"Mraa."

"Be patient, okay? This is delicate."

"Mrooooooow."

"I am *not* getting cold feet. I'm just . . . being careful."

"Mraow?"

"Fine, all right! Now be quiet."

Hobbes watched me expectantly. I took a deep breath, and channelled.

Warmth and energy flowed into me, spreading outwards from the sigl into my chest and body. Looking down, I could see the sigl pulling in free essentia and sending it into me in a flow of green. Slowly I increased the flow, scaling it up until it hit maximum. It took a lot more of my personal essentia than my Light sigls did.

It also took steady concentration. Most of the enhancement sigls in the Exchange catalogue were described as "continuous," which apparently meant that they were supposed to work automatically with no effort on the part of the user. I could already see that this sigl was very definitely *not* like that. Keeping it active wasn't hard, but it did require constant attention.

Still, concentration or not, it seemed to be working. Energy was radiating out through my body, and I did feel stronger. *Let's give this a try.* I brought my arms up and drew back into a guard, intending to throw a few jabs to get the measure of my new strength.

Everything went wrong very fast.

My arms went up unevenly, the right arm coming up more quickly than it should have. I shifted to keep my balance, but my right leg moved with more power than I was expecting, making me stumble. I threw out my arm to catch myself.

It felt wrong, really wrong. My arm went out at the wrong angle, bending further than it should, and pain stabbed at my arm and chest. I tried to compensate, and my other leg did something wrong, and I lost my balance. I twisted instinctively as I fell, trying to soften the blow, and agony flared in my chest and back. The pain was sudden and overwhelming, shattering my concentration and cutting off my essentia flow through the sigl.

I hit the floor with a thump and lay gasping. I'd lost my breath, and I struggled to get air into my lungs as I lay sprawled out on my side. Pain stabbed from a dozen places across my body. Gradually I managed to get my breathing back, and eventually I was able to drag myself up to a sitting position. I pulled the sigl out from under my T-shirt to stare at it. *What the hell?*

I hauled myself up to sit on the bed. Hobbes *mrrowed* at me and head-butted my leg; he'd been watching me with wide-eyed alarm, and I scratched his head as I pulled my thoughts together. What the hell had happened?

Once I'd had a few minutes to recover (and to reassure Hobbes), I rose painfully to my feet. My chest and back *really* hurt, and after some testing and some quickly aborted attempts at stretches, my best guess was that I'd somehow pulled a dozen small muscles all over my chest and back. Not life threatening, but very, very painful. *God damn it.* I'd only just finished recovering from the last lot of injuries!

I pulled off the sigl and held it up in front of me by its cord. "What the hell is wrong with you?" I asked the thing. This had never happened before. I'd had sigls fail to work, but nothing like this.

The sigl hung there, glinting slightly in the light.

I've got a sigl that lets me cripple myself, I thought sourly. *Wonderful.* With a sigh, I sat down to begin the long, slow work of figuring out what I'd done wrong.

AFTER FOUR SOLID hours, I was no closer to solving the problem. In the end, out of sheer frustration, I decided to go back to the person who'd told me about Life sigls in the first place.

"Stephen," Father Hawke said in greeting. He was sitting in one of the pews of the church, reading from a battered old paperback. "Did you lose a fight?"

"I don't want to talk about it," I said shortly. "Can you help me with something? I've made another Life sigl, and it doesn't work. Or it does, but very badly."

Father Hawke closed his book, set it down on the pew, and turned towards me. Even sitting, he was almost as tall as I was. "Show me."

I pulled out the sigl, still hanging by its thread and Blu Tack, then very carefully channelled the tiniest thread into it that I could. The green tendrils of Life essentia twined out from the sigl and into my arm, sinking into my muscles. I kept the flow to the barest minimum and didn't make any sudden movements.

Father Hawke studied the sigl as it glinted in the lights of the church. "Interesting."

I let the flow drop. "Can you see what's wrong with it?"

Father Hawke gave me a curious look. "See?"

Oops. "I mean, tell me what's wrong with it."

"Is it a mending sigl?"

"Enhancement."

"How did you know how to make an enhancement sigl?"

"Based it off my mending sigl."

"And who taught you how to make the mending sigl?"

"You told me how one was supposed to work," I told him. "I figured the rest out on my own."

Father Hawke studied me.

"So . . ." I said. "Do you have any idea what the problem is? I've been trying to figure out what I did wrong."

"Hmm?" Father Hawke said. "Oh, yes, the sigl. I should be able to solve your problem. However, I require something in exchange."

"How much?" I asked with a sigh. It seemed like it didn't matter whether it was the Ashfords or Maria or Ivy; no one in the drucraft world ever did anything for free. At least I wasn't broke anymore; as long as Father Hawke's prices weren't any worse than Maria's, I should be able to afford—

"Explain and answer the problem of pain."

I blinked. "What?"

Father Hawke took out a pen and a scrap of paper, wrote for a few seconds, then handed it to me. "This should give you somewhere to start."

"What's the problem of pain?"

"Read those books and find out."

I frowned. I couldn't really understand what Father Hawke was trying to do. Still, if all I had to do was answer a question . . .

"Can we do the sigl tomorrow, then?"

Father Hawke picked up his book and returned to his reading. "That depends upon your answer."

———

I DID SOME Internet searches, then came back next morning.

"Okay," I said. "So the problem of pain is asking how you can believe in God if there's pain in the world."

"And?"

I looked at Father Hawke in confusion.

"You haven't explained why this is a problem."

"I . . . don't understand."

"The use of the term 'problem,' in this context, implies a contradiction," Father Hawke explained. "The existence of pain and suffering may be *unpleasant*, but does not by itself contradict a belief in God."

"Okay."

"So what solution would you suggest?"

"There . . . isn't one?"

Father Hawke gave me an unimpressed look.

"Okay, there is one."

"Come back tomorrow," Father Hawke said. "And I suggest you actually do the reading this time."

THE NEXT DAY was Sunday. I waited for the service to finish, then entered to find Father Hawke talking to some members of the congregation. Once there was a gap in the conversation, I moved in.

"Okay," I told Father Hawke. "So the problem of pain is three things. Firstly, God is supposed to be completely good; secondly, God is supposed to be all-powerful; and thirdly, there's pain and suffering in the world. If God's good, then he shouldn't want people to suffer, and if he's all-powerful, then he should be able to stop it anytime he wanted. So there's your contradiction."

Father Hawke nodded. The two old Nigerian ladies he'd been

talking to were watching curiously. "And what is your answer?" Father Hawke asked.

"Well, if you've got a contradiction, then one of the things must be wrong," I said. "And there's obviously pain and suffering in the world. So either God isn't all-powerful, or he isn't all that good."

"Don't blaspheme, young man," one of the ladies said sternly.

"You said I had to come up with an answer," I pointed out to Father Hawke. "You didn't say it couldn't be a blasphemous one."

The old lady looked indignant, but Father Hawke raised his hand to forestall her. "True," he said. "If, for example, one believes that God is the source of all good, and that an equal and opposing supernatural power is the source of all evil, then the problem of pain disappears and is replaced with other theological problems instead. However, I asked you to answer the problem, not avoid it."

"It's still an answer."

"Yes. In the same way that a valid answer to your particular problem is 'stop using that sigl.'"

I threw up my hands, then turned and marched out. The two old ladies watched me go with satisfied expressions.

THE NEXT DAY arrived.

"All right," I said. Father Hawke and I were alone in the church again. "So if you have a contradiction, you can resolve it in two ways. Either one of the things that contradict each other must be wrong, or they're not actually a contradiction at all. Right?"

Father Hawke nodded. "Continue."

"So according to Christian theology, God's not just omnipotent, he also knows everything. Right?"

"The term is 'omniscient.' Continue."

"So since God is omniscient, that means he knows the consequences of everything," I said. "And since he's good, that means that he'd only let them happen if the consequences were good ones." I folded my arms. "So all three parts of the problem are true. There's no contradiction."

"What about events that would seem to be purely evil, with no good consequences at all?"

"Well, humans aren't omniscient, and God is, right? So we just say that if anything is happening, then God must want it to happen, which means it must be for the best."

"All according to God's plan?" Father Hawke asked. "Is that what you believe?"

It wasn't, but it was the best argument I'd been able to come up with. "It's a valid answer."

Father Hawke nodded. "If your cat had died last month, and someone had told you that it was all part of God's plan, how would you have responded?"

I felt as if I'd been slapped. "That's not fair!"

"As questions go, I'd say it's extremely fair."

I hesitated, torn between the convenient answer and the truth. "I'd probably have punched them," I admitted.

"Then I would say that your argument needs work."

"Why are you making this so difficult?" I said in frustration. "Whose side are you even on?"

"Come back tomorrow," Father Hawke said. "And I suggest you read those books a little more thoroughly."

NEXT DAY.

". . . so the reason that it isn't a contradiction is the existence of free will," I was saying. "You can have people who are free to act according to their own choices, and you can have people who never do anything evil, but you can't have both."

"But you've already conceded that God is omnipotent," Father Hawke said. "If so, surely he can do both those things."

"No, because that's mixing up two different meanings of 'omnipotent,'" I said. "There are things that we can't do because we're not powerful enough, like 'lift up this building,' and there are things that we can't do because they're self-contradictory, like 'draw a square circle.' Something that doesn't make sense doesn't make any *more* sense if you put 'God can' at the beginning of it."

"However, God could still counteract the effects of evil choices," Father Hawke pointed out. "This would allow for free will while still preventing suffering."

"Yes, but the only way he could keep on doing that would be by preventing almost everything. Because every time someone took an action that led to some consequence, there'd be some other action they could have taken instead that would have led to a *better* consequence. So every single thing that anyone ever did would end up getting overridden, and you wouldn't have any freedom at all."

"Would it not be possible for God to simply arrange the world such that everyone was equally happy and provided for?"

"No, because once you've got a fixed world, then there's no way it can ever suit everyone equally," I said. "If something's lying on the ground exactly where I want it, then it can't be lying on the ground exactly where you want it. The world we act in has to be permanent, or none of our choices matter, but if we're free to choose in a permanent world, then we can use those choices and the things in that world to hurt each other. Which is why when there's a fight, it's the stronger guy who wins, not the one who's more virtuous."

"You lifted that from C. S. Lewis," Father Hawke said.

"You were the one who put that book on my reading list," I told him. "If you didn't want me to use it . . ."

Father Hawke smiled slightly. "Take out your sigl."

Finally, I thought. I'd been carrying that Life sigl to and from this church for four days straight. I took it out of my pocket and held it out to Father Hawke. "So whenever I try to activate it—" I began.

"Your sigl is missing a regulator," Father Hawke stated.

I paused. "A what?"

"A constituent part of a sigl designed to spread its essentia flow evenly across the body," Father Hawke explained. "Mending sigls don't use them, because the whole point of a healing effect is that you want its effect to be concentrated at the location of the injury. An enhancement sigl, by contrast, needs to affect all parts of the body equally. Otherwise the sigl expends all of its energy on the closest parts of the body, or those that the essentia happens to flow to first, with the result that nearer and smaller muscles will be boosted in an uneven way. Which means that as soon as you attempt any sudden movements, you'll tear your own muscles in a dozen places at once. Quite painful, as I expect you've learned."

I stared at Father Hawke for a few seconds. "Did you know what was wrong from the start?"

"I suspected."

"You could have told me this in two minutes, and instead you had me doing theology problems for *four days*?"

"If you'd applied yourself properly, it would have taken you a day and a half at most," Father Hawke said. "Hopefully you'll perform better next time."

"Next time?"

"I'd been under the impression that you would continue to develop your drucraft," Father Hawke said. "The choice of whether to do so, of course, is yours."

I stared at Father Hawke for a minute, then turned and marched out. I didn't quite slam the door, but I came close.

As I left the church, I privately resolved that there wouldn't be a next time. I wasn't going back to Father Hawke for help. Or if I did, it'd only be after I'd tried my absolute best to fix the problem on my own.

Come to think of it, maybe that was exactly what Father Hawke had wanted.

It wasn't until much later, after I'd had dinner and was about to go to bed, that it occurred to me to wonder why Father Hawke was going to all this trouble to teach me in the first place. But no particular answer came to mind, and in the end I decided I had bigger problems to worry about.

CHAPTER 14

I woke up the next morning to some good news. While Father Hawke had been keeping me busy, Linford's had activated my account. I could finally register Wells.

I'd found a weak Matter Well a couple of days ago, and I decided to try out my new status straightaway. I headed to the Well to check that it was still there, then called it in. There was no immediate response, and after hanging around the Well for an hour, I gave up and went home.

But the next morning I got an email saying that the Well had been verified. Even more surprisingly, I got a message only a few hours later telling me that payment had been made. I checked my bank account and, sure enough, there was a payment of £220 from Linford's. I had a source of income again.

Two hundred and twenty pounds wasn't much—it wouldn't even pay my rent for two weeks—but if you've never had to live with the pressure that comes with running out of money, it's hard to explain just how big a relief it is to feel as though you're pulling away from it. I'd spent most of the past year watching my balance hover around the mid-hundreds, knowing that it would only take one or two things going wrong to put me in the red. A sudden accident or a missed payslip, and all of a sudden you can't pay a bill. Missing a bill means you get hit with penalty fees, which makes it harder to pay the next bill, which means even more punishment fees, which make it harder to pay the next bill, and so on. I'd survived this long by being obsessively careful to never let my bank account dip below zero, but the price for that had been constant low-level stress. No matter what I was doing or thinking, a part of my mind would always be worrying about money. That worry wasn't gone, but now that I had both a source of income and a few months' savings, I had more safety margin than I'd had in years. All of a sudden, I could take some of the mental resources I'd been spending on worrying about money, and use them for . . . well, anything else. It was like carrying a bunch of heavy rocks everywhere you went, and finally getting to dump some of them out.

With my newly available time and attention, I set to work on my next project: learning how to make a continuous sigl.

BY THIS POINT I'd read the Exchange catalogue cover to cover multiple times, and one of the things I'd learned was that sigls were divided into two basic categories. First were triggered sigls, like the light sigl I'd started with. "Triggered" was a reference to how they were activated—you sent a flow of essentia through them, and they did whatever they were supposed to. No matter how basic or complex the design, all triggered sigls required you to be a channeller to make them work. Without the ability to sense your own personal essentia and channel it, a triggered sigl was just a shiny rock.

Continuous sigls were different. They worked without any

need for channelling or activation, so long as they were close enough to their bearer. You didn't need to be a drucrafter or know anything or even *do* anything: you just had to pick the thing up, and as long as you kept it next to your skin, it would work.

For me, the big advantage of continuous sigls would be that they didn't require concentration. Channelling essentia was easy, but doing something else at the same time was hard. Channelling essentia into one sigl, while activating a second sigl, while *also* doing something physically demanding—defending myself in a fight, say—well, that was past "hard" and into "nearly impossible."

My experience with the Mark 1 enhancement sigl had also shown me the problems with triggered sigls. The pain from the torn muscles had broken my concentration and stopped me channelling. Which had worked in my favour that time, but if that had been a *real* enhancement sigl, having it cut out when I got hurt seemed like a recipe for disaster. If I wanted something that would keep working even if I got stunned or injured, I needed to learn to make continuous sigls. Fortunately, I had an idea about where to find one.

Maria had told me about finder's stones—continuous Light sigls that lit up in the presence of Wells. Linford's sold them to its Well locators, meaning that if I could find a locator, I should be able to get a look at one. According to the Linford's website, the company had an address in Aldgate. That seemed like a good place to start.

One bus ride later, I was loitering outside my employer's Aldgate office. I'd briefly considered just going in and asking for what I wanted, but the more I thought about it, the more I decided that *Hey, can I reverse engineer your stuff?* probably wasn't going to go down well. Instead I blended with the afternoon crowds and watched for people coming in or out who looked like locators.

After I'd been there for an hour, I spotted a pair of likely prospects: two men with Eastern European looks, dressed in run-down clothing. They disappeared into the office building, stayed for half an hour, then walked out and away down the main road.

I intercepted them a hundred feet from the office. "Hi," I said, trying my best to look friendly. "Can I ask you something?"

The two men frowned at me suspiciously.

"Are you locators?" I asked.

"Who are you?"

"I work for—" I began.

The two men walked off down the street.

"Hey!" I called, then hurried after them and started trying to talk them into helping me.

It was a struggle. The two men—Romanians, as it turned out—did *not* want to talk to some strange kid who was making weird requests. In the end I remembered what had worked with Maria and just bribed them—I told them I'd pay for their drinks for as long as they'd talk to me.

Once the two men were sitting in an Aldgate pub with pints of beer in front of them, their moods improved. But they still wouldn't show me their sigls without a good explanation, which I had trouble providing due to the language barrier. In the end a translation app let me explain that I was a Linford's locator as well. Once I'd proved to their satisfaction that I was employed by the same people that they were, they finally loosened up enough to show me what I needed.

That is really weird, I thought as I stared at the finder's stone. It was a small blue-white sphere that looked almost identical to my light sigls, set into an adjustable band that went around the man's finger. A small thread of essentia was flowing from the man's hand into the sigl, and the sigl was pulling in essentia from the surrounding air, though it wasn't lighting up . . . presumably because there wasn't enough to power it. The interesting thing was how it had happened. When the Romanian man had put the sigl on, nothing had changed at first, then essentia had started to flow into it in a tiny thread that had gradually grown stronger and stronger until it reached its maximum.

"You aren't doing anything?" I asked the man. I had to raise my voice for him to hear: the pub was cramped and noisy.

"Is fine," the Romanian man said in his thick accent. His name was Pavel, and he seemed the more willing to talk; the other was called Anton and was watching me suspiciously.

"But you're not channelling?"

I got a pair of uncomprehending looks. Yeah, that was way too technical a word. Maybe if I focused on exactly how the essentia was moving—

"Hey," Anton said. He lifted his empty glass and gestured at me.

I went to the bar, got two more beers, and went back to studying Pavel's sigl.

Pavel and Anton exchanged a few remarks in Romanian, then Pavel spoke to me. "Why you to do this work?"

"What, finding Wells?" I said absently.

"Yes. Locator."

"It's better than my last job," I told them. There was something about the sigl that seemed to make essentia trickle through it naturally, like water flowing downhill.

Pavel snorted with laughter, then said something to Anton, who laughed too. "Shit," Anton told me.

"What?"

"He says, is shit job," Pavel explained.

That made me look up. Those were exactly the words Felix had used. "What's wrong with it?"

That opened the floodgates. Anton began to talk fast in Romanian, with Pavel translating and adding thoughts of his own.

Apparently Anton and Pavel had grown up in rural Romania, near a city called Oradea. They'd been vaguely aware of the drucraft world, but there weren't any jobs, and a recruiter had told them he could get them places in London where they could work as locators for good money. When they'd got to England, though, they'd found out that the actual job the recruiter had signed them up for was at an Amazon warehouse near Bletchley. They'd skipped out and travelled to London, where they'd managed to find work with Linford's, only to discover that hadn't lived up to the promises, either. Both Anton and Pavel would spend days on end walking around London without more than a flicker from their finder's stones, returning home after dark with nothing but aching feet. And most of the time, when they did find a Well, it would turn out to be claimed already.

Even finding an unclaimed Well didn't guarantee that they'd get paid, and that was when Anton got really bitter. He claimed he'd found a Well that should have been worth thousands, called it in to Linford's, and been told that they'd check it out. He'd waited for hours, finally going home in the early hours of the morning. The next day Linford's had told him that the Well had been empty.

"Thieves," Anton said vehemently. "All thieves!"

I remembered what Maria had said about answering Well claims and finding them empty. *"They're always hoping we'll pay them anyway. We don't, of course."* At the time I hadn't given it a second thought.

At this point Pavel's drink ran out, and I had to go to the bar for more beers. By the time I got back, Anton had calmed down a bit. "If Linford's is so bad, why do you keep working for them?" I asked as I set the glasses down on the table.

"Rest are just as bad," Pavel said with a shrug.

I went back to studying the sigl. I was starting to see how it worked: it was shaped so as to create a sort of vacuum that pulled on the surrounding area. Then once a few threads of Pavel's personal essentia happened to flow in, it caused a feedback loop where the sigl pulled in more and more until it hit its maximum. That was why it had taken a few minutes to warm up. Although, if you could channel, you could just jump-start it . . .

"Why you do locator?" Anton asked me.

"You mean in general?"

Anton fired off a few sentences in Romanian at Pavel, who translated. "You don't have locator's face."

I hesitated. It would be easy to pretend I didn't understand, but the truth was, I kind of did. The people who work menial jobs in London have a specific look. No one talks about it, but everyone recognises it. It was how I'd been able to pick out Pavel and Anton.

It was just as well that Pavel and Anton weren't English, or they'd have noticed my accent the second I'd opened my mouth, and then they probably wouldn't have been willing to speak to me at all. My dad's accent is standard working class, but as I was growing up he always pushed me to speak with a more middle-class one. I didn't understand why at the time, but looking back on it, maybe he was trying to prepare me for the Ashfords. I ended up with this hybrid accent that isn't exactly one thing or the other. It's not upper class, but I still got a lot of crap at school for being "posh." There was a reason I took up boxing.

"Is shit," Anton told me again. "Get better job."

"It's not that bad," I protested. "And you can work your way up."

Pavel burst out laughing. He translated what I'd said to Anton, and Anton laughed too.

I looked between them. "What?"

"They tell you, you do well, you get promotion?" Pavel told me.

"Well . . . yes."

"All lies," Pavel said. "They say that to everyone. They say, you find enough Wells, then in six months, you get proper job. Regular hours, time off. So you work hard, do as they say, then in six months they say, oh, sorry, nothing they can do."

"But you can still make money," I said.

Pavel snorted and held up his finder's stone. "You know how long these last?"

"Uh," I said, looking at the sigl in puzzlement. "Pretty much forever?"

Pavel and Anton burst out laughing again.

I looked between the two men. "What is it?"

Pavel grinned at me. "Two years."

"What?"

"Maybe less," Pavel added.

"I don't get it," I said. "What happens after a couple of years?"

"You go to them and buy new one."

I tried to find out from Pavel why his finder's stone would break, but he didn't really know. All he knew was that after maybe eighteen months or so, the finder's stones you got from Linford's would stop working. Linford's would buy them back, but not for much.

We talked for another hour (and for three more rounds of drinks), but I didn't learn much else. Pavel and Anton mostly wanted to complain about Linford's, though when I asked, they said that they'd heard bad things about all the other drucraft corporations as well. Mostly they emphasised how insecure the job was. A few locators did strike it rich, but for most it was all they could do to eke out a living. Pavel and Anton had survived this long by working together with some other Romanians from their region—everyone chipped in and supported each other. Solo locators didn't have that safety net, and as a result they usually didn't last long. Sooner or later something would go wrong, and they'd disappear.

Pavel had some parting words as we said our goodbyes. "You should get out," he told me. "Being locator is tough, tough, tough. You're young, you're English. Find something better."

I HAD A lot to think about on the way home.

I'd got what I came for. I was pretty sure I understood how that sigl of Pavel's worked—the key was to create an essentia vacuum in its core, and once that was set up, it should be self-sustaining. I'd have to experiment, but I thought I could see how to make it work.

But mostly what I was thinking about on the bus ride back wasn't about sigls; it was about Pavel and Anton. They'd both taken for granted that finding Wells was a terrible job, and now that I'd actually had a chance to study those sigls of theirs, I could see why. Those finder's stones that Linford's sold them were streamlined, but to my eyes they looked cheaply produced and crude as hell. They'd pick up a Well, but you'd have to get *really* close, maybe twenty feet or so. I could spot even the weakest of Wells from three times that range. Three times the range meant a circle with *nine* times the area, which meant I could cover as much ground in an hour as Pavel or Anton could with a full day's work.

And then on top of that, I had my essentia sight. Which not only let me find Wells more easily, but also meant that once I *did* find a Well, I could make use of it in a way that other people couldn't. Maria had made it sound as though being a manifester wasn't particularly useful, and now that I saw the kinds of tools that most locators were working with, I could see why. If I had to find Wells the way that Pavel and Anton did, it'd take me so long that by the time I finally found one, I'd probably have to sell it just to keep my head above water.

The only kind of people who *would* get a lot of use out of being a manifester would be the ones who were rich enough and connected enough that they had access to as many Wells as they wanted. People like the Ashfords. Which would explain why they could afford to put so much value on drucraft skill.

I finally understood why Lucella had turned on me the way she had. Not that it did me much good.

Except . . . no, that wasn't true. I'd learned something important. This ability of mine was more than a way to make money—it gave me the potential to grow stronger than anyone would expect, maybe even stronger than the Ashfords. But to do that, I needed time: time to develop my shaping skills, and time to build up an armoury of sigls that would let me face them on even terms.

But how long did I have?

WHEN I GOT home, I went online to research what Pavel had said about sigl life spans. It was puzzling because I was sure I remembered my dad saying something about sigls being passed down by parents to their children, which didn't make any sense if the things only lasted a couple of years. My first few searches got me nothing useful, but I persisted.

In the end, it was a throwaway phrase from the catalogue that put me on the right track. It turned out that there were two ways of making a sigl. The old-fashioned way, the one I'd been using, was to make "solid" sigls, and those could last practically forever. But most sigls sold nowadays were "threaded," with parts of the sigl's interior replaced with empty space. Threaded sigls used less essentia than solid sigls, but the price for that was a shorter life span. A *much* shorter life span. The companies that sold threaded sigls were vague on exactly how short, but I could make a guess by looking at the warranties for the sigls that Linford's sold. They were for one to three years.

Oh, and it turned out Pavel had been telling the truth about promotions as well. I'd found an anonymous forum for locators called the Back Alley, and it turned out they had an entire thread on the subject. The complaints ran to pages, but the general conclusion was: don't hold your breath. Drucraft corporations filled their higher ranks by recruiting graduates from prestigious universities, not by promoting workers on zero-hours contracts.

Putting it all together, the whole thing made me see that interview I'd had with Maria in a very different light. If I'd followed her advice and got a finder's stone, I'd have ended up paying thousands for some piece of junk that would have lasted barely long enough to get out of warranty before breaking and forcing me to go back and buy a new one. And given that those finder's stones were pretty terrible at finding Wells in the first place, the cost of that sigl could easily have ended up being most of my take-home pay.

It also put a different spin on Maria's eagerness to sell me on the job. Back when Kiran had been working as a taxi driver for a ride-hailing company, one of the things he'd mentioned was that the company was always trying to push as many drivers onto the streets as they could. The company wanted a fleet of cars circling 24/7 so that as soon as a customer pinged the app, one would roll up in seconds. But for that to work, there had to be more drivers than customers. And drivers didn't get paid for the time they spent waiting.

It seemed to me as though the locating business worked the

same way. Linford's wanted to have a swarm of locators combing the streets so that new Wells were snapped up as soon as they appeared. But there was no risk to Linford's if they hired too many. They were the ones selling the finder's stones, after all—they were turning a profit either way.

In fact, the more I thought about it, the more it felt as though *all* the risks of the locating job fell on the locators. If you ran into a gang of raiders who put you in hospital, you didn't get compensation or sick pay. If you searched for days or weeks and never found a Well, then that wasn't Linford's problem. They only had to pay for results.

And that was assuming Linford's played by their own rules. Well registration was done in the corporation's name, not your own. If someone like Pavel or Anton *did* hit the jackpot and find a Well worth £50,000 or £100,000, what was to stop Linford's from coming up with some excuse not to pay them? They had lawyers and accountants; locators didn't. And funnily enough, when I looked on the Back Alley, there were stories about exactly that.

I came across other stories in the course of my research too. It seemed that drucraft corporations did a lot more than just sell sigls. They were involved with governments and politics, and had research projects and agendas of their own, and some of the rumours were pretty disturbing. Military corporations apparently had a history of Well raiding, using black-ops teams equipped with their own combat sigls to steal essentia from Wells owned by Houses or other corps. Medical corps had a reputation for developing their sigls using human experimentation. Some of it was legal, with controlled trials, but there were persistent rumours that the more high-risk tests were done on destitute people in secret facilities in Eastern Europe or Africa.

The more I learned, the more cautious I became about the

company I was working for. I knew I was going to keep working as a locator—I needed the money, and I didn't have any better options. But I was very glad I hadn't told Maria about my essentia sight.

The whole experience had one final effect: it changed how I saw Wells. Before, if a Well flashed purple on the registry app, I'd seen it as someone else's property. But the more that I learned about the drucraft world, the more it seemed as though the way the big corporations and Houses got their property was by taking it by bribery or by force.

Bribery and force weren't options for me. But in the course of my searching I was finding a steady trickle of claimed Wells. And some of those Wells, particularly the weaker ones, didn't seem to have much security. In fact, in the case of the D-class Wells, "security" was often nothing more than a chain-link fence.

I didn't start raiding them. Yet. But from that point on, every time I found a Well that was claimed, I'd make a mental note of its location and quietly weigh up exactly how hard it would be to take it for myself.

CHAPTER 15

I SAT ON my bed cross-legged, looking down at my laptop, and at the small box next to it. On the laptop screen was an email from the detective agency; in the box was an enhancement sigl. Both were from this morning. Funny how you can work for weeks with nothing to show for it, then two things come along at once.

The little glinting fragment of green in the box was my third try at an enhancement sigl. My first attempt, the one I now thought of as the Mark 1, had nearly put me in hospital. My *second* attempt was currently sitting in the box behind my skirting board, along with the rest of my cast-offs. Apparently I hadn't understood continuous sigls as well as I'd thought, and I'd managed to shape it in such a way that *neither* channelling *nor* wearing it next to your skin would trigger the essentia flow, meaning that there was no way to activate it at all, which made it completely useless. Another Well's worth of essentia wasted . . . but I did eventually figure out what I'd done wrong and incorporated those lessons into the Mark 3.

And the Mark 3 worked perfectly. It was a functioning continuous sigl, with a working regulator. When I slipped the cord over my neck to let it rest against the bare skin of my chest, it would gradually start to pull in essentia, starting with only a thread but drawing in more and more until a steady stream was flowing into that tiny green gem. From there, Life essentia flowed back out, charging my muscles with power. No more regulation problems: the effect was perfectly even, making every muscle in my body proportionately stronger.

Specifically, it made them about 15 percent stronger. I'd tried lifting weights, and then doing pull-ups, first with the sigl, then without. Whichever muscle group I tested, the number came out around the same. It had disappointed me a little at first—I'd had fantasies of being able to pick up people one-handed and throw them across the room like a superhero—but, then, this was from less than a month's work.

It would have been nice if I could just keep on making more and more enhancement sigls and stack them one on top of the other until I was invincible, but I could already see that it wasn't going to work that way. Life sigls seemed much more essentia hungry than Light ones, and this one swallowed up between a third and a half of my essentia capacity all on its own. At this rate, it wouldn't be long before I'd have to work out some sort of budget.

But although the enhancement sigl was a big deal, it was the email that my eyes kept coming back to.

I reached for my laptop and double-clicked the file attached to the email, reading through it for the fourth time. The detective agency hadn't been able to trace the men who'd followed me, but they *had* been able to trace the car. It had been leased by a company that was owned by another company, which after some twists and turns led to a third company calling itself Sardanapalus

Holdings. The company's owners were anonymous, but its correspondence addresses weren't. The report finished by informing me that my retainer had run out and asking whether I'd like to pay for further investigation.

I took another look at the addresses. There was an office in Southwark, an address in Ealing, and an address in Hampstead. It wasn't much, but it was a start.

My eyes fell on my enhancement sigl. I picked up the box and held it up to the light, watching the sigl sparkle. I had somewhere to look, and a new sigl to field-test.

Okay, let's see how this goes.

IT WAS LATER that night.

I was standing halfway down Keats Grove, a cramped little street in the middle of Hampstead with pavements so narrow that for two people to pass each other, one would have to step into the road. Trees and thick hedges concealed the houses behind. On the far corner was a wine bar advertising dishes with names like "Exmoor Caviar" and "Wagyu Beef Platter"; beyond, the muted buzz of the Hampstead nightlife echoed up into the sky. The air was cool, the chill of the spring still reluctant to give way to the coming summer.

The first two addresses on my list had been dead ends. The office in Southwark hadn't been there at all; the number plate for the floor had been blank, and the rooms themselves boarded up and empty. The address in Ealing *had* been there, but as far as I could see it was nothing but a postbox, with a pile of mail that hadn't been touched in weeks.

But there was a reason I'd saved this place for last. The other two addresses had been publicly available, but this one hadn't been—the agency had only found it because it had been used recently for billing. And now that I was here, it was obviously occupied.

I loitered behind a car on the far side of the street, studying the house. It was three storeys tall, red and orange and white with a black front door, most of the building hidden behind tall shrubs and a pair of birch trees. Bigger than average for a Hampstead house, but not so much as to draw attention. It didn't look the least bit unusual.

At least, not on the surface. The flows of essentia around the house were . . . strange. They weren't strong enough to indicate the presence of a Well, but they were *odd*, with a colour and resonance that I'd never felt before. They gave me a sense of . . . what?

Air. Darkness. Night.

I shook it away. Right now I had more practical matters to worry about, such as the fact that I could make out one light on the ground floor, and another behind the curtains of a first-floor window. I settled down to wait.

A couple of hours passed. I did a circuit of the surrounding blocks, getting a feel of the neighbourhood. It was pretty, but too rich for me to feel comfortable. No Wells. Usually areas with a lot of greenery are decent hunting grounds, but this spot felt dead.

Midnight approached. I checked the house again. The same two lights were on.

Maybe no one was home.

Screw it. The fence at the front of the house was black, with iron spike railings. I took a quick glance up and down the empty street, vaulted the fence at its lowest point, then walked past the flowering shrubs and the expensive car in the driveway to find a tall wooden gate blocking the way into the back garden. I could feel the enhancement sigl beneath my shirt, sending strength and power flowing into my muscles and filling me with confidence. I jumped up to catch the top of the gate in both hands, then slithered up and over to drop with a rustle of movement into the house's back garden.

The garden was dark and still. The sounds of bustle and chatter drifted over the rooftops, but the house itself was silent.

I picked my way around the side of the building, placing my feet carefully, until I could see through French windows into what looked like a kitchen and dining room. The room was unlit, but the orange glow of the London sky was just barely bright enough to pick out the shapes of a table and counter. On the table was a pale fuzzy patch that looked like papers.

I hesitated, looking at the French windows. Their white plastic handles glinted invitingly.

I cleared my mind, opening my senses wide.

The feel of that strange essentia flooded in, stronger this time. Colours in the dark, a kaleidoscope of black. Stars, cold and hungry in the void. And something more, unfolding to blot out the sky, a feather-light brush that tore the earth, the thunder of wings—

With a wrench I tore myself away. A wave of dizziness washed over me and I staggered, nearly falling before catching myself and taking deep breaths. The night suddenly felt very bright and very loud. I heard a rustle in the trees and snapped my eyes up, searching blindly, but saw nothing.

The garden felt awake all of a sudden, the air hushed and still. I looked at the French windows, and at the papers on the table inside. A few steps would bring me within reach of the door, but all my instincts were sounding a warning.

I hesitated, taking one last lingering look at those papers. It would only take me a few seconds to try the handle, maybe grab something from the table, but . . . *no*. I didn't know what was going on, but I knew I wasn't safe here. I took a step towards the gate.

The attack came from above.

Movement whispered; I glanced up, saw an open window and a falling shadow, threw myself sideways. There was the thump of shoes on grass, then essentia flared in the darkness and the shadow was on me. I dodged the first attack, jumped away from the second, backpedalling towards the gate. The shape pursued; for an instant I saw an upper body silhouetted against the street-lights, and I raised my left hand, triggering my slam sigl to send a concussion blast into the guy's head.

He shrugged it off like a flea bite and hit me with enough power to send me flying.

I crashed into the gate with a thump, pain flaring in my back and chest as I tumbled to the ground. I gasped for breath, trying to get to my feet, but before I could make it, a hand yanked me up, slamming me into the wall. "Who sent you?" the figure demanded.

It was a boy's voice, a little deeper than mine. In the shadows of the garden I couldn't make out his face. I drew on the full strength of my sigl and yanked sideways.

Essentia surged, green against black. The boy held on, matching my strength and more, then hit me across the face and slammed me against the wall again. "Who sent you?" he repeated.

Panic flashed through me. The other boy had a strength sigl too, one that was a lot more powerful than mine; spikes of pain shot through my chest as his fingers dug into my flesh. I struggled, trying to break his grip, but it was like trying to bend iron with my bare hands.

"What was that piece of crap you hit me with?" the boy asked. He grabbed my left arm with his free hand, squeezing my wrist like a vice, then held my hand up to study my sigl rings.

I twisted the finger that held my flash sigl and sent a blaze of light into the boy's face.

He yelled and shoved me away, and all of a sudden I was free. Ignoring the pain in my arms and chest, I turned and leapt, fear and my strength sigl sending me soaring over the gate and back into the front yard. I caught a glimpse of the boy bent over, clutching his eyes, then I was tearing across the driveway, over the fence and out down the street.

The thump of feet behind me made my heart jump. I took a glance back and saw a figure sprinting after me, essentia wreathing his long legs as he powered down the pavement. He looked half-dazzled, but he was coming right at me.

I reached the wine bar at the end of the road and darted right, catching a glimpse of my pursuer as he turned and realising with a thrill of fear that the other boy was gaining. I sprinted down the slope of South End Road, knowing that I had a minute before he caught me, maybe less. Off to the left was the darkness of the Heath; to the right were cafés and restaurants. Figures flashed by on the pavement. Up ahead, across a junction, were the orange and white lights of Hampstead Heath Overground station.

I made a snap decision and cut across the road. A horn blared as I dodged around a car, between two lampposts, and into Hampstead Heath station. Once I was inside, I stopped and turned.

My pursuer came racing in only a couple of seconds behind me, skidding to a halt on the tiled floor. In the bright lights of the station entrance I finally got a proper look at him. He was a couple of years older than me and a few inches taller, pale and rail-thin with short black hair, and was dressed in light clothes that looked like the kind you'd wear to bed. A thin chain ran around his neck and disappeared beneath a white T-shirt, and I could see the green glow of Life essentia flowing from the chain's lowest point. But his most distinctive feature was his eyes, dark with the flat, opaque look that you see on street kids. Even if I hadn't just seen what he could do, I would have marked him as dangerous.

The boy looked me up and down. I returned his stare, then deliberately looked up and to the right. The boy followed my gaze to a CCTV camera mounted on the ceiling. Its unblinking black eye was trained on us both.

The boy looked around. The London Overground doesn't get as many passengers as the Tube, but a station like Hampstead Heath is never empty, even close to midnight. More than a dozen people were hanging around or passing through, some of them slowing to stare as they registered that something was going on.

Frustration flashed across the boy's features. I raised my eyebrows at him in a silent message. *How badly do you want to get me?*

The boy's gaze flickered from me to the passers-by to the camera. I could sense him weighing his options and stood very still, my muscles coiled and tense. Essentia pulsed from the sigl at the boy's chest, sullen and powerful.

Then the cheery jangle of a ringtone made me jump. Without taking his eyes from me, the boy dug into his tracksuit bottoms to pull out a big expensive-looking smartphone, then thumbed it and lifted it to his ear. "Yeah."

The faint mutter of a voice sounded from the phone's speaker.

"It's fine, go ahead," the boy said.

Maybe a dozen people had now stopped to watch, middle-aged men with shoulder bags and girls dressed for an evening out. A couple had taken out their phones. I didn't quite relax, but I felt my tension ease a little. I didn't think this guy would start anything in front of this many witnesses.

The boy was listening to some question from the phone. "No," he said, giving me a contemptuous look. "Just some raider kid with really shitty gear."

I felt insulted, but kept my mouth shut.

"We're in a crowd," the boy said in reply to something.

"Hey," some girl in her twenties who'd been watching us said. "What's going on?"

"Yeah, sure," the boy said into the phone, and hung up. He stuffed the phone back into his pocket and looked straight at me. "Come here again and I'll break your fucking arm."

The cold, uninterested look in his eyes sent a chill through me. "Hey, what are you—" the girl began, but the boy turned and left, disappearing out into the night.

A man in a Transport for London uniform bustled up, looking around suspiciously. "Oi," he told me. "What do you think you're doing?"

"You okay?" the girl asked.

I nodded and backed away through the ticket gates. Once I was down on the platform, I waited for a train, watching the stairs all the time to see if the boy would reappear. Only after a train pulled up, and after I'd stepped onto it and heard the doors hiss shut behind me, did I finally relax.

THE OVERGROUND TRAIN carried me home.

By the time I arrived, the adrenaline had worn off and I was stiff and aching. The house was dark; everyone else was asleep. I wanted a hot shower to soothe my bruises, but the heater wasn't working and I got a cold one instead. I crawled into bed cold and shivering.

I felt tired and despondent. For weeks I'd been looking forward to the point where I could finally start searching for my father. Now that I'd done it, it had been a total failure. I'd lost, badly, and the only reason I'd got away was because that boy had decided I wasn't important enough to keep chasing. I curled up under the blankets until I was warm enough to stop trembling, and finally drifted off into an uneasy sleep.

I had a nightmare that night. I dreamed that Diesel and Scar were coming after me again and that they'd forced their way into my room. I fought back, but my punches didn't do anything. They tried to grab me and so I jumped out of the window, but then once I was outside, I remembered I'd left Hobbes behind, and I ran back in. Then I met Lucella on the stairs, except she'd turned into Tobias, and from there everything became confused. Diesel kept on chasing me, but somewhere along the line I realised that I was dreaming and forced myself to wake up.

I opened my eyes to see the grey light of dawn. Hobbes shifted with a sleepy meow, and I leant against the wall and stroked him for a while, feeling the softness of his fur and watching the sky change gradually from pale grey to light blue.

I felt drained and sluggish. My mind kept on going back to what had happened last night. I finally had a lead on my father's disappearance—the fact that I'd been attacked like that proved it—but what use was it? I could keep investigating, but if I did, sooner or later I'd come up against that boy again. Or someone worse.

I tried to think of how I could beat someone like that with the resources I had right now. I came up with half a dozen plans, playing them out in my head one after another, and abandoned them all. None felt likely to succeed.

I wasn't getting stronger fast enough. That was the problem. It was May 25, meaning that it had been nearly two months since I'd met that girl on the bridge. And in pretty much every way, my life was much better—I had a small but steady income from locating Wells, I had a bit of money in the bank, and I'd made more sigls in the past two months than in the previous two years. But I also had more enemies, and the events of last night had just given me a painful reminder that at any time, any one of them could just kick down my door and force me into a fight that I couldn't win. The harsh truth was that right now, if the Ashfords or that boy from last night came after me, my only real chance would be to run. And I might not even be able to manage that.

It's not fun feeling helpless. I tried to work on my ideas for new sigls, but each time I started to get into one I'd find myself wondering whether it would really help, and that would distract me again.

By the evening I was restless and frustrated. As the sun started to dip towards the horizon, I decided I'd go and meet my friends at the Admiral Nelson. It had been a wasted day.

"HEY, WHAT HAPPENED to your face?" Gabriel asked as I sat down at our usual table.

"Leg-breakers finally got him," Felix suggested.

"For the last bloody time, I'm not being chased by debt collectors," I told them wearily. "I stopped drinking last month because I got sacked."

"My dad started drinking *more* when he got sacked," Gabriel said.

"Don't give him ideas," Colin told him.

The pub chatter formed a hum in the background as Kiran and Gabriel kept pestering me with questions. I answered vaguely, not going into details. That talk I'd had with Felix had made me wary of talking too much about my new job, and so without exactly lying I managed to give them the impression that I was doing some sort of gig work where I was paid on commission (which was true) and that I'd got into a spat with a customer (which wasn't). After the usual jokes about me joining an underground boxing ring, Kiran and Gabriel lost interest. Colin, though, was watching me sharply.

The conversation moved on. Felix was having trouble with his current girlfriend, and Gabriel was bringing it up every chance he got—he was obviously loving the shoe being on the other foot for once. Kiran had got his first car and wouldn't stop talking about it. Colin's third-year exams were coming up.

The next time Felix went to the bar and everyone had to shift seats, Colin moved next to me. "You going to tell me what's really going on?" he asked quietly.

"What do you mean?"

Colin reached up and poked me on the side of my face where the boy had hit me last night. I flinched as pain stabbed from the bruise, then looked quickly to see if anyone had noticed. On the other side of the table, Felix and Gabriel were deep in an argument, while Kiran was typing into his phone.

"Feels like every time I see you lately, you've had the crap beaten out of you," Colin said while I recovered. "It's not about money, is it? If it was, you'd be doing that thing where every time you go to the bar, you dig around in your wallet like a nervous squirrel."

"I do *not* look like a nervous squirrel."

"When you're skint you do. So?"

I sighed. "It's not about money," I admitted.

"So what is it?"

"I think . . ." I said. "I think pretty soon, I'm going to have to go up against some people. And right now, I'm not strong enough to manage it."

"Some people? Like who?"

"Like the guy from last night," I said. "Or the ones who beat me up the first time. Lucella and those bruisers."

"Wait, that girl from a couple of months ago? What did you *do* to piss her off this much?"

"What do you mean, what did I do?"

"I just figured you were really bad in bed or something."

"Oh, for—no! Look, I'll explain it properly. And pay attention this time."

"ALL RIGHT," COLIN said once I was done. On the other side of the table, Felix and Kiran and Gabriel were deep in conversation and seemed to have forgotten about us. "So you have these rich relatives who don't like you. Then when you went around asking questions about your dad, you ran into *another* guy who didn't like you."

"Yeah."

"Not to point out the obvious," Colin said, "but have you considered just staying *away* from all these people? I mean, I still think this drucraft job of yours sounds dodgy as hell, but it seems to be working out for you. Why not just stick with that?"

"I don't think I can stay away forever," I told him.

"All right, so what's the problem? You don't think you can take on these guys?"

"Pretty much."

"Well . . . then maybe you shouldn't be trying?"

I frowned. "What do you mean?"

"Look, back when you were boxing, you were featherweight or something, right?"

"Lightweight," I said. "That's one hundred thirty-two pounds and under. Featherweight is one hundred twenty-five and a half. Also, I couldn't qualify for featherweight anymore, because that's only for juniors—"

"Okay, okay, I don't actually care," Colin said, waving his hand. "And it's supposed to be really hard to beat someone from a higher weight class, right?"

"Right. That's why they have them."

"And those two bodybuilder guys who broke into your room, they'd be what class?"

"Off the top of the scale. Superheavyweight."

"So doesn't that mean you're never going to beat them?"

I was silent.

"Well?" Colin asked.

"I suppose," I said, suddenly depressed. When Colin put it like that, it really did sound impossible. And I wasn't even telling him the worst part. These people weren't just bigger and stronger and richer than I was; they had more powerful sigls too.

"You don't need to look so down," Colin said when I stayed silent.

"What am I supposed to do, then?" I asked. "Give up?" I'd been working nonstop to get this far, and right now it felt as though I was no closer to my goal than when I'd started.

"No, just maybe come up with a new angle or something?" Colin asked. "I mean, you keep talking about being strong enough, but just because you have to deal with these guys doesn't mean you have to take them on in a boxing ring."

I thought about that for a second.

"Also, you could try telling me the truth about what you've been up to," Colin added.

"I *am* telling the truth."

"Dude, you can't lie for shit," Colin told me. "Okay, maybe you're not *technically* lying, but these stories you've been telling lately have holes big enough to drive a lorry through."

I looked away, embarrassed. There was a pause.

"Okay, look, don't stress about it," Colin said at last. "Just promise me that next time you need help, you'll tell me the real story, okay?"

I hesitated a second. "Okay."

———

I THOUGHT ABOUT Colin's words on the walk home. Now that he'd pointed it out, it was obvious. I wasn't going to win this with brute strength.

Back when I'd first taken up boxing, brute strength had worked pretty well. The bullies at school hadn't really cared about me; I'd just been an easy target because of my looks and accent. Once I'd proved that I was willing to fight, they'd backed off, and I'd even ended up making friends with a couple of them afterwards, which I'd found pretty funny.

But things weren't funny now. Last night had been a wake-up call. I'd been treating my drucraft as something that I could take my time over, and that wasn't going to work anymore. If I was going to keep chasing after my father or drawing the attention of people from House Ashford, then things like this—finding my-self alone on a dark night facing some big nasty guy with a strength sigl who wanted to do bad things to me—were going to keep happening. In fact, I had the unpleasant feeling that they might end up becoming the new normal.

The next time this happened, I needed an answer, and it had to be a good one. "Beat the guy in a straight fight" wasn't good enough. In fact, *any* answer that involved treating this like some sort of sports match wasn't good enough.

So what was?

THE NEXT MORNING found me sitting on my bed, looking down at three sigls laid out in a row. The Mark 1, Mark 2, and Mark 3 enhancement sigls glinted in the morning light. To my eyes, an essentia construct hovered in the air just above them.

The "supercharge" idea, I decided, wasn't going to work. My

initial plan had been to take the Mark 3 and modify it so that it could channel all its power into only the muscles I was using at one specific moment. The idea had been to multiply the sigl's power five or ten times over. Now that I'd had the chance to study it in more detail, I was pretty sure that all that would accomplish would be to cripple me in the same way that the Mark 1 had, except that the injuries would be five or ten times worse.

The problem was the regulator. *With* the regulator, the power from the sigl was spread throughout the body, causing most of it to be effectively wasted. But *without* the regulator, my body's balance got destroyed, and my muscles would tear themselves apart.

I sighed, then picked up the Mark 3, rolling it between my thumb and forefinger. Maybe there was some way to have the regulator work only part of the time? If I designed the sigl so that the regulator could be partially disabled, so that I could turn it off when I needed a burst of strength . . .

On some level, I knew that this was the wrong track. I was still going for the "brute strength" approach, just in a slightly different way. Still, like Colin had said, I had to come up with something.

I kept at it all morning without much success. I did manage to figure out a way to temporarily stop the sigl's regulator from working—there was a weird, very specific way you could channel your personal essentia into the sigl in order to suppress it. Unfortunately, as soon as I did, I ran straight back into the problems I'd had with the Mark 1. I was deliberately channelling only a thread of essentia through the sigl as a whole, in order to keep its enhancement down to the barest minimum, but even so, it made my body feel off balance and wrong. Not quite pain, but very unpleasant.

Maybe if I trained with an unregulated sigl, I might be able to get used to it, enough to use it in a fight? No, that didn't make sense—the whole problem was that it was too unpredictable to get used to. I might be able to control it, but that'd take way too much concentration. Particularly if I had to concentrate on shutting down the regulator at the same time . . .

I stopped.

Wait.

I had a way to shut down a sigl's regulator.

I went back to practising, channelling into the sigl, making the sigl's regulator go on, then off. Slowly, an evil smile started to spread across my face.

CHAPTER 16

THE NEXT FEW days were busy.

First on the to-do list was another chat with Father Hawke. He confirmed that, yes, all enhancement sigls had regulators, and, yes, they worked pretty much exactly the same as mine. He also gave me a book of apologetics to read, which I knew I'd have to do by the next time we spoke. I still found it odd that Father Hawke seemed to care so much about making me do what amounted to theology homework, but I was starting to get used to it. And I had to admit it was a nice change to deal with someone in the drucraft world who was willing to help *without* either charging extortionate amounts of money or trying to stab me in the back.

Next was design. To suppress the regulator on my own sigl, I had to touch it, which obviously wasn't practical in combat. But thinking back over what Maria had told me, I realised that if I could do this without a sigl, then it had to be a Primal effect, which meant that I should be able to make it a lot more powerful by turning it into a Primal sigl. And come to think of it, I'd found a Primal Well last month . . .

And so the following Monday, I found myself standing in a nature reserve outside London, looking down at the palm of my hand. Resting there was a tiny sphere of grey, the colour of thick cloud. The nature reserve was near Cobham, a sleepy little village in Surrey that I'd visited back in April in the hope that a less populated spot might make for a better hunting ground. As things turned out, it hadn't, but I'd managed to find one Well all the same. It had been very weak, its reserves right on the edge of being unable to make a sigl at all, but it had been enough.

Normally I tested my sigls at home, but I'd been waiting for this one for what felt like forever and I wanted to try it out straightaway. Of course, the only way to give it a *proper* test was to use it on an enhancement sigl that was actually working . . . which meant testing it on myself. I walked through the May wildflowers, buttercups forming little dots of gold against the grass, and ducked under the branches of a sweet chestnut tree that would hide me from any passersby. Then I put on my enhancement sigl and got to work.

I had to be very slow and careful, but after an hour I knew that I'd done it. Every time I aimed the stream of essentia at my own enhancement sigl, its regulator node stopped working. Crucially, though, the *rest* of the sigl *kept* working, meaning that it would send unregulated energy into my body's muscles in exactly the same way that the Mark 1 had. The range wasn't huge—maybe thirty feet—but I could probably extend that with practice. And given that it was completely invisible, most people wouldn't even be able to tell I was using it.

As far as weapons went, it was ridiculously specific. It was completely useless against every possible opponent *except* one who was using a strength-enhancing Life sigl. But weirdly, the fact that it was useless against 99.9 percent of people actually made me feel better. No normal person would carry a weapon like this . . . which meant that no one would be expecting it.

I set off for home with a spring in my step.

FROM THAT POINT on, it felt as though the tide had turned.

I went back to my training and my practice with a new energy. Whereas before I'd thought in terms of escaping or running away, now I thought in terms of fighting to win. The fight in Hampstead had taught me an important lesson: a weak weapon could be worse than none at all. My slam sigl had been a help in the battle at Victoria Park, but it had turned into a liability as soon as I ran up against someone really dangerous. This one was another story. For the first time, I felt as though I had something that let me face my enemies on even terms.

But I still wasn't going back to Hampstead. My new sigl might let me take on opponents like that boy, but only so long as I had the advantage of surprise—as soon as he figured out what was going on, he could just take his strength sigl off, at which point my new weapon would be useless. It was a good trick, but it wasn't enough.

The fact was, right now, I just wasn't punching at a high enough weight. To go up against enemies like that boy, or Scar and Diesel, I needed more than one good trick. I needed *lots* of good tricks, and that meant more sigls, which meant work and time. And that meant that, for now, I was going to have to put my search for my father, as well as any plans I had for the Ashfords, on hold. I wasn't happy about it, but at the moment my priority had to be getting stronger.

I just hoped I'd have long enough to do it.

I TOOK HOBBES back to the vet to check on his progress. The news was good, and I was told I could start gradually allowing him more freedom of movement, which led me into my new project—figuring out how to make a sigl for someone else. I didn't know how, but I knew someone who did: Maria. Her entire job revolved around supplying sigls to rich people, and I was pretty sure she'd understand the process well enough to explain it to me.

Unsurprisingly, she did. Also unsurprisingly, she wasn't willing to do it for free. I'd been expecting it this time and brought the cash with me.

"All right," Maria said once we were settled in her consulting room. "This should be easy for you to understand since you can shape sigls already. When you create a sigl, the initial construct is made out of your personal essentia. Then you layer the Well essentia on top of that, like flesh onto a skeleton. Right?"

I nodded.

"That construct is what's used to make the sigl core," Maria said. "We usually call it the kernel. When the construct is shrunk down and manifested, the threads of the construct become the kernel's strands. Now, the key thing to understand is that even once they're solidified, those strands are still made out of your personal essentia, and they still react to you. So when you channel into them, they conduct the essentia, and the whole thing works. Some people think of it like water flowing through cracks, others think of it as electricity going through a circuit, but either way, the important thing is that it's *your* essentia in the kernel that makes it function. To anyone else, it's just a piece of rock. This is called the Blood Limit, and it's one of the most important restrictions in drucraft."

"Why is it called the Blood Limit?"

"Because of the two ways around it," Maria said. "First, you can use the sigl of a blood relative. Your personal essentia is a lot like your genetic code—it's fixed at birth, and you get it from your parents. The more closely related you are to someone, the more likely the sigl will look at your essentia and say 'close enough.'"

"How closely related do you have to be?"

"Closer the better. Parent, child, brother, or sister is best. Past that it depends on attunement ratio and a bit of luck, but that's complicated and I won't get into it now. The important part is that there's a second way to get around the Blood Limit. Can you see what it is?"

I frowned. "What do you mean?"

"Your sigls work for you because they're made out of your personal essentia," Maria said. "So if you want a sigl to work for someone else . . ."

"You make it out of their personal essentia instead," I finished.

"Exactly."

"But how would that work? When you take someone's personal essentia too far away from their body, it starts losing attunement. I suppose if they were right there . . ."

"There's an easier way to do it," Maria said. "Bring a piece of their body."

I gave her a look.

"Not like that," Maria said with a laugh. "You use their blood. You can use other things too, but blood's usually best. You use it as a focus for the shaping and draw out the essentia in the process."

I thought about it. It sounded difficult, and I said so.

"It is," Maria said with a nod. "And it gets harder the more of their essentia you use. The proportion of the sigl's kernel that you shape out of the customer's essentia is called its attunement ratio. If you mix them half-and-half, that's an attunement ratio of one to one. The more of their essentia you use, the more effective the sigl will be, but the harder it'll be to make."

"What's the highest you can go?"

"You're ambitious, aren't you?" Maria said. "Board standard is two to one. If you want professional grade, you can get custom sigls that go up to three or three point five. Even four to one, sometimes, although at that point you're starting to run the risk of the whole thing failing."

"Huh," I said. I wondered how far I could push it.

"So how's the locating going? Did you manage to get a finder's stone?"

She doesn't know, I realised. Though maybe I shouldn't have been surprised. Maria's job was to deal with rich customers, not poor employees. "Not exactly."

"Did you not pass the credit check?"

"No, I just didn't apply, because finder's stones are terrible," I said bluntly. "Why did you tell me to get one?"

Maria looked surprised. "Most of Linford's Wells are discovered using finder's stones."

"But their range is awful. Why not just get someone with good sensing skills?"

"Do you know how long it takes to train someone up to that level?" Maria asked. "It's years of work, all to develop a skill with no market value. Meanwhile, you can teach someone to use a finder's stone in five minutes."

"A finder's stone that'll break in a year and a half."

"Threaded sigls are the industry standard."

"But those threaded sigls still cost around half the price of a solid one," I pointed out. "Replacing your sigls every one and a half years doesn't sound like a good deal."

"According to surveys, most locators only stay in the business for less than eighteen months before dropping out, anyway," Maria said. "It can be a bit of a transitory sort of job."

Funny how you didn't mention that part before. "You said

before that locators can work their way up," I said. "How would I do that?"

"I'm afraid I'm not very involved in the locator side of the business. You'd have to talk to your supervisor."

I hadn't even known I had a supervisor. All my contact with Linford's had been through their app, and the one time I'd stuck around at the Well, the arriving team had told me to go away. "I don't even know who that is."

"Unfortunately there's not much I can do to help with that."

I was starting to cool on Maria. At our first meeting she'd seemed like a treasure trove of information, but the longer I spoke to her, the more I was starting to get the feeling that everything she told me seemed aimed to push me into a certain lane. "Can I ask you something?"

"You've got twenty minutes left," Maria said with a smile.

"Linford's is a drucraft company," I said. "So how come they don't seem to actually care about their employees learning any drucraft? You say that locators are supposed to just use finder's stones, but if they don't learn sensing, how are they going to move on to the things they'd need for the higher-level jobs, like channelling and shaping?"

"You mostly *don't* need those skills," Maria pointed out. "I hardly use my channelling at all these days. And shapers only need to know enough to use a limiter."

I frowned.

"Think of it as like building a house," Maria explained. "You could do it yourself, but it's a lot easier just to buy one that someone else has made for you."

"There must be some good drucrafters in your company."

"Well, yes."

"So how do you get a job like that?"

"Not by walking in and applying, if that's what you're wondering," Maria said. "The people in those jobs have spent years and years at the company, working their way up."

And how are you supposed to work your way up when the company doesn't teach you anything? I thought but didn't say.

"Anyway, I think you're getting a little ahead of yourself," Maria said with another smile. "Was there anything else?"

". . . No. That's all."

I WENT HOME deep in thought.

The more that I learned about Linford's, the more it was starting to feel as though I didn't have much of a future there. Linford's might be happy to buy my Wells, but they weren't interested in teaching me anything. In fact, I was starting to get the definite impression that what they *really* wanted were worker bees who'd do exactly what they were told and nothing more. That was the point of finder's stones. They turned locating from a skilled job into an unskilled one so that corporations like Linford's could hire workers in bulk and quickly find new ones when the old ones quit. Just as Charles Ashford had said, I was a replaceable part in a machine.

For now at least, being a locator was working out. But in the long term, there was probably no more future in it than there had been in any of my other jobs. If I wanted something with actual prospects, I was on my own.

Well. It was something to think about. In the meantime, I had a sigl to make.

IT TOOK ME a while to get the hang of the technique Maria had described. Working with personal essentia that wasn't my own made the whole shaping process very different, but by this point I was getting used to figuring out this stuff on my own. It took several practice attempts with weak Wells, and yet another visit to Father Hawke, but I eventually worked out that the key was to treat the personal essentia in the same way that you'd treat the free essentia of a Well. I was pretty sure Maria had thought I'd been asking about this because I'd been hoping to start some side hustle involving selling sigls to other people. I wondered how she'd react if she found out I was doing it for my cat.

Hobbes by this point had been in recovery for more than two months, and it was getting harder and harder to keep him inside—he wasn't back to full strength, but he was bored and impatient and wanted to go out. The sigl I was making had two purposes. First, it would jump-start his recovery by boosting his weakened muscles. Second, it would give a nasty surprise to the next person who tried to hurt him.

Around mid-June, I finally found what I'd been looking for— a temporary Life Well on Blackheath. I took Hobbes out there in his cat carrier. Linford's might use blood samples, but I didn't see any reason to do the same when I could just shape the sigl right in front of Hobbes and draw the essentia out of him that way.

The shaping process went perfectly, and soon I had a cat enhancement sigl. I took it and Hobbes home, fitted the sigl into a specially prepared collar, and put it on.

At which point I discovered some things.

It turned out that cats had a much lower essentia capacity than humans. The same type of enhancement sigl that took less than half of my own capacity consumed every bit of personal essentia that Hobbes could produce. On the other hand, since the sigl was so oversized for his tiny body, all its power was concentrated into a very small volume. It was sort of like taking an electric scooter and fitting it with a jet engine: it didn't leave much space for anything else, but it was a *lot* more powerful.

Hobbes spent the first hour tripping over his own feet. He looked like a kitten that was relearning how to walk, but it didn't take him long to get the hang of it, and soon he was bouncing around the room. I took him out into the house's small back garden, but the instant I put him down he cleared the fence in a single bound and disappeared.

I spent an hour searching for him with no luck. I went to bed and slept badly, one ear open for the sound of him coming back.

I was woken up at five a.m. by piercing meows. I jumped out of bed, opened the window, and looked down.

Hobbes was on the ledge just below my window with a full-size pigeon in his mouth. The thing was about half as big as he was, and he was having to stand at an awkward angle to stop himself from falling off the ledge. The pigeon was still alive and trying to get away. "Mraaaow," Hobbes told me in a muffled voice.

"What the hell are you doing?" I demanded.

"Mraow."

"I know it's a pigeon! Come up where I can reach you."

"Mraaaaaow."

"I don't care if you lose it! Stop balancing on that ledge and get inside before you fall."

The pigeon chose this moment to start thrashing and flapping. Hobbes lost his balance and slipped, catching himself on the ledge but losing his grip on the bird in the process. The pigeon fell to our front doorstep, scrambled to its feet, and took off in a flurry of wings just as Hobbes pulled himself back up.

Hobbes looked around, saw the pigeon, and without a moment's hesitation launched himself from the ledge in a soaring leap. He hit the bird in midair, and the two of them fell to the ground in a ball of fur and feathers.

I leant forward, afraid that Hobbes had been hurt, but a second later he was up again, apparently unharmed and with the pigeon back in his mouth. He gave me a triumphant look, then went trotting off, disappearing through the railings into the grounds of the block of flats next door. Foxden Road was quiet again.

Well, I thought, *it definitely works.*

FROM THAT POINT on, Hobbes's recovery was rapid. His pelvis and one of his legs healed a little crooked, but it didn't seem to do him any harm and soon he was roaming the street again. A couple of other cats had moved into his territory while he'd been gone, and he beat them up in a pair of extremely one-sided fights. The sheer amount of raw power that the sigl gave Hobbes was astonishing—you just don't expect a ten-pound cat to have that kind of strength. The next time I took him to the vet, I'd have to be *very* careful about putting him in his carrier. But he was on the mend at last, and as I went into the summer I felt better than I had in years.

JUNE TURNED INTO July. The solstice came and went, and I spent the long, warm days roaming the paths and forgotten regions of East London. The bramble bushes on the Greenway began to bloom, white and pink flowers appearing in greater and greater numbers until they were a sea of colour under the summer sun. I found Well after Well, some claimed and fenced off, but others undiscovered and waiting to be used. Some I sold to Linford's, but only as many as I had to; the best ones I kept for myself. Gradually I began to develop a sense of the sorts of places where Wells were most likely to be found, and I built up a map that I'd study in the evenings to decide where to explore the following day.

The weakest Wells I used for my experiments. D-class Wells sold for very little, and now that I was no longer perpetually broke

I could afford to use them to try out new designs. Most were failures, producing inert sigls, useless sigls, or nothing at all, but that was okay: each failure taught me something new. I became familiar with the essentia of the different branches: the vital green glow of Life, the clear purity of Primal, the heavy thickness of Matter. No matter how many I found, though, Light remained my favourite. Light Wells were the only ones where the essentia seemed to *want* to be shaped, as though it understood what I was trying to do and responded to it.

And always, at the back of my mind, I was aware of the Ashfords and of that house in Hampstead. At least once a week I'd think of going back, and every time I'd decide against it. I wasn't ready. Not yet.

July passed. The bramble flowers began to wilt and fall, blackberries growing on their stems to replace them. As the blackberries darkened on the branches, my experiments started to find success. I had a particular sigl that I'd been wanting for a long, long time, one that I thought might finally bring me up to the level I needed, and now my skills were approaching the point where I thought I might actually be able to do it. As August came and the summer drew to a close, I started work on what would be my most difficult project yet.

CHAPTER 17

I SAT BACK on my bed with a sigh and looked down at the transparent blue-tinted sigl resting in my palm. After all this time, I'd done it.

Ever since I'd read about that Phantom sigl in the catalogue at the Exchange, the idea of an invisibility sigl had caught my imagination. Actually trying to make one based off the description, though, had been a dead end. I'd figured out (after a lot of experimentation) how to change light's frequency, but it turned out that the further you tried to move it on the spectrum, the more energy it took. Shifting visible light all the way into the radio band on that kind of scale took more power than I had available, at least not without access to some much more powerful Light Wells.

So I'd gone back to the design I'd worked out on my own all the way back in January, the one that just bent light rather than changing its wavelength. Power issues had eventually forced me to give up on the "invisibility sphere" approach—the bigger the area you tried to bend light around, the more essentia you needed, and making it a sphere resulted in too much wasted volume. I needed a shape that was as space efficient as possible, and so the design I eventually settled on was an "invisibility ovoid," centred on my waist. It covered a volume exactly big enough to hide me, while using little enough power that I could just barely find a Well that I could use to shape it.

It had still required trial and error. *Lots* of trial and error. I'd figured out a way of scaling down sigls so that I could make prototypes without having to spend as much essentia doing it, but even so, I'd gone through a *lot* of Light Wells, and I still cringed thinking of how many thousands of pounds I'd wasted on those failures. My sigl box in the cubbyhole was now full of failed diffraction sigls, a few of which would make your hand or finger invisible, and most of which would do nothing at all.

But though it had cost me more time, money, and essentia than I liked to think about, it was done. I took a deep breath, stood up, and looked at Hobbes. "All right," I told him. "We ready?"

Hobbes was sitting up on the bed, tail curled around his feet. He looked bright and alert, and I could see the essentia flowing through his muscles from the sigl at his neck. "Mrraaaaow," Hobbes told me.

"Okay," I said. "Invisibility sigls, full set, test one." I tucked the sigl into my waistband—I needed to figure out some way to clip it so that it'd stay there securely—and channelled.

The room around me seemed to darken, the morning sunlight dimming to evening, then to dusk. Hobbes faded into the shadows of the bed and wall. In seconds all I could make out was the fuzzy patch of window, and then even that was gone, leaving me standing in pitch darkness.

That's the trouble with invisibility. It works both ways.

"So, can you see me?" I asked Hobbes.

"Mraow."

"You are totally useless, you know that?"

"Mraow?"

So far so good. I'd already known that the diffraction sigl would work. It was time to test out the complete set.

I reached into my pocket and took out a cord, then tied it around my forehead. Once I had it right, I reached for the sigl set into the cord and adjusted it until it was resting on my forehead, just above my eyebrows. Then I took a deep breath. This was the moment of truth.

Invisibility on its own isn't hard. Visible things are visible because light bounces off them and reaches other people's eyes. You want to stop that happening, cut off the light. Simple.

The problem is, cutting off the light also blinds you. Bend light around you: now light isn't reaching your eyes, either. Make yourself transparent: now the light's going through your eyes without being absorbed. Pretty much everything that stops other people from seeing you also stops *you* from seeing *them*. Or anything else.

In the end I'd worked out a two-part solution. The diffraction sigl that I was using didn't bend all light, only visible light. The rest of the electromagnetic spectrum was reaching me just fine, and the job of the sigl on my forehead was to take some of the ultraviolet light passing through the diffraction field and shift its wavelength down to visible light so that my eyes could see it. Except that as soon as it *did* become visible light, the diffraction field tried to push it aside again, so I had to do the conversion very close to my eyes . . .

Well. You can see why this had taken me a long time.

I crossed my fingers, channelled a thread of essentia through the sigl on my forehead, and waited.

For a moment nothing happened, and my heart sank, but then I fiddled with the essentia and felt a flash of excitement as I saw a flicker of blue. I widened and strengthened the flow, and gradually my sight came back, the darkness resolving into the familiar image of my room.

Familiar, but weird. Everything was shades of blue: the walls were violet, the bed indigo, Hobbes a pattern of navy and black. It was like looking through a colour filter, and I spent a minute or so just looking around and staring.

But it was working! I turned to the little mirror that I kept on the front of my wardrobe, hoping to see right through myself, and . . .

. . . saw myself in shades of blue. Oh. Of course.

Damn it. How was I supposed to test it?

I spent longer than I should have done messing around with mirrors (which, as you'd expect, didn't help at all) before hitting on the obvious solution. I turned on the camera on my phone, propped it up on the chair, and filmed myself while I walked around. Then I took off both my sigls, blinking in the dazzling light as colour returned to the world, and looked at the video.

Three seconds into the video, I punched the air above me and shouted "YES!" loudly enough to make Hobbes jump off the bed and hide. The video showed nothing but an empty room.

I SPENT MOST of that day on a high, running tests and pinning down the limits of what my new sigls could do.

There were a lot of problems. For one thing, because I'd had to compromise so much on the volume of the diffraction field, my hands and feet could actually poke through the edges of the field if I moved them too far from my body. For another, the sigl didn't handle movement well—there was a noticeable shimmer, like a distortion in the air, and trying to bend light too close to a solid object caused all sorts of trouble. And the vision sigl was a massive headache—I had to keep adjusting the essentia flow on the fly to match it to the ambient conditions, and if I messed up I'd either dazzle myself with too much light or blind myself with too little of it.

It didn't take me long to realise that keeping both these sigls running at once was going to take constant concentration. It was easy enough so long as I was standing still, but trying to do anything else at the same time was going to be really, really hard. Not to mention that the two sigls combined used up half my essentia capacity.

But none of that was enough to dampen my spirits. I could turn *invisible*. I'd figured out the design, I'd gathered the materials, I'd worked and worked and worked until it did what I wanted it to, and I'd done it all by myself. I felt like a real-life wizard.

I picked up my Exchange catalogue and flipped through it to the Phantom page: £84,990 for an invisibility sigl, according to them. Well, I could make my own. It might not be as good as theirs, not yet, but it *would* be.

Now I just had to decide what to do with it.

My excitement cooled as I considered my options. I could use my new ability to spy on the Ashfords, hoping to find something that'd give me some edge. Or I could go back to Hampstead, and try again to follow my father's trail. Which to choose?

The longer I thought about it, the more I realised that it was a really hard question. I didn't know which would have a better chance of success, and I didn't know which was more urgent. Worse, I didn't know what the consequences would be if I failed. I tried tallying up the pros and cons, and had to give up. I'd just have to go on instinct.

I hesitated, weighing my two options, and made my choice.

THE ASHFORD MANSION was difficult to spy on. It was set far enough back from the road that it was hard to see, and there were no good vantage points. The best you could do was to hang around in the street, which was spacious and empty enough that anyone doing so would be very obvious. There were also a couple of discreetly positioned security cameras that looked to have been placed to catch anyone loitering.

Of course, security cameras aren't so good at spotting someone who's invisible.

I settled into the spot I'd picked, a patch of grass under a tree that gave a view of the mansion's front gate and drive. The angle could be better, but it was far enough away that I didn't have to worry too much about anyone spotting a shimmer in the air if I scratched my nose. Now all I had to do was wait.

Choosing to go after the Ashfords instead of my father had been hard. I *really* wanted to find my dad, and I was afraid that if I waited too long, I'd lose him forever. But every time I thought about what going after that address in Hampstead would actually mean—breaking into that house and searching through it room by room—a wave of unease went through me. All my instincts told me that going back to that place was a very bad idea. Spying on the Ashfords felt safer.

But "safer" didn't mean "safe," which was why I was keeping my distance. I still didn't know how heavy the Ashford family's security was, and until I knew *exactly* how good they were at detecting trespassers, I was going to err on the side of caution.

The day passed. Delivery drivers came and went through those gates, as well as some women who looked like cooks or cleaners. There were also several of those ominous black minivans, their windows tinted so that I could only guess who was inside.

By the end of that day I'd learned an important lesson about spying: contrary to what the movies tell you, it's actually really, really boring. When I finally pulled away from the tree to begin my journey home, I felt like the whole thing had been a waste of time. I wanted to give up.

I didn't. I went back the next day, and again the day after that.

If you're wondering why . . . well, it's hard to explain. It wasn't as though I knew exactly what I was trying to find, and in fact, I didn't even know for sure that there *was* anything to find. If I was being honest, hanging around the Ashford mansion and hoping that something would turn up really wasn't an amazing plan. It sounded better than searching that house in Hampstead, but I knew my chances of finding anything weren't great.

But even so, I never seriously considered giving up. The past five months had been good ones for me—my drucraft was growing by leaps and bounds, and everything I did mattered. But there was a dark side to that—my *mistakes* mattered too. Several times in the past five months I'd been in real danger, not the kind where the worst that can happen is getting beaten up or losing your job, but the kind where you don't *know* what the worst that can happen is, because when you start looking into that hole, you realise it doesn't have a bottom. The attack by Diesel and Scar. The battle with the raiders in Victoria Park. The ambush in Hampstead. All three of those had had the potential to end really, really badly, and looking back on it, the scariest thing had been how little warning I'd had. At any time, the same thing could happen again.

So at some point, at the back of my mind, I'd started wondering what I could do to make a difference. If I knew that at any point a test could be sprung on me, a test that I had to pass, what could I do about it?

And the more I thought about it, the more I kept coming up with the same answer. Every time I'd passed one of those previous tests, it had been because of something I'd done *before*. Running, boxing, channelling, shaping . . . I'd put in the work day after day and year after year, and because of that, those skills and abilities had been there when I needed them. In boxing, the fight's usually won or lost long before you step into the ring, and after the past few months I was starting to feel as though that was true for everything else as well.

I couldn't take on my enemies directly, not yet. But what I *could* do was gather information. There were too many things that I didn't know, and right now, the best way for me to get an edge was to find out what those things were.

ON THE THIRD day, I decided to switch things up. I hadn't been getting anywhere watching the mansion during the daytime, so I'd try the evening instead. I did some Well hunting in the morning, went home for lunch, then around four o'clock took a pair of buses to The Bishops Avenue. I leant against the tree in my preferred spying spot and got comfortable.

Hours passed. Running both my vision and invisibility sigls at the same time was hard, and from time to time I'd take a break, letting my concentration on the vision sigl drop and standing there in pitch darkness while I recovered. It's hard to stay focused when nothing's happening, and as the sun dipped low in the sky, my mind started to wander. Would anyone be able to see through my invisibility? Diffraction sigls seemed to be pretty common, which meant that there were probably other sigls designed to counter them. On the other hand, the strength of the Well in the Ashford mansion would make it hard to notice the essentia from my sigl. What kind of sigls could I make if I had a Well like that? Maybe that crazy-expensive active camouflage one that a couple of the high-end Houses sold . . .

The sight of the gate swinging open pulled me back to the present. A small figure came out of the Ashford mansion grounds, turned left, and walked away up the avenue. My blue-shifted vision made it hard to pick out details, but it looked like a girl wearing a long coat.

I frowned, something nagging at my memory. Why did that look familiar?

I hesitated an instant, then started following the girl. She wasn't walking particularly fast, and it wasn't hard to keep up with her. Every now and again she'd pause, as if waiting for someone to catch up, and a couple of times I thought I heard her talking.

That memory was still nagging at me, a half-remembered impression from a long time ago. A suspicion was growing in my mind, but I couldn't see her well enough to confirm it. I'd have to get a closer look.

I stepped behind a tree, then cut off the flows of essentia to my vision and diffraction sigls. Colour flared, shockingly bright after so many hours of seeing in shades of blue. The sun was setting, casting golden light and long shadows across the quiet avenue; above, the grey-purple sky was streaked with honey-coloured clouds. I sped up, passing the girl on the other side of the street, then walked quickly up the avenue. Once I was a couple of hundred feet ahead of her, I crossed back to her side of the street, leant against a tree, and waited.

Slowly the girl approached. The avenue was quiet, with few passing cars, and I could hear her footsteps clearly on the paving stones. As she drew closer, I saw that she was smaller than me, maybe sixteen or seventeen, with long brown hair, fair skin, and delicate features.

On top of that, my essentia sight was showing me something more. She had an active sigl on her left hand, a Light effect of some kind. The really odd thing, though, was that it seemed to be targeted on a patch of air just behind her and to her side, around the height of her waist. It looked like an invisibility effect, which meant it was hiding something . . . but what?

The more I thought about it, the more convinced I was that it was the same girl, but I wasn't sure. It had been a long time ago, and I'd only had a glimpse.

Well. I could think of one way to check.

The girl kept walking, angling slightly to one side so that she'd pass between me and the wall. Her eyes were down on the pavement, with a frowning, pensive look, and she walked by me as though I wasn't there.

As she passed, I spoke. "Better get stronger."

The reaction was instant. The girl whirled, jumping away from me and back like a startled cat. She came down on her toes, eyes wide and alert. I heard a growl and felt a flash of danger. All of a sudden I had a very good idea of what that sigl was hiding, and I stepped back, bringing up my hand.

Then the girl's eyes came to rest on my face with a flash of recognition. "You!"

I stayed in a ready stance, keeping a wary eye on both her and the invisible thing at her side. If she made a move, I'd have to react very fast.

And then the girl laughed and the tension was gone. "You!" she said again, but this time she sounded happy. She made a gesture with her right hand and said, "Down, down," then folded her arms, tilted her head, and looked at me. "It *is* you."

"Surprised?" I asked.

"No," the girl said, then seemed to reconsider. She put both hands behind her back, leant against the wall, and smiled. "Well, maybe. You took your time about getting here."

"Your family hasn't exactly been making things easy for me."

"I heard."

"Who sent you after me?" I asked. "Tobias or Lucella?"

"Tobias."

She seemed very relaxed for a teenage girl who'd just been

tracked down by a near stranger with good reason not to like her family very much. Then again, if I was right about what that sigl was hiding, she didn't have much reason to be nervous. "Why?"

"Who knows?" the girl said with a shrug. "Tobias is always doing this sort of stuff."

"What did he tell you?"

"Just said that Lucella might be coming after you and that he wanted to know what you could do. But after I walked right by you like that without you noticing . . . well, I felt a bit sorry for you. You really had no idea what was going to happen."

Yeah, no kidding. "How do you know Tobias?"

The girl smiled again. "Guess."

I looked at the girl, thinking. She had to be one of the Ash-fords; that was obvious. Which one? Johanna had said something about Charles choosing between Calhoun, Lucella, and two grand-children. Tobias was Charles's grandson, which meant . . .

"You're Tobias's sister," I said.

"Mm-hmm."

I paused. The girl looked at me expectantly.

"And?" the girl said when I didn't speak.

"And what?"

"You don't know?"

"Don't know what?"

The girl gave me a disappointed look.

"What?" I asked.

"Never mind."

"All right," I said. I still didn't know why this girl was so inter-ested in me, but this was my best chance in months to find out what was really going on. "Not to pressure you or anything, but this is kind of important. If I understand this right, the whole reason Tobias and Lucella went after me is because of the competition in your family about who gets to be heir. Is that go-ing to happen again?"

The girl thought for a second. "I'm not sure," she admitted at last. "Right now everything's about Calhoun. Charles has put him in charge of that new Well in Chancery Lane. You know about that?"

"No."

"Charles never used to like Calhoun much," the girl said. "Be-cause of his parents. As Calhoun grew up and kept being so good at everything, Charles started to come around, but he's never stopped keeping an eye on him. He's been acting as though giving Calhoun this job is a big honour, but I think it's another test. He wants to see if Calhoun can handle it."

"Not to be rude or anything," I said, "but I don't really care who's in charge of your family's Wells. Are they going to drag *me* into it?"

"I shouldn't think so? Like I said, everyone's kind of focused on Calhoun. I don't think they're paying any attention to you."

Well, that was something, at least.

"Tobias feels bad about what happened to you," the girl added.

"Then maybe he shouldn't have pointed Lucella in my direc-tion," I said shortly. After how things had turned out in the spring, I wasn't feeling very sympathetic towards Tobias.

"He can't really help himself," the girl said. "He always has to have some sort of clever plan, even if they never really work. It's because of the whole inheritance thing. He grew up thinking he was going to become heir. Then when that all went wrong . . . well, he's been trying to get it back ever since."

"So what about you?" I asked. "You're the last one of the four, right?"

"Four?"

"That generation of Ashfords. Calhoun, Lucella, Tobias, and you."

The girl looked at me for a second. "Oh," she said. "Yes."

"So why are you the only one who doesn't seem to care about inheriting?"

"I never thought I was in the running," the girl said with a shrug. "When I was little, I thought it was going to be Tobias, then when he got the bad news, well, it was obvious that it wasn't going to be me, either. Besides, there are plenty of things you can do even if you're not going to be the next head of House. I really wish Tobias would just give it up. Charles is never going to choose him."

"One last thing," I said. "From what Lucella told me, this whole thing started because she went to Tobias fishing for some sort of advantage. Tobias told her about me, and she thought I might be useful. Right?"

"I think so."

"Why?"

"Why what?"

"Why me?" I said. "Okay, so I'm Lucella's cousin. But from the sounds of it, your family isn't exactly short of relatives. Why would that make Lucella care about me?"

The girl studied me.

"Can you stop looking at me like that?" I said.

"No," the girl said. "It's fun." She pushed off the wall. "Well, time to go."

"Wait! Can you answer my question?"

"Figure it out," the girl called over her shoulder as she walked away. An odd clicking sound followed her, like nails on concrete.

I stared after the girl as she headed back towards the Ashford mansion. I wanted to chase after her and force her to give me an answer, but something told me that would be a bad idea. Instead I watched her go further and further down the pavement until she vanished from sight.

Once she was gone, I turned away. Only now that the conversation was over did I realise I'd never got her name. Well, since "Bridge Girl" was all she'd left me to go on, I might as well start calling her Bridget.

HOBBES MET ME at the door when I got home, twining around my leg and meowing insistently. I poured out some food into his bowl, then threw my coat on the chair, dumped out the contents of my pockets, and flopped onto the bed. Then I put my hands behind my head and looked up at the ceiling.

Well, I'd wanted to find out more, and I had. Was it any use?

I thought back over my conversation with Bridget, reviewing it line by line. So the competition to be Ashford heir was still going on, just out of sight. I didn't really see how it had anything to do with me, but I couldn't help feeling that, sooner or later, one of them was going to *make* it have something to do with me. After all, I hadn't known what was going on when Lucella showed up at my door, and that hadn't done me much good.

Why *had* Lucella shown up at my door?

I puzzled over that for a few minutes. Hobbes finished his dinner, paced over, and hopped up onto my bed. I scratched his ears absentmindedly as he leant into my fingers.

The more I thought about it, the more it felt as though there was some piece that I was missing. There had to be some other reason Lucella had been willing to believe that I might be a threat.

Start at the beginning. The whole reason Lucella and Tobias had come after me was because of my connection to the Ashfords. They wouldn't be interested in me if I wasn't related to them.

Related how?

Hobbes had climbed onto my lap. I lifted him off, reached for my notebook, and started writing notes, pausing from time to time to make sure I was remembering right. Once I was done, I looked down at what I'd written.

Family Relations

— *Charles Ashford is the son of Walter Ashford, who married someone from Johanna's family*

— *Tobias & Bridget are Charles's grandchildren*

— *Lucella & Calhoun are Charles's nephew and niece*

— *Lucella and Tobias are first cousins once removed*

— *I'm Lucella's first cousin once removed*

I checked the Internet to see what "first cousin once removed" meant, then started sketching out a family tree. After several false starts and crossed-out diagrams, I sat back to look at the result.

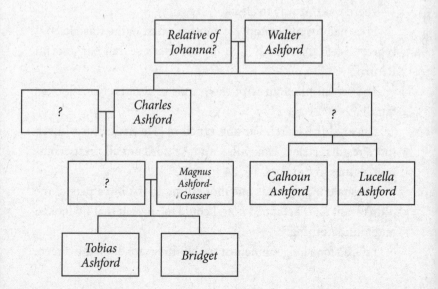

I frowned at the image. It seemed right, but there was one problem—there wasn't any place for me.

Tobias had said something about Noble Houses having "minor branches of the family" that they used to marry in outsiders, and he'd made it sound as though my mother had come from one of those. But now that I looked at the family tree, that didn't make sense. If I was Lucella's first cousin once removed, then didn't I have to be related pretty closely to Charles? Unless my mother was from the other side of Lucella's family . . . no, that couldn't be right, Charles had said my mother was from House Ashford . . .

What had Tobias said *exactly*?

"*Your mother is from one of House Ashford's branches.*"

"*Lucella's my first cousin once removed. And you're Lucella's first cousin once removed.*"

I looked at the family tree again. My eyes drifted to the question mark next to "Magnus Ashford-Grasser."

A sudden awful suspicion reared up inside me.

No. That couldn't be right.

There was one way to check.

I reached for my laptop. My mother's first name was Helen. I typed "Helen Oakwood" into my browser's search bar and hit Return.

The screen filled up with thousands of results. None looked familiar.

I cleared the search bar and typed in "Helen Ashford." Even more results. Helen, Oakwood, and Ashford are all pretty common names in England.

I hesitated. There was one more thing to try, but a part of me didn't want to. If I stopped now, I could tell myself that I'd looked and found nothing.

I stared for a long moment at the blinking cursor on the screen.

Then slowly, I typed in "Helen Ashford-Grasser." My middle fin-ger hovered over the Return key, then stabbed down.

There were only a few dozen results this time. Most were from newspapers and gossip sites. I clicked on one and scrolled until a name jumped out.

```
. . . helped the bride out of the car and held
up her long train. Arriving separately in a
silver £300k Rolls-Royce Corniche V were Magnus
and Helen Ashford-Grasser, making a rare public
appearance. The publicity-shy Ashford heiress
declined to pose for a picture but stood out
from the crowd in an off-the-shoulder blue
ruffle dress before heading into the stunning
Grade II listed church. Meanwhile, putting on a
leggy display in a smart red outfit was . . .
```

I closed my laptop and leant back against my bedroom wall.

I STAYED UP late that night.

My first reaction, once the truth had finished sinking in, was anger. All of those bastards had *known*. Lucella, Tobias, Charles, probably more. They'd known and said nothing, just sat back and laughed as they'd watched me blunder around. For so long I'd thought about my mother, wondering what had happened to her and why she'd disappeared, when all that time any of the Ash-fords could have told me.

Except it had been worse than that. They hadn't just said noth-ing, they'd *done* nothing. All those years that I'd been alone and struggling, they'd been sitting in their mansion, ignoring me.

Even the tiniest bit of help would have made so much difference. It would have been easy for them, they'd barely have had to lift a finger, and they'd done *nothing*.

The more I thought about it, the angrier I got. I paced up and down my little room while Hobbes slept on the bed.

At least I finally had the answer to the question of where my mother had been all these years. She'd been right there in the Ashford mansion. All this time, she'd been less than an hour's journey across London. That was how long it would have taken her to come see me if she'd wanted to.

She hadn't.

A little worm of resentment started growing in my heart. All these years, I'd told myself that there'd been some reason for all this, that it had made sense somehow. The more I learned about my mother's family, the harder it became to keep believing that.

I tried to shake off the anger by giving myself something to do. I went back to my notebook and sketched in a few more lines, putting myself on the family tree, then looked at the diagram. So Tobias was my half brother and Bridget was my half sister. A lot of little things about how they'd both acted made a lot more sense now.

And it finally explained why Lucella had been so willing to believe that I might be a rival. I wasn't some distant relative; I was Charles's grandson. And speaking of which, good God but that guy was a bastard. He'd acted like that to his own *grandchild*?

Thinking about the other Ashfords instead of my mother helped me calm down. Unfortunately, I still couldn't see how any of it helped. I knew how I fitted into the family now, but I didn't know what to do about it.

I puzzled over it until one in the morning, but didn't get anywhere. At last I gave up and went to bed.

———

THE NEXT DAY was a Saturday. I knew I should get back to investigating, but last night's discoveries had left me frustrated and I decided to spend a day locating to clear my head. Luck was with me, and I found a whole cluster of temporary Wells in a part of South London that everyone else seemed to have missed. All were only half-charged, and no more than D+ in strength, but if I could wait for them to fill, they'd be quite the treasure trove.

The find didn't exactly make me happy, but it helped, and I went home that night in a better mood. It was September 10; in another week, it would be my birthday.

The next morning, the black minivan was back on my road.

CHAPTER 18

I woke to the sun streaming through my window. It was a pleasant September morning, puffy clouds making a patchwork of white against a blue sky. I put down Hobbes's food, then sat on my bed reading while he ate.

Father Hawke had been branching out a bit with the books he'd been lending me, and this one was more to do with politics. It was arguing that the idea of a utopian society was impossible because humans were inherently flawed, so no matter what kind of technology or system of education you had, people were still going to be born with an inclination towards evil. Despite myself, I was actually starting to find the subject kind of interesting, although I still wasn't sure what the point of any of it was.

Hobbes finished eating and meowed to be let out. I opened the window, leaning out to look around. I supposed I shouldn't complain: Father Hawke might be weird, but he was harmless enough compared to—

A jolt went through me as I spotted the van.

Hobbes had sprung onto the windowsill and was just about to

jump down to the ledge; now he stopped, looking at me questioningly. "Inside," I told Hobbes quietly, then picked him up, dropped him back inside the room, and shut the window. Only then did I lean against the wall and take a deep breath.

So they're back.

It's funny how you can see something coming months away and still feel a shock when it happens. I'd been expecting this ever since April, but as week after week had gone by, I'd let myself be lulled into a false sense of security. Now, all of a sudden, my time was up.

But I hadn't put that time to waste. I was a lot stronger now than I had been. It was time to find out whether it would be enough.

I shut Hobbes in my room with a firm command to stay, then went downstairs and outside into our house's tiny back garden. I moved into the shadow of the wall and slipped on my invisibility and vision sigls, watching the world go black, then blue. Once I was sure that the diffraction field was working, I jumped up and scrambled over the wall into the grounds of the block of flats, then walked to the side gate and let myself out.

The streets felt strange in the light of my vision sigl, faded and washed out. I circled all the way around the block, then approached Foxden Road from the other side. Peering around the corner, I could see that the black minivan was right there, less than thirty feet away. It was the same one as last time—same number plate. Cars buzzed past on the main road, but Foxden Road was quiet.

I knew that I was taking a risk. I'd made a point of researching ways to see through invisibility, and it turned out that there were a lot. In fact, invisibility was practically an arms race, with different corporations selling sigls specifically designed to counter the ones from their rivals. If your invisibility sigl hid the part of the spectrum that the other guy was using, you were fine. If they had a sigl that let them see at that particular frequency . . . tough luck.

My invisibility sigl was pretty basic. I'd tried to make it bend away as much of the spectrum as I could, but I'd been limited by power requirements, meaning that the only thing I was *sure* it hid me from was visible light. Ultraviolet was out since my own vision sigl needed that for me to see, and I wasn't too confident about my ability to hide from infrared, either, meaning that if they had a sigl that let them see in either of those two bands, I was in trouble. For that matter, if they were watching closely enough, they wouldn't need a sigl at all, given that my diffraction field left a shimmer as I moved. Most people would dismiss it as haze or a trick of the light. Someone who knew what to look for wouldn't.

I took a deep breath, then started around the corner.

I crept towards the van, muscles and nerves on edge. The tinted windows made it hard to see in, and so I got closer and closer until the shadows in the windows took shape, becoming two bulky figures in the driver and passenger seats, facing towards my house. I might have guessed who they were just from the silhouettes, but the sigls on their chests, glowing with a web of green light, made me certain. It was the same ones who'd attacked me before, Diesel and Scar.

Slowly and carefully, I withdrew around the block, through the flats, over the wall, and back into our garden. Only once I was sure I was safe did I pull off my sigls, let my eyes adjust to the light, then go back into the house and climb the stairs to my room.

Hobbes meowed as I came back through the door, rubbing against my leg and looking up at me with concern. I slid down to the floor and stroked him, staring up through the window at the white-and-blue sky.

All right. I knew what I was up against.

Now what?

The obvious answer was to hide. Between my sigls and the back garden route, I could stay out of sight of Scar and Diesel for a long time. Unfortunately, that wouldn't work forever. Scar and Diesel might be willing to wait for a while, but eventually they'd run out of patience.

Running wasn't really an answer, either. I could lie low and avoid Foxden Road for a day or two, but, again, I couldn't do it forever. Sooner or later they'd track me down.

So if running and hiding were out, what about fighting? Pick my ground, go out fully loaded, and take them on?

The funny thing was that if I did that, I actually thought I'd have a good shot at winning. Scar and Diesel were tough, but I had a sigl specifically designed to counter them. They were just hired thugs; if I sent them packing, Lucella (or whoever was giving them orders) wouldn't care. She'd just get more thugs.

No, going after Scar and Diesel wasn't the answer. I needed to stop this at the source.

But to do that, I'd have to figure out why they were here. The Ashfords had left me alone for five months, so why were their men showing up now? I didn't think that even Lucella would do something like this totally at random. What had changed?

I puzzled over that question for a while. The best answer I could come up with was what Bridget had told me two days ago, something about Charles putting Calhoun in charge of a Well, but I couldn't see how that had anything to do with me.

The frustrating thing was that I had the nagging feeling that if I just went to the right member of the Ashford family and asked them the right questions, I could solve all this. The trouble was, I didn't know who. Lucella and Tobias were obviously out, and Charles was almost as bad. That just left Bridget and Calhoun, who for all I knew might be trying to screw me over too. In fact, there really wasn't a single member of the Ashford family who I was willing to bet *wasn't* trying to screw me over, with the possible exception of my mother, and honestly, I wasn't even all that sure about her.

And for all I knew, more than one of them might have it in for me. Hell, maybe they *all* did. After the kind of treatment I'd had so far, I wouldn't put it past them.

I sat there in my little room, feeling very small and alone.

At last, after half an hour of my mind fruitlessly going round and round in circles, I shook it off. *All right.* I couldn't solve this on my own, and I couldn't go to the Ashfords. What did that leave?

Go to someone else. That was the lesson I'd taken away from the last time Scar and Diesel had shown up, right? Don't try to handle everything on your own. If you need help, ask.

Who to ask?

I went down a mental list of everyone I knew, trying to think of someone that I could trust with something like this, and who cared enough about me that they'd be willing to help. One name came to mind.

I MADE A phone call, then sat in my room, on edge and tense. Hobbes kept on meowing to be let outside. I showed him his litter tray. Hobbes gave me a dirty look.

Eventually my phone pinged. I glanced at the text message, peeked carefully out the window to check that the minivan hadn't moved, then shut Hobbes in my room and went downstairs and out into the back garden. Then I leant against the wall and waited.

Five minutes passed.

There was the scrabbling sound of shoes on brick and Colin's head poked up over the wall. "There you are," he said breathlessly.

"Dude, this climb is a pain in the arse. Can I just use the front door?"

"No. And keep your voice down."

Grumbling, Colin heaved himself over the wall and dropped down heavily next to me. "Someone's been eating too many pies," I told him.

"It's Sunday morning! I've got a hangover!"

"Oh, right." For the last five months I'd been working more or less seven days a week. I'd started to forget that other people spent their weekends doing things like going out drinking. "Thanks."

"Yeah, yeah," Colin said, brushing himself off and looking around. "All right, you said you didn't want to do this over the phone. What's the big emergency?"

"Come upstairs and I'll show you."

"THAT'S THEM?" COLIN asked. He was next to the window in my room, craning his neck to see.

"That's the van," I said.

"You're sure it's the same one?"

"Same van, same guys."

"And you're sure they're here for you?"

"Jesus Christ. Why else would they be here? This is Plaistow, they're not coming here for the scenery!"

"Okay, okay, sorry," Colin said. "But look, you're telling me that a couple of bouncers on some rich family's payroll are trying to kidnap you. You have to admit, it sounds a bit out there."

"I know," I said, leaning against the wall with a sigh. "That's the problem. Most people aren't going to take me seriously, and the ones that will won't care."

"All right," Colin said. "So if they're here because of you, what are they waiting for?"

"My guess is for nightfall."

"What's going to happen then?"

"They'll wait for me to go for a run or something, park the van somewhere to wait for me, jump out and grab me, then drive off."

Colin stared at me.

"Either that or they'll try to kill Hobbes," I said.

"Mraow," Hobbes said. He was curled up on the bed in meat-loaf position and had been watching our conversation through half-closed eyes.

"Again," I added.

"Jesus, dude," Colin said. "What did you *do* to piss these people off so badly?"

"All right," I said. "You know that kung fu movie you showed me last year? The one where the old master takes in this young outsider, and the guy who used to be his top student gets angry because he thinks that the master's going to make the new guy head of the school? It was called *Fist of Legend* or something."

"No, *Fist of Legend* is the one where Jet Li's master gets killed in a duel so he has to go back home," Colin explained. "Then he finds out that his master was actually poisoned by someone within his own school and—"

"Okay, okay, so I got the name wrong. Point is, I'm the out-sider, and the other Ashford kids are the students who think I might be competition. Except in my case the guy in charge made it really clear that he's never going to choose me for heir anyway, but that doesn't seem to matter."

"All right," Colin said. "Let's hear it."

"Hear what?"

"Why they're so interested in you," Colin said. "You promised you'd tell me the truth, remember?"

I let out a breath. Well, it wasn't as though I hadn't seen this coming.

"Because I'm a manifester," I told Colin.

"A what?"

"An advanced kind of drucrafter. It doesn't count for much in most places, but apparently these Houses place a lot of stock in it."

"Is this that drucraft thing again?"

"Look, you know I've been working for that company finding Wells, right?" I said. "Well, one of the things I can do with them is use them to make sigls."

"Sigls?"

"You saw one last time you were here. The 'green shiny thing.'"

"And you're getting paid to make them?"

"No, not exactly, I . . . okay, look, never mind the details. Do you believe me or not?"

Colin looked at me.

"Oh, come on," I said.

"Stephen . . ."

"You said you wanted me to tell you the truth."

"Yeah, but not a bunch of conspiracy bullshit."

"It's not bullshit!"

"Look, I know you take this drucraft thing seriously, but . . . come on, dude. The only people who believe in this stuff are weird losers who live in their mum's basement."

I stared at Colin for a second. "Is that what you think of me?"

"I didn't mean it like that," Colin said with an uncomfortable look. "It's just . . . look, I get it, okay? If your life kind of sucks, then it feels a lot better if you can tell yourself that you're special and that it's all happening for a reason. But at some point you have to just kind of get over it."

I looked away. I suppose I should have seen this coming, but it still hurt.

"Look, I'll help you out with these guys, whoever they are," Colin said. "But once this is done, you need to get your life back on track, okay? Go to uni or get a real job. Not this weird multi-level marketing thing where you're selling crap that doesn't work, or whatever it is you're doing."

I thought about pulling out my flash sigl and triggering it right in Colin's face. See if he'd think *that* was multi-level marketing. But I knew that doing something like that just because I was upset and pissed off was a bad idea. "I'll tell you what," I said. "I'll show you exactly what's going on and what I've been doing. Then once this is over, if you still believe that this is all fake, I'll let you point me at a better job. Sound fair?"

"Sure," Colin said immediately. He sounded a little relieved.

"All right," I said. "So. Got any ideas?"

"About what, those guys in the van?"

"Yeah."

"Okay," Colin said. "First off, why do you think they're going to try and kidnap you once it gets dark?"

"Because that's what Lucella told me she was going to do," I said. "Also, because it was what they did last time."

"Mraow," Hobbes said.

"Okay, okay. The second-last time."

"So . . . talking things out in a civilised manner is probably not an option."

"Not very likely, no."

Colin thought for a minute. "How long you think they'll stay there?"

"Last time they did this, it was for recon, I think," I said. "Probably they hung around long enough to get a look at me and to make sure I lived here, then went and reported back to Lucella. Then she showed up the next day."

"Did they get a look at you today?"

"I stuck my head out of my window this morning, but it was only for a couple of seconds. They might have missed it."

"So you might have a bit of time."

"To do what, though?" I said. "I can keep playing hide-and-seek with them for a while, but they're going to catch on eventually."

"Well, what if we flip things around on them?" Colin suggested. "Wait for them to leave, then follow them home."

"How's that going to help?"

"Look, if these guys really are kidnapping people off the street, then I promise you they'll have all kinds of other dodgy shit that they're up to as well," Colin said. "Plus you said you wanted to find out who was giving them orders."

I thought about it for a minute. It did make sense. "How are we going to follow them?"

"I passed my driving test last year, remember?"

"I don't have a car," I said. "Neither do you."

"Kiran does," Colin said with a grin. "So, you want to call him, or shall I?"

COLIN WENT OUT the way he'd come in. Ignas and the others had gone out for the day. The house was empty and quiet.

I spent a while going through my sigls. Once I'd ruled out the ones that were too weak or weren't any use in a fight, I had six. There were the slam and flash sigls that had proved themselves in the fight against the raiders. My only continuous sigl, the strength enhancement. The Primal sigl I'd made at the end of May, which I'd nicknamed my "haywire" effect. And the diffraction and vision sigls, which worked as a pair.

I leant back from where I'd laid out my sigls, looked down at them with mixed feelings. Six months ago, I would have found a collection like this amazing. Now that I knew what I was up against, I wasn't at all sure it'd be enough.

I was also starting to run up against the limits of my essentia capacity. My slam, strength, haywire, and diffraction sigls each consumed around 40 percent of my personal essentia, meaning that I could only use any two of them at once. My flash and vision sigls had more modest power requirements, but I could already see that this was a problem that was only going to get worse as my sigl collection expanded.

Well, it is what it is. I had a good invisibility spell, two weak combat spells, the ability to sabotage strength sigls, and a weak strength sigl of my own. Those were the tools I had, so I'd just have to make them work.

Midday came and went, clouds gathering in the sky. Hobbes gave up nagging me to let him out and went to sleep on the bed. I paced back and forth in my little room, checking every few minutes to make sure that van was still there. Why was Colin taking so long?

With nothing else to do, I went back to trying to figure out why the Ashfords would be making a move on me. The only answer I could come up with was the same one as before—what Bridget had said about that Well—so for lack of any better ideas, I opened up my laptop and started searching for news items within the past month that included the name "Ashford."

To my surprise, I got a hit immediately. The article title read, "Tyr Expansion On Hold After CMA Snub."

```
Tyr Aerospace Europe's stock price fell by 4%
yesterday following the surprise decision by the
Competition and Markets Authority to block their
purchase of a 10,000-square-foot office in
Chancery Lane. The US defence contractor had
submitted plans to develop the building as a
```

```
new regional headquarters, but the CMA rejected
the proposal, instead ordering the vendor,
Camlink, to sell the property to Ashford
Holdings for an undisclosed sum. The short
notice is likely to make it difficult for Tyr to
hit its projected Q4 targets, and its plans for
an expansion are now in doubt.
    Tyr Aerospace could not be reached for
comment.
```

I read the article a few times, trying to puzzle it out. Something was going on, but I didn't know enough to be able to figure out what. For now, all I could do was wait.

AFTERNOON TURNED INTO evening, the clouds growing thicker and darker until they were covering the sky completely. The sun dipped behind the rooftops, painting the underside of the clouds blood-red.

My phone finally lit up, and I snatched it up before the second ring. "Where the hell are you?"

"On the North Circular," Colin said. "Chill."

"Just get here fast. And come around from the back."

I WAITED FOR dusk to fall, then grabbed Hobbes and put him in his cat carrier. He wasn't happy, but after I explained that it meant he'd finally get to go outside, he went along with it. Then I picked up the carrier, checked my sigls one last time, and headed downstairs to leave the house by the back door.

Colin was parked on the other side of the block. Kiran's car was dark blue, medium sized, and spotlessly clean. I crossed the road, opened the door, and dropped into the passenger seat. "What the hell took you so long?"

"You know how long it took to talk Kiran into letting me borrow this?" Colin said. "I had to promise him it wouldn't get a single scratch. Also, did you seriously just bring your cat?"

"Yes," I said, glancing ahead through the windscreen. The light had faded to a dusky purple, and the streetlights were coming on one by one.

"Come *on*, dude."

"I told you what these two guys did last time they were here," I said. "I'm not giving them the chance to try again."

Grumbling, Colin started up the car and crept forward towards Foxden Road. I scanned the street, looking for a space, then pointed to a gap between two cars. "There."

I ducked down in the seat as Colin pulled the car in carefully and parked. Once Colin had turned off the engine, I peeked up to look through the passenger-side window. The minivan was just visible.

"Can you see it well enough?" I asked.

"They'll have to come this way to leave."

"Are you even a good enough driver to follow them?"

"Of course I'm a good driver."

"You failed your test twice."

"I told you, that second time wasn't my fault."

We sat in silence for a few minutes, watching the sky darken. Every few seconds, the A-road at the top of the street would be briefly illuminated by a pair of headlights as a car flashed by. Hobbes scrabbled in the cat carrier, meowed for a while, then fell silent.

"When do you think they're going to go home?" Colin asked.

"Probably not until they think I've gone to bed," I said. "Maybe midnight."

"Midnight?"

"If we're lucky."

"You really owe me for this."

"I know."

Colin leant back in his seat with a sigh. I settled down to wait.

It was two hours later.

"I am driving in my car," Colin was singing to himself. "Doot doot doodle-oodle oot doot doo . . . It's not quite a Jaguar . . . doot doot doodle-oodle oot doot doo . . ."

"We're not driving," I told him without turning to look. I was leaning with my head propped up against the door. "And it's not your car."

"It's nice, though, right? I'd like to have a car like this."

"It's not like you need one."

"Be good for visiting my mum and dad."

I didn't answer. The car was quiet for a minute.

"I am driving in my car," Colin began again. "Doot doot doodle-oodle oot doot doo . . . It's not quite a Jaguar . . . doot doot doodle-oodle oot doot doo . . ."

For the hundredth time, I studied the minivan through the window.

"Bought it down in Muswell Hill . . . doot doot doodle-oodle oot doot doo . . . From a bloke who was from Brazil . . ."

"Can you not?" I asked him.

"Dude, this is boring."

"Yeah, welcome to spy work."

"You're not a spy."

I started to answer, then stopped. Three men were crossing the street up ahead of us, heading for Foxden Road.

Colin saw them at the same time and sat up, alert. "Those your guys?"

"No," I said. I recognised Ignas at the front. "My roommates. Damn it, why'd they have to come back now?"

Ignas and the others passed the van and disappeared from sight, heading for our house. "You think they could be in trouble?" Colin asked.

"I don't know," I said, chewing my lip. I didn't like this. Yeah, Scar and Diesel should be after me, not Ignas, Matis, and Vlad . . . but the Lithuanians had got in their way before.

I came to a decision quickly. I owed Ignas and the others; I had to warn them at least. "I'm going to sneak back in and tell them what's going on," I said. "You stay here and keep an eye on the van."

"Hurry up."

I ducked out of the car and backed off down the road, staying at a crouch until the van was out of sight before straightening up and breaking into a jog. I went through the apartment building's grounds, climbed the wall, and dropped down into our back garden, moving faster than before. It was the third time I'd done this today, and I wasn't being so cautious.

I came in through the back door to hear the familiar sounds of a football match coming from the front bedroom. I walked past the kitchen and reached for the door handle.

A deep voice spoke from behind me. "Hey."

I turned. A man was standing right behind me, his bulk filling the corridor.

It was Scar.

I froze.

"Open that door," Scar told me.

CHAPTER 19

I STOOD FACING Scar in the narrow hallway. Neither of us moved.

"Open that door," Scar repeated.

Scar was just in front of the kitchen door. Close, but just far enough that he couldn't grab me without taking a step forward. If I moved fast, I could get out of reach before he could—

My face must have shown what I was thinking, because Scar half opened his jacket to reveal the black metal grip of a handgun sticking up from his belt. "Don't get stupid."

My eyes flicked from Scar's face to that gun. Slowly, I turned the handle of the door.

It swung open to reveal the front bedroom. Ignas, Matis, and Vlad were crowded onto the bed, sitting still. Diesel was standing at the opposite side of the room, aiming a gun at the three Lithuanians. Four pairs of eyes turned towards me. The TV commentator's voice filled the room with breathless chatter.

"Close it," Scar told me.

I did. Diesel's eyes followed me, narrow with dislike. The door clicked shut, the sound of the TV becoming muffled again.

"We understand each other?" Scar asked.

I nodded.

"Get in the kitchen."

Slowly, I did as I was told. Scar backed into the kitchen ahead of me, watching as I followed him in. The room was small enough that with Scar in it already, there was barely room for me.

I focused on Scar's chest. The telltale glow of that strength sigl sprang out at me, essentia flowing through it and out into Scar's body. The ring with my haywire sigl rested on my finger, ready to be used.

"You're going to do a job," Scar told me.

I blinked. "What?"

"A job."

"What kind of job?"

"The kind where you shut the fuck up and do as you're told," Scar said. "Now, we're going to walk out the front door, get into the van, and drive off nice and peaceful. That way, nobody gets hurt. You understand?"

I'd forgotten just how big Scar was; he could probably break me in half even without that strength sigl. Having him looming over me like this was really scary.

But I had that Primal sigl ready and waiting, and that made all the difference. It didn't make Scar or his gun any less frightening, but it turned it into an energising sort of fear, the kind that sharpens your senses and readies you to fight or flee. And it gave me the courage to say the next word. "No."

Scar stared down at me with cold blue eyes. "Excuse me?"

"I'm not getting in your van."

"Don't make me do this the hard way, kid."

"Last time I talked to Lucella, she told me she'd make me disappear," I said. "And she told me the way she'd do it would be by having you guys drive me off in that van."

Scar stared at me. The silence stretched out. I held my breath.

Then Scar gave a snort of laughter and the tension eased. "Yeah, she *would* say something like that."

I relaxed slightly, but only slightly. I'd been watching Scar's right hand like a hawk. If he'd moved it even an inch towards that gun, I'd have struck.

"We're not going to make you disappear," Scar told me. "You come with us, do as you're told for an hour, then walk away."

"Walk away from what?"

"Not your problem."

I gave Scar a sceptical look.

"What, you think we're going to off you?" Scar asked. "Ashfords are a bunch of ruthless bastards, but that's not how they do things."

"All right," I said. "Say I believe you. Then why are you working for them?"

"What?"

"I mean, there's a reason they're sending you instead of doing it themselves, right?" I said. "If something goes wrong, they're just going to blame it on you."

Scar was silent, and I decided to push my luck. "What if you just go back and tell them you couldn't find me?"

Scar looked at me for a second. "You've got some balls, I'll give you that."

"So?" I asked hopefully.

"No."

My heart sank. Yeah, I hadn't really expected that to work.

"Let's go," Scar said.

"Where?"

"Jesus," Scar said. "You ask way too many questions, you know that?" He nodded to the door. "You get with the plan, or we do this the hard way. What's it going to be?"

I hesitated. I could do this, right now. Hit Scar with my haywire sigl, cripple him and take him out, maybe even grab his gun while he was down. Then head for the other room and take down Diesel the same way.

But it had the potential to go really wrong, especially the part where I used my haywire sigl on Diesel while he had a gun in his hand. Ignas and the others would probably help if it came to a fight, but this wasn't their battle. They'd helped me once already; I didn't want to risk them getting shot.

"All right," I told Scar.

Scar gestured towards the door. "Move."

WE LEFT THE house. Scar must have given Diesel some signal, because a few seconds later Diesel came backing out of the front bedroom before putting away his gun and following us out. Scar led me towards the minivan, slid open the side door, and waited. I paused, looking down the street out of the corner of my eye. I could just see Kiran's car, though it was too dark for me to make out Colin.

"In," Scar told me.

I got in.

Scar followed me into the back of the van. Diesel got into the front, then twisted to stare at me. "You going to leave him like that?" he asked Scar.

"Like what?"

"Last time he blinded me."

"He shone a fucking flashlight in your face," Scar said with irritation. "What do you want, sunglasses?"

Diesel gave me a last glower, then turned and started up the engine.

I watched silently, trying not to show how keyed up I was. I was incredibly aware of exactly how far away Scar and Diesel were, everything from the angles they were sitting at to how long it would take them to reach their guns. I'd been waiting for Scar to search me or demand I take my sigl rings off, and if he had, that would have started a fight. But as far as he and Diesel knew, I was just an amateur with a single weak light sigl.

The minivan drove away from my street and turned onto the A-road. I couldn't see behind us without craning my neck, so I had no way of knowing whether Colin had seen us. I hoped like hell he was paying attention.

We drove north towards Stratford station. Once we were there, Diesel turned left onto the A11.

"Where are we going?" I asked.

"Shut up," Diesel told me.

We headed west into Central London. Traffic lights shone red through the tinted windows. The van slowed to a stop, drove off once the lights turned green, stopped again at the next set.

It occurred to me that I could crash the van right now. Wait for Diesel to get up some speed, then hit him with my haywire sigl. He and Scar probably wouldn't even know what was happening until it was too late. But all that would do would be to put me back where I'd started.

No, I decided. *Wait.* The van drove on through the night.

We drove for maybe half an hour. I kept an eye on the landmarks, waiting for the van to turn north towards the Ashford mansion, but instead we went deeper and deeper into Central London. The traffic grew denser and the pauses at traffic lights longer.

Only when we reached Holborn did we start making turns. I took the opportunity to glance out of the side windows, trying to see if Colin was following. I saw the headlights of other cars, but between the darkness and the tinted windows I couldn't tell whether any of them was his.

It was only when I caught a glimpse of barred white-and-black walls and peaked roofs that something stirred in my memory. But before I could get a closer look, the van turned off the street. Through the windscreen I saw a yellow traffic barrier rising, then the car tilted downward and we were driving down a ramp through a tunnel with concrete walls.

We came out into an underground parking garage. Diesel pulled the van into one of the parking spaces and switched off the engine. Scar slid back the side door and got out. I followed him and looked around.

The garage was big and bleak, all grey concrete and straight lines. White paint on the floor marked out parking spaces, but few were occupied. There were only two ways out: the ramp that we'd come in by, and a single small door at the far end, with a green glowing EXIT sign.

Scar had taken out his phone; he'd dialled a number, and as I watched, he put the phone to his ear, waiting for an answer while he kept an eye on me. Diesel was getting out of the other side of the van. Something was tickling at my senses. I focused on my essentia sight—

Light surged out at me. There was a Light Well, above us and in the direction of that door, massively powerful. More than that, it was familiar. Where had I—

And then in a flash I put it together. We were under the Well in Chancery Lane, the same one that I'd found back in April, and the Well that Bridget had told me Calhoun had been put in charge of. All of a sudden I understood exactly why I'd been brought here.

"We're here," Scar said into his phone, then waited for a reply. "Yeah . . . Okay." He hung up and turned to me. "Let's go."

"No," I told him.

"I wasn't asking."

"You're going to raid this Well and blame it on me," I told Scar. "Aren't you?"

Scar's expression didn't change, but from his lack of reaction I knew instantly that I was right. It had never made sense that they'd want me to do a job. Anything the Ashfords could want, they could find someone who could do it better than I could.

Except if the "job" was to be the fall guy. Then forcing me into it made *perfect* sense.

"In there," Scar said, nodding towards the door with the EXIT sign.

"What, so I'll show up on the security cameras?"

"We don't have time for this shit," Diesel said angrily. "Just beat his arse and throw him in."

I glanced from Scar to Diesel, measuring distances. Scar was about three strides away, Diesel next to the van. Whichever one I didn't target would be free to go after me.

Okay, I decided. *Let's do this.* I felt adrenaline start to race through my body.

"Listen, kid," Scar told me. "One way or another, you're going through that door. You can do it the easy way, or . . ." Scar tailed off with a frown, his eyes shifting past me as a soft, rapid pattering echoed through the garage.

I turned.

A grey blur came racing down the ramp and then shot like an arrow towards Diesel. I had just enough time to see the glow of the enhancement sigl before Hobbes leapt onto Diesel with a banshee yowl.

Diesel yelled, staggering back. Hobbes had latched on to Diesel's leg, his feet going like four tiny buzz saws, and Diesel tried unsuccessfully to kick him off before grabbing at him. But by that point I'd sent a beam from my haywire sigl right into Diesel's chest.

All the work I'd put into that sigl—from injuring myself to learning what I'd done wrong to turning that same mistake into a weapon to be used against someone else—paid off in that moment. As my beam touched the Life sigl on Diesel's chest, the regulator in the sigl shut down and the essentia flowing into his body surged out of control. Diesel's grasping hand missed Hobbes and he tried again, but overcorrected with a jerk. I saw his eyes go wide in pain and knew he'd probably just torn half a dozen muscles; his leg went out from under him, and he went down with a crash.

I caught a flicker of movement at the corner of my eye and turned to see Scar grabbing for me. I dodged, but his fingers caught my sleeve and yanked, trying to pull me in. Instead of fighting it I went with the pull, and in the split second before I crashed into him, I triggered my flash sigl.

Light exploded and Scar swore, blinded. We bounced off each other, but Scar kept his grip on my sleeve; I twisted around and used my slam sigl, hammer blows of compressed air smashing into Scar's head. Scar took five hits from my slam sigl, shrugged them all off, then punched me in the chest.

It felt like being kicked by a horse. The impact drove the breath from my body and sent me to my knees; grey specks swam in my vision but I managed to stay conscious. Scar scrubbed at his face with his free hand, blinking, but as he turned his eyes angrily down towards me I triggered another flash burst right in his face.

Scar shouted and this time he let me go. I fell to the concrete, did a backwards roll, then came up with my haywire sigl levelled and hit Scar with it at full power.

The effect was more dramatic this time. Scar had just been straightening up; as the sigl on his chest went wild, he overbalanced and went over backwards. His head hit the concrete with a crack and he lay stunned.

I turned on Diesel, only to find him curled into a ball and staying very still. Hobbes was prowling around him, tail swishing; every time Diesel made a move, Hobbes would spring forward, claws out and ready to slash until Diesel froze again. Looking around, I saw that I was the only one left standing. The fight was over.

"Guess this was the hard way," I said to no one in particular.

Hobbes made a guttural, threatening noise.

The sound of running footsteps made me look towards the ramp just in time to see Colin come jogging around the corner and skid to a stop. He looked at me, then down at Scar, Diesel, and Hobbes.

"Nice of you to show up," I told Colin.

Colin stared at the men on the ground, then at me. "Dude. What the *hell*?"

I took a last glance to make sure that Scar and Diesel weren't getting up, then walked to the van to try to fetch Hobbes. "Okay, first, thanks for following me," I told Colin. "Second, why is Hobbes out of his cat carrier?"

"Because he ripped it open!" Colin said. "Then as soon as I opened the door, he took off like a guided missile. What have you been feeding him?"

"Long story . . . Okay, Hobbes? Hobbes! Come on. You've won. Let's go." I tried to pick Hobbes up and the cat hopped away, circling Diesel with a baleful stare. He ignored Scar completely.

Well, if nothing else, now I know which of them did it. Diesel's gun was lying on the floor a little way away. He wasn't going for it, but I kicked it under the minivan just to be sure.

"Is it safe for us to be here?" Colin asked.

"No."

Colin looked at Diesel and Scar. "Did you actually take these guys down by yourself?"

"Yes."

"How?"

"Conspiracy bullshit, remember? Hobbes, *come on.*"

Hobbes gave Diesel a threatening yowl . . . then stopped. His head snapped around and he looked towards the ramp, his ears flattening and his tail curling back between his legs. Then without a backward glance, he fled across the garage, disappearing under a car at the far side.

I looked at Hobbes, then back at the ramp. The garage was silent.

"I think we should go," I told Colin, and started walking quickly after Hobbes.

"Go where? Hey, wait up." Colin jogged to catch up with me. "Why—"

"Shh!"

I could see Hobbes's yellow eyes shining from beneath the car. He looked scared, and just as I noticed that, I heard the distant sound of footsteps from the direction of the ramp.

Colin opened his mouth to say something and I put a finger to my lips. I grabbed him by the arm, dragged him around behind the car, and pulled him down with me so that we were both out of sight. Then I poked my head up to look through the windows of the car.

Two people came walking down the ramp into the parking garage, a man and a woman. The woman was shorter, and even at this distance I recognised her instantly: Lucella. Her eyes came to rest on Scar and Diesel, and I saw her frown.

But it was the man beside Lucella who caught my attention.

He wore a black suit with a flat-brimmed hat tilted down to hide his eyes and had long blond hair that fell down his back in a braid. His clothes on their own would have been strange, but something about him made me pause.

I felt something push against my leg and looked down to see Hobbes pressed against me. His eyes were fixed on the man in the hat, and his ears were flat against his skull. I looked from Hobbes to the man.

"Hey," Lucella called, her voice echoing through the garage. She stalked over to Diesel and gave him a kick. "What are you doing, taking a nap?"

"Who is it?" Colin whispered from beside me.

"Trouble," I whispered. "Stay quiet."

"You said he was here," Lucella was saying. "So where is he?"

Diesel mumbled something.

Lucella's voice rose dangerously. "What do you mean, you don't know?"

Mumble.

"A *hellcat*? Are you high? You just called me *five minutes ago* and told me—"

The man in the black hat spoke. "Do we have a problem?"

"No," Lucella said, glancing quickly at Black Hat. "No problem." She bent down and carried out a quick whispered conversation with Diesel.

Beside me, I felt Colin trying to lift himself up for a better view. I put a hand on his shoulder to stop him.

Lucella finished with Diesel, then turned to face Black Hat and took a breath. "They lost him."

Black Hat looked back at her. "They lost him."

"Yeah."

"And how did that happen?"

"Because they're idiots!"

"If you thought they were idiots," Black Hat said mildly, "why did you give them the job?"

Lucella shot Black Hat a look, then kicked Diesel again. "Get that useless piece of shit on his feet and *find him!*"

Diesel scrambled to his feet, jogged over to where Scar was stirring, and pulled Scar up. The two of them began to look around the garage.

I spoke quietly in Colin's ear. "I'm going to hide us. Stay quiet and don't move."

Lucella had stepped next to Black Hat and the two of them were arguing, their voices too low for me to overhear. Scar and Diesel split up and began to search, Diesel limping in our direction.

The garage was big but open; as soon as Diesel got around to this side of the car, we'd be in clear view. I leant in close to Colin, slipped on my headband, and activated my vision and diffraction sigls.

The world went blue. I felt Colin go stiff; I put my hand on his shoulder and gave it a warning squeeze, then poured as much essentia into my diffraction field as I could. If I'd judged it right, it should be just barely enough to cover us and Hobbes.

Diesel came into view. I froze, holding my breath as I focused on keeping the light-bending field smooth and steady. Diesel's eyes swept over us . . .

. . . and moved on. He turned and limped away.

I heard Scar say something and Lucella replied, her voice loud and angry. "We just came from there, you meathead! You had one job! One! Job!"

Scar started to answer but was cut off by the scrape of a door. Both he and Diesel turned towards the door with the "EXIT" sign just in time to see a boy step through and start walking across the concrete. It was . . .

... Tobias?

I held very still, trusting to my invisibility field. What the hell was going on?

"Hey," Tobias called.

I saw Lucella roll her eyes to the ceiling. "Oh, for God's sake."

Tobias marched across the garage, coming to a stop a little distance from Lucella. He gestured at Diesel and Scar. "You have something you want to tell me?"

"Hello, cousin dear," Lucella said. "Everything ready?"

Tobias looked from Diesel to Scar. "Why do they look like they've been in a fight?"

"Don't worry about it."

Tobias stared at Lucella. "Did you have them kidnap Stephen?"

"No."

Tobias kept staring at Lucella for three seconds, then took a deep breath. *"Are you serious?"*

Lucella sighed. "Here we go again."

"We talked about this! As few people as possible, remember?"

"Oh, get real," Lucella told him. "You really thought Charles was going to say 'oh well' and forget the whole thing? No, he's going to go *fucking ballistic*. Someone is paying for this, and it's not going to be me."

"It didn't have to be him, either!"

"What's the matter?" Lucella said with a smile. "Feeling guilty?"

"We had a plan," Tobias said tightly.

"Yeah, and it was a stupid plan, so I changed it."

Tobias looked from Scar to Diesel, who both seemed to be trying unsuccessfully to fade into the background. "Where is he?"

Lucella scowled. "I don't know, ask Holmes and Watson over here."

"Are you telling me you lost him?"

"Fascinating as this little family drama is," Black Hat interrupted, "I'm going to have to ask that you put it on hold. Lucella, I assume this is the one you were telling me about?"

Lucella shot Tobias a dirty look, then took a breath. "Yes. My cousin." She gestured to Black Hat. "This is my . . . friend."

Tobias looked at Black Hat. "Friend."

"You've been wanting to meet him," Lucella said. "Well, here you go." She stepped back. "Enjoy."

Tobias gave Lucella a long look, then turned to Black Hat. "Nice to meet you, uh . . . ?"

"You can call me Byron," the man said, his mouth curving in a smile that didn't reach his eyes. "And what can I do for you, Lucella's cousin?"

Tobias took a deep breath. "I want in."

"To what?"

"You know what."

"That all depends on what you think you're getting into," Byron said with a raised eyebrow. "I'm more curious as to why you're interested."

"Lucella met you two or three years ago, right?" Tobias said. "Through one of the other girls at King's. That was when she started acting differently. She stopped acting scared of Charles, and she started ordering other people in the family around. And they'd do what she told them. It was like she had some new sigl that could control people."

I glanced sideways at Lucella. She was watching Tobias without expression.

"And?" Byron asked.

"And you can't *do* that," Tobias said. "I checked, and there's no such thing as a 'mind control sigl.' There are a few Life sigls that can do bio-emotion control, but nothing like what she did. I asked three different experts and they all told me it was impossible."

"Perhaps you were asking the wrong experts," Byron said. He looked amused, but was studying Tobias in an appraising sort of way. "Well, you've done your research, but you haven't answered my question. What is it that you believe we are?"

"I don't really care."

"Really?"

"You can do things no one else can," Tobias said. "I'm guessing that's how you could make this deal with Tyr, right? I want that kind of power. Where I have to get it from . . . I don't see how that matters."

Byron looked at Tobias for a long moment. Then he broke the silence with a small sigh. "How disappointing."

Tobias looked taken aback.

Byron looked sideways at Lucella. "You haven't told him?"

Lucella shrugged, studying her nails.

"Hey," Tobias said. "Did you hear me?"

"I heard you," Byron said, turning back to Tobias. "You think this is about power? Some set of tricks or techniques that you can take for yourself, then use to scheme and manoeuvre until you rise to the top of your House? Is that what you came here hoping for?"

Tobias hesitated.

Byron sighed. "Go home, little boy."

Tobias looked between Byron and Lucella before pointing at his cousin. "I can do anything she can!"

"No, you really can't."

Tobias glared angrily at Byron. "I'll tell Charles!"

Byron looked back at Tobias, then began to laugh.

Tobias looked shocked, then furious. He tried to speak, but

Byron just kept on laughing. Tobias looked around at Lucella, Diesel, and Scar; none of them would meet his eyes.

Something in Tobias seemed to snap. He ran towards the ramp, Byron's laughter echoing around him. Only once he reached the tunnel mouth, and the way out of the garage, did he turn back towards Byron and Lucella. "Someday I'll be stronger than any of you!" Tobias shouted at them, his voice cracking. "You should have helped me when you had the chance!" He turned and fled up the ramp.

Byron's laugh rang out for a few more seconds, mixing with Tobias's fading footsteps, then he stopped. "Well," he said with a chuckle. "At least that was amusing."

Lucella was still studying her nails. "Cringe," she said shortly, then looked at Byron. "So . . . ?"

"Not so fast," Byron told Lucella. "I said it was amusing. That doesn't excuse you wasting my time."

"There's still Tyr."

"Yes, yes," Byron said with a sigh. "You and your inheritance. All right, Lucella. Go play your games. Just don't forget who you really serve." He turned and walked away.

"Hey!" Lucella called after him. "What about Tyr?"

"I'm sure you can handle it," Byron said with an airy wave. He disappeared up the ramp in the same direction as Tobias.

Lucella stared after Byron. "I don't serve anyone," she said to herself, so softly that I wasn't completely sure if I'd heard. "And definitely not you."

"Uh," Diesel said. He and Scar had stayed very quiet through the conversation, looking as though they'd been trying hard to avoid drawing attention. "Boss?"

Lucella kept staring for a moment longer, then shook her head. "All right," she said, sounding as though she was talking to herself. "All right. Screw them both." She turned to Scar and Diesel.

"Get over here, and once Tyr arrive, stand behind me. Let's at least *pretend* like you've got a fucking clue."

Scar and Diesel moved to obey. Diesel was still limping.

Lucella watched them in disgust. "Jesus," she said. "Okay, stand there. Back. *Further* back, you're supposed to be body-guarding me, not trying to look down my dress. Okay, you know what, forget it. Just stand still, keep your mouths shut, and if we're lucky maybe they won't figure out how frigging useless you are."

"What's going on?" Colin whispered.

"Shh."

"I still can't—" Colin began, then fell silent as we both heard the growl of an engine. It grew louder and louder, until with a scrape of tyres something huge and heavy came bumping down the ramp and turned into the garage.

CHAPTER 20

THE VEHICLE DRIVING into the garage was a van, big and blocky and painted in dark colours. It looked like a heavier version of one of those paddy wagons the police use for football matches. Lucella, Scar, and Diesel stood watching as the van pulled into one of the parking spaces. The growl of the engine died, then the doors at the back swung open and someone stepped out.

It was a man . . . probably. He wore a rounded helmet with thick shoulder and chest plates, and as I looked down I saw that his armour just kept on going, similar pieces protecting his arms, midsection, and upper and lower legs, covering his entire body from head to toe. It looked too big and heavy to be real, far thicker and bulkier than the body armour you see soldiers wearing on the news. He was holding a gun, but the armour was so oversized that it made the weapon look like a toy.

A second man wearing similar armour emerged behind the first, followed by three more. The van creaked as they got out, though their footsteps on the concrete were surprisingly quiet. Looking at the armoured men, I felt a chill. They looked like they should be lumbering and slow, but instead their movements were smooth, almost graceful. The man at the front marched forward, coming to a stop in front of Lucella and staring down. The garage lights reflected off the black lenses covering his eyes.

"You our contact?" the armoured man said. His voice echoed through the helmet.

"No, I'm here for the scenery," Lucella told him.

The armoured man paused for a second as if listening for something, then glanced back and gave a signal. Two of the armoured men began walking towards the door at the end of the garage. "Codes," the man at the front ordered, turning back to Lucella and holding out one gauntleted hand.

"Money first," Lucella said.

"You'll get paid once we're done."

"Yeah, screw that," Lucella told him. "Money." She snapped her fingers. "Chop-chop."

Much as I hated Lucella, I had to admit that she had guts. Those armoured soldiers looked intimidating as hell: both Scar and Diesel looked as if they wanted to turn and run, and if I'd been in their place, I'd have been thinking the same thing. But Lucella was treating the one in front of her like a waiter who was giving her poor service. I didn't know whether it was bravery or sheer obliviousness, but it was kind of impressive either way.

The man stared down at Lucella for a long moment, then he turned back and called something over his shoulder. He paused for ten seconds, then turned back to Lucella. "Transfer's done. Now. Codes."

"Wait," Lucella said, then pulled out her phone and started scrolling.

There was a pause.

"So?" the armoured man said.

"I'm logging in," Lucella told him.

Another pause. Scar and Diesel shifted their feet. The other soldiers looked around.

"Can we hurry this up?" the one who seemed to be the leader said.

"Give me a minute."

The leader looked down at Lucella's phone and pointed. "The square with the fire hydrant is that one."

Lucella gave him an annoyed glance, tapped the phone, scrolled for a second, then nodded. "Okay, got it. Code for the alarms is six-seven-eight-four-three-two, everything else is switched off. Have fun."

The garage broke into motion. The leader walked back to the other soldiers and spoke with them briefly, then another man came out of the van, this one unarmoured but carrying what looked like a toolbox. The van doors slammed shut; one of the soldiers knocked on the driver's side, and the van started up again, wheeling around in a circle and driving off up the ramp and out of sight. The squad of soldiers and the unarmoured man began marching towards the door.

In the meantime, Lucella had been whispering quietly to Diesel and Scar. As I watched, all three of them pulled on black masks and then followed the soldiers at a distance. The soldiers filed through the door at the end of the garage, passing under the "EXIT" sign one by one. Lucella, Diesel, and Scar followed. The door shut behind them and the garage was still.

I stayed hidden, watching and waiting for thirty seconds before letting my diffraction field drop. Colour flooded back into the world, reds and yellows joining the blues. I stood up, stretching the stiffness out of my legs.

Colin scrambled to his feet, looking from side to side. "Okay," he asked me, his voice low. "What the *hell* is going on here? How did you turn all those lights off? Why didn't any of those other guys seem to care? And what were they even doing here?"

"First, I didn't turn the lights off. I put up an invisibility field. You couldn't see because I was bending light around us."

"Just tell me the truth!"

"Second," I said, ignoring him, "those guys are from a drucraft corporation and they're here to steal the essentia from the Well in the building above this garage. The reason Lucella got those two guys to bring me here is so that she can blame the whole thing on me. I only figured it out ten minutes ago."

"Jesus." Colin raked a hand through his hair, looking away. "I did *not* sign up for this. I thought this was just some rich girl with a grudge, not this corporate espionage shit!"

"I know. I'm sorry."

Colin looked away, then back at me. He looked rattled. "What are these guys going to do if we get in their way?"

"Well, they were carrying guns," I said. "So maybe let's not find out?"

Colin stared.

Hobbes was still crouched at my feet; he was looking around warily but didn't seem inclined to run away anymore. I scooped him up and walked quickly over to the ramp, beckoning Colin to follow. Once I was there, I peered cautiously up towards the exit. The path out to the street looked clear.

"All right," I said, turning back to Colin. "Get back to the car and get ready to leave. I might be joining you really soon, and if I do, we'll want to get out of here fast." I pushed Hobbes into his unresisting arms. "And try not to lose my cat this time."

"What about you?"

"I'm going after Lucella."

"What are you going to do if you find her?"

"Turn invisible, for a start. Don't worry, I'm not planning on getting caught."

"Look," Colin began. "Can you just talk straight to me and—"

I took a step back and activated my diffraction and vision sigls.

The world returned to its familiar shade of blue. Colin stopped dead, staring. From his perspective, I'd have seemed to vanish into thin air.

"What are you staring at?" I asked, and Colin jumped. "Go. Now!"

Colin hesitated, then turned and jogged up the ramp. Hobbes twisted around in his grip to look back at me with interest, but didn't object. I watched them go, then once they were safely out of sight, took a deep breath and headed after Lucella.

THE DOOR AT the end of the garage led into a basement with a lift and a set of stairs. I headed up.

Although I'd put on a brave face for Colin's sake, I didn't like my situation one bit. Now that the soldiers from Tyr had arrived, Lucella was going to let them drain the Well, then pin it on me. I'd get blamed for the raid, and Calhoun would get blamed for letting it happen. Meanwhile, Lucella not only got to hurt two of her rivals at the same time, she was getting paid for the privilege.

The question was whether I could do anything to stop it. I could walk out of here right now, but Lucella could just accuse me anyway, at which point it'd be her word against mine. Given that Charles Ashford already didn't like me, I didn't like my odds of proving my innocence. What I needed was evidence, something that I could point at to prove that this whole thing was Lucella's fault. But how?

I left the stairs on the ground floor to come out into an office building. It was dark and quiet, the only sound the distant rush of the Holborn traffic. I could feel the essentia in the Well, enormously strong and very close. I headed towards it.

I ran into one of those armoured soldiers almost immediately. The corridor ended in a set of glass-fronted doors that opened up into some sort of courtyard; people were moving inside, but the soldier was standing right in front of the doors and I didn't dare get too close. Instead I paused and studied the soldier, focusing on my essentia sight.

The red-brown glow of Matter essentia sprang out at me. It was flowing through the armour, coming from . . . oh, that was interesting. The man was wearing a pair of sigls, not one, set into his armour on either side of his chest. The essentia from the left sigl flowed down into the armour's left half, and vice versa for the right. A lightening effect, one that reduced an object's effective mass. So you could make a suit of armour out of solid metal, thick enough to stop a bullet, and still have it be light enough to move in. Using two sigls instead of one spread the load and probably allowed them to use lower-ranked sigls to keep costs down. Pretty neat.

I shook my head; this wasn't the time for research. The Well was in that courtyard, but getting closer would mean walking past that soldier, and I wasn't willing to bet my life on him not noticing my diffraction field. I withdrew to the stairs and went up one floor before coming out into the first-floor corridor.

That was better. There were windows looking down into the courtyard, but no soldier on guard. I walked forward and peered down through the glass.

The courtyard at the centre of the building was square. Potted bushes, paving stones, and concentric rings of grass made up a small, carefully tended garden, with a tree standing at the centre, rising up into the sky, its branches overhanging the four sides of the building around it. The Well was right there, at the base of the tree, overflowing with Light essentia, a hundred times the strength of the one on my street.

Although it didn't look as if it'd be overflowing for much longer. The Tyr soldiers were scattered around the courtyard, but the unarmoured guy had set up shop at the foot of the tree, his toolbox open and the glint of equipment coming from inside. It was hard to see through the glass; looking around, I spotted a pair of balconies looking down onto the courtyard, one to the north, one to the south. I circled around, keeping back from the windows, and slipped out through the doors onto the south balcony, coming out into the London air and the distant rush of traffic from over the rooftops.

The unarmoured man seemed to be taking a reading from some sort of device, pausing occasionally to type on a tablet. I thought I could pick up a flicker of essentia from the thing in his hand, but the Well's aura made it hard to tell. I'd never had the chance to watch someone draining a Well before, and part of me wanted to see how they'd do it—would they make a sigl right here?—but I knew this wasn't the time. I was the one who was going to take the rap for this, and I still had no idea what the hell to do about it.

My eyes flicked around the courtyard. It was maybe sixty feet square, darkened windows looking down from all four sides, dimly lit from the orange glow reflecting off the clouds. I couldn't see where Lucella had gone. Maybe I could disable her, then wait for the police to show up? No, those soldiers would murder me.

As I looked around the courtyard, though, I frowned. This close, the Light Well was dazzling; it was like standing next to a bonfire, the aura so strong that it was hard to make out anything else. But the more time I spent around these Wells, the more I was finding that I could adjust. The Well's aura was powerful, but it wasn't really any different from my own Well, just stronger.

And right now, I was noticing that not *all* the Light essentia in the courtyard was concentrated in that Well. There was a second, much smaller concentration coming from the balcony on the far side of the courtyard. It was only a tiny amount, a cupful of water set against a lake, but the more I quieted my thoughts, the more I emptied my mind and focused, the more I became sure that it was coming from *there*, that point at the centre of the balcony, exactly opposite me.

I was still staring at that spot when the air there shimmered and changed colour, revealing a young man with white hair and black clothes. His pale face stood out in the shadows. To my eyes, essentia glowed from sigls on his hands and chest, shrouding him in an aura of power.

"You are not who I expected," Calhoun Ashford told the men beneath him.

All around the courtyard, helmets twisted around, guns tilting upwards. The technician stopped what he was doing.

"Identify yourself," the Tyr leader called.

Calhoun stood on the balcony, looking down with one black-gloved hand resting on the railing. "When I discovered that the security rota had been altered, I assumed it must have been someone from my own family," Calhoun said. He seemed very calm for someone with so many guns pointed at him. "I suppose I shouldn't have been surprised that they'd bring in help."

I saw the technician look up at the Tyr leader, as if for orders. The leader made a "stay" gesture.

"I want the name of your contact within House Ashford who arranged for our House security to be sent elsewhere and who deactivated the cameras and alarms," Calhoun said. "Tell me now, and I will allow you and your men to safely withdraw."

The soldiers stared up at Calhoun. The courtyard was very quiet.

"Get the fuck out of here before we shoot you," the Tyr leader said.

Calhoun looked back at the leader. I held my breath.

"As you wish," Calhoun said. He turned and walked away.

The leader called out something to his men, but I was still watching Calhoun. As soon as the edge of the balcony hid him from the soldiers, Light essentia pulsed, and Calhoun's shape blurred and vanished. Then from where he had been, a man-sized source of essentia, moving very fast, came flying back out onto the balcony. It left a faint shimmer in the air as it vaulted the rail to come down next to one of the soldiers with a thump.

The soldier spun. He wasn't fast enough.

Motion essentia flashed and the soldier flew thirty feet to crash into the wall. The leader shouted an order, and the court-yard erupted in a roar of stuttering gunfire; Calhoun shimmered back into view, his left hand raised, a sigl set into his glove glowing yellow. Tiny flashes sparked in midair as bullets collided with an invisible barrier, pattering to the paving stones at his feet. Calhoun backed away behind his shield, eyes narrowed in concentration, until a pillar came between him and the soldiers; in the instant that he was cut off from view I felt a flash of essentia, and he was invisible again.

Shouts and gunshots filled the courtyard, a chaos of noise and movement. There was too much going on for me to take it all in; I heard the whine of a bullet, followed by the sound of shattering glass, and I ducked behind the balcony's brick walls. Calhoun shimmered into view at the opposite side of the courtyard and struck again, this time with some sort of ranged attack that pulsed outward from his hand. Plants froze, leaves and blades of grass frosting over, and one of the soldiers staggered and fell. Again the remaining soldiers sent a barrage of gunfire at Calhoun, and again he deployed that Motion shield, backing away into the shadows.

The battle was frightening to watch. I was sure that if I'd been down there, I'd have been hit and bleeding by now, just from the sheer volume of fire; the unarmoured technician had fled at the first shots, his tools abandoned at the foot of the tree. Calhoun hadn't even been scratched. That shield of his seemed able to shrug off any amount of gunfire, and he was *fast*, his reactions quicker than should have been possible. Despite the odds, he actually seemed to be winning, though the soldier he'd flung across the courtyard had got to his feet and the one he'd frozen was dragging himself towards his teammates.

But then movement above caught my eye.

It was Lucella. She and another man were on the same level as me, on the opposite side of the building. I could just make them out through the windows; the man was masked, but I had the feeling it was Scar. Lucella's face was twisted in anger as she gave Scar some order; he shook his head, then jerked, flinching back as—

A bullet slammed into the balcony. My concentration slipped and I dropped to the floor, hearing the shouts and gunfire from below. Only once I'd regained my focus did I poke my head cautiously above the railing.

In the few seconds that I'd been out of sight, Scar had come out onto the far balcony. His gun was in his hand, and he leant out over the railing, scanning the courtyard below.

I peered over the balcony to see that the battle was still raging. Calhoun was fighting hand to hand with a soldier who was wielding a baton whose tip sparked with electricity. The baton lashed out; Calhoun ducked with inhuman speed and struck; essentia flashed and the soldier went flying, tumbling over and over across the floor. Before Calhoun could follow up, one of the other soldiers opened fire and Calhoun had to bring up his shield again. I could see it now that I knew what to look for, a curved invisible barrier, flashes of light sparking on it as the kinetic energy of the impacts was converted into essentia, causing the bullets to drop harmlessly to the floor.

On the balcony above, Scar hesitated, then aimed his gun down at Calhoun.

I acted on reflex, channelling into my haywire sigl and firing in a single motion, pouring everything I had into making that Primal beam as precise and far reaching as possible. It hit Scar's strength sigl dead-on, and even at this range, the effect was instant. Scar staggered, falling heavily against the railing; his gun jarred against the metal and fell from his hand, clattering to the paving stones below.

I lowered my hand, wondering if that had been a bad idea. If anyone spotted me—

Suddenly I realised I was seeing in colour, not in shades of blue. I'd lost concentration on my other sigls when I fired at Scar. I looked down to see one of the soldiers below looking straight at me.

I threw myself backwards, landing on the balcony hard enough to jar the breath from my lungs. I heard the deadly chatter of gunfire, followed by shattering windows; shards of glass rained down, and I scrambled frantically back into the building. I could hear voices shouting orders: the soldiers below and a closer one that sounded like Lucella. I crab-walked backwards, came to my feet, and darted around the corner just in time to run into Diesel.

Diesel reached for a weapon, but I'd had just enough warning to be ready and I was sick and tired of this guy. I blinded him with a flash, then gave him another haywire blast. If Diesel had been smart, he would have taken that strength sigl off by now, but he hadn't, and he went down with a crash to reveal Lucella in the corridor behind him, staring at me with wide eyes.

Lucella turned and ran.

I started after her, then nearly fell as a half-blind Diesel grabbed my ankle. I hit him with my haywire sigl again, then kicked him in the head with my free leg until he let go. The corridor shook as one of the soldiers was slammed into the wall just outside before falling back down to the courtyard below. I ran after Lucella.

The time it had taken me to deal with Diesel had given Lucella a head start. I reached the end of the corridor and looked left and right just in time to see the door to the stairwell swinging shut. I made it into the stairwell, heard the sound of running footsteps from above, and raced up the stairs after Lucella, two at a time.

I burst out onto the rooftop thirty seconds later. The London skyline was all around, yellow and white lights against the darkness, and I had to scan the roof for a few seconds before I made out Lucella's shape fleeing through the gloom. I ran after her; the route took me around the top of the courtyard, and I caught a glimpse down to see that the battle was still going on. The Tyr soldiers were retreating, one dragging a fallen teammate while the weapons of the others spat fire back at Calhoun. Then they were out of sight, leaving only me and Lucella.

I let essentia pour into my enhancement sigl. I'd kept it deactivated until now so as to have more to spare for my invisibility, but I wasn't hiding anymore and I felt strength flow through me, my legs driving me forward through the night. We were running alongside the main road, and I saw cars driving below, their headlights sweeping over the streets.

The flat roof ahead turned into a peaked one, and Lucella clambered across it. I could see the glow of Motion essentia around her, some effect that I didn't have time to recognise, but she was moving fast and with no apparent concern for the drop. Maybe she thought I wouldn't dare to follow. *Wrong.* I went scrambling after her, slipping but managing to catch myself and jumping off the other side onto a wider roof coloured a pale blue. Lucella was ahead of me at the roof's far side, but as she drew close to it she checked, turning south.

I charged straight for Lucella and tackled her.

We went tumbling to the rooftop, bouncing off a ventilator and rolling to a stop. Lucella slashed at me with something on one of her fingers; I caught the green flash of Life essentia and twisted away, coming to my feet. All of a sudden everything was still. Lucella and I faced each other on the rooftop, maybe ten feet apart, both of us crouched and ready to strike.

The lights of the office building across the street shone down, yellow-white squares in their geometric rows, but our rooftop was shadowed and dark. I heard a flutter of wings and caught movement out of the corner of my eye as a bird alighted on one of the ventilators, but I didn't take my eyes off Lucella.

"What is your *problem*?" Lucella said viciously. Her face was twisted with anger, the lights of the city reflected in her eyes.

"What's the matter, Lucella?" I asked. "Things not going to plan?"

"*God*, you're annoying!" Lucella told me. "What are you even doing here?"

"You tried to kidnap me, kill my cat, and frame me for a raid," I said. "You really didn't think I'd have a problem with that?"

Lucella gave me a blank look. "Why would I be thinking about you at all?"

I looked at Lucella for a second, then barked a laugh. "That really is how it works in your world, isn't it? People like me, we're supposed to just disappear into the background when you don't need us. Would never occur to you that I might exist and be doing things on my own."

"Oh, get over yourself," Lucella said contemptuously. "So you managed to find someone to buy you a couple of crappy attack sigls. Who was it, Tobias? It was Tobias, wasn't it?"

I stared at Lucella, then let my lips curve upwards. "I am going to really enjoy teaching you a lesson."

I began to circle, trying to put Lucella between myself and the ventilator. Lucella reacted quickly, moving sideways; despite her words, she was watching me closely. I could see essentia glowing from both of her hands: two sigls, one Motion, one Life. I couldn't tell what they did, and I was wary of getting too close. From the way Lucella had struck at me, I had the feeling that at least one of them worked by touch.

I heard the sound of wings again as another bird came flapping down to land on the ventilator. There were five of them now, crows, watching us with black eyes. One of them opened its beak to caw.

I saw Lucella's eyes flick towards the crows; sudden confidence flashed across her face.

I took a deep breath, measuring the distance between us. I'd use my flash sigl to dazzle Lucella, then try to close the distance before she could recover. I took a step—

Two claps came from the darkness, making me jump. "All right," a voice said from our side. "Break it up."

Lucella and I turned.

The man who'd called himself Byron stepped out of the shadows, continuing to clap. "Break it up, break it up."

Lucella looked from me to Byron. "Excuse me?"

"I'll admit a duel between the two of you would be amusing, but I'm afraid blood sports just don't have the same appeal to me as they did in my younger days," Byron said. "Besides, I'd rather not have either of you falling off the roof. So let's put a pin in this, shall we?"

I'd backed up a few steps as soon as Byron had shown himself, watching the two of them warily. All my thoughts of going after Lucella had vanished; I knew I couldn't take on her and Byron at once.

Lucella pointed at me. "Get rid of him!"

"Are you giving me orders?" Byron asked mildly.

Lucella opened her mouth, then clenched it shut. I saw the muscles in her jaw work as she stared daggers at me.

"Better," Byron said after a pause.

"He's going to be trouble," Lucella said. Her voice was tight, but she seemed to have got herself under control. "The raid on the Well—"

"—is nothing I care about," Byron interrupted. "Honestly, Lucella, I'm not one of the Mountains. If you want to rule House Ashford, that's your affair, but I wish you'd stop running to me for help."

The sound of gunfire from the courtyard had stopped. I couldn't hear any police sirens yet, but I had the feeling it wouldn't be long. "You don't care about House Ashford or their Wells," I told Byron. "You don't care about money or power. What *do* you care about?"

"Ah, our mystery guest speaks!" Byron said. "So that *was* you, back there in the garage. I am interested in . . . potential."

"Potential for what?"

"For something more," Byron said. "Haven't you ever felt trapped, in your old life? Restricted, kept from doing what you really care about? As though there's something better, that you're being kept from?"

I paused.

"You've been fighting on the wrong side, Stephen," Byron said with a smile. He nodded back towards the Well. "The Ashfords are part of the old order. Do you really want to be like them, spending your life chasing money and power? Haven't you ever wanted to be something more?"

"Like what?" I said. "What do *you* stand for?"

"Freedom," Byron said. "Why should we be less than what we could be? Why should you be limited by what you were born into? We offer power, yes, but not for its own sake. Power to overthrow injustice, to break the shackles of the past."

There was an intensity to Byron's words; his voice had become resonant, deep and commanding. I could feel the pull of it, the appeal . . . but I held back. I didn't trust Byron, and I hadn't forgotten who he'd come here with.

As I thought that, my eyes lit on Lucella. There was an odd expression on her face, yearning and bitter, and a thought flashed across my mind. *Is this the same speech he gave her?*

"Sorry," I told Byron. "Not convinced."

Byron cocked his head. "Oh?"

"You were the one who gave Lucella her powers, right?" I asked Byron. "Well, as far as I can see, all she uses them for is to step on anyone who gets in her way. I don't get the feeling you're the good guys."

Byron didn't seem fazed. "If self-protection is what concerns you, then why not seek such powers yourself?"

"What, so I can be a little monster like her?"

"We don't want anyone to become monsters, Stephen," Byron said. "We're working towards utopia. A world where anyone is free to become their true self, without constraint or pain or suffering. Where the structures and institutions that restrict people and force them into unhappiness are swept away. Isn't that worth sacrificing for?"

I looked back at Byron for a moment before answering. "No."

Byron paused. "I'm sorry?"

"First, your utopia wouldn't work," I said. "You can't have a world where everyone's painless and happy, because if your world's set up to be suited to one person, it won't suit another. Second, sweeping everything away wouldn't do anything, because people have got inborn inclinations to evil as well as to good, so even if you got rid of every institution in the world, a new bunch of selfish bastards like the Ashfords would just show up and do the same thing all over again. And third, and most importantly, I don't trust you. So take your sidekick, or whatever Lucella is, and go away."

The three of us stared at each other across the rooftops for a moment. I could hear the first police sirens now, distant but drawing closer. Then abruptly and unexpectedly, Byron threw his head back and laughed.

I watched Byron sceptically. I had my invisibility sigl ready to go, but it felt to me as though the time for that had passed. If he'd wanted to attack, he would have done it by now.

It took Byron a while to stop laughing. When he finally stopped and looked at me, there was genuine mirth in his eyes, and for the first time since I'd seen him he seemed to be really enjoying himself. "You know, I really thought that line would work," he told me. "Where did you learn to talk like that?"

"None of your business," I told him. Inwardly, I was deciding that once I got out of this, I'd give Father Hawke an apology.

"You sounded like—ah, never mind. Well, I was going to save this for later, but I have to admit, this is a lot more interesting. What if I gave you a more personal incentive?"

"Like what?" I said warily. Up until he'd burst out laughing, Byron had seemed amused but detached, as though he'd done this all before. Now all of a sudden he was looking me up and down with an interested expression that I didn't particularly like.

"Work with us," Byron said, "and I'll tell you about your father."

I froze. "What?"

"What?" Lucella said. She was staring at Byron.

"Really, Lucella?" Byron asked her. "You didn't know? As soon as you heard the name Oakwood, I would have thought you'd have made the connection."

"The same—"

"*Yes*, the same one. Honestly, I know you have trouble remembering anything that doesn't directly relate to you, but this is ridiculous."

The wail of sirens sounded from below as the first police cars pulled into the street beside us. I saw the blue strobing flash of their lights reflected from the buildings. "Well, I believe that's our cue to leave," Byron told Lucella. "Shall we?"

Lucella shot me a final venomous look and disappeared into the night. Byron turned to follow her.

"Wait!" I called.

Byron glanced back over his shoulder with a smile. "Oh? Did I get your attention?" He pulled out something small and white from inside his jacket. "Give me a call when you're ready. Though I wouldn't wait too long." He tossed the sliver of white to the rooftop, then walked away, the shadows closing in around him.

I stared after Byron until I was sure he was gone, then walked forward to pick up what he'd dropped. It was a business card, black ink on a white background. There was no name, only a strange symbol that looked like a spread of five feathered wings. Underneath was a phone number.

I looked up. The crows that had been perched on the ventilator were almost all gone. Only one was left, watching me with black eyes.

"What are you staring at?" I asked.

The crow cawed.

The sirens from the street below had stopped, though the strobing blue flashes had grown stronger. The police were here, and that broke my hesitation. I was still trespassing, and if I was caught here, it'd mean trouble. I turned in the opposite direction from the one in which Byron and Lucella had disappeared, and started looking for a way down. Between my strength and invisibility sigls, I should be able to get off the roof and meet up with Colin.

Behind me, the last crow watched me go, then flew away into the night.

CHAPTER 21

IT WAS THE next day.

The morning had dawned bright and sunny, puffy white clouds floating in a bright blue sky. Despite the sunlight, the air was cool and the breeze carried enough of a chill to make me glad I'd worn my fleece. Autumn was coming.

I leant against the tree at the bottom of The Bishops Avenue and scrolled through my phone. I had five missed calls, two from an unknown number and three from Colin. I'd answered the unknown number on the third call to receive a terse message informing me that Charles Ashford required my presence, right now. In the case of Colin I hadn't picked up any of the calls, but that hadn't stopped him texting.

Colin: Hey, call me back.
Colin: We need to talk.
Colin: Dude, pick up your phone
Colin: PICK UP YOUR PHONE
Colin: PICK UP

Colin: CALL ME BACK or I swear to God I'm going to come around to your house and beat some answers out of you

I sighed. This was going to be a long conversation. I texted Colin back, telling him that I'd call him tonight, then slipped the phone into my pocket and started walking towards the Ashford mansion.

Given the sheer amount of crap the Ashfords had put me through in the past six months, I would have really liked to ignore Charles's message, but I knew that was a bad idea. I wasn't sure how things would go if I managed to seriously piss off Charles Ashford, but I was pretty sure the answer was "badly." And although I'd come prepared with my full combat sigl loadout, I had the feeling that against the kinds of problems someone like Charles could cause, sigls wouldn't help much.

I arrived at the mansion and was buzzed in. A man was waiting for me at the front door. He was wearing a strength sigl like Diesel and Scar's, and the blue-and-silver Ashford crest. "Stephen Oakwood?" he asked, and at my nod he ushered me inside.

The man led me up to Charles's study on the first floor, where I got my first surprise: Tobias and Lucella were waiting out in the hall. Lucella was leaning against the wall with her arms folded, while Tobias was slouched with his hands in his pockets. Both gave me unfriendly looks, but another Ashford armsman was watching and neither spoke. I kept a wary eye on both as the armsman who'd led me in knocked on the door, then motioned for me to enter.

"You're late," Charles told me as the door clicked shut behind me.

"Yeah, well, take it up with your niece," I told him.

The study looked much the same as last time. There seemed to be a few more glass beads on the map; looking at it, I saw a large pale blue bead pinned to a spot in Central London that I thought might be Chancery Lane.

"Give me an account of your part in last night's events," Charles said.

"Why?"

Charles Ashford gave me a level look. "Excuse me?"

"I don't work for you," I told him. "Why should I answer your questions?"

"You can answer them here, or from the inside of a cell," Charles told me. "I've heard Calhoun's, Lucella's, and Tobias's stories. The only one left is yours."

I felt a flare of resentment. I hadn't expected a thank-you, but this was the second time I'd stepped into this study, and once again Charles was treating me like a dog to be kicked around until it did as it was told. I was starting to really hate this guy.

But while I might hate him, I didn't think he was the kind to make idle threats. "Last night, your niece sent her two personal armsmen to kidnap me right out of my house," I told Charles, my voice tight and clipped. "For the second time, by the way, not that you seem to care. She and Tobias had organised a raid on that Well in Chancery Lane and got some corporation called Tyr to be the muscle. I was supposed to be the scapegoat. I escaped, Calhoun fought off the raiders, and Lucella and Tobias ran away. That's it."

Charles studied me for a second, tapping his fingers on his desk. "And do you have any proof of this?"

"Oh, yeah, the whole time those goons were abducting me, I was videoing the whole thing with a selfie stick. No, I was busy trying to survive. Go check your security cameras or something."

"The cameras were deactivated immediately before the raiders arrived," Charles said. "Anything else?"

"What do you mean?"

"Did you see or hear anyone else?"

I thought about that man in black and the business card lying on my bedside table. "Like I said, I was busy."

Charles stared at me for a long moment. I shifted uncomfortably, waiting for him to go on. "So?" I said when he didn't.

"So?"

"So are you going to believe me?"

Charles leant back in his chair. "Your story is, for the most part, congruent with Calhoun's," he told me. "With regard to Lucella's and Tobias's accounts of the night's events, there are points of disagreement."

Yeah, I bet there are. "Such as?"

"Tobias arrived on the scene shortly after the raiders had withdrawn, leading a small group of armsmen," Charles said. "He claims to have known nothing of the raid on the Well until Calhoun raised the alarm. At which point, filled with family loyalty, he rushed to his cousin's aid."

Okay, so at least Tobias hadn't *actively* tried to throw me under the bus. I suppose I should be grateful. "And Lucella?"

"Lucella claims that her personal armsmen uncovered evidence that you had sold information on one of our Wells to a hostile corporation," Charles said. "They went to your home to question you, at which point you agreed to take them to the target's location. However, once there, the raiding team attacked and you escaped in the confusion."

"Oh, screw that," I said angrily. "You believe her?"

"Why shouldn't I?" Charles asked, raising an eyebrow. "You've already admitted you can't provide proof."

I took a breath, fighting back outrage. I'd been dragged into this, I'd even *helped* Calhoun, and this was what I got for it?

No. I forced myself to stay calm. Losing my temper wasn't going to help. Lucella had been smarter than I'd thought; her story matched the facts just closely enough that it'd be hard for me to disprove it. But there were gaps.

"You just told me the security cameras were deactivated," I told Charles. "And Calhoun said the security rota had been changed."

"Go on."

"So how would I do that?" I asked. "I don't have access to your systems. Oh, and for that matter, why would I even be doing this in the first place? The whole reason for this stupid raid was for Lucella and Tobias to knock Calhoun off the top of the ladder so they could go up a rung. But you made it pretty clear last time that I'm not *on* the ladder. I don't benefit from Calhoun failing—they do."

Charles nodded. "Anything else?"

What, he wanted more? I tried to think of other reasons why . . . *Wait.* Charles was watching me calmly. Too calmly.

"You don't believe them, either, do you?" I asked.

Charles looked at me.

"You don't," I said. I was sure it was true as I said it. "What is this, a test?"

"Go call in Tobias and Lucella," Charles said, nodding to the door. "I have something to say to all three of you."

I turned and took one step towards the door, then paused. I looked back at Charles.

Charles had already turned his attention to the papers on his desk. "Today, please," he said without looking up.

"How can you let them keep getting away with this?" I asked Charles. "This is the third time this year that Lucella's tried to ruin my life. Are you going to stop her?"

"What were you expecting me to do?" Charles asked. "Slap her on the wrist and tell her to stop being mean to you? There are plenty of Lucellas in the drucraft world. They play rough. If you can't handle it, I suggest you keep your distance."

I stared at Charles for a second, then something in me snapped. "Okay, you know what?" I said. "Screw this." I walked back and put my hands onto the back of the chair, leaning over it. Charles did look up, then, his pale eyes meeting mine. "You don't like me? Fine. I don't like you much, either. But you can at least tell me what's really going on. You owe me that much."

Charles looked at me without expression, and I had to fight the urge to flinch. When he finally spoke, though, his voice was calm. "Do you know why Tyr carried out last night's raid?"

"Because Lucella or Tobias called them in," I said.

"Back in the spring, several US factions pushed for an embargo on essentia sales to non-NATO countries," Charles said. "For various reasons, the debate came to centre around a UK company called Camlink, with extensive Well holdings and a history of sales to China. Tyr took advantage of this to pressure Camlink into selling them one of their more powerful Light Wells. The war has driven up the price of Light essentia, and Tyr has recently acquired a lucrative contract to supply the US government with the active camouflage sigls they use in their stealth units." Charles looked at me. "Are you following all of this?"

"Yes," I said. *Barely.*

"To coerce Camlink in this way, Tyr had to expend political capital, which brought about resentment," Charles went on. "Some began to argue, first quietly, then openly, that selling to the US but not to China could be seen as becoming actively involved in the new Cold War. So when I approached certain figures in our government about withdrawing our support from Tyr's bid, they were willing to listen. An agreement was reached to block the sale of the Well."

I remembered that news article I'd read yesterday. "And give it to you instead."

"Correct. This placed Tyr in a difficult position. They had

counted on the supply from that Well and were now at risk of defaulting on their contracts. As a short-term solution, and to buy them time to secure a replacement source, they decided to take action. This raid was always going to happen. It was just a matter of when and where." Charles looked at me. "Last night wasn't about you. Or Tobias or Lucella, though I doubt they realise it. All of you were simply playing pieces in a much larger game."

I looked back at Charles, trying to process all of that.

"I believe that answers your question," Charles said.

"You know Calhoun nearly got shot last night, right?" I said. "Was that part of your plan as well?"

"Calhoun is being groomed to be the next head of House Ashford," Charles said. "As part of that, he has been given the best training, the most powerful sigls, and partial authority over our armsmen. If, with all of those resources, he couldn't deal with one small group of raiders . . . well. Better to know early." Charles tapped his fingers on the desk. "Still, there are limits." He pressed something under the desk and spoke into the air. "Send them in."

The door opened behind me, and I turned to see Tobias and Lucella enter. Both shot me suspicious looks. I wondered why for a second before realising that they must have been wondering what I'd told Charles.

Charles pointed at the space in front of the desk. "Stand."

Lucella and Tobias came to a stop, side by side. I stood a little way away.

"I have always believed that a certain amount of competition for positions such as the head of this House is both healthy and appropriate," Charles said. "I want the heir to this family, whoever he or she may eventually be, to be the most capable of all of the possible candidates. Some conflict is acceptable, so long as it does not go over the line. Consider this to be your official notice that you have now crossed that line."

I didn't like that I was apparently included in that, but I held my tongue.

"The events of last night have made it clear that Calhoun is the one who can be best trusted to uphold the interests of our family," Charles went on. "As such, I am now designating him as heir to the position of head of this House, effective immediately." Charles looked at Lucella and Tobias. "I hope this will remove any further temptation to cut to the front of the line. Calhoun will continue to be evaluated, and it may be that he will, in time, prove himself unfit, in which case the two of you will once again be considered for the position. But until and unless that occurs, none of the three of you will take any further hostile action, direct or indirect, against Calhoun or against one another. Is that clear?"

I shot a glance at Lucella and Tobias. Neither looked happy, but they didn't argue. They'd probably known this was coming.

"I have, however, noticed that some among you seem to have difficulty following my instructions," Charles said with a cold smile. "So this time, I will provide an additional incentive. Should any mysterious strokes of misfortune befall Calhoun while he is heir . . . even ones that appear to be entirely coincidental . . . then all three of you will be immediately disinherited from this family. Your sources of income will be suspended, your sigls will be repossessed, and you will be permanently barred from any position of any kind within House Ashford."

That got a reaction. "What?" Tobias said incredulously.

"That's not fair!" Lucella shouted.

"Life isn't fair," Charles said with a raised eyebrow. "Deal with it."

"But what if something happens to Calhoun?" Tobias said. "If he has some kind of accident—"

"Then it would be in your best interests to ensure that he doesn't," Charles said. "Wouldn't you say?"

Tobias fell silent.

"Regardless, all three of you are now in the same boat," Charles told them. "I hope this will mitigate your rivalry somewhat. If not . . . sort it out amongst yourselves." He nodded to the door. "You can go now."

Lucella stared angrily at Charles, then turned and left. Tobias followed slowly, shooting his grandfather a backward glance. I followed them out. Charles had already returned to his paperwork.

We went out into the hall, the door swinging shut behind us. The armsmen who had been outside were gone. The three of us were alone.

Lucella, Tobias, and I all looked at each other.

"Charles won't be there to protect you all the time," Lucella told me. Her voice was low but pitched to carry. "Watch your back."

I gave a sharp laugh. "You watch yours."

"Okay, okay," Tobias said. "Look, let's all calm down, all right? I think we can all agree that it's in all of our interests to—"

"Oh, for the love of God, will you *shut up*?" Lucella told him. "This is why no one likes you. You're never going to be chosen by Charles, you're never going to be chosen by Byron, you're always going to be the last one picked for the football team. So go run back to your mother and stop trying to play out of your league."

Something dangerous flashed in Tobias's eyes, but Lucella had already turned to me. "Actually, maybe you should take his advice," I told Lucella. "Because if you *ever* make another move on me or anyone I care about, I'll do the same thing to you that you had done to my cat."

"What, you think Byron's going to help you?" Lucella asked. "If you know what's good for you, you'll stay away."

"I don't need his help, or anyone else's," I told Lucella. "What are you going to do, send your goons? I went through them to get to you once already. You think I can't do it again?"

"Enough," Tobias said sharply, and this time there was something in his tone that made both me and Lucella turn and look. His face was hard. "Maybe you weren't listening back there, but Charles just made it pretty clear what would happen if you two keep this up."

"Oh, I heard what Charles said just fine," I told Tobias. "But here's the thing. I *already* don't get anything from your family. If Charles disinherits all three of us . . . well, doesn't make much difference to me. You two, though? You're a pair of spoilt brats who've probably never worked a day in your lives. So the way I see it, you've got a *lot* more to lose than I have."

"You try to undermine me here, or anywhere else," Lucella told me, "and I'll make you wish you'd never been born."

"Bring it, you psychotic bitch."

Silence fell. The two of us stared at each other.

The sound of footsteps on the carpet behind us made us all glance around. One of the Ashford armsmen was heading in our direction. "Okay," Tobias said, looking from me to Lucella. "Good talk."

I backed up. Neither Lucella nor I took our eyes off each other until we were out of each other's sight.

THE ARMSMAN ESCORTED me out. I left through the front gate and walked down the hill. As soon as I was out of sight I slipped on my vision sigl, turned invisible, went back to my old vantage point where I could watch the Ashford mansion, and waited.

Bridget appeared about an hour later, leaving the mansion and strolling away up the hill. I cut ahead of her, then once I was out of sight deactivated my sigls and waited for her at the same spot as last time.

"Oh, it's you!" Bridget said cheerfully as she walked up. I could see the active sigl on her hand, just like before: the same invisible presence was at her side. "What happened last night? Everyone's been running around, but no one's telling me anything."

"I'll tell you the story, but I need a favour in return," I said. "There's someone from your family I want to meet."

"Who—" Bridget began, then paused. "Oh."

I watched Bridget, waiting for her answer.

I WENT TO the church that evening. There was a service going on, and I dawdled outside while I waited for it to finish, watching the flowers in the churchyard wave in the wind. In my head I was turning over ideas for sigls. Seeing those soldiers in their armour had got me thinking: if they could use Matter drucraft to protect themselves, maybe I could do the same. I couldn't make a full suit of armour like theirs, but maybe something thinner and less bulky? Or maybe instead of making a sigl that reduced the mass of what you were wearing, I could make one that strengthened or toughened it? It wouldn't be as rigid, but it would be a lot more subtle.

So many possibilities, and I still felt as though I was only scratching the surface of what I could do. With my drucraft and my essentia sight, there was a whole world open to me.

The service finished, and I waited for most of the congregation to leave, then slipped through the door. Father Hawke was packing up his books near the lectern. "Ah, Stephen," he said. "Have you looked at the Ellul?"

"I haven't even finished the last book."

A woman came up to ask Father Hawke a question, and I paused while he answered. Once she was gone, Father Hawke turned back to me. "Did you have some other issue with your sigls?"

"Actually, I came to apologise."

"Really?"

"Okay, so I've got a confession," I admitted. "All of the time you were getting me to read those theology books, I thought they were kind of pointless. But last night . . . Well, long story short, I think I can see why it's useful now."

"It sounds as though you're growing up."

I nodded, then paused. ". . . Was that an insult?"

Father Hawke smiled. "No."

The remaining members of the congregation were starting to drift in the direction of the exit. "Can I ask you something?"

"Of course."

"Someone told me drucraft can't be used for mind control," I said. "Is that true?"

"Essentially," Father Hawke said. "Certain Life effects can alter a subject's emotional state, but only by flooding their system with hormones in a very crude way. It doesn't function in the sense that you're thinking of."

"Huh," I said. That was more or less what Tobias had said. "So it can't be done?"

"Not with sigls."

"What do you mean?"

The last people were leaving the church. Father Hawke started walking slowly down the nave, and I fell into step beside him. "One does sometimes come across people with unique abilities," Father Hawke said. "They can manipulate essentia without a sigl to produce effects that would usually be impossible. It's a rare thing, but not unknown."

I frowned. "Where do those abilities come from?"

"They are bestowed by spiritual entities."

"Uh," I said.

Father Hawke smiled. "You don't believe me?"

"That's, um . . . a bit hard to process."

Father Hawke nodded. "It's not a subject that is widely discussed. Still, if you move in certain spheres, you'll come across such people from time to time."

We'd reached the church doors, and I stopped on the front step. "So if someone seemed to have the power to give people orders and have them obey . . . ?"

"They could simply be unusually persuasive," Father Hawke said. "But, yes, it's possible. If so, I would advise you to be cautious. The entities that bestow such abilities do not act randomly or on whim. If they choose someone as the recipient of such a gift, no matter what it might be—the ability to see essentia, say—it is for a purpose." Father Hawke gave me a nod. "Well, until next time. Don't forget the book." He swung the door shut.

I was right in the middle of turning away when my brain caught up with what I'd just heard. I stopped dead. *Wait, what?*

I stared at the closed door. Father Hawke had disappeared behind it, and the last members of the congregation had gone. I was alone in the churchyard.

I stood there for a long time before slowly walking home.

THE ARRIVALS HALL at Heathrow Airport feels small, given the size of the terminal. A lit tunnel leads from the baggage and customs section into a long open area, divided in two by a steel railing. Passengers walk out of the tunnel and along the railing; as soon as they step past it and into the main terminal, there's no way to tell them apart from everyone else.

I got there early and spent a while hanging around. Some of the people on my side looked like family members; others were taxi drivers, holding up names. Bridget had given me the number of the Lufthansa flight, and the blue-and-yellow monitors overhead were still showing it as "due." From time to time I'd take out that business card to stare at, looking at the number written below the five wings. Each time I'd remember Father Hawke's warning and stuff the card back into my pocket, but somehow, a few minutes later, I'd find myself looking at it again.

At last the description on the monitors changed from "due" to "landed." I shoved the card back into my pocket one final time and found a spot where I could look up the exit tunnel, my eyes searching through the scattered string of arrivals.

I spotted her as soon as she came into view. She was wearing a dark purple blazer over a slim dress and was towing a small suitcase, the heels of her shoes clicking on the polished floor. There was a huge billboard behind her, and for a moment, as she walked by, her shape was silhouetted against the stylised dragon on the ad, purple against gold.

I followed her past the end of the railing. She turned towards the terminal exit, still towing her carry-on, and caught a glimpse of me out of the corner of her eye. She started to look away, then something seemed to catch her attention and she turned back to me with a slight frown.

"Hi, Mum," I said.

GLOSSARY

affinity (branch)—A talent or skill with one of the six branches of drucraft. Almost all drucrafters discover that they have at least one branch that they find particularly easy to work with, and at least one branch that they find particularly difficult. A strong affinity allows a drucrafter to use and create sigls from that branch more easily and with greater effectiveness.

affinity (country)—A natural familiarity with the essentia found in the Wells of a particular geographical region. It's almost always much easier to shape a sigl at a Well in the country you grew up in. Country affinity doesn't matter much to drucrafters who live most of their lives in the same place but causes problems for "sigl tourists" who want to fly into a country, acquire a sigl, and fly out.

aurum—The raw material that sigls are made of, also known as solid essentia or crystallised essentia. It has a density of 8.55 grams per cubic centimetre, slightly denser than steel and about the density of copper or brass. If left untouched, aurum will eventually sublimate back into free essentia, though in the case of solid sigls this can take thousands of years.

Blood Limit—One of the most important principles of drucraft, the Blood Limit states that sigls are locked at the moment of their creation to the personal essentia of whoever made them. This makes sigls nontransferable: to anyone but their maker, a sigl is nothing but a pretty rock.

There are two ways to get around the Blood Limit. First, in creating a sigl, a drucrafter can choose to mix their own personal essentia with someone else's. The higher the proportion of the other person's personal essentia that they use, the more effective the sigl will be for that person, but the harder the sigl is to make. This is the method used by all commercial providers.

The second way around the Blood Limit is to use a sigl shaped by a close relative. The more closely related two people are, the more likely it is that their personal essentia will be similar enough that the sigl will accept it. This method works well between parent and child or between siblings, but its effectiveness drops sharply with more distant relations, and anything more distant than grandparent to grandchild or aunt/uncle to niece/nephew almost never works. This method has been one of the ways in which Noble Houses have preserved some measure of their strength down the generations.

Due to the Blood Limit, all sigls effectively have a finite life span. No matter how powerful a sigl may be, there will eventually come a point at which every person capable of using it is dead, at which point the sigl is useless.

Board—The ruling body that governs all matters relating to drucraft in the United Kingdom. The Board has wide discretionary powers but is still subject to the authority of the Crown and functions in practice like a cross between a board of directors and the British Parliament.

Possession of a Well of strength A+ and above grants the holder a seat on the Board; as a result, the sale and purchase of these Wells in the United Kingdom is subject to special restrictions.

branch—Different types of Wells contain different kinds of essentia and produce different kinds of sigls. These are known in drucraft as the six branches, named after the sorts of things that can be done with them: Light, Matter, Motion, Life, Dimension, and Primal. Of all the branches, only Primal effects can be created without a sigl, and then only weakly.

channeller—A drucrafter capable of controlling and directing their personal essentia, allowing them to activate triggered sigls. Becoming a channeller is generally the point at which someone is considered a "real" drucrafter.

corporations—Most corporations are not involved in drucraft, but those that are have great influence in the drucraft world. Like Houses, corporations can buy, hold, and sell Wells, and are treated by governments as legal entities in their own right. The distinction between a corporation and a House can be fuzzy, though there is a noticeable difference in terms of organisational culture: Houses tend to be more traditional and are more strongly tied to their country of origin, while corporations are much more heavily focused on profit and are typically international, with relatively little connection to the countries they operate in.

drucraft—The art and skill of working with essentia. Drucraft consists of three disciplines: sensing (perceiving essentia), channelling (manipulating one's own personal essentia), and shaping (the creation of sigls).

drucrafter—A practitioner of drucraft. Typically used to refer to a channeller or shaper.

essentia—The raw energy that powers drucraft and creates sigls. Essentia is fundamental and omnipresent, flowing through the world in invisible currents. If depleted in any location, it naturally replenishes itself from the surrounding area.

Pure essentia is completely inaccessible to living creatures: they can no more tap it than draw upon the chemical energy in a lump of stone. However, over long periods of time, essentia can be shaped by the land around it, its currents converging at a location called a Well. The essentia in a Well is still mutable but will be inclined towards a certain aspect of existence, such as light or matter.

A living creature of sufficient enlightened will can shape the reserves of a Well into a small piece of crystallised essentia called a sigl. Sigls have the power to conduct essentia, transforming its raw universal energy into a spell effect. Over a long, long time, the sigl sublimates back into essentia; this essentia is absorbed again by the land, and the cycle begins anew.

essentia capacity—The rate at which a living creature can assimilate ambient essentia into personal essentia, and thus make use of sigls. It is measured on the Lorenz Scale and is loosely correlated with height and skeletal mass; average adult essentia capacity in the UK is 2.8 for men and 2.4 for women. For a combat drucrafter, an essentia capacity of 3.0 and over is considered ideal, allowing them to use three full-strength sigls at once, while an essentia capacity of below 2.0 is considered crippling.

essentia construct—A sketch or sculpture crafted out of essentia. Making an essentia construct is the first step towards creating a sigl. Manifesters typically use essentia constructs as blueprints, allowing them to practise the important early stages of creating a sigl, as well as adjust its design before attempting the costly process of shaping it for real.

Euler's Limit—Sigls can only be created from essentia: many substitutes have been tried and all have failed. This means that the supply of sigls is limited by the supply of locations that possess a sufficient concentration of essentia to shape a sigl. These locations are called Wells.

Faraday Point—The minimum quantity of essentia needed to consistently produce a viable sigl. Below this point, effectiveness falls off sharply: a drop of even 10 percent below the Faraday Point usually produces a nonfunctional sigl. A sigl created at the Faraday Point is rated as D-class.

The Faraday Point is used to define the Faraday Scale. A Well with a Faraday rating of 1 can sustainably produce exactly one D-class sigl per year.

Faraday Scale—The most common measuring scale for Wells, used in Europe, Japan, Russia, Australia, India, and some parts of Africa and South America. The Faraday rating of a Well is a measurement of how many D-class sigls the Well can sustainably make in a year.

The Faraday Point is a "soft" limit and as such is not considered one of the Five Limits of drucraft (which are much closer to being absolute restrictions).

Five Limits—The five most significant limitations on drucraft. More than anything else, the Five Limits shape how the drucraft world operates. In brief, the Five Limits are:

Euler's Limit: Sigls can only be created from essentia.
Primal Limit: You can't use drucraft without a sigl.
Blood Limit: You can't use someone else's sigl.
Limit of Creation: You can't change a sigl after it's made.
Limit of Operation: A sigl won't work without a bearer.

While the Five Limits significantly restrict what drucraft is capable of, all five do have workarounds and exceptions.

House—An aristocratic family of drucrafters, usually one that holds title to one or more Wells. In the past, the Great Houses of Europe had various special privileges under the law; while this is rarely the case nowadays, Houses still command great wealth and influence.

Drucraft Houses are primarily found in Europe and Asia. In countries without Houses, different institutions fill similar roles: in the United States, the place of Houses is filled by corporations, while in China, the main drucraft enterprises are all state owned. In the United Kingdom, the main significance of House status is that both Great and Lesser Houses are entitled to a seat on the Board.

House, Great (United Kingdom)—A House in the United Kingdom that possesses at least one Well of S-class and above. At the time of writing, there are eight Great Houses in the United Kingdom: Barrett-Lennard, Cawley, Chetwynd, De Haughton, Hawker, Meath, Reisinger, and Winterton.

House, Lesser (United Kingdom)—A House in the United Kingdom that possesses at least one Well with a class of A+. The United Kingdom has between thirty and thirty-five Lesser Houses (the exact number is subject to dispute).

Houses that own no Wells of class A+ and above have no special legal status, though they will often take the title of "House" regardless, particularly if they held Great House or Lesser House status in the past.

kernel—A sigl's core, made out of the shaper or wielder's personal essentia. The fact that it is *their* personal essentia is the reason that the sigl will work for them and not for anyone else.

limiter—A device used by shapers to assist in creating sigls. Limiters give two advantages: consistency (sigls produced by the same limiter are always exactly the same, without the variation created by free manifestation) and reliability (shaping a sigl with a limiter is much less demanding on the user's shaping skills). Limiters are expensive to create and as such are typically not cost effective unless the owner plans to produce many copies of the same sigl. The vast majority of sigls sold commercially are created with limiters.

Lorenz Ceiling—The maximum quantity of personal essentia that can be channelled through any sigl before its efficiency drops off sharply. Like the Faraday Point, this is a "soft" limit rather than a hard one. The Lorenz Ceiling is defined as a 1 on the Lorenz Scale.

The Lorenz Ceiling is not affected by a sigl's size. Larger sigls have more powerful amplification effects (allowing them to draw in more ambient essentia from the surrounding environment) but cannot make use of any more personal essentia than a smaller sigl can.

Lorenz Scale—A measurement of essentia flow, used to evaluate both a living creature's essentia capacity and also the amount of personal essentia a sigl requires to function at full output.

Most commercially created sigls are designed with Lorenz ratings as close as possible to 1. A sigl with a Lorenz rating of less than 1 will be less powerful but also less draining to use (this is more common with Light sigls, due to their generally lower power requirements). Sigls with Lorenz ratings of more than 1 are rare, since going above the Lorenz Ceiling brings greatly diminishing returns. A sigl with a Lorenz rating of 1.5 will be only marginally more powerful than one with a Lorenz rating of 1, despite being much more taxing on its bearer's essentia capacity.

manifester—A drucrafter capable of creating a sigl without assistance (i.e., without a limiter or similar tool). Becoming a manifester requires advanced shaping skills. Most drucrafters never become manifesters, although there is a growing feeling that limiters have become so widespread in the modern age that being unable to create a sigl without one is no longer a significant drawback.

personal essentia—Essentia which has been assimilated by a living creature and which has taken on the imprint of that creature's mind and body. With practice and concentration, personal essentia can be directed, controlled, and channelled into sigls to produce various effects.

Primal Limit—The second of the Five Limits, the Primal Limit states that it is impossible to produce any kind of drucraft spell without a sigl. Humans can assimilate free essentia into personal essentia, but without a sigl they can't transform that personal essentia into a spell effect. The one exception to this limit is (as the name suggests) Primal drucraft, which can be performed unassisted, although much more weakly than with a Primal sigl.

shaper—Any drucrafter capable of creating a sigl. In theory this is a neutral term, but in practice, if someone is called a "shaper," it usually means that they can't create a sigl without a limiter. Otherwise, they'll call themselves a "manifester" instead.

sigl—A small item resembling a gemstone, created out of pure essentia at a Well. Sigls convert their wielder's personal essentia into a spell effect and then pull in free essentia from the surrounding environment to amplify it. Larger sigls have a more powerful amplification effect, allowing for more sophisticated and complex spells.

Sigls, once created, can be used only by their makers, though there are some work-arounds to this (see **Blood Limit**). There is no known way to alter a sigl once it has been shaped.

sigl class / sigl grade—A sigl at exactly the Faraday Point is defined as being of D-class. The mass of the sigl doubles for each half grade above D (a D+ sigl has twice the mass of a D-class sigl, a

C-class sigl has four times the mass of a D-class sigl, and so on). In ascending order, and counting half grades, the sigl classes are: D, D+, C, C+, B, B+, A, A+, S, and S+. "Class" and "grade" are used interchangeably.

sigl type—Sigls fall into two types: continuous and triggered. Triggered sigls require their bearers to consciously channel essentia into them and as such can only be used by channellers. Continuous sigls are designed in such a way as to automatically pull in personal essentia from their bearers, meaning that they require no concentration and can even be used by a bearer with no knowledge of drucraft at all.

sigl weight—In casual conversation, sigls are usually referred to by their class. However, when greater precision is needed (such as when they're offered for sale), they are measured by carat weight instead. A D-class sigl has a weight of 0.18 carats, or 0.036 grams, and has a diameter of about two millimetres.

tyro—The lowest rank of drucrafter, with no ability to control their personal essentia. The only sigls a tyro can use are continuous ones.

Well—A location at which essentia accumulates. Wells are categorised by branch: for example, a Light Well collects Light essentia and produces Light sigls.

Wells can be permanent or temporary. Permanent Wells replenish themselves over time, and if properly tended can be used year after year for decades or even centuries. Temporary Wells, on the other hand, are typically one-offs: they have only brief life spans and do not usually refill themselves when drained. The distinction between the two types is sharper at higher ranks than at lower ones: Wells of class A and above will typically have storied histories of hundreds of years, while a permanent D-class Well can appear with relatively little fanfare and may disappear almost as fast, particularly if roughly treated.

Wells are commonly described by their class, which indicates the maximum strength of sigl the Well can produce when fully charged (e.g., a C-class Well can produce at most one C-class sigl before it must be left to replenish itself). Where more precision is needed, Wells are measured on the Faraday Scale.

Chris Murray Photography

Benedict Jacka is the author of the Alex Verus series, which began in 2012 with *Fated* and ended in 2021 with *Risen*. He studied philosophy at Cambridge University, taught English in China, and worked as everything from civil servant to bouncer before becoming a full-time writer.

VISIT BENEDICT JACKA ONLINE

BenedictJacka.co.uk
🐦 BenedictJacka

Ready to find
your next great read?

Let us help.

Visit prh.com/nextread

Penguin
Random
House